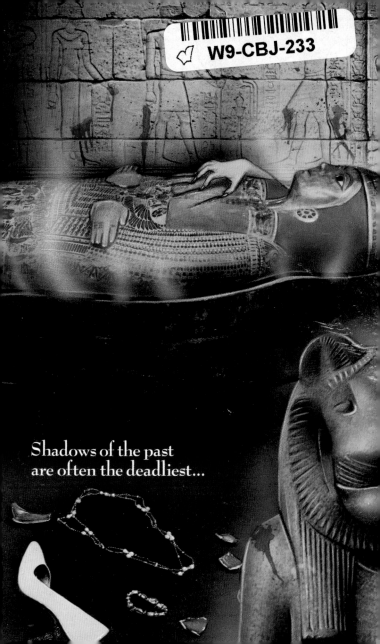

W9-CBJ-233

Shadows of the past
are often the deadliest...

Search the Shadows
Barbara Michaels

"Michaels is up to her old tricks: romantic suspense with an archeological setting. Pro that she is, Michaels wastes no time in sinking us in the story . . . The author's wit gleams."

—*Kirkus*

"Michaels has filled her latest romantic suspense novel with plenty of potential villains and lovers, and the suspense lingers until the final pages."

—*Booklist*

"The atmosphere is thick with threats and unexplained secrets, and Haskell's determination to find the truth leads to a final confrontation with a palpable enemy."

—*Cincinnati Post*

"Her adventures are non-stop . . . The only way the reader can take a breather to figure out the next step is by exercizing great willpower to set down this book."

—United Press International

"Michaels has a fine sense of atmosphere and storytelling."

—*New York Times*

"A new Barbara Michaels always means a day when I quit work early and stay up late."

—Marion Zimmer Bradley

BARBARA MICHAELS
SEARCH THE SHADOWS

B
BERKLEY BOOKS, NEW YORK

This Berkley book contains the complete
text of the original hardcover edition.
It has been completely reset in a typeface
designed for easy reading and was printed
from new film.

SEARCH THE SHADOWS

A Berkley Book/published by arrangement with
Atheneum Publishers

PRINTING HISTORY
Atheneum edition published 1987
Berkley edition/November 1988

ISBN: 0-425-11183-0

A BERKLEY BOOK ® TM 757,375
Berkley Books are published by The Berkley Publishing Group,
200 Madison Avenue, New York, NY 10016.
The name "BERKLEY" and the "B" logo
are trademarks belonging to the Berkley Publishing Corporation.

PRINTED IN THE UNITED STATES OF AMERICA

10 9 8 7 6 5 4 3 2 1

TO OLIVIA BLUMER
with heartfelt thanks for her professional brilliance
and personal charm

1

Nineteen sixty-five wasn't the worse of years in which to be born, but it certainly wasn't the best. It was, among other things, the year of Selma and of Watts. Martin Luther King went to Alabama that year; they met him with tear gas and with dogs. In Chicago they met him with night sticks. But the Voting Rights Act became law in 1965. You have to call that a plus.

It was the year of the "Great Society," which would eliminate poverty in America. An A-plus idea—if it had only worked. On a lighter level, the Rolling Stones hit it big with a song called "I Can't Get No Satisfaction," and Simon and Garfunkel swept the charts with "The Sounds of Silence." Diet Pepsi was introduced to the lucky American public; and in December, the month of my birth, Mary Quant unveiled the miniskirt.

On the minus side, there was that little far-off police action in Vietnam. By the end of 1965, U.S. planes had begun the bombing of the north, and there were over

400,000 American troops fighting, bleeding, and dying in actions that were never called a war. One of the ones who died was a boy named Kevin Maloney. For over twenty years I thought he was my father.

I don't remember anything about the trip home from the doctor's office. Not one blessed thing. I must have bought a ticket and gotten on the train at Thirtieth Street station. I must have left the train at Wayne, my usual stop, and walked home. The house was only a mile from the station and it was a pretty spring day. I do remember the weather. Partly because the sunshine and soft blossoms were in such bizarre contrast to my mood, partly because the pale pink petals sprinkling Pooch's black fur made him look so odd—like a painted porcelain statue of a cat.

He came out from under the azaleas in the front yard to bump against my ankles and mew his greeting. I had to respond—it would have been rude not to—and the necessity of acknowledging a friend shook me out of my stupor. I discovered that I had the front-door key in my hand. I put it in the lock, opened the door, and stepped nimbly aside to let Pooch in. It was pure reflex, like everything else I had done in the past few hours. Pooch weighed eighteen pounds, and he had no manners to speak of. If you didn't get out of his way, he ran right over you.

He headed for the kitchen. I stood looking around the familiar hallway, wondering why it looked so strange. I knew every object in it; I could have found my way in the dark. I had lived there for nineteen of my twenty-two years. Everything was the same—except me.

Jessie wasn't home from work yet. She had raised me from a pup, as she liked to say; she was my aunt, my mother's sister. At least I had always assumed she was. . . . We had our ups and downs—a lot of downs in those early years, and again when I moved into the typical schizophrenia of adolescence, as Jessie called it. I was a rotten kid. So Jessie said; it had become the lead line in one of our favorite routines. "God, you were a rotten kid, Haskell." Then I'd say, "Impossible. How could a rotten kid turn into such a perfect human being?" And Jessie would say, "The credit is all mine. It took a lot of nagging and spanking to turn a rotten kid into a perfect human being."

She had nagged—at least that's how I would have described it at the time. But she had never laid a hand, or a hairbrush, on me. For a single woman, dedicated to her career and having at best tepid feelings about children, she had been a superb mother substitute. I adored her. If she didn't adore me back, she was the world's greatest actress. How could she have lied to me? She must have known. She, of all people . . .

From the kitchen, Pooch's voice rose and fell in piteous complaint. His food dish must be empty. Instead of rushing to comply with his demands as I usually did, I went up the stairs. My feet automatically avoided the worn spot in the carpeting that Jessie always meant to fix. We never closed doors in that house. Hers stood open. I went into her room.

It was an austere bedroom, almost monastic in its lack of feminine furbelows. She always made her bed before she left for work; the plain white spread lay smooth and unwrinkled, marred only by a stubborn scattering of black cat hairs. The dresser top held her brush and comb and an eight-by-ten photo of me. The desk was organized with the same efficiency; a compartmentalized file held bills and unanswered letters. I sat down and opened the top drawer.

I didn't know what I was looking for, but I was still looking for it when I heard the sounds of Jessie's arrival—the scrape of the key in the locks, the slam of the door, a thud as she dropped something, and a loud "Damn!" She was as clumsy physically as she was well organized mentally, always dropping things and banging her shins on the furniture.

I had left my purse on the table in the hall. Jessie must have seen it; she yelled, "Hey Haskell, I'm home," and then continued, scarcely drawing breath, "All right, you damned pushy cat, give me a break, will you?"

I went on searching the drawers. The lowest on the left was twice as deep as the others, containing files. Methodically I went through them—insurance forms, papers on the car, tax returns, receipted bills. Downstairs, Jessie's footsteps clumped from room to room, accompanied by the rattle of utensils as she fed Pooch and mixed her evening martini. She called again as she started up the stairs. "Haskell—where are you? Are you coming down? Do you want something to drink?"

Impatient as always, she didn't wait for answers. She went to my room first. Hers was farther down the hall, away from the head of the stairs. I was looking through the file marked "Legal Papers" when she came to the open door.

"What are you doing?" she asked.

Her voice was mildly curious rather than outraged, though she had every right to be angry. We respected one another's privacy; she hadn't opened a drawer or a closet door in my room since I was thirteen.

She stood staring from the doorway, her glass in her hand. She was an inch shorter than I, exactly five feet four; and until a few years ago, we had worn the same dress size. Recently she had begun to put on weight. Her graying hair waved naturally. It was cut short, not as a statement of anything in particular, but to save time. Her gray pin-striped suit and tailored white blouse suited her position as head buyer for a large Philadelphia department store. I stared back at her as if I were looking at a complete stranger.

Her nose wrinkled and her eyes narrowed. She was getting nearsighted but hated to admit it; she refused to wear glasses except when she drove. But she knew me too well to miss the signs of distress.

"What's the matter?"

"I went to the doctor today."

"I assumed you had, since you told me this morning that your premarital exam was scheduled." A typical, cool Jessie response, but the deepening wrinkles around her eyes and a betraying tinkle of ice cubes from the glass she held were substitutes for the agitated questions another person might have asked. I could read the fears boiling up in her mind. An embarrassing social disease? A grislier, more ominous set of symptoms?

I said, "I have it. Tay-Sachs."

"What the hell is . . . Oh, you mean that exotic disease your future mother-in-law insisted you be tested for?" Jessie's full cheeks darkened as relief and rising anger replaced concern. "What are you trying to do to me, Haskell? You can't have Tay-Sachs. If you did, you'd be dead—years ago. Babies who get it don't live past two or three."

"You looked it up."

Jessie shrugged.

"I never heard of the damned thing till Mrs. Feldman mentioned it. Of course I looked it up. Sorry I did; of all the awful, ghastly diseases . . . And there's no cure."

I might have expected that Jessie would "look it up." That was one of her most admirable characteristics—a need to know the truth, find out the facts, however unpalatable, and face them head-on. I hoped it was one of my characteristics, too. Like Jessie, I had looked it up.

I said flatly, "Eighty-five percent of Tay-Sachs victims are children of eastern European Jews. The Jewish community started screening for it in the seventies and reduced its incidence enormously. Mrs. Feldman was right when she insisted we both be tested; it's a genetic disease and it does occur, rarely, in other groups. A cruel disease—no cure, no treatment. Blindness, paralysis, mental deterioration, death within two to four years of birth."

"I know," Jessie said. "You don't mean . . . You're a carrier?"

"Yes."

"What about Jon?"

"He isn't."

Jessie let out a long breath.

"Well, that's all right, then. It's a recessive gene: unless both parents carry it, there is no risk to their children." Her face had cleared, but she was still annoyed with me. Glancing at her glass, she announced irritably, "My damned drink is half water by this time. I'll have to throw it out and start again. Come downstairs and talk to me."

"Where did I get it?"

"What do you mean, where did you get it? You ought to know enough basic biology to answer that one. Children get their genes from their parents, who get them from *their* parents, and so on, ad infinitum."

"Most carriers are eastern European Jews. Ashkenazim."

My aunt, the child, like my mother, of Pennsylvania Dutch stock, contemplated me—whose father had been named Maloney. At least that was what the birth certificate I was holding claimed.

She knew what I was driving at, but she clung to the pretense of bewilderment. Her eyes shifted, her tone was truculent. "Most doesn't mean all. There are exceptions. The book I read mentioned them. A group in Nova Scotia—"

"It isn't just that. Look at me. Look at them." I gestured, stupidly, at a photograph that wasn't even in the room, but on the piano in the living room, where it had been for years. A wedding picture, in full color: Leah Emig, fair-haired and blue-eyed, her square jaw softened by the froth of lace framing her face; Kevin Maloney, lean and fit in dress uniform, unruly red hair blazing, green eyes bright with laughter. A nearby mirror reflected my image, if I had needed to see it—eyes so dark they looked black, olive skin, heart-shaped face framed by masses of thick black curls.

Jessie sighed. "Are you going to start that again?"

"You make it sound as if I brought the subject up once a week. I haven't mentioned it for years."

"That's right. You got over it. A lot of kids, especially those who are orphaned early, develop fantasies about their 'real' parents. Think they're the long-lost heir to the throne of France or something. You forgot that nonsense—"

"I was brainwashed into forgetting it, by you and Dr. Whitaker. Maybe she believed it was a typical adolescent fantasy, but you knew better. You must have known. No, don't interrupt, let me finish. I'm well aware of the fact that statistics are meaningless when applied to individuals. I realize that though it is a rare occurrence, two light-eyed people can have a dark-eyed child. I know that although Tay-Sachs is a hundred times more common among eastern European Jews, I could be one of the exceptions. I know all those fascinating facts; what I don't know is the name of my real father."

Jessie's lips parted, but she didn't speak.

"You must know," I went on. "She was your own sister. My mother. Or is that a lie, too? Am I a casual and inconvenient souvenir of a brief encounter—hers . . . yours . . ."

Moving briskly and without her usual clumsiness, Jessie stepped forward and slapped me across the face.

We stared at one another in mutual consternation. I'm sure she was as surprised and horrified as I.

"You're hysterical," she said hoarsely. "How dare you say that?"

"I'm not hysterical. I'm just very confused."

Leaving the file drawer open, I stood up and walked out of the room.

• • •

Over the years, my bedroom had been redecorated several times. Posters of rock stars had replaced prints of Winnie the Pooh and Mr. Toad, to be replaced in their turn by Degas dancers and Monet water lilies. I had grown up in that room—soaked the pillows with bitter tears of frustrated adolescent love, giggled and whispered with friends, consumed countless bowls of milk toast and chicken soup during bouts of normal childhood ailments, studied and dreamed and played.

Memories permeated that room, memories good and bad. But mostly good.

The kitten under the bed. I was eight years old. Jessie had always refused to let me have a pet. I was too young to understand her reasoning—"Baby, we're both gone all day, me at work, you at school and at the sitter's; it wouldn't be fair to an animal." So when the hungry, bedraggled kitten followed me that day, it didn't have to follow far. I kept it hidden for almost twenty-four hours before Jessie discovered it. I should have known she'd wonder why I spent so much time in my room that sunny Saturday. She was afraid I was ill or unhappy. The kitten was sitting on my lap when she walked in. She let out a loud whoop of sheer surprise and, in sheer surprise, the kitten promptly wet all over my jeans. I screamed, the kitten lost control of another vital bodily function, and Jessie collapsed into a chair and laughed till she cried. Pooch had been a member of the family ever since and Jessie often said she didn't know how we had managed without him. "But, oh, Haskell, the look on your face when he pooped on your lap . . ." Both of us had laughed about it many times since.

Sitting on the edge of the bed I heard Jessie's retreat, quick blundering footsteps descending the stairs. I knew she was angry at herself, bitterly regretting her impulsive blow. I didn't resent it. It had not been a hard or calculated slap. She had an explosive temper and had delivered quite a few tongue-lashings when I was younger, but she had never struck me in the face. I wasn't angry; I felt nothing except a vast bewilderment. I couldn't remember my parents. I had lost both in infancy—my mother in an automobile accident, my "father" in war. Worst of all, I had lost myself. I didn't know who I was.

The photographs had hung on the wall, one on either side of the dressing table, ever since I could remember—the first things I saw when I woke in the morning, the last things I saw before I turned out the light. Hers was a studio portrait, taken on her twenty-first birthday. As the day of my own majority approached and passed, I had studied her young unmarked face, trying to see a resemblance to my own. Except for a vague similarity in the curve of the smiling lips, I couldn't find one. A light behind her made her hair glow; in the black-and-white photograph, it looked like silver. I had never thought she was pretty, but I liked her face; it had strength and humor and a touch of veiled melancholy. Or was that romanticizing, knowing as I did that the fair hair would never turn true silver, or the smooth cheeks be marred by wrinkles?

The face of Kevin Maloney had been enlarged from a snapshot, so it was a little blurry, but it was a far better likeness than a posed studio photograph. His head was thrown back in laughter, strengthening the lean line of the jaw, exposing even white teeth. A handsome face, heart-breakingly young and happy; in every picture I had ever seen of him, he was laughing or smiling. Below the photo-graph, set against black velvet, was his Congressional Medal of Honor—posthumously awarded. How I had ideal-ized that face, and the gallant young man who had earned his country's highest award by sacrificing his life for others.

The tears were streaming down my cheeks. I heard footsteps and reached for a tissue.

After a moment's hesitation, Jessie sat down on the bed—

not too close, a careful distance from me. "I'm sorry," she muttered.

"I know."

"Want something to drink?" From behind her back, with the air of a puppy offering a cherished bone, she produced a glass of white wine. Seeing my expression, she went on, "Or a cup of tea? Or—"

"No, thanks."

Jessie looked at the glass with faint surprise, as if it had just materialized in her hand. She raised it to her lips and drained it in one gulp.

I started to laugh. At least I thought I was laughing, until the sounds turned harsh and ugly and tears splashed darkly onto the fabric of my skirt.

"Oh, baby—don't do that. . . ." She reached out for me.

"It's all right. The last shower." I blew my nose and found I had been right; like the final cloudburst of a thunderstorm, the tears were done with.

"I don't understand you." Jessie didn't follow through on her tentative effort to hug me; my tone, though calm, had been as negative as physical recoil. "Honest to God, Haskell, aren't you being a little melodramatic? You've always been such a well-balanced person—"

"Thanks to three years with a shrink."

I used the word deliberately because I knew Jessie disliked it, particularly when applied to her old friend. She frowned. "Most people would be better off for a few years of counseling. Any child who lost both parents and who was raised by a crusty old spinster aunt is bound to have problems. Normal problems."

"You aren't old and crusty."

"Thanks a heap," Jessie said. "Whatever happened to your sense of humor? You used to tell me about that funny little voice in your mind that made rude comments whenever you wallowed in theatrics."

"I killed it," I said, unsmiling. "The way Mark Twain murdered his conscience. I know just how he felt when he wrote that story. It would be so comfortable to live without a nagging inner voice that won't let you dramatize yourself and your feelings. Most people don't seem to be handicapped by such a thing."

"Your mother was." Jessie faced me squarely. "She *was* your mother, Haskell. She lived with me all those months; I watched her get bigger; I felt you move in her womb. I drove her to the hospital when the pains came on. I was in the waiting room when the nurse brought you out."

"You were the only one there," I said.

"Your—" She faltered, but went resolutely ahead. "Your father was dead. We had received the telegram only a few days earlier; I thought that was why she went into labor prematurely."

"Until you saw me—fat and dark and fully developed."

"Haskell, please."

"Sorry."

"You were such a beautiful baby." Her eyes dropped to her clasped hands. "A perfect little face, without the blotchy skin so many newborns have; a head of dark curls, and long black lashes. You smiled at me. The nurse said it was gas, but it wasn't; it was a real smile."

I had never heard her talk that way before. The facts weren't new to me, but the emotion behind them was. I wanted to throw my arms around her and hold her tight, but something held me back—a new obsession that dulled every feeling except a desperate need to know the truth. I had to hear the whole story over again, for if one unquestioned assumption had proved false, how many others were lies, not facts?

"My grandparents weren't there?"

"You know that."

"Tell me again."

Jessie's hand moved in a gesture of acquiescence.

"Your—Kevin's mother was dead, his father had remarried; he had other children and wasn't much interested. There wasn't time for my mother and father to come. Not that they would have. Papa didn't believe in doctors, especially when it was a case of a woman doing what she was made to do, as he would have expressed it."

The smile that had softened her lips when she spoke of me hardened into a tight line. Already she had told me something I had not known before—how she really felt about her father. She hardly ever mentioned him. Strange, that I had never wondered why.

"And Gran?" I asked.

"He wouldn't let her come."

"Let her?"

"That's the sort of man he was. And," Jessie added bitterly, "the sort of woman she was."

I said, groping, "But you let them take me. After Mother died."

"I couldn't stop them. He was ready to take the case to court, and what chance would I have had against them—an unmarried career woman, tough as nails, probably 'queer'— that's the word he would have used—against a pair of doting, God-fearing, cookie-baking, ideal grandparents? He died when you were three, and I got you back—but only because your grandmother didn't fight me." Jessie got to her feet and began pacing. "I don't want to talk about them. She was your mother, Haskell. Have I ever lied to you?"

"I . . . No. No, you never did." Except about Santa Claus and the tooth fairy and heaven, where my mother and father had gone, to be together and to wait for me. But those weren't lies, they were scraps of comfort, desperately needed and gallantly given, by a woman who had never believed in any of them. But it had never been necessary for her to lie about the identity of my parents. It had never occurred to me to ask. I said, "So now I'm asking. Who was my father?"

Her face paled, but she didn't hesitate. "I never knew anything that would lead me to suppose it wasn't Kevin Maloney."

The very phrasing was a kind of admission. I continued to press her. "You might not have known, but you must have suspected. Are you trying to tell me you never asked her? That she didn't confide in you?"

"It was none of my business."

"But it's my business. Jessie, the odds are piling up. Tay-Sachs, the fact that I don't resemble either of my supposed parents, the fact that I was a seven-month child—"

"Where did you hear that?" Jessie demanded.

"For God's sake, Jessie, I can count to ten—or nine. Besides . . ." I frowned, remembering. "I heard the phrase somewhere—sometime. . . . I didn't know what it meant, but there was something about the *way* it was said that made it stick in my mind."

Jessie's lips compressed, but she didn't enlighten me. "Suppose you are right. To coin a phrase, so what? What difference does it make?"

"A lot of difference. I want to know who I am."

"You'll find that out," Jessie said. "Eventually. And it won't have much to do with who your parents were."

"Oh, sure, give me the old routine! I am what I am, I am the master of my fate and the captain of my soul. . . . But the damned genes do count, Jessie. Tay-Sachs proves that they count. How do I know what other lethal factors are swimming around in my bloodstream?"

"That's just an excuse."

"Maybe. Probably. I don't care if it is. I want to know."

"Suppose you never know?"

"Then I'll deal with not knowing. But if there is a chance—"

The telephone on my desk set up a strident squawk. We both started and Jessie swore.

"Damn, look what you've done to me. Aren't you going to answer it?"

"No."

"It's probably for you."

"I don't want to talk to anyone."

"Goddamn it. . . ." Jessie bounced to her feet and ran out. The telephone kept ringing. It stopped in mid-peal, and I heard her voice from the extension in her room. I couldn't make out the words.

When she came back I was lying down looking blankly at the ceiling.

"That was Jon," she said.

"I figured it might be."

"He wanted to talk to you. I told him you were lying down."

"Thanks."

"So I said he could come over after supper."

"Thanks again." I made myself sit up. It felt like lifting a fifty-pound bag of topsoil. "I suppose I might as well tell him sooner or later."

"Tell him what?"

"That the wedding is off."

That wasn't the end of the argument. Jessie tried everything she could think of to make me change my mind. While I prepared and served a meal of which I ate almost nothing, she kept after me, until finally I said, "For heaven's sake, Jessie, you never wanted me to get married in the first place. I'd think you would be pleased that I've decided to postpone it."

"I thought you were too young, that was the only . . . Did you say postpone?"

I shrugged, poking at fragments of meat loaf with my fork. "That's up to Jon. I may feel differently in a few months, but I can't expect him to sit around waiting for me to make up my mind."

Jessie nodded vigorous agreement and cut herself another slice of carrot cake. Catching my eye, she grimaced. "I know, I know; I said I was going to cut down on sweets. It's your fault; I always gorge when I'm upset. If you wouldn't—"

The doorbell rang; Jessie dropped her fork. "Damn, just look at me. I'm a bundle of nerves. He's early."

"You said after supper," I reminded her.

"Yes, but . . . Are you going to answer the door?"

"Of course." I rose. "Coming?"

"Hell, no. Don't count on me for moral support; this is between the two of you."

"How nice of you to admit it."

Jessie crammed her mouth full of cake and rolled her eyes heavenward.

I went straight to the front door, without stopping as I usually did to glance in the mirror and make sure my hair was smooth and my lipstick unsmudged. When I opened the door, Jon's back was turned to me. His raised arm and the shouts of the children playing catch in the park across the street told me he had just pitched their ball back to them. He had already made friends with the neighborhood menaces, as Jessie called them; sometimes when he was early or I was late, he'd join their game. Kids liked him. So did I.

"Presenting my best side, as usual," he said, before turning to face me.

His features weren't conventionally handsome. Though he was only in his late twenties, his hairline was receding; his nose was outsized and his eyes were deep-set, half hidden by heavy lids and shadowed by protruding brow ridges thickly furred with dark hair. But I had admired his face even before I fell in love with him and lost all aesthetic judgment. He had wonderful bones, sculptured and pronounced, and the severity of his long, strong face was offset by a surprisingly gentle mouth. At least it was always gentle for me.

After the way I had bolted out of the doctor's office, ignoring his anxious questions and refusing his offer to drive me to the station, he must have known something was wrong; but at first he tried to pretend it wasn't serious. I let him kiss me. That was all; I let him. Then I ushered him into the parlor and offered him a chair.

We were like two people trying to communicate without a common language. The things I said made no sense to him; the arguments he produced had no effect on me.

He was so damned reasonable! He said all the right things, making point after unanswerable point with his deadly lawyer's logic. Tests like the ones we had undergone only indicated probabilities; they were not conclusive for individuals. Any of my western European ancestors could have picked up an eastern gene somewhere along the way. And even if my (I should forgive him) overly emotional suspicion was correct, what possible difference did it make? We were the same two people, weren't we? We loved one another, didn't we?

Right, right, and right again. I said, "I don't know who I am."

"But you just agreed—"

"Don't treat me like a hostile witness!"

"I'm not. I only expect a little consistency—"

"I am being consistent, damn it! On one level, I am the same person. On another level—call it psychic, call it emotional—I'm all at sea. Adrift on an ocean of possibilities."

"I understand." We are sitting side by side on the sofa, facing one another. He reached for my hand, like someone grasping at a rope that dangled just out of reach.

I pulled my hand away. "You don't understand. If you did, you wouldn't be trying to make me change my mind."

His lips folded over, no longer gentle. When he spoke, his voice was even. "If you want to search for your roots, that's fine. I'll help you. We'll do it together."

"I have to do it alone."

"Why?"

Why? A good question. I wished I had a good answer.

I might have claimed I was being generous—freeing him of a commitment he would feel bound to honor until I was certain my unknown family tree contained no rotten apples. But that would have sounded absurdly melodramatic in this day and age; there were solutions to all such problems, even genetic anomalies as grisly as Tay-Sachs. I might have repeated the equally melodramatic statement I had already made: "I don't know who I am. The woman I *was* loved you. This woman is someone else." But that was just too corny—even if it was partly true.

I didn't know all the answer, but I knew part of it. This was something I had to do myself, without help, without false comfort, without leaning on someone else's strength. I had always had someone to lean on. First Jessie, a strong woman who solved her own problems and those of others. Then Jon. Was that, perhaps, why I had been so glad to accept Jon's proposal instead of facing the alternative— independence, departure from home, responsibility?

I wasn't thinking that clearly at the time, but I knew in my heart, if not in my head, that now if ever I had to go it alone. And because I was so afraid of being alone—because I ached to take the hand he offered—because I had to fight myself as well as Jon—I fought cruelly and unfairly.

"Why?" he repeated, and I said, "Just because. If you really loved me you wouldn't ask why."

Distressed as I was, I felt a faint stir of wry amusement as I spoke the words; that's the sort of statement that drives men to scream, "What the hell do you women want, for God's sake?" Jon never yelled or lost his temper. Sometimes I wished he would. Right then I wanted him to scream. A good loud fight might have cleared the air. If he had been equally unreasonable I wouldn't have felt like a sulky child being handled, oh, so gently and kindly, by a superior adult. After all, why couldn't he admit that my feelings were important simply because they *were* my feelings? Why couldn't he back off and give me some breathing space, instead of demanding quick, cool-headed reasoning in a situation that was essentially an emotional one?

I won't repeat the rest of the argument. I'm not too proud of my remarks, even though I still think I had a point. He never cracked, he never shouted. His final comment was a quiet "We'll talk again when you are calmer."

When he left, he didn't slam the door. The click of the latch was succeeded by a thud as a baseball hit the door, and I laughed out loud. "I think you're out of luck tonight, kids. Your pal is in no mood to play games."

"Talking to yourself?" Jessie peered cautiously through a narrow slit in the door that led to the dining room. Cake crumbs clung to the corners of her mouth. I didn't answer; after a moment she opened the door all the way and edged in.

"Looks as if you've cooked your goose there," she said. "I hope you won't regret it."

"I hope so too."

"What are you going to do now?"

I hadn't thought about it consciously, but all at once the general outline was as clear in my mind as a military campaign.

"I'm going to take a sentimental journey."

"Where?"

"Not where—when. I'm going to travel in time."

For the next few weeks, I spent my days in various libraries. I had completed most of the requirements for my degree; I finished the rest mechanically and meticulously, because I didn't want to damage my chances of graduating with honors. Without a degree, I didn't have a prayer of succeeding in the wild plan I had concocted. Even with a degree, it was going to be tough.

Most of the time was spent in time traveling. That's how I learned all those fascinating facts about 1965. In one way, that recent period was as remote as the history of the ancient Near East, which was my college major; in another way, it was painfully immediate. My primary concern was what that year had meant to one woman—besides being the last full year of her life.

I didn't attend my own graduation. I didn't have time. Besides, it would have been too awkward, with Jessie sitting there trying so hard to play the proud guardian when we were barely speaking to one another.

Wary neutrality is the best way to describe our relationship. It was the first time I had seen her floundering, unable to deal with a problem. If I hadn't been so wrapped up in myself, I would have realized it wasn't only my problem that had thrown her into a paralysis of indecision—that she carried a weighty bundle of worries of her own. She volunteered nothing and I asked nothing. I meant to question her eventually, but I had been well educated, I knew how to establish priorities; background research came first. I knew how to do that, too.

I had expected to hear from Jon, but he didn't write; and if he called, Jessie didn't tell me. She didn't tell me about the call from his mother, either, but I happened to overhear the conversation—Jessie's end of it—and it wasn't pretty. Having failed to tell me what she thought of me, Mrs. Feldman wrote me a letter.

She had never liked me much. Jon was her treasure, her darling, and she thought he deserved better than a girl from an undistinguished background, with no particular talents or social graces. Jon's father was the senior partner of one of Philadelphia's leading law firms, and there was family money; Mrs. Feldman was a patron of the symphony, the museum, and everything else that had patrons. Her well-bred friends on the charity boards would have been a little surprised at her vocabulary—or maybe they wouldn't have been surprised. I threw the letter into the wastebasket, but I didn't blame her for letting off steam. I had behaved badly, and I knew it. The person I blamed was Jon, for crying on Mama's shoulder.

One afternoon I came home early to find not only Jessie's car, but another one, in the driveway. I recognized the second vehicle; it belonged to Ann Whitaker, one of Jessie's best friends, and—not so coincidentally—my ex-shrink.

A rush of anger sent the blood burning in my cheeks. If I had not killed my conscience, it would have told me that anger was illogical and unfair. Jessie had a perfect right to discuss her worries with an old friend. She also had the right to discuss me—the biggest of her worries. Some such acknowledgment stirred in my mind, like a dying echo from a reproachful ghost, but I squelched it.

Jessie must have assumed I wouldn't be home until five or six o'clock, as had been my recent habit. If I walked in on them, they would pretend that Jessie had decided to take the afternoon off and Ann had just happened to drop in. But I knew this was a consultation, not a social call. They were talking about me. Heads together, voices hushed—"Poor Haskell, what can we do to get her trolley back on the track?"

My first impulse was to rush in and confront them. It would have been so satisfying to yell at someone who would yell back. Satisfying but stupid.

I tiptoed up the walk and circled the house, walking on the grass. I was in luck; the back door was unlocked. Jessie must have let Pooch out and neglected to bolt the door again. She was careless about such things, probably because she couldn't imagine a burglar having the chutzpah to bother her.

Pooch squatted near the birdbath behind a miniature rosebush that wouldn't have concealed a mouse, much less an eighteen-pound cat. He could never understand why the birds never dropped by for a drink or a swim when he was there, but hope sprang eternal in his furry breast. Seeing me, he hoisted his tail in greeting and grumbled low in his throat—I was scaring the birds.

"Sssh," I whispered. Pooch looked puzzled; my greeting was usually more enthusiastic—but decided I was heeding his warning. He watched benevolently as I eased the door open and slipped inside.

A murmur of voices from the living room reached me, but I couldn't make out the words. I would have to get closer. Stepping out of my shoes, I crept down the hall and took up a position near the open archway.

They say eavesdroppers never hear anything good about themselves. That may be because anyone low enough or desperate enough to eavesdrop hears exactly what he expects to hear—the worst. As a matter of fact, the first thing I heard was Ann's voice saying, "Jessie, you're asking me to make bricks without straw. How can I talk to Haskell if she won't talk to me? I can't telephone and suggest we meet for lunch; she'd see through that in a second and resent you all the more for consulting me— behind her back, as she would view it."

Jessie grunted. "You're a hell of a lot of help."

"And you are no help at all. I assume you're familiar with that well-known psychiatric adage: Just because someone is paranoid, it doesn't mean people aren't following him. Haskell's reaction is not abnormal or unreasonable. How would you feel if you discovered that you had been adopted in infancy by the people you always believed to be your natural parents?"

"I'd throw a big party and celebrate."

"Yes, you probably would at that. I've told you before, Jessie, that someday you must come to grips with your anger toward your parents. You sent Haskell to me with her emotional problems, but when I suggested you could do with some counseling . . ."

She broke off. I realized Jessie must have registered her dislike of the subject with a wordless gesture. I was sorry she had stopped Ann. So Jessie had problems too, did she? And about her parents. That made two of us.

After a moment Ann said, "All right, I won't belabor the point. We're talking about Haskell, right? In some ways her feelings resemble those of an adopted child. Many of such children want—need—to locate their birth parents. I don't understand why you can't accept that."

"It isn't what she's doing; it's the way she's going about it. She's changed, Ann. She's become secretive, hostile— not only toward me, toward everyone. She won't tell me what she's planning to do. I'm afraid it's something dangerous or illegal or . . . Look at this."

There was a pause. I was dying to see what they were looking at, but I was afraid to take the chance. After a moment, Ann said, "I'm not sure what this means."

"It means she's going back there. She isn't stupid. She's figured out that it has to be one of them—that group—"

They must have discussed this point before I arrived; Ann obviously knew what she was talking about. So did I, of course. It was typical of Ann that instead of answering directly, she should attack from another direction.

"Has to be? Then you admit Haskell is correct in her assumption that Kevin Maloney is not her father?"

Jessie was silent. Ann pressed her. "You've avoided that issue all along, and it is the most important one. What about it, Jessie?"

I was so anxious to hear Jessie's reply that I leaned forward, brushing the lamp on the nearby table with my arm. I caught it in time to keep it from falling, but the glass baubles hanging from its shade rang a musical chime.

They must have heard it. Rather than be caught in a

humiliating position, I decided to brazen it out. I went to the door.

"Good question, Ann. Maybe Jessie will tell you. She certainly hasn't confided in me."

I thought I was being pretty cool until I saw the paper on the table. Snatching it up, I turned on Jessie.

"How dare you snoop in my desk?"

"I got the idea from you," Jessie snapped. "You started it—first snooping, now eavesdropping. . . ." She faced Ann, her hands spread in appeal. "She was never like this, Ann. She was the most honest, forthright child. What's come over her?"

Ann cleared her throat and shifted her weight slightly. That was all it took to shut both of us up. She was a big woman, tall and heavy-set, who made no attempt to minimize her size; instead she used it to dominate other people. It wasn't so much a question of sheer physical bulk as of the projection of an image—that of the Earth Mother, the wise woman who knew all the answers and was in communication with higher powers. Her clothes, always in exquisite taste, supported the image—traditional, perhaps a little old-fashioned, but always intensely feminine. She had favored shawls and scarves long before they came into style; she wore her hair coiled around her head like a coronet, silver twisting through the brown in a regal glimmer.

"I'm glad you're here, Haskell," she said calmly. "It's a pity you didn't arrive a few minutes earlier. . . ." Her eyes shifted to my bare feet, and a slight knowing smile curved her lips as she went on. "You would have heard me tell Jessie I was in full agreement with you."

I threw myself ungracefully into a chair and scowled at both of them impartially. "I didn't hear Jessie answer your question."

"Maybe she doesn't know the answer."

"She must know. She's told me over and over how close

she and Mother were—closer than sisters, closer than best friends. How is it possible that my mother wouldn't confide in her adored, supportive big sister?"

"That's enough," Ann said. She glanced at Jessie. Some signal must have passed between them; Jessie jumped up and went quickly out of the room, but not before I caught a glimpse of crimson cheeks and lips pressed tightly together.

"Why did you do that, Ann?" I demanded. "Why not let her answer back—yell at me, if she felt like it. You don't have to spare my feelings—"

"Your feelings?" I had never seen Ann lose her temper, but she was on the verge of doing so now. Her hands twisted and clasped as if she were trying to keep them from doing something she would later regret. Such as giving me a good hard smack?

She caught herself; leaning back in the chair, she let out a little breath of amused surprise. "That was close. I'm trying not to be angry with you, Haskell. You've had a severe shock and your behavior is quite typical. You're using Jessie as a whipping boy, knowing you are perfectly safe in doing so because you'll never lose her love no matter how you abuse her. A classic mother-child relationship."

I wished she had slapped me. Her speech hurt even more because I knew she was right. And the word that hurt most was the single, non-pejorative noun, child.

"I know how you feel, Haskell, but it's difficult for me to be cool and professional where Jessie is concerned. Couldn't you see that what you said was rubbing salt in the wound? That if she didn't know the truth—and I assure you, she did not—the discovery must have shocked her as severely as it did you? The person she loved best in the world deliberately deceived her; the person she trusted most didn't trust her. You, of all people, ought to know how that hurts."

I couldn't look at her. My eyes were burning with tears of

shame, but I made a last-ditch attempt to defend myself. "She's always been against the things I wanted to do."

"Like going camping in the Adirondacks with the campus drug pusher and two of his friends?"

"It wasn't the way you make it sound," I gasped.

"I know. You honestly believed your saintly trust would turn the druggies from their wicked ways."

"So I was a fool. I was only sixteen."

"Everyone is a fool at sixteen," Ann said with a smile. "Even you?"

"Especially me."

I was familiar with Ann's methods, but she was getting to me all the same. There was an odd sense of relief in being forced to face facts, however uncomfortable. Even the fact of my own selfishness.

"All right," I said. "So I'm a no-good, ungrateful rat. I owe Jessie an apology, and she'll get one—from the heart, and on my bended knee. But dammit, Ann, I wish she wouldn't fight me every time I try to make a decision and carry it out by myself. Even if the decision is wrong. Isn't that how people learn—by making mistakes and suffering the consequences?"

I detected a gleam of sympathy in Ann's eyes, but she shook her head. "It's difficult for any parent to watch a child rush headlong into disaster without attempting to interfere. Especially a parent as tough and realistic as Jessie."

"I know. I mean, I suppose it must be. But my decisions weren't all disastrous. First she tried to talk me out of majoring in Egyptology—"

"You know why."

"But I wasn't trying to imitate my mother. Well . . . not entirely. Then, when I decided to get married after I graduated instead of going on for my Ph.D., she objected to that."

"She thought you were too young."

"And now I've proved she was right."

"I wish you'd stop thinking of this as a contest," Ann said forcibly. "There is no way either of you can win if you go on fighting each other. If I may make a suggestion . . ."

"You will anyway."

Ann grinned. "Quite right, I will." She glanced at the closed door to the dining room and called, "Come in, Jessie, it's safe now."

Jessie came in. She was carrying a tray. Another of Ann's ideas, I felt sure—drinks and canapés, setting the scene for a normal social occasion. Ann accepted a glass of sherry, the only drink she allowed herself, and then I saw what Jessie had brought for me. It was my favorite kind of beer—imported, expensive, and hard to find. It couldn't have been that silly bottle of beer that made me want to cry; it must have been the look on Jessie's face as she gave me a shy, sidelong glance from under her glasses. She was wearing them for once; they didn't succeed in concealing the redness around her eyes.

I said, "I'm sorry, Jessie."

"I'm sorry, too, baby."

Ann sipped her sherry and smiled her enigmatic Earth Mother smile.

2

I wish I could say that confrontation cleared the air between me and Jessie, but it didn't, not entirely. Life is never that simple. Thanks to Ann's analysis I had a better understanding of my aunt and of what I had done to her. Inadvertently I had wrenched the lid off Jessie's private box of horrors—memories she had suppressed for decades. Once released, they could not be imprisoned again. She had to do battle with them, and the process was painful to watch. It was also frightening. A child hates to admit that mothers and fathers aren't solid, safe authority figures but suffering, vulnerable human beings. The worst of it was that there was nothing I could do to help her. Each of us has to fight her own demons.

I knew the bare facts about Jessie's background, and Mother's. Actually it wasn't so much a question of knowing the facts as of accepting them, without thought or question, like knowing you'll get wet if you stay outside in the rain. They had been born in a small town in Illinois. When they were eleven and six years old, respectively (Jessie was the elder), their father, a carpenter by trade, had moved to a suburb of Chicago. I knew Jessie had gone straight into the labor market after high school; that Mother had not only attended college at the University of Chicago, but was working on her doctorate when she dropped out of school to get married.

That sudden decision had seemed very romantic to me. I remember asking Jessie about it when I was twelve or thirteen—that quintessentially romantic age. Jessie had carefully tailored her answers to my age and mood, telling me what I wanted to hear—that my mother had thrown her career aside in order to spend a few bittersweet weeks with her young husband before he marched off to serve his country, God, and apple pie. It made perfect sense to me at the time. I'd have done the same for a gangling boy named . . . I forget his name. That is, I'd have done it if there had been a war, and if What's-his-name had asked me.

So much for the facts, so called; now I had to hear them again, interpret and dissect them. In the beginning, Jessie bitterly resented my questions. Sometimes she would jump up and run out of the room, her face flushed, her lips shaping words she didn't want to utter.

A breakthrough of sorts came one evening when we were sitting in the living room after supper. It was Saturday night; Jessie didn't have to go to work the next day, so she was indulging in a postprandial glass (or two) of brandy. Pooch was on her lap, purring like a thousand crickets.

We had taken out Jessie's old photo albums and were looking at Mother's wedding pictures. She had been married in this very room by a justice of the peace, but Jessie, not Mother, had insisted on white satin and lace. The traditional tokens of virginity have ceased to mean anything, if they ever did; but the irony of the symbols struck me rather forcibly in this case, and I found myself studying my mother's slim figure with particular interest.

"You never suspected she was pregnant?"

I tried to keep my voice neutral, and apparently I succeeded, for Jessie answered readily. "Not at the time. It did dawn on me a few months later when she began to show. Not that I cared. Your generation wasn't the first to invent premarital sex."

"Didn't you have the pill?" I asked curiously.

Jessie tickled Pooch under his chin. He rolled over, paws curled and eyes closed, in an ecstasy of feline abandon. I could see that the question had bothered my aunt, which surprised me; she had certainly been blunt enough when informing me about the facts of life. After a short pause she said, "You have to understand, Haskell. Your mother and I never talked about things like that. Growing up the way we did . . . I never said much about your grandfather, did I?"

"I don't care about my grandfather. I want to know—"

"Shut up," Jessie said equably. "If you want to understand your mother, you'll have to hear a few painful truths about the old—man."

"You didn't like him?"

"I hated his guts," Jessie said. "I still do."

The cold, ruthless tone was more shocking than a scream of rage. I stared at her, chilled. "You never said—"

"Oh, I said plenty. You just weren't listening." Pooch let out a squawk of protest, and Jessie's taut grasp on his fur relaxed. She laughed self-consciously. "Even after all these years I clench my fists when I think of him. He's probably the reason why I never married. He may have been the reason your mother rushed into a hasty marriage. And if he hadn't died when you were three years old, I would have . . . I honestly don't know what I would have done—kidnapping, patricide—anything, to get you away from him."

"I never understood how he got custody in the first place.

Weren't Mother and I living with you when she—when it happened?"

"Yes. She moved in with me when your—when Kevin went overseas. Papa was furious; he expected she'd come home. Home . . ." Jessie gave a mirthless little laugh. "He couldn't do anything about you while she was alive, of course. The day after the funeral—I had to go to work, I'd taken too much time off already—you were with a sitter—and in they came, Mama and Papa—she couldn't stop them—she called me, but it was too late, they'd already left."

The jerky, disjointed sentences were broken by gasps, as if she were having trouble breathing. I hated myself at that moment; she was not remembering, she was reliving a time that still hurt, hurt like hell. After a while her breathing quieted and she said, "The day after the funeral. We had a fight about that too. He wanted her buried in Illinois, in the sanctified cemetery of the holier-than-thou church where he planned to lay his own bones. Assuming, of course, that he wasn't transported bodily to heaven, as I think he expected to be. I won that battle. I knew she'd rather burn in hell than join him in *his* hereafter."

"Why didn't you ever tell me?"

Jessie reached for her glass and took, not a genteel sip, but a good healthy swallow. "I tried not to dump on you. You were just a baby—and what would have been the point? I slipped, now and then. . . . But I guess you weren't paying attention. It's amazing how seldom people actually listen to other people. And kids never listen to parents or guardians."

"Only when it concerns their selfish interests," I muttered, in new-found (and unfortunately temporary) humility. "I don't remember him very well, but I have a vague impression of a bearded Santa Claus figure. Did he—was I abused or what?"

Jessie shook her head and licked a drop of brandy off her

lip. "No, not at all. He was a doting grandfather—by his standards. He loved children. It was women he hated."

"You and Mother?"

"And Mama," Jessie said. "God help her. . . . Do you know what my name is?"

"Jessie," I said, bewildered. "Jessica . . ."

"Jezebel. Jezebel and Leah—two of the most unappealing women in the Bible. We lived by the Book—or rather by Papa's interpretation of it. He censored our reading, selected our playmates—we weren't allowed many—and watched us like Big Brother. We went to church three times on Sunday; between services we had to sit and listen to Papa read from the Bible. He boasted that it was the only thing he ever read. I went to church school for the first four grades. The girls all wore the same uniform—dark print dresses down to our ankles, with long sleeves and high necks, winter and summer. Our hair was cut short because Saint Paul said a woman's head should be shorn if it was not covered. The older girls and women all wore caps or bonnets; I never saw my mother without one. That's the good part. Shall I go on?"

"I get the picture." I looked wonderingly at my aunt, sprawled comfortably on the couch with a cigarette in one hand and a glass of brandy in the other. "How did you get away?"

"I might never have had the courage if we hadn't moved to Chicago—Oak Park, rather. A cousin of Mama's had died and left her the house, and Papa was having a hard time getting work; he was such a cantankerous old so-and-so that most people in town wouldn't hire him. It would have hurt his pride to go to work for someone else in a small town where he had always considered himself a leading citizen. He had no trouble finding a job in Chicago; he did good work and I guess he had learned to keep his mouth shut instead of lecturing everybody about their sinful ways.

"It was the first time I had seen how the normal world

lived. There was no branch of Papa's church there, and he wouldn't attend any other—he conducted services himself, every Sunday, all day Sunday. We had to attend the public schools. And of course we had to wear the same clothes we wore at home, including the thick stockings and heavy, clumsy shoes. Papa cut our hair himself."

"Oh, Jessie," I said, from the heart. "What grade were you in?"

"Fifth. Lee was just starting first grade; she had never attended kindergarten. Oh, it wasn't the era of fishnet stockings and miniskirts, but you can imagine how we looked compared to the others—and what they said and did to us." Her face was pinched and pale with remembered suffering. "Nothing else that happened to me was as bad as that. Sounds vain and foolish to you, I suppose."

"No. Oh, no."

Jessie gave herself a little shake. "Well, being a weak vessel of corruption, I allowed the devil to enter my sinful heart. In others words, I dared to differ with Papa on some issues. They were minor acts of rebellion, but retaliation was swift and painful; it didn't take me long to realize my only hope was to bide my time and work for the day when I would be legally free of him. He didn't hold with education for women; the only reason he sent us to school was because the law said he had to. I knew he'd take me out the minute I was sixteen. With the help of some sympathetic teachers— God bless them—I worked my fanny off and managed to finish high school early. On my sixteenth birthday I walked out of the house and never went back. With the help of one of those wonderful teachers and a lot of lies, I got a job as a trainee at Marshall Field's. I was a department head when I was twenty-one—Field's thought I was twenty-three. I'd kept in touch with your mother, on the sly—Papa had, of course, officially cast me off and expunged my name from the family Bible. On her sixteenth birthday, Lee followed my sterling example, with the difference that she had *me* waiting for her, with my own little apartment and a salary big enough to support the two of us. I was determined she should go to college. Oh, I was bright enough, but it was mostly hard work and desperation that got me where I was. I knew she was different. And I was right. She had no trouble getting scholarships. Even with that help, it was a struggle, but we made it.

"Then, when Lee was twenty-one, I was offered a job in Philadelphia. Lee was in her first year of graduate school. That was a funny thing, the way she settled on her major. I tried to talk her into teaching or business school—something practical. No way. She had always been interested in archaeology, but the day she walked into the Oriental Institute, it was like Fate—love at first sight.

"I wanted Lee to come with me. She could have transferred to the University of Pennsylvania. But she was so happy where she was, and she had just won a big fellowship that paid most of her expenses. I wasn't worried about leaving her. She was twenty-one years old, after all. Parents send children away to college when they're much younger. They do it all the time."

It was dark outside. A single lamp behind her shone on her silvery hair but left her features hidden in shadow. "Of course they do," I said. "You've no reason to blame yourself—"

"Who says I blame myself?" Jessie moved so suddenly that the sleeping cat rolled off her lap and thudded to the floor. She reached down apologetically; Pooch snarled and stalked away. "I don't blame her either. It was her life, her decision. It just came as such a surprise. She was so gung-ho about getting her degree. And Kevin, of all people . . ."

"Did you know him?"

"I had never actually met him. I knew her other friends; most of them were students in the same department at the Oriental Institute. The first time I ever heard her mention

Kevin was when she came here for Christmas that last winter—the winter of 1964. He was a business major, but he signed up for some courses at the O.I., just so he could be near her. She was flattered, of course, but a little—well, I have to say contemptuous. Not that she didn't like him, but she couldn't take him seriously. At least that was what I thought. . . . I wouldn't have been so surprised if it had been one of the others. When she called and said she and Kevin were getting married, I thought she was joking. I was absolutely thunderstruck.''

And hurt, I thought. You were closer than most sisters, closer than best friends, because she owed you so much. It wouldn't be much of an exaggeration to say she owed you her very life—for what sort of existence could she have looked forward to without your help and your example? All your fierce intelligence and ambition had been poured into advancing her—her career, her success. Wasted. Down the drain.

And now I was repeating the same pattern.

Placing her glass carefully on the coffee table, Jessie rose. "I'm drunk," she announced seriously. "I'm going to bed. I hope you have enjoyed this conversation, because I sure as hell have not."

She went to the door, weaving a little but not without a certain forlorn dignity. I couldn't be cruel enough to detain her, but I felt horribly frustrated. We had gotten so close to the heart of the matter.

Usually Pooch slept with Jessie and went upstairs with her. That night, offended by her cavalier treatment, he climbed into my lap and fussed around, nudging and shoving, until I arranged myself to his satisfaction. I sat there for a long time, stroking him until his rumbling purr faded into the quiet breathing of sleep. For the first time— though certainly not the last—I wondered if I was about to make the mistake of my life. Why not let sleeping dogs—or cats—lie? Even as the question entered my mind, I knew the answer. I couldn't do it. There was a gaping hole in my life, and monsters lurked in the dark depths. Look what was happening to Jessie because she had tried to ignore her own dragons.

The dragons were awake and breathing fire, and as the days passed, I watched Jessie fight hers. What I had done to her was tantamount to throwing someone into the deep end of the pool instead of offering him swimming lessons. Not that Jessie would have accepted the offer; Ann had tried, more than once if I had understood her oblique reference correctly, and had been refused. Jessie's very strength was a kind of weakness. She hated to admit she needed help.

I didn't have the kind of training that would have let me help. I blamed myself, often and bitterly, for being the unwitting instigator of her war with the past but—I'll be honest—even if I had known how it would affect her I'm not sure I could have acted any differently. At any rate, the damage was done now, and I think the rough and ready catharsis helped her. Having once let down the barriers, she talked more freely; I had sense enough to keep quiet and let her set her own pace. She'd get to the point in her own good time.

The thing that did it were the old photo albums. I had looked at them often. I had few-enough mementos of my mother. Jessie had given me her books and papers and notes, but there was nothing from her childhood—no toys or dolls, no trinkets or treasures dear to the heart of a little girl. Not even early pictures of her. It was as if she had not existed before her sixteenth birthday.

Jessie had taken a lot of snapshots after Mother came to live with her; she must have gloated over them, seeing her young sister smiling and happy at last, prettily dressed, surrounded by friends. Later, after they were separated, Mother had been conscientious about sending photos, accompanied by long, affectionate letters that described her activities. It was a means of reassuring Jessie that, though they were separated physically, they remained close.

These were the pictures that interested me—the ones that showed Mother with her friends of that last significant year. Thanks to her letters and—in some cases—to previous acquaintance, Jessie knew them all. I knew them too. I probably knew more about them than Jessie did.

Jessie hadn't lied to me. She had lied to herself, unwilling to admit a breach of faith with someone she loved. Now, after hearing her bitter reminiscences, I knew there was another reason why the truth had been, and still was, so hard to face. Early-childhood conditioning leaves an indelible stain. Her father had believed that fornication was a sin and that it was better to marry than to burn—but not much better. Now I was demanding that Jessie discuss which of the men in my mother's life might have fathered her child— a child who was, by "Papa's" moral standards, illegitimate.

She kept returning to those old photo albums, like someone rubbing a healing wound. (I could only hope the wound was healing.) Her need suited my own, because the albums were the heart of my inquiry. One in particular—the one labeled 1964–5.

There were a few baby pictures of me at the end, filling out the blank pages. The other photos were of Mother and her friends—the men in her life.

We were sitting, as we had so often before, in the living room. Jessie had a glass in her hand, as usual; she was drinking more these days and I was sorry about it, but there wasn't much I could do to stop her.

The earliest pictures in the album had been taken on the steps of a building identified, in Mother's neat handwriting, as the Oriental Institute. It was winter; snow frosted the broad balustrades, and the subjects of the photos were bundled up in heavy coats and jackets. One showed my mother, standing between two men. She was twenty-two years old; the smile that rounded her cheeks and narrowed her eyes made her look even younger. A scarf covered her head and was tied under her chin. Her arms were clasped around a pile of heavy books.

The men also carried books. One was hatless, his hair wildly windblown. He looked like an amiable hippopotamus, his body round as a barrel, his sleepy smile and plump cheeks narrowing his eyes to slits.

I read the label under the photo aloud. " 'Phil, Dave and me in front of the O.I. March 1964.' Which one is Phil?"

I knew, but I hoped the question would start Jessie talking. She didn't answer at first; her eyes were fixed on the miniaturized smiling face of her sister. When she spoke, her voice was slurred and soft. "Phil is the short one. I've forgotten his last name. He left school the next year; took over his father's business, your mother said. Somewhere out west."

Phil's last name was Cartwright. That was all I knew about him—so far. Tracking down a "business, somewhere out west," wouldn't be easy, but if my initial inquiries turned up a blank, I'd have to try. I pointed to the other man.

"That's Dave?"

"David Wertheim. He was a few years younger than Lee. Smart as a whip, though. He's a professor now."

Full professor of Egyptology at the Oriental Institute. It had not been difficult to trace David Wertheim; his articles appeared in professional journals from time to time. I wondered if I would recognize him. He was much taller than Phil, and as thin as the latter man was squat and chunky. A shaggy black beard covered the lower part of his face, a knitted cap was pulled low over his forehead. One long, spidery arm was draped over Mother's shoulders.

The same people appeared in all the pictures, Phil and Dave and a few others. "There were never more than a dozen grad students in Egyptology," Jessie explained. "Usually fewer. It isn't like engineering or economics; there aren't many job openings. I remember going to one of Lee's classes, where she and Dave were the only students. They were reading some weird text—hieroglyphics, she called it."

"Hieroglyphs," I corrected automatically.

"Yeah." Jessie smiled. "She always corrected me when I said that. Anyhow, I fell asleep. I couldn't help it; I didn't have the faintest idea what they were talking about."

"Was Mother embarrassed?"

"She laughed her head off." Jessie grinned reminiscently. "Dave kidded me about it; he always called me 'Sleeping Beauty' after that. The teacher laughed too. He was a nice young fellow; I can't remember his name."

I felt my nerves tightening as I turned the pages, approaching the most vital group of pictures. Jessie was in a good mood, talking freely. I prayed I wouldn't do or say anything to stop her.

These photos dated from the fall and early winter of 1964. They were indoor photos taken at informal parties. There was a lot of mugging and horseplay; some of the humor eluded me, presumably because it involved departmental personalities and private jokes. The ambiance was always the same—the interior of a small house or apartment; kitchen, bedroom, and living room.

"Steve Nazarian's apartment," Jessie said. "He was the only one who had his own place, so they always held their parties there. That's him."

It was a face one would not easily forget. The features were pronounced and distinctive—full lips, high cheekbones, strong aquiline nose. But the most striking thing about the face was its intensity. The pictured eyes were no bigger than pinpoints, but they blazed at the camera.

"His father was a multimillionaire." Jessie added casually, "Is, I should say; he must be pushing ninety, but I believe he's still alive."

I studied the next snapshot. It was one of a series

depicting an amateur play or charade, ancient Egyptian in theme, as one might expect. The costumes were impromptu and hilarious, concocted from sheets and tablecloths and kitchen implements. Steve was the central feature in this one; stripped to the waist and adorned with fake jewels, a striped towel wrapped around his head in a fair imitation of the pharaoh's nemes headdress, he pointed a basting spoon at a kneeling captive, while his court stood around in attitudes expressive of awe and adoration. The captive was Dave Wertheim; his bare chest and arms were thickly furred with dark hair, and his face was a mask of mock terror, eyes rolled up and tongue protruding.

"Dave was the biggest ham of them all," Jessie said fondly. "I suppose it looks silly to you. . . ."

"No."

The laughing young faces didn't look silly; they struck me as unutterably sad. They were so young. . . . I reminded myself that it hadn't been that long ago; most of them would only be in their forties by now. Those that had lived.

Mother played queen to Steve Nazarian's pharaoh. A tablecloth wrapped tightly around her body was held at the waist by a wool scarf. Her tall, Nefertiti-type crown had been shaped out of a rolled newspaper. She looked delicious.

Another series of photographs depicted a case of royal adultery. Kevin Maloney played the part of the guilty lover, first clutching Mother in a passionate embrace, then cringing in terror as pharaoh caught the lovers in flagrante. He had not been a very good actor. He couldn't stop grinning, even when pharaoh struck an attitude and condemned him to die.

"They were all crazy about Lee," Jessie said proudly. "Not that she had much competition. There was only one other woman in the department. That's her—Margaret Maxwell."

Margaret was always on the fringes of the group. Thin and hollow-chested, her long face frozen in a stiff smile, she suggested an old-maid teacher trying desperately to join in the children's game.

"I wonder what she was supposed to be," I said, studying Margaret's costume. It hung awkwardly on her, its bed-sheet origins only too obvious. Mother managed to make her tablecloth look authentic—and sexy.

Jessie shrugged and poured another drink. "It would be a supporting role, you can bet on that. She was always second banana to Lee, in class and with the guys. She'd have taken any of them, but it was Steve she really wanted."

I could understand that. Even without the Nazarian millions, Steve would have knocked most girls off their feet. He played the part of a god-king to perfection. A lean, spare body like those of the idealized royal statues, features bold and arrogant. Those features seemed oddly familiar to me; I had often studied them in the past few days, trying to pin down the elusive resemblance, wondering if I had seen it in my own mirror. All of a sudden, I got it. He reminded me of Jon—the same prominent nose, the same structure of jaw and cheekbones.

"That was sad," Jessie muttered. "Poor Steve . . ."

"What happened to him?" I knew. I wanted to hear her version.

"It made the national news," Jessie said, staring into her glass. "One of those radical student groups, protesting the war. That was the Vietnam War—"

"I know."

"Weathermen, Black Panthers—he wasn't one of them; his group called itself the Front for the War for Peace, or some such thing. He was killed in 1968 when a house in New Jersey blew up. The kids were planning to set off the explosives in some demonstration. It was a demonstration, all right."

She drained her glass.

"Ironic," I said.

"Yeah. Violence for the sake of peace, murder to stop the killing."

"More than that. Kevin Maloney died fighting that war. Stephen Nazarian died fighting against it."

Jessie continued to study the depths of her empty glass. "So that's what you believe."

"What do you believe?"

"I don't believe in anything these days." She reached for the brandy. I caught her hand.

"Please, Jessie. Don't. Talk to me; help me."

Her fingers writhed in mine and then went limp. "What are you going to do, Haskell?"

"You know."

"Yes, I know. It follows logically, doesn't it? You're going to Chicago—to find him—whoever he is." Jessie added in a voice so soft I could barely make out the words, "That's what she did. She went. But she never came back."

Shocked and speechless, I let my fingers relax. Jessie grabbed the bottle and refilled her glass.

My mother had been on her way back from Chicago when her car went out of control and slammed into an abutment, killing her instantly. I had been only three months old at the time. She had left me with Jessie. Luckily for me . . . But now it occurred to me that it was a little strange that she had not taken me with her. Traveling with a child can be a pain, but an infant, who sleeps most of the time anyway, isn't much trouble.

She had left me with Jessie and I had taken her place in Jessie's life and in Jessie's love. No wonder Jessie had reacted so violently to my quixotic but essentially harmless plan; she saw the same pattern repeating itself and feared it would have the same fatal end. The fact that her fear was unfounded, pure superstition, didn't lessen its force. At first I couldn't think what to say.

I began, "But I thought she went to Chicago to see my grandparents. To make up with them."

"Oh, yeah, that's what she said," Jessie mumbled. "Mending fences, she said. And to look for a job. Kevin was dead; she had to find something to do with her life. I was praying she wouldn't find anything. I wanted her to stay with me. But I couldn't talk her out of going; she was as stubborn as you are. Just lately I started wondering if she had another reason. . . . Oh hell, don't listen to me; I'm not making sense."

"You're upset," I said. "And it's my fault. I'm sorry, Jessie. I'm sorry about everything."

"But not sorry enough to change your plans."

"I can't! Is it so terrible, what I'm doing? I'm not going to hurt anyone. If what I suspect is true, there is no one living who can be hurt."

"Steve," Jessie said.

"You agree?"

"I just don't know," Jessie said heavily. "Even now. Isn't that a sweet thing to say about your own sister? I don't know whether she was sleeping with one of them or all of them, or half the goddamn city of Chicago. Good night, Haskell. I think I'm drunk enough to sleep now."

So once again I watched my aunt retreat, her feet unsteady, her face drawn with pain—and all because of me. There was nothing I could say to console her or convince her that her suffering was senseless.

I decided I had learned all I could from Jessie. If there was veritas in vino, she had told the whole truth as she saw it. It would take someone cleverer or crueler than I to probe deeper; and perhaps after all, there was nothing more to discover from that source.

She hadn't asked about my plans. Oh, I had plans. I had been working on them for weeks.

Theoretically it was possible that any one of a million or so men could be Mother's long-ago lover. People sometimes lead secret lives unknown to their closest friends and relatives. However, the most likely candidate was one of her former fellow students. Several of them were still in Chicago. Philip Cartwright had left the area, but another member of the group, Vladislav Wtysinski, was listed in the Chicago phone book. With a name like that, it was safe to assume it was the same man or a near relative. Wertheim taught at the Oriental Institute and so did Margaret Maxwell. She didn't look like the sort of person Mother would have chosen as a best friend, but she was the only other woman in the group; being on the spot, she might have seen or heard something that would give me a clue. I couldn't eliminate any of the men on the basis of their names or their presumed ethnic backgrounds. Many Americans are individual melting pots, fascinating mixtures of diverse races and nationalities.

Steve Nazarian was a special case. I had known about his family long before I realized he was one of Mother's friends; the Nazarian name was famous—or notorious—in archaeological circles. Steve had followed a family tradition by majoring in Egyptology. Both his father and his grandfather had been collectors of antiquities, patrons of institutions involved in excavation and research. The Nazarian Collection was one of the biggest and richest of all private collections. Housed in the old mansion on Chicago's South Side, it was a source of constant frustration to scholars because old Nazarian refused them access to it. Now and then he would allow a photograph to be published or let some favored scholar study a particular object, but this only whetted the appetites of those who knew full well that there were even finer pieces hidden away in the hundred-odd rooms of the family home where Nazarian lived in virtual seclusion.

There had been considerable speculation about what would happen to the collection after he died; his only heir was a daughter, childless, married to a scholar who was the curator of the private museum. Apparently Nazarian had begun to worry about it too. He was over eighty, and in failing health; a series of strokes had finally convinced him that he was as mortal as any man. There had never been an official announcement of his decision, but rumors had spread the way they will in any small, closed community. Nazarian had decided to make arrangements for the disposal of the collection while he was still alive to supervise. His daughter would inherit the bulk of his fortune—enough to maintain the inhabitants of a small country in comfort—but the museum and its contents would be taken over by a foundation set up for that purpose (and, I assumed, for the purpose of saving a bundle in taxes). The eventual beneficiary would be the Oriental Institute of Chicago—logical enough, because of Nazarian's long and close association with that institution—but when the word got out, there was a lot of wailing and gnashing of teeth in other places, including the University of Pennsylvania museum. One of my teachers had literally shed tears of frustration, and it was to her I went when the far-out idea occurred to me.

Professor White was probably the only person who received the news of my broken engagement with unmixed delight. She wasn't opposed to marriage because she hated men; she simply believed that the life of the mind took precedence over all else, and that love and marriage were as fatal as smallpox to feminine intellectuality. She'd have been perfectly at home in the commons room of Dorothy Sayers' imaginary Oxford College during the innocent twenties, when the lady dons sat around solemnly agreeing that the restoration of a lost breathing in Euripides was more important than petty emotions like love or loyalty. She even looked like Sayers' lady dons—tall and vague, hairpins bristling from the untidy bun of hair at the back of her neck.

When I told her I wasn't going to be married after all, a smile rippled out across her face and only inherent good manners kept her from yelling "Hurrah." She had been crushed when I told her I was giving up graduate school, at least for the immediate future. She knew, as I did, that I'd probably never return to the field. It's hard enough to combine a career and marriage; when the career demands long months of absence from spouse and possible offspring, the combination is virtually impossible.

Once her raptures were contained, her smile faded. "But Haskell, dear, it is too late to apply now. All the grants and scholarships will have been awarded."

I explained what I had in mind. She looked even more dubious when I showed her the notice that had appeared in various periodicals the past fall. "But, Haskell, that's out of the question. Not only has the position been filled, but you would never have qualified. They want a Ph.D. with field experience."

She was still unconvinced when I finished talking but she agreed to write the recommendation I requested. It was a copy of this letter that Jessie had found in my desk. "I've never heard of anyone refusing free labor," Dr. White said, with a touch of humor. "But at best you would be typing, filing, and making coffee. Not the sort of training you want."

I fed her a lot of high-minded talk about how all experience was valuable, about making useful contacts, about proving myself worthy of better things by being humble, trustworthy, loyal, and God-fearing. She'd have been horrified if I had told her my real reason for wanting that recommendation.

The day before I left, Jessie wasn't speaking to me. I mean literally. She glowered speechlessly when I asked if she wanted one or two pork chops for supper, and walked out of the room without having spoken a word after she had eaten. Not until I was loading the car next morning did she relent.

The car was the ostensible reason for her anger. I had taken the money for it and for my summer living expenses from the bank account she had built up for me over the past eighteen years. Strictly speaking, the money wasn't mine. It had come from Kevin Maloney's G.I. insurance. Jessie had conscientiously banked every penny. It had built up into a tidy nest egg—enough to give a person a good start in graduate school or put a down payment on a house or start a small business. But I needed the money. I would have to live all summer without income, paying my own way, and I wanted my own wheels.

Of course it wasn't really the money that bugged Jessie. That was just the straw that broke the camel's back. She didn't want me to go. She considered my quest foolish and hazardous and childish; and fight it as she would, she was haunted by the memory of another beloved young woman who had set out on a similar journey and who had never returned to her.

When I said, "Good-bye, Jessie," her expression didn't soften, even when I added, "I love you." But when I picked Pooch up and cuddled him and told him to take good care of the boss, her face crumpled. We rushed into one another's arms.

"Damned stubborn kid," she muttered. "Just like your mother."

"I'm not going to the moon," I said. "You know how to reach me—through Gran."

"You weren't really serious about staying with her?" Jessie blew her nose in a crumpled tissue.

"Initially. I may find a place of my own later—depending on how things work out."

"You won't be able to stand it," Jessie warned. "The way she lives—"

"You said she had loosened up since Grandfather died."

"Some. But she has a long way to go. Damn it, Haskell, she doesn't even have a phone."

"I'll call as soon as I get to Chicago, and we'll figure out some method of communication. I may not stay there for long, Jessie."

Jessie was obviously afraid to pursue that idea. Thinking of me on my own in the wicked city scared her even more than picturing me held lovingly incommunicado by my grandmother. If she had known what I had in mind, she'd have blown her stack, but mercifully the possibility never occurred to her; it was such a farfetched scheme only an optimistic idiot—like me—would have considered it.

"I should know better than to argue with you," she muttered. "You think you know everything."

"Not yet."

"Haskell." She put a tentative hand on my arm. "Please. Be careful."

"I will." There was one more question I wanted to ask. I had put it off until the last minute—and now, seeing Jessie's red eyes and quivering lips, I couldn't ask it. I repeated, "I will. Don't worry, Jessie. Everything is going to be all right."

"Sure."

"You do understand—"

"Yes. I guess I'd do the same thing if I were in your shoes."

"I know you would. It's a family trait, isn't it? Determination?"

She gave me a watery but valiant grin, and we chanted in chorus, "'I'm determined, you're stubborn, he's bull-headed. . . .'" Then she hugged me again, squeezing so hard it hurt, and then bolted back into the house.

I felt pretty rotten as I started for the car, but the worst was yet to come. He must have parked down the street. I didn't see him until I went around to the driver's side.

Jessie must have called him; it was too much of a coincidence that he should happen to turn up at that strategic moment.

I said brusquely, "Good morning," and opened the car

door. Jon took the suitcase from me. I grabbed for it; we wrestled, briefly and absurdly, over the wretched thing until he released his hold and I stowed it in the car.

"Why didn't you return any calls?" he asked. His voice was the voice of calm reason, but a pulse beat frantically at his temple.

"I didn't know you had called."

"That's because you never answered the phone."

It was the closest Jon had ever come to one of those delightful non sequiturs that mark a debater too angry to think sensibly. I found the lapse rather touching, and it made me all the more anxious to get away before I felt even sorrier and more guilty than I did already.

"What's the sense in talking?" I asked. "I have nothing to say—"

"I do."

I couldn't open the car door, he was leaning against it. "All right," I said. "Go ahead, say it."

"I had nothing to do with that letter. My mother wrote it without my permission and sent it without my knowledge."

"Oh."

I had almost forgotten about the letter, it mattered so little to me. "I assumed that, Jon."

"Thanks for that much."

"I also assumed you wouldn't want to see me or hear from me again."

"For that I don't thank you. You think my feelings for you were so shallow I can throw them away like a burned-out light bulb?"

"You're doing it again," I said.

"What?"

"Cross-examining me. How can I answer a question like that?" He started to speak and I put up a hand to stop him, noting with disgust that it wasn't as steady as I would have liked. "Please, Jon. Don't—don't bug me, not now. Don't start a long argument, just when I've finally worked myself up to the moment when . . . Don't try to talk me into changing my mind at the last damned minute."

"Is that how it strikes you?" I didn't answer. He thought it over; then he said coolly, "Yes, I suppose it would. All right, Haskell."

He opened the car door for me and I got in. His apparent capitulation hadn't fooled me, I knew he wasn't finished, and I was right. Holding the door, he said, "Will you call me?"

"I'd rather not. Your mother might answer the phone."

It wasn't a joke, and neither of us smiled. "At the office, then," Jon insisted. "If you need anything—"

"Thanks. I will. I'll call—if I need anything. Jon, I really must get started, I've got a long drive ahead of me—"

Unexpectedly he caught my face between his two hands and planted a quick, hard kiss on my lips. Before I could react, or object, he had released me and stepped back. "Oh, Haskell," he said softly. "You are so damned young."

It was the meanest thing he could possibly have said. If anyone but Jon had said it, I would have thought the insult was deliberate. But not Jon. He was never deliberately nasty. He couldn't have known that words like child, childish, and young were knives piercing the chink in my armor, poisonous fangs sticking into my Achilles' heel. The only way I could fight my own insecurity was to be cold and unfeeling. If I had weakened, even the least little bit, I'd have had to admit that I was scared to death.

3

After I reached the turnpike, I had to switch on the windshield wiper to clear away the spray flung up by other cars. It had rained hard during the night, and lowering clouds held the threat of more rain to come.

The question I had not dared to ask lay heavy on my mind, dark and ominous as the clouds shrouding the hilltops. The weather had not been so dismal when Mother started out on what was to be her last earthly journey. According to the old newspapers I had consulted, the whole eastern half of the U.S. had been fair and dry that week.

Slippery road conditions had not caused the accident, nor heavy traffic. No other vehicle had been involved; no one had seen the car go off the road. The call to the state police had come from a truck driver who had come over the crest of a rise after the car had hit the abutment. "Mechanical failure" was mentioned as a possibility in the yellowing letter I had found in Jessie's files; but it couldn't be proved, since the front end of the car had been smashed to bits.

Philadelphia to Chicago and back was a long haul for a woman alone with an infant. But one of her ostensible reasons for going was to mend fences with her parents. Wouldn't she want to show off her baby—their only grandchild?

I didn't know where my mother had gone, or what she had done, during those days in Chicago. Tracing her route was one of the things I hoped to do. But I knew she must have visited her parents. What had happened during the hours she spent in her father's house? A happy, successful reconciliation—helping Mama cook dinner and wash the dishes, listening patiently to Papa's lectures, displaying my baby pictures? Or a failed attempt, a renewal and strengthening of old resentment? Anger strong enough to fester and grow in her mind, blurring her eyes, distracting her attention and slowing her reaction time?

I don't know when the idea came to me, but it was firmly planted now, and I couldn't get it out of my mind. Perhaps I was looking for a scapegoat—someone to blame. God is too remote and invulnerable to be a satisfying villain. Perhaps Jessie's uncritical adoration had given me a false impression of Leah's competence and intelligence, but I just couldn't believe such a woman would take chances with a vehicle that wasn't in proper repair, or would drive under the influence of alcohol, fatigue or drugs. After all, she had responsibilities. Me, for one. Jessie claimed she had been crazy about me. . . .

If true, that would seem to rule out suicide. But there are moments of black despair and irrational depression even in the sunniest of natures. There are clinical conditions like postpartum depression. A momentary impulse, easily overcome under normal conditions, can be deadly when there is a deadly weapon at hand. And a car is a deadly weapon.

I wondered if Jessie suspected that my journey was not only a quixotic quest for a missing father, but something uglier—a search for the ultimate cause of my mother's death. And as the gray day darkened and the rain grew heavier, I knew I had to stop thinking about it, at least while I was driving.

The ghost-memory of the girl who had driven that same route over twenty years ago rode with me, and she was a distracting companion.

I had planned to drive straight through, but the foul weather and my fouler mood changed my plans; after a near miss from a tractor-trailer, I decided to pull off and spend the night in a motel on the Indiana-Ohio border. I had a good night's sleep and woke to find the sun breaking through. A positive omen. I needed it.

I had written Gran to tell her I was coming but had received no reply. That didn't surprise me; over the years I had received only a few letters from her, painful scrawls that betrayed both arthritis and semiliteracy. She sent presents for Christmas and birthdays—batches of cookies, mittens badly knitted out of coarse yarn in inappropriate colors, deep purple and sullen brown and khaki. I never knew whether those were her ideas of proper colors for the young or whether she got the yarn on sale.

Chicago boasts a good-looking lake and a handsome skyline bristling with tall buildings. I learned to know and admire both on later occasions, but I didn't see much of either on that trip; I was too busy watching the traffic, which was heavy, and the signs, which were confusing. Tollways flowed into freeways and expressways and skyways; I flowed along with them, from the Dan Ryan to the John F. Kennedy. I was well on my way to Wisconsin before I realized I shouldn't have been on the John F. Kennedy. I never did locate the Eisenhower, which was the one I should have taken, but it's easier to find one's way in Chicago than in Philadelphia; everything is all straight lines and squares once you get off the freeways, skyways, and expressways.

It was shortly after noon when I reached Oak Park, one of the near-in suburbs, due west of the Loop.

I was still lost. I had only the vaguest memories of the house where I had spent most of my first three years of life, and I had been back only once since—when my grandmother had a bad bout of pneumonia and wasn't expected to live. I don't know who it was who didn't expect her to live; as we learned shortly after we arrived, the doctors had never said any such thing. However, it was the kind of summons that could not be ignored, and Jessie had taken me with her. I was eight at the time, too young to realize that Jessie's rotten mood was due to exasperation, not worry. She had suspected the truth all along—that Gran saw no reason to spend money on doctors and hospitals when it was a daughter's bounden duty to tend an ailing mother, never mind such minor matters as a job. When we arrived at the hospital, we found Gran dressed and packed and ready to go.

Jessie put up with it for about a week, until she could locate a practical nurse.

I had a good time during that week. While Jessie scrubbed and swore and cooked and cursed, I played in the backyard or sat with Gran. I liked Gran. One day when Jessie was out shopping, she sneaked out of bed and whipped up a batch of cookies. She told me stories about what a good girl my mother had been, and about Jesus, and how He loved the little children. It was the first I had heard about Jesus. He did not figure prominently in Jessie's conversation. Gran had a picture of Him on her bedroom wall. He had a sweet, sad face and a halo of light around His head. Gran cried when we left. So did I. Jessie didn't.

I had to stop at a gas station and ask how to find Kenilworth Avenue. Once I reached it, memories began to stir. The houses were simple but substantial, dating from the twenties and thirties; and the tall trees arching over the street must have been almost as old. The houses were fairly close together; there were yards in front and in back of them. I saw a few small children playing, under the supervision of adults; the older ones would be in school, of course.

Gran's house was a narrow two-story affair with brown wood shingles and an open front porch. I pulled in to the curb and sat there for a few minutes, trying to figure why it looked so different from the others on the street. It was of the same date and architectural style; the house and yard were well maintained. Too well maintained, too neat—that was the difference. There were no tricycles or children's toys on the front lawn, no open windows, no signs of life.

I climbed the stairs to the porch. On it were two chairs with a table between them. Chairs, table, and floor were spotless, speckless; they had to have been swept only minutes before, because as I stood there a catkin from a maple tree drifted over the railing and settled, alone of all its kind. My footprints left faint but visible dust marks. After looking in vain for a doorbell, I knocked on the door.

Nothing happened. Gothic images swarmed in my brain, despite the bright sunshine and homely middle-class ambiance. Would I find my grandmother laid out in the parlor, candles at her head and feet? "You came too late. . . ."

More likely she was deaf and hadn't heard the knock. I pounded with my clenched fist. Finally I heard sounds of life—footsteps, slow and heavy. They were followed by more Gothic sound effects—chain rattling, keys turning. At least the door didn't creak when it swung open.

I found myself confronting not one old lady but two, so much alike that they might have been twins and sisters to all the sinister black-clad housekeepers of fiction. Mrs. Danvers would have looked like a chorus girl by comparison; both of the women I faced were dressed in long, shapeless dark gowns, and they were wearing black bonnets that covered their hair and shaded their faces.

I said uncertainly, "Gran?"

The pink, crumpled old faces broke into broad simultaneous smiles, but only one of them spoke. "Haskell, honey. Is it you?"

"Didn't you get my letter?"

"Why, sure," said the other old lady. "We expected you last night."

"We didn't expect her," said the first old lady, scowling at the second. "I told you she wasn't gonna come till today."

"No, now, you sure didn't. You said—"

My head was beginning to spin. I knew one of the old ladies must be my great-aunt Ella; she had come to live with Gran a few years after my first, long-ago visit. But I didn't know which was which, and I wondered how long they were going to stand there arguing before they let me in.

"I had hoped to get here last night," I said. "But the weather was bad, and I was running late. I didn't want to disturb you."

"There, I told you," said the two of them in chorus.

They weren't as much alike as I had thought; it was the bizarre, identical garb that made them look like twins. Both had blue eyes but one was a few inches taller than the other, and the lock of hair that had escaped from her bonnet was dark, filmed with gray. Similar wisps eluding the other bonnet shone silvery fair.

"Well, why don't you let her come in?" demanded the taller woman. "You always did talk too much, Mabel. Here's the poor girl, tired and hungry after a long trip, and you keep her standing on the doorstep."

Having been given the necessary clue, I said again, "Gran," and kissed the shorter of the pair. Her cheek was as soft as velvet and smelled like soap. The other old lady looked hurt, so I kissed her too; and in a mood of temporary amity, they moved aside and waved me in.

They argued all the time, over everything—the time of day, the weather, what they had had for supper the night before. It was their favorite form of entertainment; God knows they had few others. They had an antiquated black-and-white TV set, but Gran made a point of explaining that they only watched religious programs.

They weren't unkind. Quite the reverse: they overwhelmed me with compliments, affection, and food. The lunch they had ready and waiting would have fed a crowd of hungry truck drivers, and they kept apologizing for their cooking. Not like it was back on the farm, no, it sure wasn't; without cream straight from the cow, them butterbeans just didn't taste right, and the awful eggs from the supermarket didn't make the kind of noodles Mama used to make. I wondered how they kept their figures, for both ate voraciously, and though they were decidedly chubby, they were not as badly overweight as such a diet would have suggested. I soon found out. They cleaned. I cleaned, too. We swept the porch and wiped the porch furniture; we washed and dried the dishes; we scrubbed the table, the kitchen floor, and the counters. They cleaned the entire house at least once a day, and when they got through, they went out and cleaned the yard. Dead flower heads had to be removed—not dropped onto the dirt but placed in a plastic bag and put in the trash—the walks had to be swept, the slightest hint of a weed had to be ruthlessly exterminated, and the dog's—er—had to be removed.

According to Gran, the dog was the cause of all this excessive labor—Aunt Ella's dog, which she had insisted on bringing with her. The dog was a gray-faced, wheezing, fat beagle with a pleasant smile and no bad habits that I could see. Gran never referred to him by name, but only as "that dog" and insisted that she had admitted him only because two women living alone needed a watchdog, but it was obvious that she was fond of him. She kept sneaking him tidbits. So did Aunt Ella, which accounted for his girth, and perhaps for his smile.

Toward evening, when my anatomy was beginning to

ache in odd places, we settled down on the porch to watch the neighbors. This was obviously part of the daily routine and gave the old ladies a necessary contact with the outside world. Nothing escaped their evil old eyes. Mr. Albans was half an hour late; must have stopped at that bar again. Them terrible kids of the Delaneys were riding their bikes on the sidewalks, and Miz Marks hadn't swept her porch for at least a week.

Supper was early, and again they apologized for the food. They had their dinner in the middle of the day, so there was only enough food for two hungry truck drivers. Afterward, we retired to the parlor. Aunt Ella spread the dog's rug at her feet, and all three of them settled down, Ella with her crocheting and Gran with a pile of photo albums.

If I had been stuck in that house with no means of escape, I probably wouldn't have been amused by the dear old ladies—I would have been aghast. It hadn't taken me long to realize that Jessie had been right on the mark; I'd go crazy if I stayed more than a few hours. I think it was when we started washing the porch furniture that I made up my mind to leave; after that I could enjoy the pair for what they were—sweet and engaging and funny and pathetic. Gran's timid compromises between the life-style her husband had forced on her and the one she would have preferred if marriage had not sunk her in a rut thirty years deep, fascinated me. The picture of Jesus was a classic example. It still hung on Gran's bedroom wall, and she prayed to it every night. Seeing it now, as an adult, I realized that Grandfather would have considered it an abomination. For one thing, it was a Catholic picture, complete with Sacred Heart. But I could understand why Gran preferred the gentle, girlish face to the God of wrath Grandfather had worshiped. Perhaps she also preferred it to Grandfather.

Most of the relatives had broken away from the dying old fundamentalist sect in which they had been raised. Gran showed me their pictures, aunts and uncles and cousins, dressed in ordinary clothes and doing ordinary things like visiting Disneyland and putting on fancy weddings. Jessie had not kept in touch with them; she detested them, lock, stock, and barrel, because none of them had dared or cared to help her break free of her father's dominance.

Not until the hands of the mantel clock neared 8 P.M. and the old ladies started making comments about how late it was, did I force myself to introduce the subject that was my principal reason for being there. I felt the fascination of an anthropologist visiting an alien tribe; I could only imagine how much worse it must have been when Grandfather was alive. Gran kept saying, "Mr. Emig didn't approve" of this or that. I got the distinct impression that he didn't approve of anything any normal person might enjoy.

A few old school pictures gave me the necessary lead. They were the only pictures of Mother and Jessie. (Mr. Emig hadn't approved of cameras.) How Gran had talked him into paying good money for the school photos, I could not imagine—and I was afraid to ask.

The pictures were enough to make you cry—all the little girls in pretty fluffy dresses and hair ribbons, except for Mother and Jessie. The most pathetic thing about them was the way someone—Jessie, undoubtedly—had tried to spruce Mother up a little, so she wouldn't look so out of place: a borrowed ribbon or pinafore, hair fluffed up and twisted into little spit curls around her face. Granddad must have raised Cain when he saw those curls. Perhaps that was why he had ordered the photographs, as a means of checking on his daughters.

They affected me so poignantly that my introduction wasn't as smooth as I had intended. Both old ladies looked startled when I said abruptly, "Mother was here that day— just before the accident—wasn't she?"

They talked about it freely enough, however. Aunt Ella had not been present, but that didn't keep her from putting her two cents in. She drove me to distraction; every time she interrupted, she and Gran got into one of their endless, pointless arguments, and I had to nudge Gran back onto the subject.

"She brought along nice pictures of you," Gran said, staring sadly at the pages of the photo album. "But she wouldn't let us keep them. I felt so bad—"

"I thought Mr. Emig didn't approve of photos," I said.

The implied criticism was wasted on Gran. She said placidly, "Oh, he didn't mind if other people gave 'em to me. That's how I got all of these here. Your Aunt Jessie did send me some, other times. This one here, you must of been about ten—"

"Eleven," said Aunt Ella firmly. "You said she was eleven."

"I never did. She must of been ten, because it was that same year—"

"Was that why Mother came?" My voice was getting shrill, try as I would to control it. "To tell you about me—show you the pictures? Or was there some other—"

"We was so disappointed she didn't bring you," Gran said. "Mr. Emig just loved babies; he was real disappointed. He told Leah she should just come on back home with us, since she was widowed and alone in the world. He had a man in mind for her—"

"She didn't agree, though," I said. Figuratively I wiped my brow, imagining the sort of stepfather Grandpa would have picked for me.

"To come home? Well, not then, but he'd have persuaded her in time. It wasn't right for her to go out to a job and leave her baby with strangers. With what the gov'mint was giving her, she could of lived here and not had to work, till she got herself another husband. Mr. Emig didn't believe in all those gov'mint handouts, but I said her husband was a hero, he died for his country, and so—"

"A woman's family ought to take care of her," opined Aunt Ella. "Not the gov'mint. I always say—"

"Well, isn't that just what Mr. Emig said? He said—"

I was so distracted by this nonsense I was slow to accept the fact that my questions would have been futile even if the old dears could have kept on track. Gran didn't remember what had happened; she remembered what ought to have happened. If there had been discord between her husband and her daughter, she would have wiped it out of her mind. The best I could hope for was a slip, not of the tongue but of the understanding, like the unconsciously damning comments she had made about Mr. Emig.

And perhaps nothing significant had happened. Perhaps I was searching for a mythical monster in a zoo full of harmless ordinary animals.

So I stopped asking questions and eventually they wound down and we all retired, the old ladies clucking about how late it was. It was eight forty-five. After we had prayed and Gran had tried to lend me one of her flannel nightgowns— "You'll catch your death in that flimsy thing, child, and besides, what if there was a fire?"—they finally left me alone. The room was small, bare, and clean; the single window was tightly shut and heavily curtained; the overhead light held a 40-watt bulb, dim enough to have cast ghoulish shadows over a face reflected in the mirror—if there had been a mirror.

I sat down on the single straight-backed chair and fought a desperate desire to smoke. I had never smoked in my life, mind you; I was suffering from mental claustrophobia, a need to break out of the cocoon into which the old ladies were winding me. I had a novel in my bag, but unless I stood on the bed and held the book next to the light bulb, I wouldn't be able to see the print. Finally I managed to wrestle the window open, though layers of ancient paint had hardened in the cracks. That helped a little; but it was all I could do not to climb out the window and run for my life.

• • •

The ladies rose at five, which should not have surprised me. It was still dark outside. After we had cooked and eaten an astonishing breakfast, the sun started to rise, Gran started laying out the chores for the day, and I told them I had to go.

They were hurt and unbelieving. They had counted on a nice long visit. I discovered that they had also counted on using me as a chauffeur. "It would save all that money on taxi-cabs," Aunt Ella mourned. She added darkly, "You can't ever tell what them drivers will do to helpless women."

Torn between laughter and guilt, I questioned them and learned that except for rare visits to doctors and dentists, their errands consisted of a weekly trip to the grocery store. "We always go on Wednesday afternoon. The stores ain't so crowded, and the vegetables are fresher than on Monday, and by Thursday—"

I never did find out why Thursday was a bad day for grocery shopping. I was in full flight, fumbling for the doorknob.

They followed me to the car, squeaking out agitated warnings about the perils of the big city. As I drove away, I saw them standing on the curb, twin figures of blackness on that beautiful morning. They weren't looking after me; they were facing one another, and from the movements of their hands and heads I deduced they were arguing. Perhaps about whether I would be raped and murdered or only murdered.

I headed straight for the nearest all-night drugstore. One of the astonishing things about that breakfast, besides the quantity of food, was the fact that neither tea nor coffee had been offered. I drank two cups of coffee and bought a city map. With its help, I had no trouble reaching the university.

In their heyday, Hyde Park and Kenwood were among the most affluent and elegant of Chicago's suburban areas. That day was long past. The burgeoning city had swallowed up both subdivisions before the turn of the century, and even in my mother's time, the surrounding "depressed areas" (a pretty word for slums) had made nocturnal strolls hazardous. However, the neighborhood had held its own, thanks in large part to the university and the museums and the professional schools that filled the area. Hyde Park claims to be Chicago's most successfully integrated community and the handsome old houses on its tree-lined streets include the work of some of America's best architects, including Frank Lloyd Wright and Henry Ives Cobb. Kenwood is even fancier; around 1900, it rivaled the Gold Coast and Evanston as a haven for Chicago millionaires.

If that sounds like an excerpt from a guidebook, it is. I had done my homework like a good little student. But it's one thing to read about an area; quite another to see it with one's own eyes. For me the immediacy was direct and personal. Greatly as it must have changed in twenty years, the major structures and landmarks were the ones my mother had known. She would have felt as if she were coming home, to the place where she had spent what were unquestionably the happiest years of her life.

I recognized the Oriental Institute from Mother's pictures. Wide, shallow steps flanked by low balustrades led up to the heavy double doors. I opened one of them and went in.

The museum was on the first floor; I ignored it and went straight up the staircase to the second floor. Chicago was on the trimester system, so its academic year ran longer than that of the University of Pennsylvania. This was the last week of classes, though; I had had to hurry my final preparations so that I'd be sure of catching the man I wanted to see. He was teaching that quarter. I had taken the trouble to check the catalogue, since archaeologists are even more peripatetic than other academicians.

Assuming that the catalogue was accurate, I had about fifteen minutes before the class in which I was interested let out. I looked into the library. It was familiar ground, more classically attractive than more modern libraries, but reassuringly the same in atmosphere. Long tables filled the room and books lined the walls. It was so quiet you could hear a fly, trapped and frantic, at one of the high windows.

I asked one of the librarians where Professor Wertheim's class was meeting. She told me; I went out and sat down on the steps leading up to the third floor. The classroom I wanted was directly to my left.

I hadn't called or written to ask for an appointment. It's too easy to turn down a petitioner who is only a voice on the phone or a name on a letter. If you are there in person, eye to eye and face to face, you can smile and wheedle, argue, persuade.

A hubbub of voices from the museum below rose and then diminished: a grammar-school class, herded by vigilant teachers. The second floor was unnervingly quiet. All the doors lining the hall remained closed; there was no sound, not even from the library.

Finally the door of Wertheim's classroom burst open and the first wave of students appeared—those who had other classes or who were in imminent need of refreshment. The rest followed at their leisure, laughing and talking. The professor was the last to emerge, juggling an armful of papers and accompanied by a die-hard apple polisher who followed him down the hall peppering him with questions.

I followed, too, congratulating myself on having had the foresight to identify David Wertheim's classroom. I never would have recognized him. The gangling, lanky boy had grown up and filled out; he was still on the thin side, but his arms and legs no longer seemed disproportionately long in relation to the rest of his body. The disappearance of the beard bared features I had never really been able to study. He moved so fast I didn't get a good look at him, only an impression of bushy eyebrows and a formidable scowl. The one thing that hadn't changed was the complete absence of sartorial elegance; instead of a suit, he was dressed in faded jeans tucked into clumsy work boots and a khaki shirt that was neither drip-dry nor vexed by the pressure of an iron. The casual clothes and the quick way he moved made him look more like a student than a distinguished professor.

At the door of his office he disposed of his follower with a brusque "Forget it, Sue," and slammed the door practically in her face.

The girl said, "Damn," and stamped her foot. Turning, and finding herself nose to nose with a stranger, she looked startled and then gave me a self-conscious smile.

"Sorry. I didn't know you were there."

"That's okay."

Instead of moving away she stood her ground, between me and the door, and studied me curiously. Her smile had faded.

"You looking for Dave?"

"Professor Wertheim—yes, I am."

My use of the formal title seemed to reassure her, but her eyes remained narrowed. They were pale blue eyes, enhanced by make-up that had been applied with considerable skill and care. Though she wore the standard uniform of jeans and shirt, both garments were cleaner, fancier, and tighter than the occasion demanded. She looked as if she were dressed for a date instead of a class. I began to understand why she was regarding me with such lack of favor, and in spite of the butterflies flapping around in my stomach I was amused.

"He seems to be a little grumpy today," I said.

"Oh, no. No, that's just his manner. He treats everybody like that. He's really a very sweet person. . . ."

My amusement must have shown on my face; she stopped, biting her lip with vexation. Mumbling something that might have been a courteous farewell, but probably wasn't, she left. She walked slowly, shoulders rigid, trying not to look back; she wanted to know whether I would gain admission where she had failed.

Poor thing, I couldn't give her that satisfaction. Come hell or high water I was going into that office. But I waited till she was out of sight before I knocked on the door.

A wordless grumble responded. I opened the door. The scowl on his face faded when he saw me, and he half-rose. "Sorry. I thought you were . . . Well, anyhow. Can I help you?"

"I hope so. May I sit down?" He hesitated, glancing at his watch, and I added, "I promise it won't take long."

"Well . . . I have a lunch date shortly, but I can spare a few minutes." Without rising, he extended an arm as long and almost as hairy as a gorilla's and cleared the chair beside his desk of a pile of papers by the simple expedient of sweeping them off on the floor.

I sat down, knees together and primly covered, hands clasped in my lap. I had spent a lot of time deciding on the proper attire, wavering between a tailored gray suit and a more casual outfit—print skirt and matching scarf in shades of black, gray, and saffron, with a short-sleeved knit top in the same bright yellow. I had made the right choice; formality wouldn't have impressed this man. His rumpled shirt, open at the neck and rolled to the elbows, exposed an amazing amount of body hair. The hair was black, untouched by gray, like the tousled curls on his head. He needed a haircut. He also needed a shave. Either he was starting another beard or he was one of those unfortunate men who have to shave several times a day; his jaw and chin were dark with stubble. The luxuriance of hair extended to his heavy brows, which shadowed his eyes so that I couldn't see them clearly. The underlying bone structure was surprisingly delicate in a man of his bulk—small, sculptured ears folded neatly against his skull; a thin, sharp nose. His lips were thin too, and long; they cut across the lower half of his face like a line drawn by a ruler.

He studied me as openly as I studied him, his eyes lingering appreciatively on the area below the scarf I had twisted around my neck. After a moment, his smile took on a faintly puzzled tinge. "Should I know you? I have a lousy memory for faces—"

"No, we've never met."

"I see." He was getting impatient. One hand beat a tattoo on the edge of the desk.

I handed him Professor White's letter. His long fingers continued to thrum on the desk as he read. It didn't take him long. He put the letter aside.

"Hmmm. Well."

He pulled a crumpled pack of cigarettes from his pocket and pretended to search among the litter on the desk for an ashtray. It was only an excuse, to avoid meeting my eyes. There were several ashtrays, all of them overflowing; the air in the room was acrid with smoke, ancient and modern. Still not looking at me, he mumbled, "She speaks highly of you. Er—how is she?"

"She's well."

"Good. Good! Nice woman, Alice. Fine scholar. She—er—she thinks highly of you."

He was going to turn me down. That didn't dishearten me; I had expected he would. In fact, his behavior was encouraging. He was a kind man, reluctant to hurt people. That made my job easier.

I laughed. He glanced up at me, his eyebrows rising. I got a good look at his eyes. They were his best feature, big and brown and oddly innocent.

"Please understand," I said. "I didn't expect you to offer me the job."

"I'm glad of that, because I couldn't even consider you. Aside from the fact that you lack the necessary qualifications, the appointment has already been made."

I nodded. "I know. I'm offering myself as an unpaid drudge-assistant. I type very well, and I take a little shorthand. I've had some museum experience; I wield a mean dustcloth; and I make superb coffee."

Grinning, he leaned back in his chair. "I see."

"I want the experience," I said pleadingly. "It won't cost the Institute a cent. How can you lose?"

"Ouch." He started violently and squashed the cigarette into an ashtray. "Damn," he muttered, shaking the burned finger.

"I'm sorry."

"You should be sorry. I have heard a lot of outrageous propositions in my time—"

"I don't see anything so outrageous about mine."

"Honey," he leaned forward, his elbows on the desk. "Do you have any idea how many starry-eyed treasure seekers come into my office, offering me everything up to and including their fair young bodies for a chance to get into archaeology? Frustrated Indiana Joneses, looking for the Ark of the Covenant or, at the very least, another Tutankhamon—"

"That's not fair." My cheeks were flaming with embarrassment. "I didn't offer you—"

"No. I'd have turned you down." He added, his smile broadening, "Regretfully."

"Thanks." I settled back in my chair. Like a rock, like a boulder, immovable.

He studied me thoughtfully. "Determined, aren't you?"

"Yes. You can't scare me off by treating me like those moonstruck romantics. You know I'm not one of them."

"No?" He picked up the letter again. "No," he said after a moment. "If Alice says you're good, then you're good. All the same, can you give me any reason why I should break the rules of the Institute about accepting volunteers, and my own common sense, and make an exception for you?"

"There is one reason." I took a deep breath and clasped my hands tight to keep them from trembling. "I'm Leah Emig's daughter."

"Leah . . . Lee? No. You can't be." His eyes widened. "You don't look anything like her. . . ."

I didn't look like him either. Which didn't mean a damned thing. Looking for resemblance is a game for grandmas.

His reaction had been natural enough—amazement, doubt, interest. Well, I asked myself, did you expect your unknown father to turn pale and faint dead away when you confronted him?

"Leah," he murmured, reaching for another cigarette. "Yeah, that's right—she married that Irish guy. No wonder I didn't recognize your name. So you're following in your mother's footsteps, is that it? If you're half as good a scholar . . ."

His voice trailed off. He smoked in meditative silence for a while, and I watched the play of memories across a face that was, for all its lack of symmetry, very easy to read. Eventually his musing half-smile faded.

"How did you know Lee and I were—friends?"

"I have her things—notebooks, papers, letters, photographs. Naturally I'm familiar with your work."

"Naturally," he agreed dryly. "So this is a variety of emotional blackmail."

"Exactly."

I smiled at him. He never knew how much that smile cost me. My heart was pounding so hard I felt he must see it, and my mouth was dry. If I misread his nature—dangerously easy to do on such short acquaintance—if I played it the wrong way—I was finished. This was my last, best shot.

And it paid off. He burst into a great shout of laughter.

"You're Lee's daughter, all right. Look, kid, you must realize I can't make a firm commitment even if I wanted to—and I don't want to, not on the spur of the moment like this. There are other people whose approval you would need. But . . . we'll talk about it. Come on, I'll buy you lunch."

"You said you had a lunch date. I don't want to interfere—"

"Like hell you don't. Leah would have knocked me down and walked the length of my prostrate body to get a chance like this." He leaped up from the chair and grabbed my arm. "The person with whom I am lunching is one of those others. You'll have to sell him, and without the . . . Let's call it sentimental appeal, shall we, instead of emotional blackmail. Such an ugly word. . . ."

I felt like a prisoner as he towed me down the stairs and along the street, holding my arm in a bruising grip. My spirits were bruised, too. I had visualized the interview as climactic, dramatic, and final; either he would throw me out of his office (kicking and screaming and arguing all the way to the door), or he would get misty-eyed and choked up and welcome me to the team. I should have known better. In today's world, failure is simple, but success is not; one person's "no" can end your hopes, but approval depends on a long hierarchy of individuals. I was limp with emotional exhaustion after talking to Wertheim; now I had to gear myself up for another effort with someone entirely different—someone whom my mother's name, the magic token that had won a reluctant "maybe" from her old friend, would not affect in the slightest.

I wanted to question him about the person we were going to meet, get some clues that would help me plan my strategy. He didn't give me the opportunity. Instead he questioned me, in a rapid-fire, mobile oral examination. What did I think of Samson's theory about Smenkhkare and Nefertiti? How would I read the doubtful passage in the Teachings of Amenemopet? And what did I think of his article discussing the use of the *sedjemtify* form?

Some of the questions were just plain unfair. After all, I was still a lowly B.A. and I had taken only two years of Middle Egyptian. Increasingly exasperated and distressed at what I realized must be a poor performance, I finally snapped, "I haven't read your article."

"That doesn't surprise me. It hasn't been published." He chuckled wickedly.

I stopped short in the middle of the sidewalk and pulled my arm free of his grasp. "You don't have to resort to trick questions. I didn't claim to be James Henry Breasted. Or even Leah Emig."

He didn't answer. Pushing me ahead of him, he turned abruptly into an open doorway.

The restaurant was slightly more pretentious than your average hamburger-and-fries short-order house; there were plastic tablecloths on the tables, and a bar. It was apparently a favorite hangout for students and faculty alike; Wertheim greeted several people as we made our way between the tables.

Sitting alone at a table in the corner was the man who represented my next, but probably not my last, hurdle.

He reminded me of a photographic negative. The colors were all reversed—skin tanned to coffee-brown, hair bleached to whiteness. The drooping cavalry-style mustache matched the hair. His head was bent over a book that lay on the table in front of him, and his horn-rimmed glasses had slipped down to the end of his nose. His attire was as casual as Dave's—wrinkled khakis, no tie. The book must have been fascinating. He didn't look up until Dave greeted him with a jab in the ribs. When he saw me, he pushed his chair back and rose, not to his full height, but to a semi-crouch. A token gesture at best, but I hadn't expected even that.

We sat down, and the waiter appeared with a bottle of beer and a glass, which he deposited at Wertheim's elbow. He looked inquiringly at me, and I said, "The same. Please."

The pause that followed was decidedly awkward. It was Wertheim's move, but he didn't make it; he sat drinking his beer and smiling benevolently at both of us. I opened the menu and pretended to be absorbed in it. Sneaking a glance from under lowered lashes, I saw the younger man wriggle his sandy eyebrows and jerk his head toward me. He appeared only mildly exasperated; obviously he was accustomed to Wertheim's unorthodox manners.

Wertheim plucked the menu from my hand. "The only things fit to eat here are the hamburgers. Right, Joe?" The waiter gave me my beer, grinned, and walked away, taking this for an order—which it was. Wertheim said, "Haskell, this is Carl Townsend. Carl, meet Haskell Maloney."

It was an unexpectedly formal introduction, which he promptly ruined by adding, "Hell of a name to give a nice little girl. A tribute to the predecessor of the O.I.?"

"So I've been told." The Haskell Oriental Museum had been the first home of the Department of Egyptology, before the construction of the Oriental Institute.

Carl looked baffled, as well he might. "How do you do, Miss Maloney."

"I'm pleased to meet you, Mr. Townsend. Or is it Dr. Townsend?" I gave him my best smile, complete with dimple. He blinked, but there was no other reaction, pro or con; the upper rims of the glasses, riding low on his nose, hid his eyes and the mustache frustrated my attempt to watch his mouth.

"He has a Ph.D.," Wertheim said. "But we don't go in for academic titles at the O.I.; you can call him Carl. And you can call me Dave. After all, we're old friends."

"Are you?" Carl asked.

"In a way," Dave said coyly. He raised his glass. "A toast."

"What are we drinking to?" Carl demanded.

"Your new assistant." Dave gestured at me.

"My what?" The glasses fell off Carl's nose. He grabbed at them and missed; lifting them out of a puddle of beer, he repeated, "My *what?*"

"Haskell just graduated from Penn," Dave said. "She studied with Alice White. She's also the daughter of Leah Emig."

The mention of Mother's name was deliberate, intended to demonstrate how little effect it would have on other people. It certainly had none on Carl Townsend. "Who?"

"An old friend of mine. A fellow student in the days when I was young, handsome, brilliant, and noble. One of the most promising students the O.I. ever had."

"Oh."

"Haskell has offered her services," Dave explained. "For free. She'll do anything. Type, file, dust . . ."

Carl dipped a napkin in his glass of water and got to work on his glasses. "If she's so great at typing, filing, and—er—dusting, she can work for you."

"Just a damned minute," I said. I knew Dave was baiting me, trying to make me lose my temper, but I couldn't keep my mouth shut. "How about letting me say something?"

Carl gave up on the glasses; he folded them and slipped them into his shirt pocket. "You probably make more sense than Dave," he said. "Go ahead. Talk."

His eyes were an odd shade of brown, so light they were almost gray. Fine wrinkles fanned out from the outer corners; they must have resulted from habitual squinting against a bright Near Eastern sun, because he couldn't have been more than thirty. Probably younger—about Jon's age. He was better-looking than Jon, with regular, finely cut features. He needed a haircut, and his mustache needed trimming; but I detected a quiver of interest or amusement of the lips barely visible under the brush.

I took a deep breath. "I'm interested in museum work. I've had some experience at Penn. I can read hieroglyphs—a little—and I've had a general grounding in Egyptian history, principles of archaeology, ancient art. I want practical experience. At my level that isn't easy to find. If I work in a museum office or a university, I'll end up doing nothing but routine office work. With the Nazarian Collection, I'll at least get the chance to see the objects and watch an experienced person handle them."

"Not bad," said the man on my right. "Smooth talker, isn't she, Carl?"

The man on my left sighed ostentatiously. "Why do you do this sort of thing, Dave? She seems like a nice girl. She doesn't deserve to be toyed with and then cast aside—"

"Who says I'm toying with her? The trustees have the final vote on anything to do with the collection; and I, my boy, am a trustee, and you, my boy, are a paid employee of the Foundation. You don't have anything to say about it. I'm exhibiting a rare and touching consideration by consulting you."

"Rare indeed," murmured Carl. "Okay, if you're determined to foist this cute little teenager on me, why bother to ask?"

By that time I couldn't have said which I resented more, Dave's sly innuendoes or Carl's tolerance. "My turn," I said. "I want this—I can hardly call it a job, can I, when I won't be getting paid? I want this position. I admit that sentiment enters into it; my mother studied at Chicago, and although I can't claim to be the scholar she was, I—"

"What did she do, quit and get married?" Carl asked.

"She died. In a car accident, when I was three months old."

The pause that followed was just as uncomfortable as I had hoped it would be. Dave pursed his lips in a silent whistle and gave me a look in which respect and disapproval mingled. The effect on the other man was more dramatic. Color flooded his cheeks, darkening them to mahogany. "I'm sorry," he mumbled.

"It's a little late for condolences," I said. "I don't want them. I want to work. I only mentioned the fact so you would understand why I picked the Institute instead of some other museum. I gather you're the one who is doing the

actual work. I'll work for you or with you. I'll take orders—
of a professional nature—and, if I must, insults. I won't like
them, but I won't talk back. Why don't you give me a
chance? You can always kick me out if I don't suit. I won't
have a contract."

The argument made sense, but it wasn't my logic that
silenced Carl. He resembled a lowly freshman, not a lordly
Ph.D., still flushed with embarrassment at his faux pas and
squirming in his chair.

"It's not my decision," he muttered. "If the trustees
agree, I'm stuck with you."

"How rude," Dave said, shaking his head reproachfully.
"Cheer up, Carl, it might have been one of Victor's ex-lady
friends."

"Yes, Victor," said Carl, brightening. "That's what it
comes down to—Victor Nazarian. He still calls the shots.
You're not home free, Miss—er—Miss Maloney. You'll
have to convince the old man."

A jeering smile made his mustache wriggle. He didn't
think I could do it. As for me, I could have slumped with
relief. Victor Nazarian was over eighty years old. If I
couldn't charm a doddering, sentimental old man, I didn't
deserve the position.

At least Carl didn't harp on a subject. Having said his say,
he took out a notebook and addressed Dave.

"I made some preliminary estimates. We'll need at least
250,000 square feet. That will mean a new wing, even if the
mansion itself turns out to be suitable."

Dave's reply gave the topic a sideways twist that brought
me into the conversation; I couldn't be sure whether he did
it to be polite to me or perverse to Carl. "Those estimates
don't mean a damned thing, because we don't know how
much of the original collection is intact, much less worthy
of being put on exhibit. Some of the storage areas haven't
been investigated for half a century; God only knows what
condition the objects are in." He turned to me, his eyes

twinkling. "It will be just like a treasure hunt, won't it, honey? There could be any number of wonders down there."

"More likely a wonderful collection of forgeries," I said. "You're referring to the objects collected by Mr. Nazarian's father? To judge by some of his finds, he wasn't very discriminating. The Khufu statue, for instance; nobody but a rank amateur would have been taken in by that."

"Breasted was taken in," Carl said.

"Even the great James Henry bought his share of frauds."

"The Khufu statue is a damned good forgery," Carl insisted. "Good red Assuan granite; you can't use carbon dating on stone, so—"

"Stylistically it's way off base. One of the ideograms in the throne name is wrong."

We went on arguing, while Dave leaned back and watched in open amusement. Carl wasn't so much testing me as objecting to the effrontery of a tyro making dogmatic statements and casting aspersion on the expertise of the great Breasted, founder of the Oriental Institute and Egyptologist extraordinaire. We were going at it hammer and tongs and having a fine time—at least I was—when he glanced up and then jumped to his feet.

"I didn't realize it was so late. Got to go."

"We haven't finished talking," Dave protested.

"There's no sense in a business discussion when a third person is present." It was said without rancor, a simple statement of fact; he added, "I'll come by your office later, okay? Good-bye, Miss—er. I'll be seeing you."

"Or not, as the case may be," I said.

"Right." Snatching up a shabby windbreaker that hung over the back of his chair, he headed for the door.

I watched him walk away, and I noted, as even the best of us do, that his build was nothing to complain about—broad shoulders, lean hips, long legs. Then I saw the reason for his precipitate departure. She was waiting for him just inside the door, arms folded and eyes narrowed in the classic pose of a lady who has been kept waiting. She was almost as tall as he, and although I wouldn't have called her pretty—her features were too sharp and her face too long and narrow—she had a certain style. The blond hair may have been natural. I couldn't tell from where I was sitting.

He said something to her—apologizing, I presume. She frowned and took his arm possessively. As they went out, she turned her head and looked directly at me. Her expression was not exactly friendly.

Dave was shaking with laughter.

"Score an extra point for you," I said. "You managed to infuriate not two, but three people. Congratulations."

"Now, now, that's not a nice way to talk to someone from whom you want a favor," said Dave, trying to compose his features.

"Who is she? His wife?"

"Ex officio. I believe society, despite desperate efforts, has not yet found the mot juste for a relationship which, though increasingly common and generally accepted, has no specific legal foundation."

"I see."

"I thought you'd be crushed."

"No, you didn't. When can I see Mr. Nazarian?"

"Christ, you sound just like . . ." He broke off, not at all amused. "I am not going to say that again. To answer your question, I don't know. When are you free?"

"Anytime. Today."

"No, no." He shook his head. "You don't just drop in on Victor Nazarian. All other considerations aside, the old boy is dying."

"I didn't realize he was that ill."

"Oh, yes. He's a tough old bastard, but the end can't be far off. I'll call him this afternoon and try to make an appointment."

"Thanks." I added, "I'm really awfully grateful."

"Okay, okay. Aren't you going to eat your hamburger?"

I picked it up and took a bite. It was lukewarm, the grease congealing. Half an hour before, I couldn't have eaten the finest filet, but I was suddenly very hungry. I chewed away at the disgusting object while Dave consulted a tattered notebook, held together with a rubber band.

"Eat up," he ordered, his eyes on the scribbled page. "I'm supposed to be meeting one of my students in five minutes."

"I'm sorry."

"Can the apologies, you little hypocrite," Dave said amiably. "You're not sorry, and I know you're not sorry, and you know I know you aren't sorry." He slipped the rubber band back in place and shoved the notebook into his sagging pocket. "You through?"

I decided I had better be through.

Once outside, he set a pace that soon left me breathless. "Where are you going?" he asked, as I trotted along at his heels.

"I thought I'd spend a little time in the museum."

"I mean later. Where are you staying?"

"I don't know. Where's the nearest hotel?"

He smiled reluctantly. "Keeping an eye on me, are you? The Hyde Park Hilton is your best bet—Forty-ninth and Lake Shore Drive."

"Forty-ninth and Lake Shore," I repeated. "Shall I call you or will you contact me?"

"Call me."

The warm sunlight had brought people outdoors. A group of students sat on the Institute's broad steps; one had a book open on his knee, and I recognized the bible of the beginning (and advanced) student of ancient Egyptian, Gardiner's *Egyptian Grammar*. A couple of others were kibitzing as he worked on a translation exercise. The casual poses and easy laughter brought back the memories captured in Mother's old photographs. Perhaps Dave remembered too. He stopped at the top of the stairs.

"I'll speak with you this evening, Haskell. If you select another hotel, call me and tell me where you are. If I don't hear from you, I'll try to reach you at the Hilton. Stay there, don't go out."

"I'll wait for your call."

"When I say don't go out, I mean don't go out." He took me by the shoulders and swung me around to face him. "It isn't safe, especially after dark."

"All right." I grimaced and tried to free myself.

"What's the matter with you?"

"You're hurting me."

"Oh. Sorry about that." His grip relaxed, but he didn't let me go.

"And those people—there—are staring at us."

Dave grinned. "Who stares? They stare? Let them stare."

"I suppose they're accustomed to your eccentric performances," I said, glaring at one of the men who was watching us.

"Eccentric, hell. I'm just trying to finish a conversation; you keep squirming like a worm on a hook. What's your hurry?"

"I thought you were in a hurry."

"I am. I'm late." But he continued to hold me, fingers digging into my skin, and gradually his smile faded into a frown. "I have a funny feeling about you," he said. "Are you holding out on me?"

I countered with a question of my own. "Do you think I'm a liar, is that it?"

"No. I can tell when people lie to me." Unexpectedly his eyebrows quirked and he shook his head, as if responding to an inaudible comment by an invisible listener. "Okay, so I like to think I can tell. It's a common delusion. I don't doubt that you are Lee's daughter; you wouldn't be stupid enough to lie about something that can be readily checked."

"If you'd care to see my birth certificate—"

"I said I believed you. It's something else. I don't know what it is, but . . ."

"Your masculine intuition," I suggested sweetly. "Or your crystal ball. Do you tell fortunes?"

He shook me, none too gently; my head snapped back, and one of the staring students laughed and made a remark I didn't catch.

"Watch your mouth, kid," Dave said. "As a matter of fact, I used to tell fortunes. It was one of my better parlor tricks—the old tarot cards, and a turban made out of a kitchen towel, and a lot of patter about seventh sons."

That explained one of the snapshots I had not understood. The cards on the table had not shown clearly, but I well remembered the towel; it was the same one that, differently draped, had provided Steve Nazarian with his nemes headdress. I nodded, knowingly, and Dave's eyes narrowed.

"You know too many things," he said softly. "Or do you? Ah, the hell with it. Scram, Haskell, you make me nervous. Go bug somebody else for a while. I'll be in touch."

The heavy door opened and swung shut, practically in my face. I rubbed my aching shoulders, pretending to ignore the grinning audience, waited a few seconds to give Dave time to get out of sight, and then followed him into the Institute.

I didn't spend any time in the museum. That last unnerving exchange had finished me; I was so tired, my knees wobbled. I bought a few books at the museum shop, including one I owned but had neglected to bring with me. I figured I had better do a little homework. Art history wasn't my specialty; I had only known about the Khufu bust because of the reading I had done on the Nazarians. I needed to bone up.

I got a room at the Hilton, though the price horrified me. I would certainly have to look for cheaper lodgings. But that could wait; everything depended now on the "old bastard." What an engaging term—and how peculiarly appropriate. I tipped the bellboy, collapsed onto the bed, and fell sound asleep.

It was dusky dark when I awoke. I felt much better, physically and mentally. So far, so good. Very good, in fact; having actually succeeded with Dave, I could admit how far-out my chances of success had been. As for his dire hints and vague threats, I could dismiss them as the peculiar joke they had—probably—been meant to be.

I felt too lazy to get dressed and go downstairs for dinner. It's boring to eat alone, and as I knew by experience, there was a good chance someone would try to convince me I didn't have to eat alone. I called room service and ordered a club sandwich and a glass of milk; after it arrived I decided I would treat myself to a phone call before I settled down with *The Art and Architecture of Ancient Egypt*. I missed Jessie. Even if she lectured me, which was more than likely, I wanted to hear her voice.

It didn't occur to me that she had a legitimate reason to lecture, though her "Hello?" was sharp with anxiety.

"It's me," I said cheerfully.

"Well, it's about time! Where the hell are you?"

"In Chicago."

Jessie used a few words she had labored to expunge from my youthful vocabulary. "Where in Chicago?"

Meekly I reported my location.

Jessie repeated, "Hyde Park," in a voice heavy with implicit criticism, but decided to let that go for the moment. Instead she said, "I told you you couldn't take it at Mama's."

"You were right. Not that they weren't sweet to me. But they haven't a telephone."

"Or anything else that makes life interesting. Never mind

the old ladies. I almost hate to ask this, but what have you been up to?"

"I think I may have a job."

I explained.

"The Nazarian Foundation," Jessie repeated.

I waited for her to go on, but she didn't, so I said inanely, "That's right."

"Right? What a word . . . Oh, I knew what you were planning, but I never imagined it would work. Don't get your hopes up, Haskell. The old man is supposed to be a nasty customer."

"I'm taking it one step at a time."

"Uh-huh. How long are you going to be at the Hilton?"

"Just a couple of days. Once I'm sure of the job, I'll find a cheap room somewhere."

"For God's sake, Haskell, be careful. That's a terrible neighborhood."

"Most city neighborhoods are terrible. Chicago is no worse than Philadelphia."

"So who says I'd be any happier to have you wandering around Philly on your own?"

"I'll be careful. I'm not a child, you know."

Jessie snorted. "Jon keeps calling. Twice last night."

"Call him, then, and tell him I'm fine."

"Why don't you call him?"

"Because I don't want to."

"I'm going to give him your number."

"Wait till tomorrow, okay? I'd rather not talk to him, Jessie. Not tonight."

"Why? What's wrong?"

"Nothing's wrong!" I forced a laugh. "I'm tired; I have to pick out the right clothes to wear tomorrow, and do some boning up, in case Mr. Nazarian decides to quiz me."

She persisted. "You aren't going out tonight, are you?"

"Now who would I be going out with? I don't have any

friends here, and I'm not stupid enough to roam the city streets alone."

"You would if you wanted something badly enough," said Jessie in tones of profound pessimism. "And it seems to me you met two eligible men today."

"So I should be in hot pursuit of one or both?"

Jessie said soberly, "The other way around. You're an unusually pretty girl, Haskell. I never talked much about your looks because I didn't want to make you vain; but you're the kind men go after."

"Thanks for the compliment, but I think you might be just a teeny bit prejudiced. Neither of the gentlemen appeared to be impressed by my gorgeousness. One of them has a good friend, of the live-in variety, and the other . . . Aside from the fact that he's a few years my senior, there is that nasty little possibility of incest."

Jessie groaned. "Don't be vulgar."

"I'm not. The *situation* is vulgar. And not without a certain black humor."

"I can't see anything humorous about it. What's he like now?"

"Dave?"

"Oh, you're on first-name terms already."

"He's sweet, Jessie. I wouldn't be disappointed if he turned out to be the one."

"He's not too old," Jessie muttered.

"No, I guess not," I agreed, laughing. "What are you driving at, Jessie? Don't tell me, let me guess; he's the secret sex maniac of Chicago, the Don Juan of the Oriental Institute—"

"That is not funny, Haskell."

"No, it isn't. Sorry, Jessie. And I'm flattered that you consider me so irresistible. But believe me, darling, nothing could be farther from my mind right now than romance. Or even sex."

"All right, all right," Jessie said. "Are you eating decent meals? Getting your rest?"

I had to accept the retreat into banalities; poor Jessie, I had hassled her enough. We discussed my health and habits; I asked about Pooch and promised again to call her immediately if I changed my quarters.

After I had hung up the phone I got out of bed and crossed the room. It was furnished in basic hotel style—a few uncontroversial prints on the walls, two double beds with matching blue spreads, bedside tables, a bureau, a TV. There was a mirror over the bureau. I switched on the light and stared at my face.

I hadn't thought about my appearance for a long time—not since I fell in love with Jon. He thought I was beautiful, and that was enough. For years before that I had suffered from the usual afflictions of adolescence, including what is politely called baby fat, and the inevitable consequences of a dark, oily skin. Dark—and my mother was fair. Perhaps that was why I had never been vain about my looks. According to Jessie, my mother had been perfect, everything a woman should be. If I didn't look like her I wasn't attractive. If I didn't behave like her . . .

I turned impatiently from the mirror. So I was pretty. Fine. Senile old men are reputed to be suckers for pretty young girls, and Nazarian had been a notorious lover in his day. There wouldn't be much of his vaunted virility left by now, only wistful memories; if it would get me what I wanted, I would let him pat my hand and boast about his conquests and tell me that older men were much sexier than callow youths.

Dave telephoned a short time later. He was brisk and businesslike. Nazarian had agreed to see me at eleven the following morning. If I cared to come to the Institute at ten-thirty, he would drive me.

I started to thank him, but he said, "See you tomorrow," and hung up.

One more hurdle, I told myself. Surely it would be the last. I was so keyed up, I had to force myself to turn off the light, but I knew that if I didn't get enough sleep I'd have ugly purple smudges under my eyes next day. I didn't want to look wistful or sexy; I wanted to look fresh and young and intelligent and alert.

I lay in the dark thinking and plotting—trying to anticipate what he would say, deciding how I should respond. But my last thought, before I drifted off to sleep, had nothing to do with Victor Nazarian. I had laughed at Jessie's obscure hints concerning Dave Wertheim. Perhaps I had misinterpreted her meaning. Perhaps her reasons for warning me to keep my distance from him were not so frivolous as I had supposed. Did she know something she hadn't told me?

4

I woke at the crack of dawn and couldn't get back to sleep. As it turned out, I needed the extra time. My self-confidence about charming Mr. Nazarian had been eroded by Jessie's pessimism, and I was so nervous I couldn't get my eyeliner on straight. I did my face three times, changed my hairstyle twice, and tried on every outfit I had brought with me. It was a good thing I only had four choices (the rest were work clothes, pants, shirts, and jeans), or I would have drowned in a bog of indecision. The tailored suit was out; I wanted to look adorable. The frilly blouse and gathered skirt were no good; I wanted to look efficient. The outfit I had worn the day before was my favorite, but Dave had already seen it. . . .

I wore it anyway. It was the most becoming thing I owned. When did a man ever remember a woman's dress?

After all that, I had to cover my glory with a raincoat. It was a gray, mizzling day, but Dave was waiting for me outside the Institute, pacing up and down like a caged tiger and chain-smoking.

"You still want to go through with this?" he demanded, lighting another cigarette from the stub of the one he was holding before he tossed it away.

"Of course. If you can't spare the time, I don't mind going alone. So long as he's expecting me—"

"He's expecting you," Dave said grimly. He reached for my arm, but I stepped nimbly aside. I didn't want to be pushed or dragged, like a recalcitrant schoolgirl. Besides, his grip hurt.

"My car's this way," he grunted, and started off without waiting for me.

I trotted meekly behind him until we reached the car, a disheveled and ancient MG. It was typical of its owner— plenty of class, but not well maintained. He helped me in, and off we went in a cloud of burning oil.

I knew where the Nazarian mansion was. There was very little public information about the man and the family I didn't know. The house was on Prairie Avenue, a plebeian name for what had once been the abode of millionaires— "The Sunny Street that Held the Sifted Few." Among the sifted had been Marshall Field; George Pullman of railroad fame; and John Sherman, "the Father of the Stockyards." Almost all the grand old mansions were gone now, destroyed, not by the Great Fire, which they postdated, but by that indifference to the past which its enemies claim is characteristic of Chicago.

One book I had consulted contained photographs of the mansion, including some of the interior—the Grand Gallery, twenty feet longer than the famous Art Gallery of Mrs. Potter Palmer; the dining room, twenty square feet larger than Cyrus McCormick's dining room; the glass conservatory, which had held twice as many exotic plants as the hothouse of George Pullman. The house had been built by Anton Nazarian, founder of the family fortunes (railroads, steel mills, stockyards) and father of the present incumbent, in the last decades of the nineteenth century, perhaps the most opulently ostentatious and richly vulgar of all eras in American history. Everything Anton Nazarian owned had to be bigger, longer, and grander than the possessions of his rivals.

But the photographs were all old ones; they didn't prepare me for the present look of the house, or for the deterioration of the neighborhood. There was little left except warehouses and boarded-up houses, weedy broken sidewalks, and—worst of all—the decaying wrecks of the few remaining homes of the Sifted Few. Not so much sifted as winnowed out; aside from the Nazarian estate, the only survivor was the Glessner House, now a museum. One once-glorious old mansion was being dismantled or restored, I couldn't tell which; sections of fluted marble columns, monumental as those of a Greek temple, lay in forlorn abandonment on the overgrown lawn. The ruins were more appalling than those of an ordinary house because they had been so much more spectacular to begin with.

The Nazarian mansion was an insane, arrogant blend of conflicting styles, with the medieval predominating. It was an imitation (larger, of course) of the Potter Palmer mansion that had once dominated Lake Shore Drive. Nazarian had hired the same architect—and paid him more.

Now the house was surrounded by a steel fence like that of a prison, even to the electrified wire atop it. A thick bristly hedge inside the fence formed a second barricade.

A guard emerged from the fortified gatehouse, and although he must have known Dave by sight, he checked an appointment sheet before admitting us.

"Where are the nuclear warheads?" I asked, as we proceeded along a curving drive. "Or does he just keep the pots of melted lead boiling?"

"It wouldn't surprise me," Dave admitted. "But security

precautions are necessary. The contents of one room of that house would enrich a dozen burglars, and the old man has a few enemies, business and personal. He's the last of the Sifted Few of Prairie Avenue. The others moved out long ago, but not Victor or his father before him. Did you know old Anton commissioned a family crest? The bird is supposed to be an eagle, but it looks more like a vulture, and the motto he selected was 'Teneo Tenuere Majores.'"

"'I hold what my ancestors held,'" I said, showing off. "A slight exaggeration, surely? Isn't he Armenian? He's a long way from the ancestral acres."

Instead of stopping in front of the monumental front door, Dave drove on and halted under a porte-cochere that fronted a less imposing but handsome side entrance. The wheels had hardly stopped turning before the door opened and two men emerged. They were dressed in a sort of livery—dark suits with a crest (the bird did look like a vulture) on the pockets of the jackets; but they were built like wrestlers, and one slipped his right hand inside his coat as he took up a position at the top of the stairs. The other man opened the car door. Dave got out, leaving the keys in the ignition; and as we mounted the steps, the guard drove the car away.

"A precaution against car bombs or terrorists concealed in the trunk," Dave explained, straight-faced.

"But that's paranoid. I can't imagine living like that!"

"Ah, but you've never been very, very rich. Or very, very unpopular. Morning, Al. How's it going?"

The guard at the top of the stairs touched his cap but did not reply. He opened the door for us and stood back to let us precede him. As we entered, a buzzer went off. Dave stopped.

"Damn, I keep forgetting. Too much loose change again." He plunged his hands into his baggy pockets and pulled out fistfuls of coins, which he deposited in a tray proffered by the silent Al. Next time he made it through. I followed, cringing a little.

I was too confused and intimidated to pay much attention to my surroundings, though they were well worth studying. The walls were paneled in mahogany, rosewood, and other woods I could not identify. Oriental rugs were scattered about. Alcoves illuminated by concealed lights held pieces of sculpture—a greater-than-life-sized granite statue of a pharaoh wearing the Double Crown, a "reserve head" in plaster, a dark slate Horus-falcon whose crown appeared to be of pure gold.

The place was preternaturally quiet. Except for our footsteps—and believe me, I was tiptoeing—the only sound was the regular ticking of a clock near the foot of the stairs. Then a door opened with a soft click, and the next line of defense appeared—a slight, bespectacled man whom Dave introduced as Frank Burke, Nazarian's personal secretary. He led us up the stairs and down miles of corridors to the inner sanctum.

There he paused, his hand on the glass—or more probably rock-crystal—knob. "The young lady understands the rules, Dr. Wertheim?"

Dave scowled. "What the hell, Frank, she isn't going to kiss him. Not on a first date."

The secretary permitted himself a polite half-smile. "Yes, sir. If I may . . . ?"

Dave rolled his eyes speechlessly.

I was, I learned, to take the chair offered me and remain on it. On no account was I to approach Mr. Nazarian. I was to speak loudly and slowly, facing him at all times. Abrupt movements and gesticulations were not permitted. Joking references to the security precautions were frowned upon, as were any references to bombs, plastic explosives, and the like.

"I think I can handle it," I said, trying to sound more confident than I felt.

The secretary's soft knock was answered by a figure as intimidating as any I had yet seen. He was over six feet tall, but the extraordinary breadth of his shoulders and chest made him look short—a gigantic dwarf. His squashy ears and crooked nose suggested that he had been a boxer, and not a very good one. He was dressed in a more elaborate version of the uniform the guards had worn, distinctly military in cut and verging on musical comedy with its gold braid and rows of shiny buttons. The jacket bulged here and there. One of the bulges might have been a gun, but he didn't really need one; the other bulges were all muscles.

I would have backed away if Dave hadn't been right behind me. The giant's queer, dreamy eyes passed indifferently over me and brightened at the sight of Dave.

"Hello, Professor."

"Hello, Jerry. How's every little thing?"

Jerry's thick lips parted in a smile. "Just fine, Professor. We're just fine today."

Dave introduced me, adding, "Jerry is in charge here, Haskell. He's the boss, so treat him with respect."

The big man giggled. "You're a real kidder, Professor. You can come in now. Mr. Victor is expecting you."

That room destroyed the fragile remnants of my self-confidence. Here Nazarian's fascination with ancient Egypt and his royal arrogance met and blended in a fantastic display.

The bed dominated the room. It was triple-king-sized, draped like a throne in purple velvet trimmed with gold fringe and tassels. The walls were painted with copies, superb ones, of scenes from Egyptian tombs. Not the depressing underworld and judgment scenes, but bright images of hunting and fowling in the marshes, lavish banquets, dancing girls and musicians. It was too much; I couldn't absorb any more, though isolated impressions assaulted my dazzled eyes—a painted alabaster lamp on the mantel, a delicate little head of a woman on a carved table.

In a far corner, twenty feet from the bed, sat a nurse dressed in hospital whites. She was reading a book and she didn't look up when we entered. After the first glimpse, I forgot her presence; like all the others who served the monarch, she knew what she was supposed to do—keep quiet and look like part of the furniture until she was summoned.

But of all the astonishing things in that room, the most incredible was the old man himself. The great bed would have dwarfed a normal-sized individual; age had shrunken and withered him, but even the opulent furnishing could not diminish the sheer force of his presence.

Propped against satin pillows, he was absorbed in a newspaper, sections of which were carelessly scattered over the velvet counterpane.

He bore an uncanny resemblance to one of the best-preserved of the royal mummies—Ramses the Second, builder of Abu-Simbel and other modest memorials. A low, sloping forehead fringed with fine white hair, a nose sharp and prominent as the prow of a ship, withered lips drawn back over surprisingly well-preserved teeth. Even the best mummies have shriveled and shrunk; the skin covers the bones like stretched leather. His skin was like that, the wrinkles of old age petrified and permanent.

He went on reading for a full minute while we stood humbly waiting for an audience. Then he raised his eyes and I got another shock. Though sunken in deep sockets and half covered by withered lids, they were a brilliant black, and they blazed with life. His son's eyes must have been like that.

"What are you standing there for?" he demanded. "You, girl—sit there. That chair. Don't move it. Sit."

I obeyed. The chair was heavily carved, in the pseudo-Egyptian style popular in the mid-nineteenth century, and it was also damned uncomfortable. I couldn't have moved it if I had wanted to; it must have weighed a hundred pounds.

There was a long painful pause while the old man

inspected me from head to foot. His hearing might be poor, but his eyesight seemed to be excellent.

"Go away, Dave," he grunted, without taking his eyes off me. "Wait outside."

"But I thought—"

"You were wrong. As usual." The rusty creaking sound that issued from his lips must have been laughter.

"You're a rude old son of a bitch," Dave said.

"I am. I am." Nazarian's frail body shook with mirth.

"Okay, I'll go. This room gives me the heebie-jeebies anyhow." Dave went to the door—but not before he had given me a meaningful look and a tiny half-nod. I felt a surge of gratitude for the hint; he was telling me that the old man didn't mind a touch of his own rudeness. In fact, he probably found it a refreshing change after the subservience of his attendants. I would have to be careful, though. Every tyrant has sensitivities which it is not safe to touch.

After Jerry had shown Dave out, he took up a post by the door, his eyes watchful. There was another pause, even more painful. In some societies the first one to speak loses prestige. In others, the social inferior doesn't speak until spoken to. In either case, I had nothing to lose by keeping quiet. I was less nervous than I had expected; the old man fascinated me, and I stared back at him as candidly as he was examining me.

If the contest was to see who would speak first, I won. Maybe he wasn't used to being subjected to the searching scrutiny he gave other people. It wasn't long before he moved his head slightly—in a man so infirm, it was the equivalent of a restless change of position—and said querulously, "Well, young woman? Didn't your mother teach you it is rude to stare? What's so fascinating about this old face?"

I could hardly tell him the truth—You might be my grandfather. "It is a very interesting face. You remind me of—of—"

"Well? What?"

I decided to risk it. "The mummy of Ramses the Second."

The fleshless lips stretched farther than I would have believed possible. The teeth had to be false! "Not Ramses himself, but his mummy? That's damned insulting."

"Oh, no. It's a very well-preserved mummy."

The old man wheezed with laughter. "You're absolutely right. First person who's had the effrontery to mention it."

"He must have been a fine-looking man, if one can judge by his statues."

"Can't judge by his statues. Not portraiture. None of the royal statues."

"In some periods, certainly. But there are individual cases—"

"Don't bring up Akhenaton. Can't even tell him from his wife unless there's an inscription." He cut off my reply with a feeble but autocratic twitch of one bony hand. "Don't argue with me, young woman. Nobody argues with me. You've proved you know a little something about Egyptology—that's what you had in mind, wasn't it? No more than any well-educated layman, but something. What did you come here for?"

"Dr. Wertheim said he'd need your permission before taking me on."

"Damn right. I make the decisions. Always have. Always will, while there's breath in my body. I didn't mean that. I meant, why are you so set on the job? It's menial labor, you know. If you think I'd let an amateur like you touch my prize pieces, you're sadly mistaken. And don't think you're going to find anything you can use for an article or a dissertation. Nobody publishes without my permission."

"I wasn't thinking of doing that."

"You should." Another fleshless disconcerting grin.

"You'll never get ahead by being honest. The trick is not to be caught."

"It's only the rich who can afford the risk," I said. "If they are caught, they go to nice country-club jails or are fined a small percentage of what they have managed to steal. Poor people get shafted."

"You've got a point," said my . . . grandfather?

I felt oddly at ease with him; there was definitely a rapport. Was it an unconscious recognition of kinship? Nonsense. But he was enjoying himself; I could tell. We had something in common. I hated to think it might be a shared personality trait—stubbornness, ruthlessness, a single-minded determination to have one's own way at all costs.

He decided we had chatted long enough. "So you're Leah's daughter. You don't look like her."

"Everybody tells me that. Did you know her?"

"Nothing wrong with my memory," the old man muttered. "Yes, I knew her. Knew all of them. They didn't like me—not even my own son; he despised me and everything I stood for—but they had to be civil. A few times I entertained them here. They couldn't refuse my invitations."

"No," I agreed. "You were one of the Institute's biggest patrons. I suppose even their scholarships—"

"Right. Including your mother's. Nazarian Fellowship, the most prestigious of all. I was against giving it to her. Don't believe in women working."

"What made you change your mind?"

"I thought she was different." The old man's lips twisted. "The brightest of the lot—no question about that; she had brains. But she betrayed me in the end. Ran off and got married. Just like a woman. Not even a scholar, a damn-fool soldier! I thought she and Stephen . . ."

The wrinkled lids drooped, hiding his eyes. I waited with pent breath; when it became apparent he wasn't going to finish the sentence, I ventured, "Were they—were they in love?"

"Love?" His eyes snapped open. "How would I know about that? He didn't confide in me. He told me nothing. Maybe she was right to turn him down. He was a failure. You know what happened to him, don't you?"

"I . . . Yes, I know. I'm so sorry."

"Got what he deserved. Perfect case of poetic justice. Trying to destroy society, destroyed himself."

His voice was noticeably weaker. Jerry cleared his throat, like a miniature volcano announcing an imminent eruption, and the nurse rose to her feet. Quiet as it was, the movement startled me; I had forgotten she was there. "You must leave now," she said softly. "Mr. Nazarian is tired."

He didn't move or speak when I started toward the door. The knowledge of failure weighed heavily on my spirits. He had been playing with me the whole time; he had never had any intention of granting my request. If he could speak so callously and cruelly about his own son, that memory unsoftened by the passage of years, he would not have forgiven my mother for "betraying" him. In a way, I wasn't sorry to be dismissed. The bright, opulent room was as grisly as any tomb, and my initial sympathy had been replaced by disgust.

Jerry opened the door for me. His face was as blank as a mask, even when I murmured "Thank you." He seemed a strange person to be the intimate personal servant of a man like Nazarian, but perhaps his physical strength and devotion made up for his lack of intellectual abilities.

Dave was waiting for me in an alcove furnished with a table and chairs and innumerable potted plants. The Venetian glass ashtray was filled with cigarette butts.

"No dice, eh?" he said, studying my crestfallen face.

"He didn't say, one way or the other."

"I didn't expect he would. He likes to keep people dangling. Are you ready to throw in the towel?"

"No." I had one last card up my sleeve. If I had not been so summarily dismissed, I might have been tempted to try it—flinging my arms around the old rascal with a glad cry of "Grandfather!"

Actually, that might not have been such a smart move. I had been warned not to approach the throne, and Jerry was just the man to pull his rod and fill me full of holes if I disobeyed orders. Besides, the direct attack might have backfired. A sentimentalist the old man was not; he had hated his son and disliked my mother; why should he feel any kindlier toward an alleged grandchild?

I wasn't ready to give up, though. Fall back and regroup, that was the thing to do. Now that I had seen and spoken with him, I could revise my approach, plan a more appropriate strategy. Half to myself, I said, "He didn't say no."

"Don't get your hopes up," Dave grunted. "He probably will say no, but he'll make you sweat for a few days before he does."

It wasn't a few days, it was only the length of time it took us to traverse the long corridors and descend the stairs. The guard-butler had already opened the door when a voice called from the top of the stairs. "Will you wait, please? Mr. Nazarian would like to speak with you again."

We waited. And waited. I was too restless to sit, as Dave did, pulling a paperback novel from his pocket and becoming absorbed in it. Al didn't like my prowling the hall; he watched me like a hawk. My spirits went up and down like a yo-yo. Was this a further refinement of torture, as in the Poe story, when the tormentor allows the prisoner an illusion of escape before recapturing him?

Almost an hour had passed before the secretary reappeared and led us back upstairs. This time there were three chairs arranged near the bed. One faced the other two. Even before I was ordered to take it, I knew that was my place—on trial, facing my judges.

Standing behind one chair was a man I had never seen before, but whose face was familiar. That didn't mean a thing; lately, everyone I had met reminded me of someone—or, in Nazarian's case, of some *thing*. You can't really call a mummy "someone."

Taken as a whole, the man's face was attractive, verging on handsome, though the individual features were flawed. His cheeks were sunken, his chin was elongated. His lips were beautifully shaped, but the lower one was rather too full. His hair was black except for a wing or a plume of pure white over each ear. Over the entire countenance lay a faint, indefinable film of melancholy.

I don't often notice men's clothing, but his was smashing—a heavy silk tie, a three-piece suit of gray wool so soft you wanted to stroke it like a cat's fur.

Nazarian's idea of an introduction was to mumble, "This is the girl. Girl, this is my son-in-law. He's the other trustee."

Dave was annoyed and didn't care who knew it. "Damn it, Victor, I wish you'd quit playing cat and mouse. I've wasted the whole morning on this business, which isn't worth an hour of anyone's time. Haskell Maloney, Paul Dunlap. Paul, I presume you know who Haskell is and why she's here. Haskell, Paul is vice-president of the Foundation that has been set up to handle the collection. Now let's get on with it."

As soon as I heard the name I knew why the pensive features were familiar. I had seen them on the back of a book jacket—translations of Egyptian love poetry—which some quirk of popular fancy had transformed into a semi-bestseller. His articles, published in professional journals, were few in number but outstanding in quality. I also knew that Dunlap was the curator of the Nazarian Museum and that he was married to Nazarian's daughter. Maybe that explained his sad look. Being Nazarian's son-in-law had to be a disheartening experience.

"I've read everything you ever wrote, Dr. Dunlap," I said. "It's an honor to meet you."

Nazarian cackled. "You're a good judge of character,

young woman. Flattery will get you everywhere with this one. Sit, Dave, sit. I call the meeting of the board to order—"

"We can't act without consulting the others," Dave objected.

"How many are there?" I knew I shouldn't have spoken, but I couldn't help myself; the prospect of going through more interviews like this one brought a note of pure horror to my voice.

Dunlap's narrow face broadened into a smile. He knew exactly what I was thinking. "Don't worry, Miss Maloney. The Director of the Institute is a member, as is my wife. But you won't have to face them; they will abide by our decision."

"Thank you," I murmured.

"Don't thank me yet. I must be honest; I cannot really approve of this. A young woman of your abilities must have better ways of passing the summer. It would be a waste of your time."

It was the first time any of them had considered me, but I wished he weren't so damned thoughtful.

"No, sir, really, I want—"

"Quiet," Nazarian snapped. "You talk too much, girl. Well, Dave?"

"I'll make it short and sweet," said Dave. "I'm in favor of taking her on. Since Paul is against, that leaves you to break the tie, Victor. Let's get this over with."

The small black eyes regarded him without favor. "You're a sentimentalist, Dave."

"I'm not going to debate with you," Dave said. "Yes or no?"

The old man's head fell back on the pillow. The nurse hurried forward, reaching for his wrist. He shook her off and sat up, alert and lively. He had done that on purpose— one more delaying tactic. But he was tiring.

"Yes," he said abruptly. "Why not? Never turn down the

chance to get something for nothing. You won't get paid, girl. Not one red cent. If you thought you'd sweet-talk me into a salary—"

"No," I said. "I don't want any money. I'm very grateful, Mr. Nazarian. Thank you—thank you very much."

"In that case, I withdraw my objection," Paul said, with a pleasant smile. "You'll be a great help, Miss Maloney. But I still think we are taking advantage of you."

"Get out, all of you," the old man growled. "Nurse— where's that damned woman, always butting in when she's not wanted, never around . . . when I need her. . . ."

Lips compressed, the nurse returned to the bed. Nazarian's eyes had closed; his breath came in gasps. That moment of weakness hadn't been pure pretense after all.

Jerry showed me and Dave out and then hurried back to his master, his heavy features creased with concern. Paul Dunlap remained behind too.

"Well?" Dave said. "Pleased with yourself?"

"Let's just say I'm pleased, period."

We waited. I didn't know what we were waiting for, but it wasn't my place to ask. Dave was in a sour mood; if I hadn't been present during the voting, I would have assumed it was he who had opposed my appointment and Dr. Dunlap who had supported me. After the single sharp query, he did not speak until Dunlap finally joined us.

"Well, my dear, would you like to see the scene of your future labors? You may change your mind once you've gotten the full effect."

"I won't change my mind," I said. "But I don't want to take your time."

"No trouble, I assure you. In fact—" He glanced at his watch. "Why don't you plan to stay for lunch? I'm afraid Victor has kept you longer than you expected. You too, Dave."

"Might as well," Dave said ungraciously. "I want to have a word with Carl anyway."

"We'll ask him to join us. I'm sure he'll be delighted to learn he has acquired an assistant. This way, Miss Maloney."

Dunlap kept up a courteous flow of conversation, pointing out some of the prize pieces of the collection as we passed them and commenting on the architecture and décor of the house.

"It's a little overpowering, isn't it?" I ventured, as we turned a corner into another long stretch of corridor hung with paintings.

"Yes, I suppose so. There aren't many of these old mansions surviving, much less occupied. This one is already half museum. After Victor dies, it will house his collection."

Dave, stamping along behind us, grunted, and Dunlap smiled. "Dave doesn't approve."

"The place is impossible," Dave said. "The design is all wrong, the location stinks, and the cost of maintenance will be prohibitive. It would save money in the long run to construct a new building."

"I agree. But Victor doesn't; and it's his house, his collection, and his money." He stopped in front of a door that looked as if it had been stolen from an Italian palazzo and pressed a scowling carved head. The door slid aside, disclosing a tiny room lined with red velvet, like a jewel box. Dunlap waved me inside.

"I don't know where Carl is at the moment. Let's try his office first."

The jewel box turned out to be an elevator. After a somewhat bumpy descent, accompanied by the wheezing of the antique mechanism, we emerged into a long, empty corridor. There were no windows, so I cleverly concluded we must be underground—in a tunnel, in fact.

I had no time on that first occasion to make much sense of the plan, but later I learned to know it well. The tunnel took us to the basement of the museum proper—a separate structure built by Victor Nazarian in the nineteen-thirties to house his increasing collection. Though small in size, the museum was equipped with all the usual amenities; the basement contained offices, laboratories, and storage rooms. The room into which Dunlap led us had been fitted up as an office, with desks, filing cabinets, and metal shelves containing a hodgepodge of books mixed with cardboard boxes filled with small antiquities—beads, cylinder seals, fragments of pottery. If the office was Carl's, neatness was not one of his characteristics. Both desks and several chairs were piled high with papers.

"He's not here," Dunlap said blankly.

"Probably in the cellar," Dave grunted.

"I expect you're right. We may as well go and drag him out. I don't know, though . . . That's a very pretty dress, Miss Maloney, and the old cellars are filthy."

I assured him I didn't mind. I spoke sincerely; I knew he was referring to the lower regions of the mansion itself, wherein were stored the most fascinating and enigmatic of the antiquities—those acquired by Mr. Nazarian's father, some of them before the turn of the century, when there were no laws governing the export of antiquities, and exploration of the ancient lands of the Near East was at its peak.

The elevator didn't go down to the cellars. We had to traverse a long, gloomy passageway and descend another flight of stairs. I will never forget my first sight of that dusty, dimlit region.

The long, vaultlike underground room had been part of the original house. It had been sealed against damp and rodents, and it was equipped with massive doors that rendered it virtually airtight. Over the years, the collection had overflowed into the other subterranean areas, even into the erstwhile wine cellar. As new pieces were acquired, they replaced the ones on display upstairs and the latter were shoved haphazardly into storage. It was an astonishing and depressing sight—a mammoth jumble of boxes, barrels, and packing cases, furred with gray dust and swathed in cobwebs. Some of the cases looked as if they had never been opened. I remembered reading about the warehouses in which William Randolph Hearst, another fanatical collector, had stored his acquisitions, many still in the original packing. With men like that, who could afford to buy almost anything they wanted, the collecting instinct became perverted. They were like greedy children, grabbing with both hands, less interested in the worth of the object than in the sheer pleasure of owning it.

I shouldn't have been surprised or discouraged; but in the back of my unregenerative imagination there had been a vision of something different—Ali Baba's cavern, with jewels spilling from open chests, rich tapestries, vessels of gold and cut crystal. Dunlap looked at my wan face and laughed aloud. "Disappointed?"

"No. It's—it's fascinating."

"You won't be working down here, Miss Maloney. Eventually we will move the packing cases upstairs, where there is better light and sufficient space. It will be a slow, tedious process; every object has to be recorded, cleaned, examined, tested, appraised. . . ."

"I see."

He put a friendly hand on my shoulder. "It's frustrating, isn't it?"

"I'd love to just sail in and start rummaging around," I admitted. "It's like a gigantic junk shop. You never know what you might find."

Dave snorted, and Dunlap said quickly, "A very natural instinct. I feel the same way. But of course that would be fatal. We must try to match the pieces themselves with Anton Nazarian's records—which are haphazard in the extreme—in the hope of getting some clue as to where and when they were purchased."

"Yes, of course. I wouldn't dream of doing anything without orders."

"Where the devil is Carl?" Dave asked, peering into the gloom. "He's supposed to be working on the journals."

"He's no more immune to the treasure-hunting urge than anyone else," Dunlap said, smiling. "I'll give him a call. No need for us to descend into the grime. Brace yourself, Miss Maloney; there's quite an echo."

I was glad he had warned me. The echo picked up the long vowel and turned it into a mournful, reverberating wail. It was answered from somewhere deep in the vault, whose doors stood wide open. Before long a shadow appeared and moved out into the light. Carl's hands were black with dirt. He drew his sleeve across his face, dislodging the cobwebs that swathed his head like a veil.

"Looking for me?" he asked.

"Time you took a break," Dunlap said. "Come and have a spot of lunch—and meet your new assistant."

"Oh, yeah?" Carl came to the foot of the stairs. "Well, well. That's—uh—that's great. Welcome aboard, Miss— er—Maloney."

"Thank you," I said demurely. I couldn't keep a faint note of triumph from my voice. He had been so supercilious and so sure I wouldn't succeed.

Carl tried to turn down the luncheon invitation, pleading his disheveled condition, but Dunlap waved his apologies aside. "I'll have them bring sandwiches and drinks to your office. My wife is lunching out, so we can relax."

He made it sound like a picnic, but it definitely was not; the cloth covering the table was damask, the dinnerware was fine porcelain, and the sandwiches were open-faced and decorated like a floral display. There were fresh-baked rolls and salad and a tall slim bottle of pale wine, which I refused out of some notion of impressing my new superiors with my sobriety. Carl shook his head at the wine too, but Dave drank half the bottle and Dunlap had several glasses.

Most of the time they talked over and around me, discussing details of the work with which I was not familiar, and I was content to listen. Carl wasn't exactly verbose; I knew he was dying to get Dave off by himself and ask what happened during the interview.

We had reached the stage of coffee when the door opened and a woman entered. Her appearance galvanized Carl, who sat facing the door and was the first to see her. He was out of his chair so fast that it would have toppled over if he had not caught it.

Dunlap turned. "Ah, my dear. I thought you'd gone out."

"I'm going to be late, but I couldn't resist stopping by after I'd heard the news."

So this was Mrs. Dunlap. She wasn't at all what I had expected. Except for Jon's mother, who was not exactly at the pinnacle of the social ladder (though a good many rungs above the likes of me), my only acquaintance with the wives and daughters of the rich and socially prominent was via television. Though beautifully groomed and dressed, Mrs. Dunlap was not ashamed to look her age. She had kept her figure, though I suspected it owed something to corsets and uplift bras. Her soft wool suit was a heavenly shade of blue, with matching pumps and hat. Fluffy lace-edged ruffles cradled her chin and perhaps concealed a few sagging muscles. She had never been pretty; her hair was all soft curves and rounded outlines, with full cheeks and a soft, vulnerable mouth. Her hair was pure silver, her eyes small and dark and warm with good will.

The men had risen, and of course I had too. The effect she had on them interested me. Dave's frown of concentration relaxed into a half-smile, and Carl's expression was almost fatuous. She greeted both of them affectionately; but when she looked at her husband, there was a glow of something deeper and more intense, almost visible in the air between them. Years of marriage hadn't dulled that love affair.

She refused the chair Carl offered with the clumsy eagerness of a puppy. "I must run; I can't stay. I only wanted to tell Miss Maloney how happy I am to have her with us. I told Father long ago that Carl ought to have help; the poor boy has been working himself to death. I understand, Miss Maloney, that you are the daughter of an old friend of Father's."

"A friend of your brother's, actually," I said. "They were students together, years ago."

"Of Stephen's?" Her pretty smile wavered, but only for a moment. With determined cheerfulness she went on, "Yes, of course. Well, my dear, don't let these men work you too hard. If one of them tries to bully you, just tell me."

"Don't waste your maternal instincts on this one, Katherine," Dave said. "If there's any bullying around here, she'll do it."

Mrs. Dunlap laughed. "Poor Dave; people are always trying to take advantage of you, aren't they? Where are you staying, my dear?"

"I'm at the Hilton right now. But I'll have to find a cheaper place as soon as possible—a room or a small apartment, perhaps a summer sublet." An idea I had considered, and then dismissed as too much to hope for, revived in the light of Mrs. Dunlap's kindly smile. Disingenuously I said, "Could you perhaps suggest a cheap hotel, here in the neighborhood?"

"My dear girl, you can't live in this part of the city! A young woman alone, coming and going at odd hours as you may do. . . . She'd better stay with us, don't you think, Paul?"

Dunlap was obviously startled and not too pleased. "Why, Katherine, I don't believe . . . She would probably prefer to be independent, so she can come and go as she pleases."

"She can certainly do that here. You can't say we don't

have ample room! One of the guest cottages—that would be ideal. Away from the main house, with its own entrance."

"The cottages haven't been used in years," Dunlap objected.

"All the more reason why they should be cleaned and put in order. Let's see. Today is Friday. I suppose Father will want you to begin on Monday, Miss Maloney. Just bring your luggage with you when you come, and we'll get you settled. That will give me two days to get the place cleaned and ready for you."

"Oh, Mrs. Dunlap, I couldn't," I began.

"Really, Katherine, I'm surprised," Dunlap said seriously. "It's not like you to rush into a decision like this. You've placed Miss Maloney in a position where she couldn't refuse even if she wanted to."

"I don't want to," I said quickly. "It would be wonderful."

"All right, then," Mrs. Dunlap said briskly. She turned to her husband. "You don't really mind, do you, Paul? I'd worry about her otherwise, and I'm sure her family and friends would feel much better about the situation. She's too young to be on her own in a strange city."

"Katherine, my dear, you know it's impossible for me to refuse you anything," he murmured, looking fondly down at the face upturned to his.

It was a touching exchange, but I couldn't help thinking that, after all, this was her home, not his. She didn't have to ask his permission. Ah, well, tact is necessary in a good marriage. Maybe that was why my single tentative move in that direction hadn't been successful.

Dave drove me back to the Institute, where I found myself sucked into a whirlwind of bureaucratic fuss. Victor Nazarian didn't tolerate delay; once he had made up his mind to do something, he wanted it done now—or preferably yesterday.

Most of the papers I was given seemed to be disclaimers. By the time I finished with them, I had signed away everything except my right to remain silent. I could be summarily dismissed if and when the Foundation chose; I was to receive no compensation for my services nor reimbursement for expenses, even those incurred in the line of duty; and if I broke a leg or had a nervous breakdown, I couldn't sue the Foundation, the Institute, or Nazarian. The old man thought of everything. No doubt there was, buried in pages of fine print, a paragraph giving Nazarian the legal right to have me decapitated and dismembered, should the mood seize him.

I signed everything. The final transactions took place in the Director's office; Professor Jones was pleasant enough, but his attitude was obviously a case of "Why me, Lord?" It was almost a relief to meet someone who had not known my mother. Jones was not an Egyptologist, but a specialist in Assyriology who had come from California to work on the great Assyrian dictionary. I think he'd forgotten my name by the time I left him.

Dave escorted me back to his office and waved me to a chair.

"Now what?" I asked wearily.

"That's it for now." He lit one of his smelly cigarettes. "Uh—want to go get a cup of coffee or something?"

"Thanks, but I've taken up enough of your time. I'm sorry to have been a pest. I wish . . ." I stopped myself on the verge of a damning and damaging confession. Fatigue was washing over me in great heavy waves, and I felt, absurdly, as if I wanted to cry.

"I'm sorry, too," Dave mumbled. "I haven't been exactly sweetness and light myself. Forget it, okay? I'm sure you'll do a good job."

"I will. I intend to. You've nothing to apologize for. You've been much nicer to me than I had any reason to expect."

"I wasn't especially nice. This was a crazy idea of yours, but what the hell—it worked, didn't it? Even if it had failed, there was nothing wrong with trying."

"I took advantage of you," I murmured. "Using my mother's name . . ."

Dave shrugged. "Connections are important in any business or profession. They'll get you a hearing, and that's half the battle." His forehead creased. "It's not you, honey—it's me. Why do I have the feeling that you're making a big mistake—and that I'm making a bigger one?"

"Because you're the seventh son of a seventh son?"

Dave grinned and gave me a friendly slap on the back that almost knocked me out of my chair. "Let's just say my biorhythms are out of synch, that makes about as much sense. Get along, you saucy wench. I have work to do."

"Thanks again, Dave."

"Think nothing of it. Want me to go with you on Monday?"

"I'm a big girl now. You don't have to hold my hand."

"Are you set for the weekend? Got everything you need?"

"Yes."

"See you around, then."

He opened a book and bent over it. The last thing I saw before I closed the door was the gleam of sunlight behind his head, like a well-merited halo.

It was late in the afternoon; most of the classes were over. The hall was cool and empty and quiet. Tired as I was, I headed for the library, intending to pick up a few books. One of the perks of my new position—virtually the only one—was an ID card giving me access to the library. I had nothing else to do for the next two days, and it wouldn't hurt to refresh my memory on a few subjects—pottery and cylinder seals, for example.

A scattering of readers occupied the chairs at the long desks; one was struggling to lift a folio almost as long as she was tall. It slipped from her hands and landed on the desk with a thud; nearby students looked up, frowning at the noise.

After checking the card catalogue, I found my books; most were on open shelves and accessible. As I carried them to the desk I saw a woman rise from one of the tables. She was beside me when I turned away, my books in my arm.

"You're the girl," she said, in a low-pitched murmur. "Lee's daughter."

"That's right." I didn't have to ask her name. Twenty years had added lines to her face and streaked her hair with gray, but her features were not the sort that alter greatly with age. She hadn't even changed her hairstyle. I had not realized, from the snapshots, how tall she was. She was standing uncomfortably close, so that she seemed to look down at me from a considerable height.

"You're Miss Maxwell," I said.

"Doctor Maxwell." Her voice rose. The librarian frowned at us.

"Excuse me. Dave said you didn't use academic titles."

Dr. Maxwell's long nose quivered. "Wertheim is a victim of reverse snobbism. If one earns a title, one should use it."

The librarian bore down on us, shaking her head and scowling. Margaret Maxwell returned the scowl but gave in. "Let's go out into the hall. That woman is always on my back."

She walked ungracefully, the heels of her low, sensible shoes clumping decisively at every step. I couldn't help noticing how badly she was dressed. The drab colors, brown and beige, were all wrong for her; and in an attempt to minimize her height, she had selected a print with wide stripes that ran horizontally around her lean body. She looked like an old sepia photo of a barber pole.

I followed her through the swinging doors and to the head

of the stairs. She stopped there and turned to face me, but then she seemed to forget what she had meant to say.

"I was looking forward to meeting you," I said. "I've looked at those snapshots so often I feel I know you and Mother's other friends."

"Oh—is that how you recognized me? I assumed that any halfway competent student of Egyptology would be familiar with my work."

Ouch, I thought. "I am. I mean, I've seen your articles in the journals. But pictures are so much more personal."

"So Leah kept those old snapshots. I can't imagine why. I haven't looked at my old copies in twenty years. We were very young and very silly."

"But very happy," I suggested.

"Happy?" She considered the idea as if it had never occurred to her and then dismissed it. Irrelevant and immaterial. "I suppose it's natural that you would waste time brooding over old pictures. You can't remember her very well."

"I don't remember her at all. I was only a few months old when she died."

"Oh, yes. She showed me pictures of you. Leah had a thing about photographs."

"Pictures of me as a baby? When was that?"

The urgency in my voice startled her. "She came back to Chicago one weekend, not long after you were born. We all saw her. She stopped by the Institute, the way people do when they've something to show off or brag about. Why shouldn't she come to see us? We were her friends—her only friends."

"Yes, of course. The thing is, I know so little about her—and that last visit to Chicago. I'd like to believe she was—she was happy."

That word again. Maxwell shrugged. "She was proud of you. She flaunted those snapshots. Is that what you wanted to hear?"

I didn't know how to respond. She had been pleasant, if distant, when she began the conversation; but I must have said something to rub her the wrong way.

Imperceptibly she had edged closer, so close that her sleeve brushed mine. It might have been prompted by some impairment of hearing or vision, but I didn't think so; there was something subtly intimidating about the way she crowded in on me. I moved back a step.

"You and my mother must have been particularly close," I said. "You were the only women in the department then, weren't you?"

"Not in the Institute itself, but in Egyptology—yes. I can't say we were close, however. Leah was always more interested in the men."

Again, she had left me with nothing to say—nothing civil, at any rate. As I fumbled for words, trying to control my resentment and to find another opening, she said, "I hear you're going to be working with the Nazarian Foundation."

"Yes, that's right."

"You'd better not."

"I—I beg your pardon?"

She had crowded in again. Her face hung over mine, so close I could see the pores in her cheeks. "You had better not do it," she repeated. "It won't help your career—or you. Give it up. Go back to where you came from."

I couldn't retreat any farther, my back was up against the balustrade. Before I could reply, she turned on her heel and walked away.

It had sounded very much like a threat. But as I watched her rapid retreat, I was more puzzled than frightened. Maxwell was still the awkward, homely girl on the outskirts of the group. To think of that jealousy rankling and growing for twenty years . . . Mother had not only been a better scholar, she had compounded the injury by being prettier and more popular, by marrying and having a baby.

"Flaunting" my baby pictures . . . A strange and revealing word.

There was something deeper and more dangerous than ancient jealousy bothering her, though. Her rival was no rival; she had been dead and buried for two decades. But perhaps the dead are the ones who rankle most. You can't revenge yourself on someone who is beyond your reach.

I wasn't afraid of Margaret Maxwell, even if she had transferred her frustrated jealousy of Mother to me, my mother's daughter. There was nothing she could do to hurt me. Sticks and stones may break one's bones, but words—that was the only weapon she had, hateful words. I had hoped she might have been Mother's confidante. I no longer believed that, but I might learn more from an enemy than a friend.

It was odd that Dave had not mentioned Mother's last visit. A long talk with Margaret Maxwell was definitely in order.

The curious undercurrents in that conversation made me forget how tired I was; not until I was in my hotel room, with the door closed and only my thoughts for company, did it hit me again. The big beds looked awfully tempting, but I knew if I dropped off, I'd probably wake up at 3 A.M., unable to go back to sleep. There is nothing worse than being hopelessly wide awake in the middle of the night in a strange hotel room in a strange city.

With dragging feet, I went to the window and stood looking out. There wasn't much to see. Instead of the towering structure I had expected, the hotel was low and sprawling, with separate rows of rooms separated by parking areas, like a suburban motel. Westward lay block after block of drab buildings, apartments and shops and littered pavements. A few patches of green and a church spire or two did very little to brighten the view. Smoke belching from factory chimneys melted into the layer of polluted air and gave the impression of a city under enemy attack. A battleground.

Which was what it was for me. And I had a feeling I was already losing the war.

Dave's acerbic question came back to me. "Pleased with yourself?" I hadn't had time to think about it earlier; the strain of the interview, then the whirlwind of activity, a barrage of new impressions and new people. Now I knew why I had that feeling of flatness.

Against all odds I had succeeded in the first stage of my plan. I had never admitted to myself how slim the chances of success were; if I had done so, I probably wouldn't have had the gall to try. I had concentrated so fiercely on that one first step—winning entree, by one means or another, to the Nazarian household—that it had become an end in itself. I hadn't really thought beyond it. I didn't know what to do next.

As I turned from the window, I saw a red light on the telephone blinking. That meant there was a message for me. I had not stopped at the desk, since I always carried my hotel key with me. Jessie had drummed that rule into me: Never leave your key, because an inattentive clerk may hand it over to the wrong person. I had kidded her about that precept, and others that struck me as hopelessly old-fashioned: "Sure, right, okay; I won't accept candy from strange men either, or leave the house without clean under-wear." But now that she wasn't around to wrap me in pro-tective advice I found myself clinging to those old rules.

The message was probably from Jessie, asking me to return her call. I wanted to talk to her, and I didn't want to talk to her. Not in my present mood. The least I could do to relieve her anxiety was to sound upbeat and cheerful. At the moment I was neither—and I didn't know why.

I was sitting in the chair by the window, hands limp in my lap, mind spinning like a hamster on a wheel, when the phone rang. The room was dusky with twilight. I took my time about answering, switching on the lamp and moving slowly, but the phone kept on ringing. I picked it up. "Yes?"

"Hello," a voice said brightly.

He expected me to recognize his voice. How could I not, when it was the one I had waited most eagerly to hear for almost a year? I was tempted to pretend I didn't, but I was too tired to play games.

"Hello, Jon," I said warily.

"How are things going?"

"Fine." I cleared my throat and tried again. "Just great."

"Good. Want to tell me about it?"

A dire suspicion entered my mind. "Where are you?"

"Downstairs. May I come up?"

"No. What are you—"

"Then you come down."

"No! How dare you come chasing after me as if I were a runaway teenager?"

"Such conceit," said the familiar voice coolly. "I'm here on business, as it happens. I told Jessie that if I had time, I'd check to make sure you hadn't been mugged or massacred."

"Well, I haven't. I really don't want to see anyone tonight, Jon. I'm awfully tired."

"You have to eat," Jon said reasonably. "We'll have dinner here in the hotel, if you prefer; then you won't have to worry about being forced into a car and driven to a motel where two grim-faced men will try to brainwash you into sanity."

I realized that I had been thinking along those lines, and the picture was so absurd I felt rather sheepish. "Well . . ."

If he had continued to argue, I might have refused. But he knew me too well; with that awful, ineffable patience of his, he simply waited in silence until finally I muttered, "Oh, all right. I'll have to shower and change. It may take a while."

"I'll be in the bar." He hung up. Smart move—he gave me no time to reconsider.

I had only one dress with me that was suitable for dining out in a big hotel—a soft silk print, ruffled and feminine. It was Jon's favorite dress—so I didn't put it on. Surveying the alternatives, which were either too casual or already worn, I reminded myself I must ask Jessie to send the rest of my things. Then I put on my tailored gray suit.

He was sitting at a table in the bar, facing the door. The light was seductively dim, as it always is in places like that, but I had no trouble finding him. As he rose to his feet, with the compact efficiency that marked all his movements, I felt a corresponding lift of my spirits. I suppose that sounds paradoxical, after I had fought so hard to push him out of my life, but anyone who thinks emotions are simple and straightforward is kidding herself. One day I would have to sit down and figure out how I really felt about Jon. But not now, not until I had settled the other business. I didn't have the energy to deal with more than one emotional mess at a time.

The warmth and immediacy of my reaction to him warned me I'd have to keep my distance. Not that I was really afraid a single kiss would turn me into a limp acquiescent jellyfish—"Oh, Jon, yes, of course, Jon, whatever you say, Jon. . . ." It had happened once or twice before, though. When he leaned toward me I pulled away, too late to avoid a chaste peck on the brow—which was not what I had expected. As soon as I sat down, the waiter appeared with a glass of Chablis, my usual drink. "I don't want wine," I said, glowering. "I want vodka. A vodka martini."

Jon nodded at the waiter.

He had one-upped me again. The wine was his; when it was too late, I saw the empty glass at his elbow. I went through the tedious ritual with the waiter: "On the rocks or straight up?" "Olive or twist?" "Dry, very dry, extra dry?"

"Now that you've gotten that out of your system," said Jon, "can we talk—just talk—like ordinary, amiable human beings?"

"How is Jessie?"

His eyebrows tilted. "She's doing all right. The mother-hen syndrome is reasonably well controlled. You can't blame her."

"Your theory of life is that nobody can be blamed for anything," I said.

"And you want to blame somebody—or is it every-body?"

There was too much truth in that for me to deny it. Jon went on, "I have a statement to make that may clear the air. I've had time to think things over, and I have decided you were right."

"About what?"

"About your need to learn the truth. And," he added calmly, "about breaking our engagement."

"Oh?"

"Oh. You aren't ready for marriage—at least not with me. There were signs; I should have seen them. Instead I pressured you into it."

"Swept me off my feet," I suggested.

The phrase wasn't as far off the mark as it might have sounded to someone who knew Jon only in his public persona. When he let himself go, he could be the gentlest and most passionate of lovers. But it wasn't only his love-making that had swept me off my feet.

"In a sense," Jon said pedantically. "I think you made the right decision, and I accept it. But I still care about you as a person; I like you, as a friend." He hesitated; I could see he was choosing his words carefully. "Sometimes it helps to talk to someone impartial and disinterested. I would be happy to listen."

"And give me useful advice that will keep me out of jail?"

"I hope it won't come to that."

"You never know."

If anyone else had made a speech like that one, I'd have laughed in his face. It was too noble to be believed. But it was just like Jon to turn the other cheek and render good for evil. Nobility was his middle name.

I hated that. I resented the time he spent with the Boys' Club and the legal-aid societies because it was time away from me. I got sick and tired of hearing him make excuses for assorted criminals, his mother, and a lot of degenerate politicians. His overwhelming, disgusting, altruistic nobility was one of the qualities I found most annoying.

The realization slid into my mind so neatly and painlessly, I realized it must have been bobbing around under the surface of my consciousness for a long time—unrecognized, of course, because who wants to admit she despises a person for being nice? It was true, though. And let's face it, saints are not easy people to live with. That's probably why so many of them were single.

I contemplated this revelation with openmouthed astonishment. Jon's hand went nervously to the knot of his tie. "What's the matter, is my nose growing, like Pinocchio's?"

"I wasn't staring at you; I was staring at myself. Figuratively speaking."

The waiter came to tell us our table was ready, and we moved into the dining room. Jon hid behind the menu—tactful as always, blast him—while I waged a silent struggle with myself—common sense against stubborn pride. After a while, I realized that he had lowered the menu and was peering owlishly at me over the top of it.

"I don't want to get you involved," I began, disarmed in spite of my reservations.

"Involved in what? Are you contemplating a spot of blackmail?"

"Of course not!"

"Burglary? Fraud?" I sputtered indignantly, and Jon

went on, "Then why are you hedging? I don't think you know yourself what you intend to do. That's the truth, isn't it?"

"Damn it!" I threw my hands out in a furious gesture; the waiter, who had glided gracefully up behind me, let out a smothered yelp and backed away.

"Oh my God," I muttered. "Did I—"

"Missed him by that much." Jon held up his hand, thumb and forefinger almost meeting. His lips were twitching.

For a moment it was touch and go, but my sense of humor wasn't dead after all, just comatose. I smothered my laughter in my napkin and Jon watched, grinning, until I recovered myself.

"Okay," I said. "Truce terms accepted."

Jon's eyebrows lifted. "I haven't proposed any terms."

"Nor have I. Nor will I. You wouldn't agree to keep Jessie in the dark."

"I couldn't agree to that."

"Maybe you will when you hear what I have to say."

"Maybe."

"You've talked to her, haven't you? You know what I plan to do."

"I know what Jessie knows," Jon said cautiously.

"I got the job."

I watched him to see how he'd react. He knew what I was talking about, all right.

"With the Foundation? You're kidding."

"Nope. I saw the old man—I mean, Mr. Nazarian— today. He approved my application, and everything is settled. I start Monday. And—get this—his daughter has invited me to stay at the house. Well, not exactly in the house—in one of the guest cottages."

"You surprise me," said Jon. "I know him by reputation. It's quite a reputation. How did you do it?"

"Mother," I said briefly.

"He knew her?"

"Everybody knew her. One of her former buddies is a full professor at the Oriental Institute. I went to him first. He tries to be tough, but he melted like a Popsicle on a hot day when I told him I was Leah's daughter. He got me in to see Nazarian."

"He—the professor—is one of your candidates?"

"Yes. His name is David Wertheim."

"And Nazarian?"

"The old man? Don't be disgusting, Jon. He's over eighty. He looks like a mummy."

"He does now. Twenty years ago he was in his sixties."

"And my mother was twenty-two! She wouldn't . . ." The waiter edged cautiously toward us. I waited until he had served the first course. Then I said reluctantly, "Well, I suppose it's a possibility. But an even better one is Nazarian's son. Was, I should have said. He's dead. But he was one of the group Mother hung out with."

"The Nazarians aren't Jewish," Jon said thoughtfully.

"They're from the same part of the world as the Ashkenazim—one branch of them, at any rate. Turkey, Armenia."

"True. So what's next? You can hardly ask your candidates if they'd mind being tested for Tay-Sachs. And it's not an easy question to work into a casual conversation."

"Speaking of artichokes . . ." I smiled wryly. "I feel like the lost baby bird in that book Jessie used to read to me. It went from animal to animal squeaking, 'Are you my mother?' The duck said, 'I am not your mother; I am a duck.' And the pig said . . . Well, you get the idea."

"Hmm," said Jon, unmoved by this pathetic analogy. "That's not such a bad idea."

"What isn't?"

"Asking them point-blank. I know, Stephen Nazarian is

dead. So ask his father. Ask his sister, his former friends. One of them must know or suspect something."

"I can't do that."

"Why not? Are you ashamed of it—or her? You can't be so self-righteous." His good-humored smile had been replaced by what I called his legal face—stern, inflexible. "Or is there some other reason? What are you really after, Haskell? It's not just the name of your physical father. If that were your only aim, you wouldn't be going about it in such a stupid fashion. You are not a stupid woman. What is it?"

I put up my hand to stop the relentless beat of questions. Corporate law was his field, but he'd have made a first-rate criminal lawyer; a guilty witness would have howled and confessed under such a barrage.

"The accident—the car crash that killed her. What if it wasn't an accident?"

"Good Lord." His tight mouth relaxed. After a moment he said gently, "I'm sorry. No wonder you've been in such a state."

"You don't think it's silly of me?"

"No. The death of a parent is hard enough on a child. Suicide is the ultimate desertion. Did Jessie tell you—"

"Oh, no. No. I couldn't even bring myself to ask her about it; it would have been too cruel. But now you see why I can't trot around emulating that damned baby bird. Mother told Jessie that she was going to Chicago to make things up with her parents and to look for a job. That doesn't make sense, Jon. She had no intention of moving in with her father; why didn't she look for work in Philadelphia, near her sister, whom she loved? I think she went back to see him—whoever he was. Her husband was dead; she had a child to support and no training except in archaeology. An Army pension doesn't go very far, and Mother wasn't the sort to sit around with folded hands waiting for the Lord to provide. Why shouldn't she ask the father of her child for help? If he sent her away—rejected her . . ." I couldn't go on.

"You've no evidence whatever of that," Jon said. "It's only one of a number of possible scenarios."

"I know. But I have to find out. It won't be easy to trace her movements over those few days, it was such a long time ago. But I'm going to try. Maybe I'm wrong. I hope to hell I am wrong. But if he does have something to hide, if he has her death on his conscience, he won't admit the truth about their relationship."

"Mmm." The sound conveyed reluctant agreement. After thinking it over, Jon said, "There is another approach that might resolve your doubts—one way or the other. Where did the accident take place?"

"Some little town in Indiana, just over the Illinois line. She didn't get far," I added softly.

Jon ignored the comment. He was all business now, his voice brisk and unsentimental. "There must be records in local or state police files. A coroner's report, results of an autopsy."

"I suppose so. I guess I should try to find them, but it will probably be a tedious, frustrating process." I made an involuntary grimace of distaste. "You know what the bureaucratic process is like; you end up telling the same story to a series of bored officials who either pat you on the head or refuse to take the trouble."

"They wouldn't pat me on the head," Jon said.

"You'd do that?"

"I'll try. You might also consider hiring a private detective. Oh, I know what you're thinking, but they aren't all sleazy, unshaven booze hounds. I can get you the name of a reliable firm if you like."

"The trail is too cold," I argued. "And people clam up when they're approached by somebody calling himself a detective. It puts them on the defensive if they have anything to hide."

"Most people have something they want to hide," Jon said seriously. "That's why . . ." He checked himself and busied himself with the remains of his salad.

"That's why what?"

"Eat," Jon ordered. "The waiter has tried twice to serve the main course."

Obediently, I forced food into my mouth. "What were you about to say?"

"I'm afraid you'll get mad and yell."

"And you're so terrified of me? Okay, I promise I won't make a scene."

"Have you thought what you're doing? Has it occurred to you that you may be opening up a super-sized can of worms? Passions, jealousies, secrets that have nothing to do with your inquiry, but that people don't want dragged out into the light of day?"

"I'll be tactful."

"Uh-huh," Jon said skeptically. "Well, I had to say it. Quit picking at that salad and eat your dinner like a good girl. I have a feeling you're going to need your strength."

He turned the subject, and for the rest of the meal we talked of neutral things—politics (if politics can ever be neutral), his father's health, architecture, which was one of his hobbies. "While you're in Chicago, you ought to see the Frank Lloyd Wright houses. A major part of his work is here, in the city and the suburbs. Didn't Jessie tell me her mother lives in Oak Park? Wright's home and studio are there, and the neighboring suburb, River Forest, has half a dozen of his finest houses. Get the old dear to take you on a tour."

"I doubt that my grandmother ever heard of Frank Lloyd Wright." I told him about the brief, horrific visit; he laughed heartily and heartlessly. "Broaden her horizons, why don't you? If she doesn't have a car, she'd probably enjoy a Sunday drive—my granny did—it wouldn't be as hard on you as sitting around the house."

Another typical Jon-type assumption—that I would visit my grandmother every weekend. I had no intention of doing so, but I saw no reason to admit it to the paragon. The idiosyncrasies of the two old ladies kept us occupied for the rest of the meal, and he did not again refer to The Subject, as I thought of it.

He walked me to the elevator and then said formally, "Thank you, Haskell. It was good to see you."

"How long are you going to be in Chicago?"

"I'm catching a plane first thing in the morning. Don't know when I'll be back. I'll let you know if I learn anything in Indiana. I assume I can reach you through Jessie?"

"Yes. I—thank you, Jon. I really do appreciate—"

"Not at all." He turned away, without so much as a peck on the forehead, leaving me with my mouth open and my thanks incomplete. He couldn't have given a more convincing demonstration of polite indifference.

Well, what had I expected? What had I wanted? Exactly what I got and more than I deserved—kindness, sensible advice, an offer of friendship.

The red light was still blinking when I entered my room. It had a reproachful look; I felt as if I ought to apologize for keeping it active so long.

It was earlier than I had thought, only a quarter to ten—a quarter to eleven, Philadelphia time. I figured Jessie wouldn't have gone to bed, especially if she was hoping to hear from me.

I anticipated her question by informing her I had had dinner with Jon. I didn't elaborate, and she knew better than to ask pointed questions. But when I told her I had been—hired isn't the right word, I guess—taken on by the Foundation, her agitated reaction told me that she had never expected I would succeed.

"Oh, Haskell, are you sure you ought to stay there? I won't know how to reach you!"

"For heaven's sake, Jessie, I won't be a prisoner." Even

as I spoke the memory of the heavy, guarded gates and the electrified fence came back to me, with dark overtones I hadn't considered. Fences can keep people in as well as out. I added firmly, "I'm sure they have modern amenities like telephones. I'll call you as soon as I'm settled and give you the number. Okay?"

We had nothing more to say to one another. Recalling the many times we had chatted for hours about everything under the sun and nothing in particular, I felt guilty and depressed. But I didn't offer to do the one thing that would have restored the old loving relationship—return home, abandon my search, live with unanswered questions for the rest of my life.

After I hung up, I remembered that I had neglected to ask her to send my clothes. I was about to call back when it dawned on me that I couldn't give her an address. I didn't bother looking in the phone book; I had a hunch Victor Nazarian would not be listed. I would have to wait until Monday.

I spent the rest of the evening washing lingerie.

In the dark, dead hours of the night, I came awake with tears streaming down my face. The dream that had prompted them was fading, but I knew why I was crying. My mother was dead. Not twenty years ago, but now, today; the pain was as fresh and raw as if I had just learned the news. In my dream I had seen her. She was dead, and I knew it; but I saw her walking slowly away from me along a long, straight road that stretched across dusty plains to a dim horizon. I tried to run after her, but my feet were rooted to the ground. I called her name. I knew she heard me, but she didn't stop walking or turn her head to look back.

5

I had intended to apply myself to my studies all that
weekend, like a dutiful little spy. Instead I spent Saturday
shopping and seeing the sights. I definitely needed a lift.
Aside from all the other questions that haunted me, I
couldn't shake the effects of that depressing dream. When I
woke in the morning, I imagined I could actually see it
hanging over me, like a dark cloud. I had a pretty good idea
what Ann Whitaker would say about it. That didn't make
me feel any better.

There were no actual clouds in the sky; the weather was
sensational, clear, and sunny, with a cool breeze off the
Lake. As I wandered around the city, I began to understand
why Chicago has its passionate supporters as well as its
detractors. Unlike the cities of the East, with which I was
familiar, it lacked the charm of historic buildings and quaint
communities. It was a new city, brashly and defiantly
modern; one had the impression that every fifty years or so
Chicagoans got bored with the place, tore it down, and built

it up again. The Great Fire of 1870 did start in the O'Leary backyard, but the cow must remain innocent until proved guilty. The Fire didn't destroy the whole city, by any means, but some of the handsome hotels and elegant mansions that would be regarded as treasures of the city today had succumbed to the flames. (Critics of Chicago might claim they would have succumbed to something else anyway.) The structures that had replaced them constituted an outdoor museum of twentieth-century architecture. I knew some of the names from Jon; he was interested in the subject and waxed rhapsodic over people like Frank Lloyd Wright and Mies van der Rohe. Their work was three thousand years too modern for my tastes; even if I had been interested, I'd have avoided the starred buildings because they would have reminded me of Jon. I didn't want to be reminded of the people I had injured. I stuck to the Loop and the North Side, avoiding the University of Chicago and the near South Side, where the Nazarian mansion squatted among the ruins of its neighbors like a bloated toad.

There isn't any East Side to speak of in Chicago. Lake Michigan is its east side. Beaches and parks lined the water for miles. It was still too cold to swim, of course, but I took a walk along North Avenue Beach, watching the gulls swoop and cry and the little boats scooting through the choppy waves.

That activity soon palled; birds and blue water and solitude lead to introspection, which was what I didn't want. I headed back to the bright lights of downtown. I had heard Jessie talk about the Loop, and I knew what it meant: the central downtown area enclosed by the elevated commuter railroad, where the lines from north, south, and west met in a rough circle. Nostalgic it might have been to a returning son or daughter, but attractive it was not; trains rattled past overhead and rusty ironwork shadowed the littered streets. I paid a visit to Marshall Field's, where Jessie had gotten her start. It could not have changed a great deal since her time; it was still dignified and unostentatiously expensive.

For someone who was not a native daughter, I carried too many memories with me in those streets. Wishing to avoid them, I walked north along Michigan Avenue. The Art Institute tempted me, but I decided to leave the museums for another day. Utter frivolity was my motto; I found it in the elegant stores north of the river, along the stretch Chicagoans modestly refer to as the Magnificent Mile. Branches of New York department stores rubbed elbows with fancy boutiques and specialty shops. I had had lunch at McDonald's before I headed north, so I decided to treat myself to afternoon tea at the Drake. It was served in the English Great Hall lobby (the words were capitalized in the guidebook, and deservedly so). Stuffed with cucumber sandwiches, cakes, and Earl Grey, I headed homeward. Home . . . a nondescript hotel room and William Flinders Petrie, on cylinder seals.

At least I didn't dream that night.

A long, empty Sunday stretched before me. I had had enough of Petrie; it was probably pure boredom that made me decide to visit Grandma, but it's possible that Jon's comment had something to do with it. I expected to be received with delighted surprise. Instead, my grandmother greeted me with "Where have you been? The dinner will be cold. Come, hurry, wash your hands."

Even the dog wheezed reproachfully at me.

I immediately regretted my decision and swore I wouldn't repeat it. That's the trouble with being nice to people. They don't appreciate it; they expect you to go on being nice and then hate you if you aren't.

Yet I was touched when I saw the meal they had prepared. They must have been cooking all morning and half the day before. Home-baked bread, apple pie, cole slaw, pickled eggs dyed red with beet juice—part of the seven sweets and seven sours that are considered necessary to any Pennsylvania Dutch meal—fried chicken and cream gravy, mashed potatoes, noodles that had never seen a pasta machine—I ate till my eyes, and other parts of my anatomy, bulged. After we had washed up, I suggested a drive—what I really needed was a long walk—but the offer was refused, with a pointed reference to the Sabbath and the impropriety of unnecessary activity on the day of rest. I wasn't altogether sorry to hear that; it meant I wouldn't have to help them clean house. I might have wondered why cooking constituted an exception to the rule, if the answer hadn't been so obvious. Grandfather, not God, had enforced the rules, and Grandfather relished his dinner.

We settled down in front of the television set to watch a religious program. Before long, Gran's head began to nod. Even the passionate exhortations of the evangelist demanding we acknowledge Jesus as our Lord and prove our commitment by sending him a contribution failed to keep her awake.

Aunt Ella had taken out her crochet, but at Gran's first snore, she tucked it into the bag and beckoned to me.

"What is it?" I asked.

She put her finger to her lips. "Come upstairs. She'll sleep for an hour. We can talk."

Wondering, I followed her up the narrow stairs and into her room. She closed the door; and with that barrier between her and her sister, she became a different person. The first thing she did was whip off the black bonnet and toss it carelessly onto the bed. The stiff laced shoes went next. Then she disappeared into the closet. After a brief period of rummaging and mumbling, she came out carrying a bottle and two paper cups.

Catching my astonished eye, she gave me a conspiratorial wink. "A little wine for the stomach's sake," she said complacently. "It's in the Bible."

I didn't so much sit down as collapse into the chair she indicated. Carefully, she poured wine into both cups. It was

a variety I had read about but never tasted, one of the
supersweet types with a generic name, "Port Wine." It
tasted as foul as I had suspected it would.

Aunt Ella smacked her lips. "It's good for my sciatica.
Medicinal."

"Uh—yes. How often . . . I mean, do you do
this . . ."

Aunt Ella sat down and, with an agility that bore out the
effectiveness of the port on her sciatica, hoisted her
stockinged feet onto the bed. "I have a little glass every
night. Helps me to sleep. No harm in it, it's in the Book.
She's such an old stick-in-the-mud, so I don't let her know."

"No harm," I agreed, taking another cautious sip of the
revolting stuff. She had none of the obvious stigmata of the
secret drinker; I was inclined to believe her when she
claimed that she drank very little. Perhaps half the pleasure
in the wine was the idea that she was putting one over on her
sister.

But I had not yet plumbed the full depths of Aunt Ella's
wickedness. With a devilish nod, she opened the drawer of
the bedside table and took out an ashtray and a pack of
cigarettes. She offered me one. I started to shake my head,
and then thought better of it; she was so enjoying our shared
debauch, it would have been a pity to refuse. We lit up. I
didn't inhale—and I noticed that she didn't either. Cautiously I asked, "How do you manage, Aunt Ella? Living
like this, with all the rules and regulations—doesn't it drive
you crazy?"

Aunt Ella had been looking forward to a good gossip.
"Well, child, it wasn't easy, I can tell you. When I first
come here I thought I wouldn't be able to stand it. Not that I
was ever one to smear on make-up or dress fancy; we was
good God-fearing folks, even if we was Lutherans."

"What's wrong with being a Lutheran?" I asked, amused
at the resentment in her voice.

"To your granddad, everybody was a heathen except him

and that church of his." Aunt Ella took a hearty swig of her wine. "Your gramma was one of the prettiest girls I ever seen. I could never see why she married him. Not that he wasn't a tall, well-set-up man in his time. He got worse as he got older. Made her throw out all her pretty clothes and her magazines that she liked."

"She could have gone back to her old ways after he died."

"Too late by then. You know how it is—people feel like they'd be disloyal to the dead. Especially when they didn't like 'em much when they were alive."

She was a shrewd woman, and I thought she was probably right. I'd seen the pathetic parents being interviewed on TV, desperately denying that the dead child was less than saintly. "She was a quiet girl with no men friends." "He'd never touch drugs or drive drunk, not my boy." And the widows who remembered a marriage made in heaven, denying the mutual cruelties and disagreements.

"She didn't like him?" I asked.

"Now, child, what woman in her right senses would like a man who took away every harmless little thing she enjoyed and threatened her with hell-fire if she dared to disagree with him? Only she can't admit now she made a mistake. The worst thing she done was let him do the things he did to your mama and Jessie. That was downright cruel. She could of stood up to him, but she never did."

"Aunt Ella, how do you know about that? You weren't here then."

"Land, no. I wouldn't of come when he was alive. He didn't approve of me either. My own Henry died a few years after him, and I was having a hard time getting by. So when Sis asked me to come, I figured why not. We make out well enough together, my little bit of money with hers. And the house is hers. That's why I go along with her notions. It don't hurt me to wear that awful bonnet or do some praying.

"As for how I know what went on before—why, she told

me. She told me lots of things. She'd deny now she ever said 'em. Time sort of smooths out the past."

"You're right," I said respectfully.

There was no clock in the room, but Aunt Ella had her orgy down to a routine. "One more cigarette," she announced. "Then we'd best go back downstairs; she'll be waking up pretty soon. I figured you had a right to know about certain things. She didn't lie to you on purpose. She didn't even know she wasn't telling the truth."

"About what?" I asked.

"About the last time your mama was here. They had a terrible fight, her and her dad. She went running out of this house in such a rage she didn't even close the door after her. She was crying, Sis said."

"What was the argument about?" My throat was tight with the tears my poor young mother had shed that day.

"I'm not too clear on that," Aunt Ella admitted. "Something about you. She'd come, I think, to try to make peace between her and the old man. Brought all those pictures of you to show him. He wanted to keep them, but she said no, there was other people she wanted to show 'em to. That made him mad, but it wasn't the reason they fought. I think he was saying she should come back home to raise her child. He'd think he was making a right Christian gesture, offering to take care of the both of you so she wouldn't have to go out to work for her living. She had better sense, of course. That would make him furious, if she turned him down. Could be that was what caused it. Sis wasn't sure herself. He'd sent her out of the room when tempers started to flare."

"He *sent* her out?" I repeated incredulously. "And she obeyed?"

"She always obeyed." Aunt Ella swung her feet to the floor and stood up. If I hadn't been in such a state of confusion, I would have been amused at how she hid the evidence of her debauch. She went into the bathroom with the ashtray; after a moment I heard the toilet flush and she returned with the ashtray, cleaned and dried. It went back into the drawer with the cigarettes and matches; the bottle went back into the closet; the paper cups, carefully wrapped in a brown paper bag, went into the wastebasket. Then she opened the window wide and turned on the electric fan. Reassuming shoes and bonnet, she gave the room a careful scrutiny, and then nodded in satisfaction. "There. We don't go into each other's rooms, but I figure it's better not to take any chances."

She had timed it to perfection. Gran was stirring and mumbling as we tiptoed into the room.

Both of them assumed I would stay for supper, but I felt I had done more than my duty—not to mention the fact that the very idea of more food appalled me. I pleaded the need to reach the hotel before dark; it was an excuse they had to accept, since they were convinced that as soon as the sun went down the streets filled up with criminals—an assumption that had some truth to it. However, I didn't get away without a "care package"—cold chicken, pie, bread, and— though I tried to resist—several disgusting pink eggs.

"We will see you next Sunday," said Gran. I started to say no, they wouldn't, but I couldn't bring myself to do it. Listening to Aunt Ella's story, I had felt considerable bitterness toward my grandmother; but as she confidently offered a wrinkled cheek for my kiss, I realized she was more sinned against than sinning. There was nothing left of the pretty laughing girl my grandfather had married. What a wasted, empty life—what a burden of guilt and regret! The blame lay rather with that rigid, old domestic bully, my grandfather. But I supposed Jon would have found some excuse even for him; how could I know what forces had gone into making him what he was?

They waved good-bye from the porch. Behind Gran, Aunt Ella was grinning and winking like mad.

I promised myself I would write them a note—get it in

the mail tomorrow, so they wouldn't waste a whole day cooking for someone who never showed up. I'd think of some excuse.

Now that it was over, I could admit I felt better for having gone, even though I was determined not to be a good girl every Sunday. The revelation of Aunt Ella had been worth the trip. I could become rather fond of that old lady. . . . But the glimpse she had given me into the past had raised troubling questions. It was an indication that my preconceived notions about my mother's motives and actions on her last journey had not been so far wide of the mark. What had happened between her and her father to send her running away in a passion of angry tears? Had she, disarmed by her father's response to the unfailing charm of baby pictures, confided the truth to him? And had he driven her from the house with thundering denunciations culled from his favorite literature? The Bible teemed with epithets for fallen women and children born out of wedlock. The fact that Mother had been married wouldn't cut any ice with Grandfather if he learned that her husband was not the father of her child. In his eyes I would still be a bastard, and my mother . . . Had the cruel, cutting names he called her distressed her to such an extent that it affected her ability to control the car?

If he had done that, he was a murderer—morally, if not in the eyes of the law.

I told myself I was being melodramatic. (But I had almost run a red light at the last intersection, absorbed in my bitter speculations.) Aunt Ella wouldn't remember; she had never known precisely when that visit had occurred. If she had quoted Mother correctly, however, it could not have been her last stop before leaving Chicago. She had spoken of showing the pictures to other people.

I forced myself to concentrate on what I was doing. Sunday-afternoon traffic was heavy—people returning from weekend trips or from visits to friends and relatives. As evidence, Aunt Ella's story wasn't worth much. It was second-hand testimony, distorted by the failing memories of not one but two aging women, each with her own prejudices and preconceptions. And what an ugly story it was. If Stephen Nazarian had been my mother's lover, neither of my grandfathers was anything to brag about.

Despite a restless night, vexed by scraps of dreaming, I was up bright and early on Monday morning. I wanted to make a good impression, and I didn't dare be late.

It was ten minutes before nine when I drove up to the heavy iron gates. I couldn't help being a little impressed with myself when the guard waved me in without even consulting his checklist, but my vanity received a rude check when I stopped the car under the porte-cochere and got out. I was not allowed to enter the house. The guard waved me back into the car—on the passenger side. He got behind the wheel.

A driveway circled the house and ended in a paved area with a garage on one side. The guard—I remembered his name now—George—came to a stop next to a gas pump. Taking my suitcases, he motioned me to follow him.

Without his guidance, I might not have found the way. I couldn't believe the size of those grounds. Perhaps Victor Nazarian had bought the property of his neighbors after their houses had been torn down—or perhaps he had bought the houses themselves and watched, cackling with delight, as the wrecking balls swung and shattered the walls. That would be in character.

The garage area was enclosed by high walls, so that no ugly utilitarian view would spoil the gardens. We went along a path walled in by shrubs—azaleas loaded with blossoms of rose pink and lavender and white.

Over the enclosing walls and shrubbery, I caught glimpses of a low building made of mellow brick and draped with ivy. We emerged into a grassy area behind this building, and then I recognized it from the pictures I had seen. The museum—Nazarian's own private museum. It was close enough to the main house to be considered a wing of that structure, but it was separated from it by a covered walkway. I had been in the basement of the museum on Friday; the offices and work areas would of course be subterranean, accessible from the main house by means of the tunnel we had traversed. I wondered when I would get a chance to see the museum itself.

George was the strong, silent type; he hadn't spoken a word so far, but the next piece of information he had been instructed to give me couldn't be conveyed by gestures alone. He indicated a door at the back of the museum. It was below ground level, reached by a flight of concrete steps.

"That's where you go. To work."

"Now?"

"No."

"Then what—"

I didn't finish the question; he was already moving away from me, cutting across the grass instead of following the path that circled the museum enclosure. A gate in a brick wall led into another enclosed area. He held it open for me, and I passed through.

Everything was overgrown and untended, but the drooping boughs and tall grass spotted with wildflowers only added to the fairy-tale charm of the place. Three little houses stood in a row, half-timbered and stuccoed, with diamond-paned windows on either side of their small front doors. They looked like the sort of thing a wealthy, doting father might build for three little daughters—dollhouses, playhouses, for the spoiled children of the rich.

The path underfoot was of brick, half-hidden by sprouting emerald grass. It split into three in front of the houses. We followed the right-hand path. George opened the door—it was unlocked—and preceded me into the house. He had to duck his head, the lintel was so low.

Well! I thought to myself; his mother certainly didn't teach him manners. . . . And then I realized he was only doing what he had been hired to do.

He gave the room a slow, comprehensive survey— looking for armed terrorists, I guess. "Maid's been here," he said. "Phone's hooked up. You wanna unpack?"

I didn't wanna unpack; I was already officially late for work, but I was getting into the swing of things. In silence I opened both suitcases and removed the contents, piece by piece. A tall wardrobe provided the only closet facilities; I hung up my scanty wardrobe while George stolidly inspected the empty suitcases. No plastic explosives, no armed terrorists. He nodded at me and walked out, leaving me to inspect my new quarters.

It didn't take long. There was only one room, though a partition cut off enough space for a tiny bathroom, with a shower instead of a tub, and a Pullman-type kitchen. The shelves and the small refrigerator had been stocked with food—eggs, milk, bread, instant coffee, and a miscellaneous assortment of canned goods, mostly soup, baked beans, and tuna. I deduced that I would not be asked to dine with the family—which was no more than I had expected.

The room was clean. That was about all that could be said for it; a faint musty odor, rising above the mingled scent of bleach and ammonia, suggested that the little house had been uninhabited for a long time. The furniture looked like castoffs—a once-handsome Louis Quartorze armchair, whose needlepoint upholstery needed repairs, a mahogany table bearing the overlapping rings of wet glasses, a cheap studio couch. The rug was a tattered but beautiful Bokhara, the curtains at the windows were plain muslin, obviously new and obviously ready-made. The same incongruous blend of worn antiques and brand-new catalogue stuff continued throughout, from the motley collection of pots and pans to the silverware and china.

At least I wouldn't have to worry about damaging the

furnishings. I was relieved, but I was also a little deflated. That damned imagination of mine had misled me again; I had visualized being escorted to a stately chamber, draped in velvet and brocade, and being told that this was the room in which my mother had stayed when she visited. . . .

But she had never stayed overnight, at least I had no reason to suppose she had.

It took me less than sixty seconds to reach the museum. I descended the steps and hesitated, not knowing whether to knock or just walk in. The question settled itself when I tried the knob. The door was locked.

I found a button and pressed it. I didn't hear a bell ring inside or the sounds of footsteps; when the door finally opened, I realized why I hadn't. It was metal sheathed in wood, several inches thick.

Carl blinked at me from the threshold. "So there you are," he said.

I turned my eyes from the door and caught him in the middle of one of those long insulting surveys that go from head to toe and back again. "I see you're dressed for work," he remarked.

I was—jeans and sneakers and a tailored shirt—neat but not gaudy. It wasn't his comment that set my temper flaring; it was the damned steel door—the culmination of all the security measures protecting the house and the old man who inhabited it like a spider in the heart of his web.

"Did you expect me to show up in silk shantung and four-inch heels?" I inquired.

"Uh—"

"Are we going in, or do I work out here?"

"Uh—yeah. I mean, no. I mean—come in."

The door closed with a thud and a snap of the lock. A tile-floor corridor stretched away from me. Carl led the way, his shoulders rigid, his hands clenched. He wasn't too pleased with me, but I didn't care; he had never wanted me as an assistant anyway.

Some of the doors we passed stood open, and I caught glimpses of fascinating things within—tables and shelves containing antiquities in various stages of disrepair, sinks and cabinets, photographic equipment. Most of the doors were closed, however. I knew what lay behind them—storage rooms for objects that had not been deemed worthy of exhibition or that required restoration. These objects would be the ones collected by Victor Nazarian; the neat, professionally correct manner of their disposition was in striking contrast to the total chaos that reigned among his father's acquisitions. Perhaps the contrast wasn't coincidental. The Nazarians, father and son, had a lot in common with certain predatory animals, and in the animal kingdom the patriarch of the pride or tribe inspires no small amount of jealousy among his young rivals.

By the time we reached the office, I had oriented myself. The closed door at the end of the corridor was the one that led to the tunnel and the elevator.

"This is your desk," Carl said briefly.

A desk, a straight chair, and an old typewriter—that was the extent of the equipment I had been given. I studied the ensemble without enthusiasm.

"Right."

"The john is across the hall."

"Thanks."

"The coffee maker—"

"I see it."

"And this," Carl said, "is what you'll be working on."

He opened a file drawer. Inside were a number of old-fashioned leather-bound ledgers. They smelled of mold. When Carl removed the topmost volume, a fine rain of brittle brown scraps sprinkled the desk.

"These are the journals of the late Anton Nazarian," Carl explained. "He began collecting in the 1890s. He was a contemporary of Petrie and Maspero—"

"I know."

"Oh, yeah?"

"Naturally I read up on the collection and its founder." It would have been more tactful to listen to his lecture in humble silence, but I couldn't do it; his tone had been so damned patronizing. "Like Schliemann, the elder Nazarian was a self-made man, independently wealthy by the time he was forty years old. Unlike Schliemann, he was poorly educated. A trip to Egypt in 1885 aroused his interest in antiquities. Petrie despised him because his methods of collecting were as ruthless as his business methods. He had no taste and no real understanding of the culture; the fact that someone else wanted a particular object was enough to make him go all out to possess it."

I had to stop for breath at that point. Unimpressed, Carl said coolly, "Since you're so well informed about the old robber, you'll probably find this little task fascinating. His journals are a hodgepodge of miscellaneous information, written in the vilest handwriting you will ever encounter. Buried among scurrilous statements about other people, complaints about prices, and notations regarding his business deals, you will find records of his purchases. We need those records. No doubt you can tell me why we need them."

I said reluctantly, "One would like, if possible, to establish the provenance of a given object. It's almost hopeless with material like this, purchased from dealers or from illicit excavators; but if you can match the object with the entry he made, you might get some clue as to when and where he bought it."

"That's part of it." Carl adjusted his glasses. "But only part. The Oriental Institute follows the UNESCO agreement of 1969, which prohibits institutions from accepting gifts unless there is documentary evidence that the object was removed from the country of origin before that year."

"Well, of course," I said, trying to look as if the information were not new to me. "But surely it's obvious that Anton Nazarian's collection has been here for decades before 1969.''

'' 'Obvious' isn't the same as legally documented. We've always been on good terms with the Egyptian government and we want it to stay that way. Another Nefertiti-type scandal would raise some nasty questions.''

This time I knew what he was talking about. The famous and exquisite bust of Nefertiti had gone on display in the Berlin museum some years after a German expedition had excavated at Tell el Amarna. In accordance with the laws of the time, all its finds had been shown to the Egyptian inspector, who had selected the best for the Cairo Museum and allowed the others to be taken to Germany. After Nefertiti showed up in Berlin, the Egyptian government insisted that no inspector would have overlooked an object so uniquely beautiful. The Germans claimed that the bust had been so battered and dirty that they had not realized what they had until after it had been cleaned and restored; if the inspector had lacked the sense to recognize its value, that was his hard luck. They refused to return the bust, and as a result the Egyptians refused to allow any German expedition to work in that country.

"You don't expect to find anything as valuable as that, do you?" I asked, half scornfully, half hopefully. To be in on a discovery like that one . . .

"Not really, no. But Anton was the original pack rat, and the cellars are in a hopeless mess. If we can document a purchase and match the object with the entry in the diary, we may save ourselves a lot of trouble."

Carl opened the journal. I groaned aloud.

"You want me to transcribe this? I can't even read it. His spelling . . . 'Vilanus—' is that supposed to be villainous?"

"Probably. It was one of his favorite words." Carl's face was preternaturally bland. "Cheer up, it's no worse than demotic."

SEARCH THE SHADOWS 143

"I haven't studied demotic."

"Then this will be excellent practice."

"But I thought—I expected—"

"No, no." Carl shook his head. "No playing with the pretty antiquities, not for a while. If you're a good girl and do your job, maybe in a few months I'll let you wash some pots. Let's see—you should have everything you need. Paper, pencils, typewriter—there should be a ribbon for it somewhere—"

"I'll find it."

"I'm sure you will." Carl started out. Pausing in the doorway, he gave me a cherubic smile. "I'll be back for a cup of coffee in ten minutes."

For the entire week I sweated over the journal—and made coffee. Most of the time, I worked with a photocopy, not the journal itself—it was too fragile to endure much handling— but sometimes I had to refer to the original, when, for one reason or another, the copy was indistinct. My eyes burned, my back hurt, and my head ached most of the time.

I didn't get within touching distance of an antiquity, except for the boring scraps on the shelves in the office. Adding to the tedium of my work was my awareness that only a few inches of plaster and planking separated me from the museum upstairs—that treasure house of rarities which I had so looked forward to seeing, as one of the Sifted Few. Nazarian maintained that old Prairie Avenue tradition, at any rate.

Except for Carl, who never spoke to me except in the line of business—"How about another pot of coffee?"—I didn't see a living soul all that week. I had no key to the museum, so I had to arrive in the morning after Carl was there and leave before he did; he never left me alone in the building. I decided I was being tested and flung myself into the work with grim determination. I even took some of the copied pages home with me at night. There wasn't much else to do—no TV, no radio. After darkness fell, I might have been alone in the wilderness, miles from another house.

Sometimes I crept to the door and opened it, hoping to catch a glimpse of light from the house or hear the reassuring, normal sounds of city traffic. There were plenty of lights; the area around the museum was lit up like a Christmas tree, or, more accurately, a top-security agency. But walls and thick foliage kept the illumination from penetrating into my enclosure. It required very little imagination to feel that I had been caught in a time warp, trapped on the Prairie Avenue of a century ago. The far-off noises were so muted by distance that they might have been echoes from the past—rolling carriage wheels and horses' hoofs, carrying the Sifted Few from their palatial homes to glamorous parties, opera first nights, dinners at fine hotels with others of the Sifted Few. What an arrogant, offensive phrase that was! But time had sifted them indeed; they were only shadows now, no more immortal than their humbler brethren. Yet those shadows lingered in the dark gardens of the last survivor. When a brush (it must have been a brush) creaked in the wind, I fled back into the cottage.

I knew it was foolish to be afraid. All I had to do was cry out in order to have an indeterminate number of security guards rush to the rescue with drawn weapons. To be honest, I was almost as afraid of the guards as I was of rustling bushes. I felt sure they must patrol the grounds; sometimes late at night, peering lonesomely out of the window, I could have sworn I saw a dark form, shapeless as a nightmare, pass silently through the shrubbery and melt into the night.

Only stubborn pride kept me going. If I was being tested, then I would pass the test; if they wouldn't come to me, I was damned if I would go to them. Not that I had much choice in the matter; I could hardly march up to the front door and demand an interview with Mr. Nazarian. I had no right to complain; I had been warned what to expect—i.e., nothing. If I didn't like the situation, I could quit. I wondered if that was what they wanted me to do.

By Friday, I was about to crack. The food supply was running low—I was down to a can of tuna fish and a box of crackers—and I was so lonesome I would have tried to adopt a snake, if one had shown up. I even found myself regretting that I had written Gran to tell her I wasn't coming on Sunday—which shows how far down I had sunk. The nights were the worst. I kept thinking I heard footsteps on the path outside, and I could have sworn that once a face peered in through the narrow window. Of course, when I went to look, there was nothing there.

Late Friday afternoon I was plugging away at the damned journal, as usual. Carl was at his desk, but he wasn't working. I was only vaguely aware of him, leaning back in his chair, hands clasping the back of his neck as he stared dreamily at the ceiling. I sensed that he was sneaking glances at me out of the corner of his eye. Finally he said, "Almost quitting time."

I grunted. After a moment, he tried again. "I'm taking tomorrow off. How about you?"

My self-control, which had been wearing thinner and thinner, collapsed. The pencil I was holding cracked between my clenched fingers. "Nice of you," I snapped. "No, I'm not taking tomorrow off. Or any other day off. That's what you want, isn't it? You want me to give up. Well, I'm not going to do it!"

"You're all wrong," Carl exclaimed. "I wasn't trying—"

"You've treated me like a leper all week! You and everybody else. Nobody has come near me, nobody has spoken to me—except you, and all you ever said was hello and good-bye and 'How about some more coffee?' What is this, some kind of ordeal? I didn't expect to be welcomed with open arms, but I didn't think you'd be so low—"

"Wait—wait. Hold on a minute."

I pressed my lips tightly together, clutching my anger to me as a defense to keep from crying. That was the last thing I wanted to do.

"I thought you knew," Carl said. "Mr. Nazarian had another stroke. He's going to recover—the old boy has incredible recuperative powers—but it was nip and tuck for a while, and naturally Mrs. Dunlap and Paul have been occupied with him."

"Oh," I said, deflated. "I didn't know."

"Dave's out of town," Carl went on. "He won't be back until the weekend. He said to tell you he'd be in touch when he got back."

"You didn't tell me. Why didn't you?"

"Now look, dammit," Carl exclaimed. "You haven't been exactly forthcoming yourself. If looks could kill, I'd have been in and out of rigor mortis by this time, and every time I said a civil word, you bit my head off."

"I did not. At least—I didn't mean to . . ."

"Did too, did too," Carl chanted. "Furthermore, in case you didn't know—and I'm beginning to think you didn't—I was warned to keep a respectful distance."

"From me? By whom?"

"Everybody," said Carl, with great feeling. "Tactfully by Mrs. D. She feels responsible for you, a young, inexperienced girl, and she wouldn't want anything unfortunate to happen. Less tactfully by Paul, and profanely by Dave. What he actually said was 'Keep your hands off the kid or I'll break your back.'"

"I don't believe it! I'm not sixteen years old, for God's sake."

"I don't know," Carl said, studying me with his head on one side. "You have a sort of dewy, untouched look at times. It brings out the paternal instinct in some old guys. . . . What did you say?"

"Nothing. I'm just surprised. I guess I should appreciate

their concern, but sometimes I have the feeling that everybody is trying to run my life. I wish they wouldn't."

"I wasn't too happy about it myself," Carl admitted. "I like to think of myself as a normal, healthy, enthusiastic-type male, but a heartless seducer of reluctant virgins is not a role I want or deserve. Then, when you were so nasty all week, I started to wonder—uh—if maybe you . . ."

"Had accused you of attempted rape or something equally pernicious?" I didn't know whether to laugh or be angry.

"Something equally pernicious," Carl said, smiling. "I assumed you were sending me a message, that's all. I guess we've been at cross-purposes. I apologize."

"It was mostly my fault, I guess," I said slowly. "I'm a little overly sensitive these days. I'm sorry."

"New kid on the block," Carl said, nodding sympathetically. That was only part of it; but I could hardly explain why I was so on edge. He went on, "Let's forget it and start again. After all, we'll be working together all summer. No sense in fighting." His smile and outstretched hand were persuasive, even if I hadn't had other reasons for wanting to cultivate his friendship. I took his hand in a firm, no-nonsense, let's-be-buddies clasp.

"I did intend to work tomorrow," I said. "I wasn't sure what my hours were supposed to be."

"It's a pretty loose arrangement. Dave and Paul are our nominal bosses, but they let me set my own hours and schedule. I usually work on Saturday—sometimes on Sunday as well—but I've got other things to do this week. You're certainly entitled to some time off. You've busted your butt this week."

It wasn't the most graceful compliment I have ever received, but it sounded sincere, and I couldn't help being pleased. "Thanks, I was trying to impress you."

"You succeeded. I've worked on those journals myself. I thought I'd go crazy or blind or both. I wouldn't have blamed you if you had started foaming at the mouth and made confetti of the papers."

"The damned things are growing on me," I admitted. "His personality comes through so strongly; I've learned to detest him, but he's fascinating in a clinical sort of way. And his comments about people I've revered as pioneers in the field are real eye openers. It's a pity the journals can't be edited and published."

"The family would never allow it," Carl said. "There's too much dirty linen. Maybe you could talk them into it. You seem to be the golden girl around here."

"You resent me for that, don't you?"

"For what? Oh—you mean because you used personal connections to wangle a job? Hell, no. That's what makes the world go 'round, honey, in academia as in every other field of endeavor. If I'd had any connections, I'd have used them. Instead I had to depend on my charm, my brilliance, and my talent for flattery."

A wide, jaw-cracking yawn interrupted the list of talents. "Let's close up shop," he said. "I'm pooped, and I'll bet you are, too."

"Okay." I gathered up the loose sheets.

Carl said, "You don't have to take homework with you. It's Friday night."

"I haven't anything else to do."

"Nothing? The whole weekend? I thought Dave said you had friends or relatives here."

"My grandmother and great-aunt live in Oak Park. They are dear, sweet, little old ladies, but . . ."

"But they are dear, sweet, little old ladies. I get it. Look—uh—I'm busy tonight—some loose ends that have to be cleared away—but if you aren't doing anything tomorrow, maybe we could—uh—do something. Together."

I thought I understood the reason for his hesitation. "Aren't you afraid you'll get in trouble with my guardians?"

"My dear young woman!" Carl's eyes widened. "I am proposing a nice, harmless visit to the zoo. What could be wrong with that?"

"The zoo?"

"I love the zoo," Carl said dreamily. "Lions and tigers and bears, gorillas, popcorn, hot dogs . . ."

"I haven't been to a zoo since I was eight years old."

"High time you went, then. What do you say?"

"Well . . . all right. It sounds like fun."

"Great. I'll pick you up around eleven. Okay?" He locked the door and put the key carelessly in his pocket. I hadn't replied; Carl gave me a sidelong glance and inquired gravely, "Are you having second thoughts?"

"In a way. I just remembered . . . Are you sure your— your friend won't mind your spending the day with me?"

"That's the loose end I mentioned. I'm moving out of the apartment tonight."

"I'm sorry."

"Don't be. It's her apartment." He grinned, then quickly sobered. "We lived together last summer. Then I went off to Egypt for the winter—I was with the Epigraphic Survey at Luxor. I got back a couple of months ago; I'd left my stuff there, and I had nowhere else to go, so . . . It was a mistake. She had changed, and so had I."

"Oh. Have you found another apartment?"

"Yes." He opened the gate for me. "That one. I'm going to be your new neighbor."

He pointed at the third of the guest cottages.

I don't know why I should have been surprised. Carl's status was higher than mine, and the family had provided housing for me. But I *was* surprised. And I wasn't sure I was altogether happy about the news.

When we reached my cottage, I took the key from my purse and unlocked the door. Carl let out a whistle of surprise. "You lock your door?"

"Yes, I do. Is there any reason why I shouldn't?"

"No, of course not. It's not necessary, though; the security system here is tighter than Fort Knox." After a moment he went on, in a voice that was no longer friendly. "If locking your door was a hint, you needn't have bothered. I'm no more interested in starting something than you are. I don't believe in mixing professional and romantic relationships. Things can get—well—sticky."

"I didn't mean that—honestly. It's lonely here at night, and I keep hearing things. Like footsteps." I forced a laugh. "My imagination is too good."

His face relaxed. "Maybe it was me you heard. I've spent the night here a few times; sometimes I get restless and go out for a walk. I'm sorry if I scared you."

"That's okay. I'm glad you're going to be next door. I won't be so nervous."

"Feel free to scream if the bogeyman bothers you. Is it on, then—tomorrow?"

"I'd love to."

"Good. See you then." He walked away, hands in his pockets.

The conversation changed my perspective and made me feel something of a fool. It was stupid and childish to assume, as I had done, that the whole world revolved around my insignificant self. I had been sitting there wrapped in self-pity the whole week when there was no need for it; people were occupied with other matters, some of them literally life and death. They weren't even troubled by the thought of me, much less trying to work on my nerves. Carl had had a few other things on his mind, too. Ending an intimate, long-term relationship isn't pleasant (I ought to know), and a man who had just broken up with one woman has good cause to be wary of another. It was no wonder he hadn't been forthcoming—especially, as I could now admit, when my own prickly temper had made me suspicious of his every word. I felt particularly guilty about

Mrs. Dunlap. I had assumed she was deliberately ignoring me, while all the time she had been hovering over what she believed was her father's deathbed.

Surveying the empty shelves in the kitchen, I felt even more foolish. There was no reason why I couldn't go shopping, or anywhere else I chose to go. A telephone call to the butler or the housekeeper would probably have procured any supplies I needed. No doubt they had been waiting for me to call; it wasn't their job to take the initiative. I had no intention of doing that. I preferred to remain as independent as possible. That may sound illogical, after all the low-down tricks I had used to wangle my way into the household; but logic had very little to do with my present activities. Anyway, I wanted to get out of the house. One of my problems was an acute attack of cabin fever.

I spent a fruitless ten minutes looking for my car keys before I remembered I had left them with the guard at the garage. It's hard for us poor folks to become accustomed to such arrangements. Despite my renewed confidence, I locked the door when I left.

The garage doors were open. I saw several cars inside—a sleek black limo about twice as long as a city bus, a gray Mercedes 220, and some humbler vehicles, presumably used by the help. My little Honda was the humblest of the lot, but it was sparkling, glittering clean, the dust of long travel gone. Well, but of course, my dear—that's part of the service. No doubt the gas tank had been filled, too.

At first there didn't seem to be anyone around, but I was still a good twenty feet away from the garage when a door opened and a man stepped out of a small office. I had never seen him before, but I knew what, if not who, he was. He might have been George's brother.

"Good evening. Could I have my car keys, please? That's mine—the blue Honda."

He knew that, too. He had already reached for the keys.

They hung with a row of others on hooks inside the door of his den.

"I suppose if you—if no one—is here—I can just take the keys?"

It had been a stupid question. He answered, unsmiling, "Someone is always here, miss."

He backed the car out for me. I had intended to ask him how to find the nearest grocery store, but he made me uncomfortable—like a large guard dog whose ferocity was leashed and controlled, but who might turn, even on its owner, if the training failed. So I asked the gatekeeper instead. He gave me directions and then asked when I expected to be back. "I suggest you finish your shopping before dark, miss. This neighborhood isn't too safe."

It might not be safe and it was certainly shabby, but I found it more appealing than my silent cottage. There were people in the streets, vulgar ordinary people who went to work every day and worried about bills and had fights and made love. Live people.

After I had bought my groceries, I lingered in a neighboring drugstore, collecting an armful of miscellaneous unnecessities—inexpensive odds and ends that add a superficial but pleasant glow to one's life. I reached the gates before dark. The guard at the garage insisted on helping me carry the grocery bags to the cottage. I let him unpack them, too. You never know when an eggplant may turn out to be a bomb in disguise.

It was amazing how much more cheerful I felt with a couple of candy bars and a nice sloppy romantic novel. I was curled up on the studio couch deeply immersed in the frustrations of the heroine and wondering why she didn't have sense enough to see that the ruggedly handsome man who kept sneering at her was really desperately in love with her, when the phone rang.

I assumed it must be Jessie. I had called her on Monday to give her the address and telephone number and ask her to send my books and clothes. We had not talked long; I had told her not to call unless it was necessary, giving as my excuse the fact that I would be working odd hours and didn't want to use the phone for social purposes. It was a feeble excuse and she must have known the real reason: since all calls went through a central switchboard, there was a chance someone might overhear what we said.

I almost dropped the phone in surprise when the caller identified herself. "This is Katherine Dunlap."

"Oh. Oh—hello, Mrs. Dunlap."

"I want to apologize for neglecting you all week. My father has been ill—"

"I just heard about it. I'm so sorry; if I had known earlier, I would have done something—sent flowers—"

She was too polite to laugh, but I heard the amusement in her voice. "It would have been wasted effort, Miss Maloney. My father despises 'weeds,' as he calls them. But thank you for the thought."

"I hope he's better?"

"Much better. The doctor keeps telling him that his next stroke will be his last, but Father always proves him wrong. He's a remarkable man. . . . I'm calling, Miss Maloney, to ask if you will come to a little party on Sunday afternoon. Nothing elaborate, just an informal gathering of a few friends who are working in, or interested in, Egyptology. You should feel quite at home."

The invitation was not one I could refuse even if I had wanted to. Things were definitely looking up. A glamorous date on Saturday with a man who must know all the current gossip, and on Sunday, entree into the house. However, I rather doubted that I was going to "feel quite at home" in a drawing room the size of Jessie's whole downstairs, with people whose interest in Egyptology was measured by the number of degrees they held or the amount of money they had contributed to various museums.

6

I was in my bare feet and sans make-up when the knock came at my front door. I assumed it was Carl, half an hour before the appointed time. Before I could call out and tell him to wait, the knock was followed by the sound of a key in the lock.

The girl who halted on the threshold was as surprised to see me as I was to see her. She was a pretty little thing, with shining black hair and olive skin; the load she carried, linens and towels and a bucket filled with cleaning materials, looked too heavy for her thin arms.

I shouldn't have been surprised, because she, or one of the other maids, had been there before. I'd been trained to make my bed and tidy my room before I left it, so it had been several days before I noticed the signs of additional housework—a wastebasket emptied, a special shine to the stove.

She started to back out, apologizing in an embarrassed mixture of English and Spanish.

"No, that's all right," I said quickly. "Come on in." She hesitated, obviously not understanding. I wished I had studied Spanish instead of French: almost the only word I knew was *gracias*, which didn't seem appropriate at the moment. I resorted to sign language—a broad smile and a sweeping gesture of welcome—and relieved her of the bucket. Then she said *"gracias."*

I had already made the bed. When she began stripping off the blanket and sheets, I moved without thinking to help her. Her startled look told me that the kindest thing I could do was let her go about her business and ignore her. Still in my bare feet, I retreated into the tiny bathroom and began applying make-up.

Carl arrived prompt upon his hour, as someone (Shakespeare?) has said. I was putting on my sneakers when he knocked; the girl rushed to answer the door. The change in her expression when she saw him was astonishing. White teeth flashed, dimples dented both cheeks, and she responded to his *"Buenos días"* with a flood of melodious speech, high and chirping as a bird's song. Carl made a stumbling speech in what even I recognized as atrociously accented Spanish; she giggled and corrected him. The top of her smooth dark head barely reached his chin.

I stood up, feeling unusually large and clumsy. "Have you met?" Carl asked. "This young lady's name is Maria. Maria, this is Señorita Maloney."

"Haskell," I said, offering my hand. Instead of taking it, the girl bobbed a quick curtsy, and Carl said, "That's against the rules of the house, señorita. You'll just confuse her. Ready?"

"Yes, I'm ready. Uh—*adiós, Maria. Gracias.*"

"I don't own a car," Carl announced, as we left the house. "I hope you're not too aristocratic to ride buses."

"I have a car."

"You do? Great. I don't mind being aristocratic when I get the chance."

The guard didn't offer to back the car out. He handed the keys to Carl, who gravely passed them on to me. "Male-chauvinist type," he explained, indicating the guard, who stared at him blank-faced. "Hopeless case."

"Don't you want to drive?" I asked.

"Not especially." He got in on the passenger side, folded his arms, and leaned back with a pleased sigh. "I love having people do things for me."

Two of the cars were gone—the Mercedes and a Ford coupé—so I had ample room to maneuver. I made a rather neat job of it, if I do say so, conscious of the cold, critical eyes watching me. Once we were past the gates, Carl said, "Head for the Drive. We're going to Lincoln Park; know the way?"

"Vaguely. You'll have to tell me where to turn off. I thought you were talking about Brookfield Zoo."

"It's good, but it's too big. Lincoln Park Zoo is cozier. It's also free."

"An important point," I agreed.

"It is when you're one of the working poor," Carl said. "I make less money than a janitor—pardon me, custodial engineer."

I thought he was putting me on when he waxed so eloquent about the zoo, but I have never seen a grown man enjoy himself with such wholehearted spontaneity. Once we were inside, he headed straight for the nearest refreshment stand and bought the biggest box of popcorn on sale. We shared it as we went through the exhibits—first the gorilla house, where he identified each animal by name and commented on its appearance. "Koko looks a little depressed. I hope he isn't coming down with something." The lions and tigers and bears . . . His favorite was the polar bear. A heavy plate-glass window set in the wall enclosing the pool allowed visitors to watch the animals swimming underwater. I gasped and exclaimed and started back a step when the great sleek white body exploded out of the blue depths and slid sinuously along the inner surface of the window, as graceful as a seal and just as at home in the aqueous element. Carl, who by his own admission had seen the same thing a dozen times, stared in openmouthed wonderment, eyes wide. It was a marvelous sight; we stood gaping like a couple of kids until a querulous little voice behind us remarked, "Daddy, I can't see, that man is in my way."

It was a gray day, with occasional brief showers, but that didn't deter us; we ate hot dogs and sipped nauseatingly sweet sodas as we sat on a bench near the mammal house. Carl didn't object when I offered to buy the second round of hot dogs.

"What are you grinning about?" he asked when I returned.

"Nothing. I'm having a good time, that's all." In reality, I had been comparing this meal, if it could be called that, with my last date—if it could be called that. Jon in his three-piece suit, genteelly sipping soup in the dining room of the hotel; Carl in faded khakis, his shirt sleeves rolled to the elbow. The warm wind had tumbled his hair and his sneakers had holes in both toes.

It was a reminder of reality I could have done without. For two hours I had almost forgotten my mission. I came out of my frowning absorption to find Carl was watching me. "Want to talk about it?" he asked.

"About what?"

"Whatever it is. You look like somebody whose dog just died."

"I don't have a dog."

"Ah," Carl said seriously. "That's probably your trouble. Everybody should have a dog."

"Do you?"

"No. That's probably *my* trouble." I laughed, and he shook his head reproachfully. "It's no laughing matter. Pets are emotional and psychological necessities. They do wonders for a bruised ego. I knew a dog once, name of Jim MacAllister. . . ." He babbled cheerfully on about remarkable dogs he had known; it was a tactful gesture, giving me time to recover from whatever was worrying me—or to make up my mind to confide in him. I could do neither. For a few hours I had almost forgotten my Mission. Call it that; capitalize the word, give it the solemn significance of a quest—for without that significance, my behavior, past and present, was contemptible. I had accepted Carl's invitation in the hope of gaining information about the Nazarian family and about Dave. It would have been easier if Carl hadn't turned out to be such a nice guy. A cold academic snob, such as I had believed him to be, wouldn't have made me feel guilty.

I said abruptly, "Mrs. Dunlap called me last night."

The change of subject brought him to a stuttering stop. "Oh. Uh—she did?"

"Yes. She apologized for leaving me on my own all week."

"Under the circumstances, that was a very courteous gesture," Carl said. "But it's typical of her."

His face had taken on the softened expression I had seen before, when Mrs. Dunlap had joined us at lunch.

"You like her, don't you?"

I hadn't intended the question to sound critical, but Carl's reply was defensive. "She's been damned nice to me. And I—well, I guess you could say I admire her. She's had a hard life, but it hasn't made her bitter or unsympathetic."

"A hard life," I repeated.

Carl replied not to the words but to the tone in which they had been uttered. "You're awfully young to be so cynical. Money doesn't bring happiness—trite, but in this case, painfully true. Her family life has been one tragedy after another. Her mother died when she was a child; her father is devoted to her in his own weird way, but he isn't exactly your normal, caring dad. Her only brother was a rebel from the start, the old man handled him badly; there were violent confrontations between the two, with Mrs. Dunlap help-lessly watching the people she loved best trying to destroy each other. Steve ended up as a fugitive, wanted by the police and the FBI. His death was the ultimate in horror; there wasn't even a body to be decently buried, just bloody pieces."

I had known most, if not all the facts, but I had never thought about them as anything more than that—facts, statistics; Carl's emotional speech brought them to life. "At least she's happily married," I said, subdued.

Carl shrugged.

"He's devoted to her," I insisted. "You can tell by the way he looks at her. Why don't you like him?"

Another shrug. "I don't dislike him. I guess I'm prejudiced. He's considered something of an intellectual lightweight. Hasn't published anything in years."

"But some of his earlier articles are first-rate. The one on the co-regency question—"

"That's true." Carl made a visible effort to be fair. "I suppose I'm unconsciously parroting the opinions of—well, of other people. Reacting to stereotypes. A man who lives off his wife's money and who got his job because of that relationship—and whose major publication is a book of love poetry."

"I never expected you, of all people, to be such a macho snob. The poetry is beautiful."

"Sentimental," Carl said stubbornly. "Romanticized. Egyptian love poetry is extremely erotic. His translations gloss over that element; they're almost feminine. You know what some of the professors call him behind his back? Waenre."

"Waenre—Akhenaton? There is a resemblance, isn't there? Especially to that beautiful little head in Cairo."

"They don't have children."

"That's too bad." At first I thought he was adding

another to the list of Mrs. Dunlap's misfortunes, but his sheepish, embarrassed expression gave me the clue. It wasn't only Paul Dunlap's physical resemblance to the controversial pharaoh and religious reformer that had prompted the nickname. Some scholars believed Akhenaton had suffered from a degenerative disease that had rendered him sterile.

"Of all the malicious, petty-minded gossip," I said hotly. "That theory is as full of holes as—as your sneakers. Not only is there not the slightest shred of evidence for it, but it overlooks the fact that Akhenaton had at least six children. Who calls him that? Not Dave, I hope."

Carl ignored the question. His head dropped lower and lower. "I am the lowest of vile slaves. Petty malicious gossip is a sin and a vice. I grovel."

But petty malicious gossip was exactly what I had been hoping to get. In a milder voice I said, "You certainly do. Sit up straight, you look ridiculous doubled over that way."

"I don't know why I'm telling you these things," Carl moaned.

"Because I'm plying you with hot dogs. How about another?"

That cheered him. "Sure, why not?"

There was a long line at the refreshment stand; the clouds were being blown to shreds by a brisk breeze off the Lake, and the improving weather had brought people out in droves. Children predominated, children of all sizes, shapes, and shades; their high, shrill voices formed an incessant background babble. One moppet in a frilly pink dress with pink bows in her hair attached herself to me with a wad of cotton candy, and a little boy spilled cola on my sneakers. When I returned to Carl, he was on his feet and the bench we had occupied was filled to overflowing by a large, cheerful black family.

"How do you feel about reptiles?" he asked, accepting the hot dog.

"Lukewarm. At best."

"Don't be a sissy. Crocodiles are delightful creatures; no animal has a bigger smile. You'll learn to love them if you go to Egypt. They come to Chicago House all the time, begging for scraps. We kept one as a pet last year; taught him to roll over and play dead—"

"Oh, all right. Just let me finish my hot dog first. It's the smell I really hate."

He said no more. Eating hadn't interfered with his powers of speech before; I was afraid his silence indicated a resolution not to redescend into idle gossip. Choosing my words with care, I said, "Thanks for telling me those things, Carl. I can see why you admire Mrs. Dunlap. It's so easy to be smug about people when you don't know the facts."

Carl turned his head to look at me. His cheeks bulged ludicrously but his eyes were narrowed with suspicion. He swallowed.

"You knew some of the facts, though, didn't you? I didn't go into detail about Stephen Nazarian's death, but you didn't ask me to elaborate. You knew."

I was ready for that one. Glibly I said, "Yes, I knew about it. I was interested in him because he was a friend of Mother's—years ago, when she was at the Oriental Institute. I have a lot of old snapshots she took of him and the other students."

"Is that right?" The explanation seemed to satisfy Carl. "Who were the others?"

"Dave, for one. That's why I picked him to work my wiles on. You wouldn't recognize him, Carl; twenty years ago he was a long-legged, bearded, spidery-thin kid. And quite a comedian, to judge by some of the poses."

"He still thinks he's a comedian," Carl said with a smile. "I'd get a kick out of seeing those pictures. I don't suppose you brought them with you."

"Yes, I did. I'm sentimental about those old pictures. She

was almost exactly the age I am now. They were all so—so young."

Carl put his arm around me. It was a lovely gesture, one of simple comfort and empathy. "I know what you mean. Sometimes I get the feeling from looking at old photographs. If they had just known what we know, about what was going to happen. . . . Just be glad they didn't know."

"Right." Unconsciously I stiffened my shoulders and Carl's arm fell away. "Sorry, I didn't mean to be maudlin."

"No problem. Will you show me the pictures? Then we can be maudlin together. I," said Carl, "am rather sentimental myself. In case you hadn't noticed."

"Yes, I had noticed." I smiled at him. "We'll have a nice sloppy session when we get back."

"Good. Now come and see the snakes. That will cheer you up."

They didn't cheer me, but they certainly distracted me. I held my nose throughout, while Carl pointed out the beauties of the cobras and the charm of the crocodiles. To make amends, he took me to see the baby animals, who had a special house all their own. The small chimpanzees and gorillas had a proper nursery, fitted out with bassinets and high chairs; attendants changed their diapers and cuddled them while feeding them their bottles. There were rabbits and other furry animals in a central enclosure, within petting range. It was absolutely enchanting; I graciously forgave Carl for the snakes and told him all about Pooch. Then Carl announced he was hungry.

"You just ate three hot dogs," I said in disbelief.

"That was two hours ago."

"Oh, well, in that case . . . I'll treat you to supper. McDonald's or Roy Rogers?"

"Big spender," said Carl with a sneer.

"You may enjoy a modest stipend, but I have none at all."

"True." Magnanimously he added, "We'll go Dutch. I

know a place where the hamburgers are better and where we can get a beer. Okay?"

I handed over the car keys, since he knew where he was going and I didn't. His driving was awful, even by my uncritical standards; when I protested, he explained that it was the inevitable result of driving in Egypt. "Out in the desert there's nobody around but an occasional donkey, and in Cairo, everybody just heads straight down the middle of the road blowing their horns like mad and never touching the brake."

We ended up on the South Side, near the university; it was Carl's home turf, after all. The place he chose was obviously a popular student hangout; two patrons had their heads bent over a chessboard and I noticed a row of encyclopedias on a shelf behind the bar. It reminded me of a place where I used to go in Philadelphia, before I met Jon and moved up into higher social circles.

We were early, so we were able to get a table; and there we sat for three solid hours, drinking beer and talking shop. When your specialty is something as esoteric as Egyptology, you don't often get a chance to do that. Not that Jon hadn't been nice about it. He had an educated layman's knowledge of archaeology, and he was a lovely listener. But it isn't the same. Best of all, Carl didn't condescend or lecture, though he knew infinitely more than I did. When we disagreed, which was often, he argued like an equal.

His stories about his winter in Egypt were fascinating and hilarious. He had been with the Epigraphic Survey, copying texts from temple walls; and when he claimed to have spent the entire time squatting on a scaffold fifty feet off the ground with the sun beating down on him, I knew he wasn't exaggerating a great deal. I had read about the copying process developed by the O.I. It began with large-scale photographs. The merciless sunlight of Egypt provides excellent lighting, but photographs can't always capture small details that have been worn away by centuries of weathering; so the photographs are used as the basis for line drawings, which are corrected by artists who compare the prints, line by line, with the marks on the actual wall. Their additions and corrections are inked in; then a copy is made of the corrected print, and an epigrapher takes it up the ladder for another check. Since the epigrapher is familiar with the ancient language, he may spot errors or make deductions about missing signs that the artist fails to see. The photos are checked again and again before a final print is made.

I had seen the results in large-format, extremely expensive volumes. "Is it worth it?" I asked.

"Sssh." Carl had had several beers; he put his finger to his lips and looked warily over his shoulder. "It's heresy to ask that question. Personally, I can think of better things to do with my time than perch on rickety ladders high above a very hard, very rocky surface squinting at cracks in a stone wall. But accuracy is important. You can't translate the text if you don't have a reliable copy."

"What would you rather do? Excavate?"

"No, that's uncomfortable, too. Dusty and hot. I'd like to be the guy who translates the texts—in a nice, air-conditioned library, close to bars, soft beds, and other civilized amenities."

"I'd rather dig."

"That's what all you bushy-tailed youngsters think," Carl said. "Even if you stumbled on an unrobbed tomb—the odds against which are about a million and a half to one—they wouldn't let you run the dig; you'd probably end up typing and filing. You ought to talk to Sue Gravelly. She spent last winter at . . . Well, maybe I'd better not say, except that it was a site in Lower Egypt, ten miles from the nearest metropolis of four hundred people. She still has dysentery, but the doctors have decided the skin disease wasn't leprosy after all, and her hair is starting to grow back."

"Are you trying to scare me off?"

"Of course. Jobs are few and far between. I don't want any more competition."

"Seriously, though."

"Seriously, though . . ." His smile faded; when he went on, his voice had a sober passion I had not heard from him before. "We don't need more excavation; we need to preserve what we already have. We're closing history every day, all over the world—stained glass, architectural monuments, manuscripts, inscriptions. The Parthenon sculptures are almost gone, the Colosseum is collapsing—the list is endless, and what's happening in Egypt is not the least of it. If we can't preserve the past, we can at least copy the records before they disappear forever."

"That's why you wanted this job. It's a variety of preservation, too."

"I wanted the job because I enjoy eating three times a day."

"Seriously, though . . ."

He grinned—a comradely, affectionate grin. "Seriously, you hit it right on the head. When I think about what may be rotting away in those cellars I get frantic. I want to dig in with both hands and drag the stuff out into the light of day before further deterioration occurs. That's silly, of course; a few more days or weeks or months won't make that much difference, not after a century. But . . . There was one entry in the journal I worked on before you took over—a reference to 'ladys fancy underclothes.' (Can't you see the old reprobate leering as he wrote it?) Well, of course, it couldn't have been underwear; the Egyptians didn't use it. Maybe—probably—some sharp crook conned him into buying up a set of Parisian doodads, carefully aged and stained. But just suppose they were robes like the ones Carter found, fine linen embroidered and spangled? We'll never know; fabric that might have survived for three millennia in the climate of Egypt will be rotten dust by now, after eighty or ninety years in a packing case."

We had to talk loudly in order to be heard over the rising din. People stood in the aisles, and at least four animated conversations were going on within six feet of us. When the gesticulating arm of one debater narrowly missed his head, Carl said, "We'd better go. Things get raucous around here when the *rekhyet* start crowding in."

I was pleased with myself for recognizing the word—it was the one that ancient Egyptians used for the common people, the peasants—and I had to show off. "Hasn't the meaning been challenged?"

"You're too smart for your own good," Carl said. He was joking, but for me, the words had a meaning he hadn't intended. Sobered, I followed him through the noisy, good-natured crowd. The night air was heavy with the usual city contaminants, but it felt fresh after the heat and smells inside.

Carl handed over the car keys without argument when I pointed out I had had fewer beers than he. "I could use a cup of coffee," he said.

"If that's a hint, consider it taken. There won't be any problem, will there—if you come in for a while?"

"There damn well better not be. I don't mind a certain amount of fatherly advice, but I won't sell my soul for any job, even this one."

There it was again—a word that held meanings he had not intended. Or had he? Did he know something I didn't? Dave had been Carl's adviser, and they were obviously on friendly terms.

"You'd better turn left here," Carl said. "It's a one-way street."

I flipped my turn signal back from right to left and determined to concentrate on my driving. I had to stop reading hidden meanings into harmless statements. The situation was confused enough without that.

It was the first time I had been out at night, and as we left the Outer Drive and headed for Prairie Avenue, I realized why people kept warning me to stay put after dark. The bars and all-night eateries were doing a brisk business despite a faint mist that smeared greasily on the windshield, but the so-called Historic District, bounded by Eighteenth and Cullerton and by the weedy slopes of the railroad embankment, was as dark as a tomb except for the uncanny reflected glow from the Nazarian estate. It lit the trees like a cold fire.

Before he opened the gates, the guard looked inside the car and turned his flashlight into the back seat. George was on duty at the garage that night; he greeted me with a small contortion of the lips that might have been meant as a smile, and I handed him my keys.

"They could put a few lights in this part of the grounds," I said, stumbling over a stone as Carl and I approached the cottages.

He took my arm. "There's no way anyone could get over the walls. Don't get in a tizzy if you hear the alarm; it's always being set off by squirrels and birds and such."

Since the maid had been in the cottage when we left, I expected to find the door unlocked. However, it was not, and I fumbled to find my key and insert it in the lock. Carl made no comment. I reached for the light switch inside the door and turned it on.

Carl headed for the easy chair and was about to drop into it when I said sharply, "Wait a minute."

"What? What?" His derriere only inches from the seat of the chair, he sprang back into a standing position and stared wildly at the space he had been about to sit on. "What's the matter?"

"Someone has been here while we were gone."

Carl collapsed into the chair. "I thought I was just about to sit on a tack or a bat or something. Of course someone has been here. Maria."

"Besides Maria. She wouldn't leave marks like that."

The marks of dusty footprints across the floor were clear, to my eyes at least. Carl's male vision was less critical; his eyes followed my pointing finger and then returned to me with open disbelief. "I can't see anything."

I followed the marks to the corner where I had put my suitcases. Closet space was limited; I had had to leave them stacked against the wall. The one on top was empty. I laid it aside.

"The lock has been forced," I said, examining the other suitcase.

That got Carl out of the chair. Squatting beside me, he peered at the lock. "You lock your suitcase too? What do you keep in there, the family jewels?"

"Just papers. Family papers." I lifted the lid. When I saw the contents, I knew I had been right. The large manila envelope had not been sealed, but I had tucked the flap inside. It was outside now, and the corner of a paper protruded.

"Is anything missing?"

I pulled the papers out far enough to check them but not so far that he could see what they were. There weren't many—my birth certificate, some of my mother's letters, and the lab report giving the results of my blood tests.

"No," I said, closing the envelope. The only other thing in the suitcase was the old photo album with Mother's snapshots. I took it out.

Carl jiggled the protruding metal tongue of the lock. It moved readily under his touch. "These locks are as flimsy as paper," he said. "Any casual kick or blow could snap them. Maybe she hit the suitcase when she was vacuuming."

"Maybe."

He could tell I didn't believe it. "Are you going to report this?"

"I don't know."

"I wish you wouldn't."

"Why not?"

"It would just get the kid in hot water. People are always ready to suspect 'the servants.' She'd probably lose her job."

I wondered why he was so concerned about the maid. Could be he was only being kind and fair-minded. But she was a very pretty girl, and obviously admired him. . . . "You mean nice, kind Mrs. Dunlap would fire the girl without even trying to find out whether she was guilty?"

"You don't understand people like these," Carl said. We had both risen to our feet; his face was flushed with emotion. "Mrs. Dunlap wouldn't even know about it. The butler and the housekeeper handle minor domestic matters, and girls like Maria are a dime a dozen, they're so desperate for work. It would be easier for them to fire her than investigate." He saw I was weakening, and pressed harder. "I can't believe she deliberately broke the lock. Probably it was weak and snapped when she moved the suitcase, and she couldn't resist the temptation to see what was inside. But she wouldn't take anything. She wouldn't risk her job."

"I don't have anything worth stealing."

"Then why not give her a break?"

I knew Maria hadn't looked through those papers, and I liked Carl for being so vehement in her defense.

"Okay," I said.

"Thanks, Haskell."

"For what? I should thank you, for keeping me from doing something stupid and unfair. Sit down, I'll make coffee."

He did as I asked. When I went to the kitchen I realized I was holding the photo album close against my breast. I laid it on the counter and put the kettle on.

No, it had not been Maria who had searched my things. In a way I was glad the incident had occurred. It was the first evidence I had had that someone in the house was curious about my background and suspicious of my motives.

I was still waiting for the water to boil when the phone rang. The voice was one I didn't recognize.

"This is Elise, miss, at the main house. I was to tell you that you received a telephone call while you were out. The gentleman left a number at which he can be reached and requested that you return his call tonight or tomorrow morning. Have you a pencil?"

I found one eventually. After writing down the number, I thanked her and hung up.

She had not given an area code, so it must be a local number. Jon? He was the only "gentleman" of my acquaintance who might be in Chicago. Dave would have left his name. I wondered why Jon—if it was Jon—had not.

Carl broke the silence. "Go ahead and call if it's important. Don't mind me."

"It's not important. Just a friend. I think."

"Want me to leave?"

"No. They sure keep close tabs on us, don't they? We haven't been back five minutes."

"That's one of the disadvantages of this cozy deal," Carl admitted. "All calls come through the central switchboard; after midnight, when the poor damned house servants are finally let off duty, the telephone is switched over to the guard at the gate. It does arouse certain delusions of persecution."

"I thought you looked guilty," I said maliciously.

Carl pretended to wipe a perspiring brow. "I was afraid it was Mrs. Dunlap, telling me we had forgotten to leave the door open. Where's that coffee? I need a fix."

He got a charge out of the old pictures, especially those of Dave. "Have you shown these to him?"

"Not yet."

"He may or may not appreciate them," Carl said,

grinning. "Especially these. They must have been high on something."

The series he referred to had been taken at another of the parties, and again they were all wearing costumes. Dave had certainly been the life of that party; tastefully attired in a loincloth and a paper crown, he had been caught in a number of undignified, not to say indecent, poses. The one that amused Carl most showed Dave holding a flustered Margaret Maxwell in a lascivious embrace. The bed sheet in which she had draped her body was wildly askew, baring her long thin legs to mid-thigh, and Dave's hands were not where a gentleman's should be.

"Drugs?" I said.

"More likely beer. Dope wasn't as easy to get in those days, was it? Look at that old goat."

Someone other than Mother had taken the picture; she was prominently featured, again with Dave. His features were contorted into a satyr's goatish leer and his lips were pursed exaggeratedly. Mother had one hand spread over his forehead; her thumb was in his left eye and her face was alight with laughter.

"That's her?" Carl asked. "Your mother?"

"Yes."

"She was beautiful."

I studied the picture again. "No," I said thoughtfully. "She wasn't really beautiful. But she had something—a kind of spark. Maybe it was just simple happiness."

"She was certainly the belle of the ball," Carl said. He was looking at another photograph, where Mother sat between two of the men. Both had their arms around her and both were looking, not at the camera, but at her. She was laughing. In those pictures she was always laughing. One of the men was Dave. The other . . .

"That's him," I said, careless of grammar. "Stephen Nazarian."

"Good-looking guy, isn't he? Not much family resemblance to his sister or his father."

"No."

"Not that I'd know," Carl said. "I never met the old man until he was over eighty and petrified. They say he was quite a devil with the ladies in his time. To judge from the leer on Stephen's face—"

"That's not a leer."

"No, it's more like he was getting ready to bite her neck. Dave looks a little bloodthirsty, too. I wonder if he . . ." He didn't finish the sentence.

I said, "I wondered myself. He's not married—"

"He was."

"I didn't know about that. I guess his heart wasn't broken then."

"Who knows? He's been divorced for years. The marriage didn't last long; maybe he was on the rebound, at that." Carl pursed his lips and pondered. "Yeah, it's possible. He was married in 1967—"

"Two years is pretty long for a classic case of rebound," I said, amused at his solemnity.

"He was only eighteen. Couldn't have taken the fatal step much before that, could he? Especially on an academic stipend. Not," Carl added, with a meaningful look at me, "that two starving students can't starve together a lot more pleasantly than they can starve apart. . . . By all accounts, she preferred not to go hungry. Wanted him to quit school and go into something 'practical.'"

"Is there any dirt about these people you don't know?" I demanded.

"Not much," Carl said coolly. "When someone has as much power over you as a professor has over a student, you fasten on any tidbit that reduces him or her to human terms. You are not even averse to a spot of blackmail, should the opportunity arise."

"If you're going to threaten Dave with these pictures, I'll

be sorry I let you see them," I said—knowing full well that the pressure I had put on Dave was hardly more defensible.

"I couldn't blackmail Dave with these; he'd just laugh. But I know a couple of Mad Meg's students who would love to get their hands on them."

"You mean Professor Maxwell?"

"Uh-huh. She's a little loony, you know."

"I didn't know."

"Oh, nothing certifiable, more's the pity. She has absolutely no sense of humor and—what's the current jargon?—a very low self-image. She never forgives an insult, real or fancied, and she can fancy quite a bit. One guy I know had to transfer to Brown to get his doctorate; she'd taken a dislike to him for some unknown reason. Some people said it was because he wouldn't—"

"Never mind." I knew what he was about to say; I had heard stories about repressed spinster professors and male graduate students before. Malicious, sexist, unfounded stories—in most cases.

"If she's that difficult, why do people choose her as an adviser?"

"Boy, are you naïve," Carl exclaimed. "Little girl, you don't pick an adviser because of her pretty face or his charm. You are supposed to work with the specialist in your field—archaeology, linguistics, history, whatever. The faculty makes damned good and sure that everybody shares the load."

I had hoped to learn something from Carl about the two other men in the group, but he didn't recognize their names. His only comment was "Must have left the field."

It was almost midnight before he glanced at his watch and announced he had better go. "It is a common delusion of the middle-aged, though unsupported by statistics, that sexual hanky-panky only occurs between the hours of twelve midnight and six A.M. I don't want to endanger my reputation."

"You have your nerve accusing other people of being paranoid," I scoffed. "Do you really think Mrs. Dunlap's spies are taking notes on your comings and goings?"

"One can never be too careful," Carl said. "Are you attending the tea party tomorrow?"

"Yes. Is that what it is, a tea party?"

"Various beverages, spiritous and otherwise, will be consumed. She holds these little get-togethers, as she calls them, every few weeks. Carrying on the tradition—the old man used to do it twice a month."

My mother must have been one of the guests. Hadn't he said they could not refuse his invitations?

Carl ambled to the door. "See you tomorrow, then."

"Okay." I added, "Thanks. I enjoyed it."

"Me too. Next time I'll introduce you to the breathless excitement of Brookfield Zoo. Or how about a murder tour? The garage where the St. Valentine's Day Massacre took place, the alley on North Lincoln where Dillinger was gunned down, and, of course, the site of the 1968 Democratic Convention."

"I can hardly wait."

I left my door open so that the light spilling out would help him find his way home. After I had closed and locked it, I took the manila envelope out of my suitcase and went carefully through the papers. They were all there, but I had no doubt that someone else had done the same thing earlier that evening. Someone I could visualize only as a faceless shadow—sitting in the easy chair, whose cushions had held the imprint of a human body. I wondered why "they" had waited until today to carry out the search. I had been absent from the cottage every day. However, I had not been far away, and a trespasser would not be able to count on being uninterrupted, if I decided to return for lunch or for something I had forgotten. Today was the first occasion on which I had spent the entire day away from the estate.

Was it only a coincidence that Carl had suggested the

excursion and made sure I was absent until late in the evening?

In the cold light of day—a gray, gloomy, chilly light—I decided my suspicions of Carl had been groundless. He was the one person who had no connection with my mother; he couldn't have been more than five or six years old when she died. The intruder had to be one of a small number of people, though. A stranger couldn't enter the grounds; a stranger would not have a key to the cottage. Possibly the searcher was one of the guards, checking on my bona fides at his boss's request. If that was the case, Nazarian now knew that I was who I claimed to be. The theory didn't make sense, however. If the old man had doubted my identity, he had only to ask for proof.

The weather felt more like March than mid-June. I found a laundromat that was open on Sunday. It had the grimy, used look of most such establishments, and as I put my clothes into one of the chipped machines I reflected bemusedly on the paradoxes of my situation. I was living on the grounds of one of the most vulgarly ostentatious mansions I had ever seen—doubly vulgar because of its location in the midst of poverty and despair—with daily maid service and armed guards to protect me, but I was eating out of tins and doing my own laundry. Which was, of course, no more than I deserved.

The contrast was not limited to my own position; there were other peculiar exceptions to the luxurious life style of the Nazarians—the neglect of the cottages, for example. The gardens were not as well tended as I would have expected in such an establishment either. I was willing to bet there would not have been weedy flower beds or unpruned shrubbery when the old man was up and about. Obviously Mrs. Dunlap and her husband were not as fussy. No reason why they should care, if the house and grounds had been left to the Foundation. In fact, they were probably looking forward to the day when they could leave Prairie Avenue forever. That day could not be long distant.

Aside from the necessity of doing my laundry, I had left the house that morning because I wanted to return Jon's call from a pay phone. The phone in the laundromat was out of order. Since a conspicuous sign warned patrons that the management bore no responsibility for clothes left unattended, I had to wait till mine were done; I couldn't take the chance of losing them, since practically every stitch I had with me was in the machine. I sat twiddling my thumbs and watching the other customers—tired housewives with their hair in curlers; girls who looked like junior-high students carrying babies who should have been, but probably weren't, their younger siblings; a ragged man sleeping on a bench and surrounded by a palpable fog of alcoholic fumes. When the dryer finally stopped, I gathered up my clothes and went in search of a telephone. I finally found one that worked, in a drugstore, and placed the call.

Jon wasn't staying at a hotel. The voice that answered was that of a young woman. When I asked for Jon there was a perceptible pause before she said, "Just a minite." She continued to hold the telephone when she called him. "Jon! Jon, darling, it's for you!"

I didn't ask where he was staying. It was none of my business. I went about it in a sneakier fashion, apologizing for having disturbed him. He ignored the hint.

"That's quite all right. I was expecting you to call."

I could hear voices and music in the background and people laughing. One woman had a particularly loud and inane laugh, a sort of high-pitched whinny. I decided it must belong to the girl who had answered the phone.

Jon didn't waste much time. "Are you free for dinner this evening?"

"Well, not really. Mrs. Dunlap has invited me to a party. Some of the trustees and officials of the Foundation will be there. It starts at five, and I don't know how long—"

"Yes, that's all right. What about tomorrow evening?"

"That would be better. Have you—"

"Excuse me a minute." He may have tried to muffle the telephone, but he didn't succeed; she shrieked, practically into the mouthpiece, "Do hurry, Jon, the others will be at the club by now." I didn't hear his reply. Then he said to me, "I'll pick you up at six. Is that too early?"

"No. I mean—why don't I meet you?"

"Because, for a number of obvious reasons, I prefer to pick you up," Jon said, in that eminently reasonable tone that irritated me so.

"You won't be able to get in."

"I've gotten into places with higher security ratings."

"I doubt it."

"That bad, eh? Suppose you tell them I'm expected. I'll leave my submachine gun at home."

I knew that voice; it meant that argument was futile. "I'll meet you at the gate," I said. "At six. Jon, you aren't going to keep me in suspense until tomorrow evening, are you? Did you—were you able to talk to the police in Indiana?"

"Yes. I'd prefer to tell you in person—"

"Oh, Jon, for God's sake!"

I heard her whinnying laugh again; she must have been standing right beside him. Caught between two demanding females, even Jon showed signs of strain.

"There was nothing definite, Haskell. Still no answers. But I was able to talk with the police officer who responded to the call. . . . Yes, Miriam, all right; I'll be there in a minute."

"Oh, how inconsiderate of me," I said. "I'm keeping you from your friends."

"Yes, you've heard me speak of them," Jon said smoothly. "Morrie Abrams, my old friend from Harvard Law. He's teaching at Northwestern now and living with his parents in Winnetka. I'll see you tomorrow, then."

I bought myself an iron and went home—to use that word

loosely. The sky dribbled droplets of rain and a cold wind set the branches thrashing.

At least I didn't have to worry about breaking Jon's heart. He had sought consolation quickly; good old Morrie had a sister whom he had been pushing at Jon ever since law-school days. "Push" is not the right word; she didn't have to be pressured. Not that Jon ever said so, he was too much of a gentleman, but the impression was clear—as was the fact that his mother would much prefer Miriam to me as a daughter-in-law.

I pressed my best blouse and skirt, made myself a sandwich for lunch, and spent the rest of the afternoon working on the journals. Around four o'clock I began to get nervous. Slipping into my raincoat, I dashed over to Carl's cottage.

He looked more surprised than pleased to find me on the doorstep. "I thought you'd be primping," he remarked, stepping back to let me in. "What's up?"

"A slight attack of stage fright," I admitted. "I don't know what to wear."

"You came to the wrong person," Carl said. "I'm not up on the latest styles. Something simple and black, with a discreet string of pearls—"

"I don't have anything simple and black, much less a string of pearls, discreet or otherwise. . . . Oh, you're joking, aren't you? Damn it, Carl, this is serious."

"No, it's not. Wear anything you want. What's wrong with what you have on?"

"Jeans and a T-shirt?"

"That's what I'm wearing." He looked down his nose with a comical air of pride. "I did press my pants, though."

"Carl—"

"Look, it doesn't matter. Some men will be wearing business suits, some won't. The women . . . How the hell should I know; I never notice clothes. Dresses or slacks . . ."

"That's a big help."

"You don't have to get all gussied up. Mrs. Dunlap usually wears something long and—well, long. You know. Sit down and relax. I'll make you a cup of coffee."

"No, I can't come in. Now I'm more confused than ever. Good-bye."

"Hey, Haskell—"

"What?" I stopped.

"We'll go together. I'll bang on your door at five."

"Thanks. Thanks, Carl."

He was a few minutes late, which was just as well, because I had changed clothes three times. I was in the bathroom putting on earrings—silver, small, tasteful— when I heard his knock, and I yelled, "Come on in."

The door opened. "What, no locks, no bars, no chains? Come on, let's go, you look . . ." I emerged from the bathroom. He stopped and gave me a long, unsmiling examination.

"You look gorgeous," he said.

I was glad of Carl's company, not only because I needed the moral support but because I wouldn't have known where to go. "Where" turned out to be the front door. An insecure person (who me? no, not me) would have fainted with awe before he ever reached the top of the marble stairs with their curling balustrades and carved statues. The servant who admitted us was one I hadn't seen before, an honest-to-God butler in striped pants and tails. I wondered how many other attendants lurked in the farther regions.

He took my coat—Carl had not worn one—and we passed along silent corridors into a room at the end of one wing. It wasn't as overpowering as I had expected—only half the size of Jessie's house, furnished in an informal, feminine style. Soft pastel chintz covered the chairs and couches. The furniture was French provincial, and a fire burned brightly under a mantel of exquisitely carved pink marble.

We were not the first to arrive. Small though the room was by Nazarian standards, it was large enough to make the dozen or so guests look like a sparse sprinkling. Prominent among them, to me at least, was Dave. He wore a proper business suit, but his tie was under his ear and his pants had lost all but the faintest remnants of their original creases. His hands moved emphatically, punctuating his comments, as he talked with Paul Dunlap. Since he held a glass in one hand and a cigarette in the other, I could understand Paul's expression of alarm; his suit was another superb example of Italian tailoring and Dave's cigarette darted around like a firefly, endangering the waistcoat.

Seeing us, Dave stopped in mid-comment and shouted, clear across the room, "Hi, kids. Come over here, Carl, I want to ask you something."

"His manners are always so refined," Carl said out of the corner of his mouth. "Excuse me, Haskell." He gave me a gentle shove in the direction of Mrs. Dunlap, who was enthroned on a sofa behind a low table.

She looked queenly, her silver hair piled high and surmounted by an antique comb glittering with rhinestones—or maybe they were diamonds, how would I know? Her long gown of pale pink chiffon had full, fluttering sleeves; ruffles framed her face and her skirts overflowed the small couch. Smiling, she indicated the chair beside her.

"How nice to see you, my dear. Do you know Dr. Maxwell?"

Margaret Maxwell's shabby, ill-fitting dark dress made me feel less like a visiting peasant. I had a feeling it was her best, Sunday-go-to-meeting dress, and the attempts she had made to look more attractive only emphasized her worst features. The string of pearls around her neck drew one's eyes to the loose skin and stringy muscles; she had already chewed off most of the inexpertly applied lipstick. Little flecks of red adhered to her teeth. I didn't want to feel sorry for her, but I couldn't help it.

I admitted I had met Dr. Maxwell. Maxwell's response was a brusque nod, a hard stare, and silence. A maid glided up, offering a tray, and Mrs. Dunlap said, "If you prefer something other than sherry or Chablis, Parks will get it for you."

"Sherry will be fine. Thank you." I took one of the fragile glasses and another maid, complete with ruffled cap and frilly white apron, appeared with a tray of hors d'oeuvres. I refused, feeling sure I would drop the tidbit or spill the wine, but Maxwell helped herself to shrimp and ate greedily.

"I feel bad about neglecting you," Mrs. Dunlap said pleasantly. "Mrs. Adams—the housekeeper—tells me you haven't telephoned. Isn't there something you would like?"

Naturally I was quick to deny that I lacked anything on earth below or heaven above. Mrs. Dunlap went on, "I'm afraid the guest cottages aren't as well equipped as they once were. They haven't been used for years. Father did a great deal of entertaining at one time, but of course the state of his health doesn't permit that now, and Paul and I lead very simple lives."

"Oh, yes," I murmured, watching the maid move around the room. There were no antiquities on display here, only rare and priceless ornaments as delicate as the woman who had selected them—figurines of Meissen and Dresden, Chinese vases and crystal sconces. Obviously Mrs. Dunlap did not share her father's and her husband's passion for Egyptological bric-a-brac.

"I've always loved this room," Margaret Maxwell said, putting her glass on the table and using both hands to reach for canapés.

Mrs. Dunlap moved her glass aside and gestured to the maid to leave the plate. "It's my favorite room—as you know, Margaret. I will miss it; but candidly, it will be the only thing I'll miss when I leave this house."

"Oh, that won't be for a long time," Maxwell said. There was a little smear of mayonnaise beside her mouth; she licked at it with a long, pale tongue. She had not taken her eyes off me or spoken to me directly.

"I hope not," Mrs. Dunlap murmured. "But sooner or later . . ."

"How is Mr. Nazarian?" I asked.

"He has made an amazing recovery," said Mrs. Dunlap. "It was at his insistence that I entertained this afternoon. Can you imagine, Margaret, he announced his intention of joining us? Of course the doctor absolutely forbade it."

"That doesn't surprise me," Maxwell said. "He's never been one to give up . . . on anything."

"You know him so well," her hostess murmured.

"Twenty years." Margaret Maxwell continued to stare at me. "Twenty-three years, to be exact."

The fixity of her gaze made me uncomfortable. I finished my sherry. Mrs. Dunlap refilled my glass from the crystal decanter on the table and topped off her own drink.

"It hardly seems possible it was so long ago," she said reminiscently. "I'll never forget the first time you all came here. My brother Stephen and David—dear David—and you, Margaret; your mother, of course, Haskell; and the other young man—I forget his name. I was newly married, and so happy. . . ."

Her voice caught—nothing so distinct as a sob, just a little intake of breath.

"Don't think about it," Margaret said gruffly.

"I like to think about it, Margaret. About the time when we were all young, with our lives ahead of us. It doesn't seem fair that I should have had such a wonderful life, when poor Stephen . . ."

Margaret patted her hand. "He was a wonderful person, Katherine. We all loved him. Misguided, perhaps, but very—uh—lovable."

Mrs. Dunlap raised a filmy handkerchief to her eyes. "He was an idealist. So young, so dedicated . . . Poor Stephen."

I had the feeling that this was a familiar routine, the words themselves formularized by constant repetition. And I am ashamed to admit that my reaction was not one of sympathy. Poor Stephen the idealist, my foot. Blowing up innocent people may be one way of expressing one's ideals, but it wasn't mine. What about poor Leah? Mrs. Dunlap was as bad as my grandmother, not only living in the past, but rewriting it to suit her own needs.

Her eyes misty, Mrs. Dunlap continued to stare into space and Margaret Maxwell continued to pat her hand mechanically while shooting spiteful glances at me. I was infinitely relieved when Dave came toward us.

"On your feet, Haskell. You've loafed long enough."

"Yes, she must meet some of the others," Mrs. Dunlap said with a smile. "I shouldn't monopolize her."

Dave towed me to a spot near one of the windows. The curtains were drawn, shutting out the dreary twilight, but I could hear rain hiss against the panes. "Here," Dave said, thrusting his glass into my hand.

It looked and smelled like straight Scotch, with only a few ice cubes to weaken it. I protested, "I've been drinking sherry."

"You need something stronger to dull the agony of that conversation. She was talking about Steve, wasn't she?"

"How did you know?" The Scotch went down smoothly, and my taut muscles began to relax.

"She gets that sad, sweet look," Dave said rudely. "And Meg pats her hand like a damned robot. I guess I shouldn't be so hard on her; it's one of the poor woman's few weaknesses. But I hate to see someone make a fetish of a dead man."

"Or woman?" I took another sip.

"Or woman. If I see that nauseating expression on your face, I'll belt you one. Lee would belt you one herself. She wasn't a saintly idol; she was a real person. A mensch."

"I thought that means 'man.'"

"It means 'person.' More than that—someone with guts and character and integrity."

"That's nice."

"I don't think I've ever known anyone who was as happy as she was, that last year," Dave said musingly. "There was a kind of glow about her. Not too surprising, I suppose, after the rotten childhood she had had."

"You knew about that?"

"Oh, sure. We talked a lot, Lee and I. I was probably her closest friend."

"Were you in love with her?"

The liquor had gone to my head, or my tongue; I had not meant to be so blunt. Dave didn't seem to mind.

"No—strangely enough. I don't know why I wasn't. Well, maybe I do know. Rampant male chauvinism. She was good, you know. She and I were the most promising students in the department; we both knew it, and so did everybody else. I could take the competition in a friend, but not in a lover. That stinks, doesn't it?"

"At least you're honest about it."

Dave made a wry face. Somehow he had acquired a glass of his own. "It took me years to acknowledge the fact. I couldn't admit it at the time; I was too young and insecure. If I had had the sense then that I do now . . . But it probably wouldn't have worked; she didn't care for me that way either."

"What about Steve?"

"Steve and Leah." Dave considered the question. "I don't know. She wouldn't have talked to me about that; she was a very private person in some ways. I guess Steve loved her—in *his* way. He wasn't capable of loving a woman; his passion was spent on causes—and on hating."

"His father."

"Yes. The poor bastard didn't know that was what drove him—not love of his fellow man, but loathing of the one man who just happened to be his father. In the end it drove him to death." Dave shook himself, or perhaps he shivered, I couldn't be sure. "That's enough morbid stuff. Carl tells me you've been moping all week because we ignored you. Poor little abused thing."

"Carl is a lousy rat fink for squealing to you."

"I dare you to say that to my face." Dave had seen Carl approaching; I had not. I turned.

"I said, you are a lousy—"

"I heard you. I also told Dave you'd been doing a super job."

"Oh. Well, in that case I forgive you."

"Get us something more to drink," Dave ordered, handing Carl his empty glass.

"Not for me," I said.

Carl winked at me and wandered off. When he came back, a glass in either hand, he was accompanied by Paul Dunlap. Trailing them was Margaret Maxwell. She was still on the outskirts, on the fringes—just beyond the pale. Dave's glance, noting and dismissing her in the same breath, was more cruel than a deliberate insult because it was completely unconscious.

"Just in time, Paul," Dave said. "Time for a toast."

"Sure, why not?" Paul said agreeably. "Wait a minute—Margaret, what are you drinking?"

Her sallow cheeks flushed as he handed her a glass, and her stammered thanks gave away more than she realized. Dave's rudeness hadn't hurt her; she was as little concerned with him as he was with her. She probably wasn't the first awkward, unattractive woman to fall for Paul Dunlap's courtly manners and unfailing kindness.

Dave took a glass from Carl and put it in my hand. "Here you go, Haskell."

"No, really," I began.

"Let's drink to—*ein Mensch*." Dave lifted his glass.

It was a toast I couldn't refuse to honor. The liquid was not Scotch; I didn't know what it was, but it was awfully strong. I made an involuntary grimace after I had swallowed, and Paul said, "What are you trying to do to the girl, Dave? I usually switch to tea at about this stage, Haskell; will you join me?"

"Yes, thank you," I said gratefully.

He turned to a table behind him and asked, over his shoulder, "Lemon—milk—sugar?"

"Just plain tea, please."

Maxwell edged in, pushing me aside. "Tea for me too, Paul."

"With pleasure." He handed her her cup first; only proper, she was the older woman; but she shot me a glance of spiteful triumph, as if she had scored a victory.

Paul seemed unaware of the byplay. He had a special smile for me when he gave me my tea. . . . But that's what Maxwell had believed—wasn't it? That the soulful, deep-set eyes warmed at the sight of her, that his pensive face lost some of its sadness . . .

I was beginning to feel a little giddy. Maybe the tea would help. I sipped it and tried to concentrate on what Paul was saying.

"Now that we've settled the question of where the collection is to be housed—"

Dave interrupted, his lip curling. "We didn't agree, we were blackjacked. The old bastard has things tied up in such a way that we are forced to use this house. Sorry, Paul, but he is an old bastard even if he is your father-in-law."

"Dave, you know I agree that the house is completely unsuitable. I'm all in favor of a new building. But aside from the fact that Victor insists on having his own way, it would take years to build. The Oriental Institute hasn't enough space—"

"How do we know that? We haven't the faintest idea of what is in the cellar. If the rest of it is like the junk I've seen so far—"

"That's just like you, Dave," Maxwell said loudly. "Jumping to conclusions without sufficient evidence. The Institute has seventy thousand objects in storage as it is. We need more space too. I'm surprised you aren't pushing our interests more forcibly."

Dave's face went blank. If I had been Margaret Maxwell, I'd have hit him. Any other reaction would have been preferable to his refusal to respond to her needling, or her very presence.

Paul put a friendly arm around her shoulders. "I wouldn't say he was jumping to conclusions, Margaret. It's true that we don't know what may be down there—"

"Which is why I believe we ought to make a complete inventory our first priority," Dave argued. "You're dragging your feet on that, Paul. We ought to be in the cellars digging with both hands. We need more staff, and we are wasting the resources we already have. Haskell shouldn't be working on those journals, she . . . Haskell? What's wrong?"

What was wrong was that the tea was splashing from the cup into the saucer and dribbling onto the floor. Paul snatched it from my hand. "Haskell?"

His face was a long way off, like something seen through the wrong end of a telescope. I felt hands on my shoulders; the touch was as soft as the brush of cobwebs, and the floor had sunk away from under my feet. Vertigo twisted my insides as I floated in empty air. From a vast distance voices hissed, "She's drunk. The girl is drunk. Disgusting . . ." Faces hovered over me, faces twisted in contempt, in malicious laughter. Or was it one face, multiplied by my failing vision? The voices joined in a hateful chorus. "Drunk, disgusting, ought to know better—can't have someone like that around here . . ."

Then another voice rose over the sly whispers, dominating and overpowering them. A man's voice, deep with concern. "She's not drunk; she's ill. Help her. . . ."

"Help," I agreed, and fell through infinite depths into darkness.

7

Someone had twisted a cord tightly around my head. I had seen old prints showing the technique; it was part of the torture of the Middle Ages. The tormentor turned a stick to tighten the cord and make it bite deep into the victim's flesh.

I tried to call out. "Stop it. Make them stop." But my mouth was stuffed with cotton and it tasted foul. There was an endless period of pain and humiliation, which I prefer not to remember. Every time I vomited, my skull split apart and clapped back together again. Finally I heard someone say, "That should do it," and I passed out again.

When I woke, the headache had subsided to a dull throb. I was almost afraid to open my eyes for fear that the slightest movement would start the whole horrible process again; when I did so, one eye at a time, I found myself in a strange room. I couldn't see much of my surroundings because the only light came from a lamp some distance from the bed in which I lay. It was a big bed, and deliciously soft; the sheets felt cool and smooth, like fine silk.

I stirred cautiously. Footsteps whispered, and a face appeared, looking down at me. It was Mrs. Dunlap, still dressed in fluttering pink chiffon. "How are you feeling?" she asked.

"Better. What—what happened?"

She sat down on a chair next to the bed and took my limp hand. "The doctor thinks you had an allergic reaction to something. What were you drinking?"

"I wasn't drunk," I said feebly. "Honestly, I wasn't. All I had was a glass of sherry, and some Scotch—not much—and tea, and a sip of whatever it was Carl brought. . . ."

"Don't try to talk. I believe you."

"Somebody—Dr. Maxwell—said . . ."

"You are mistaken, my dear. No one blames you. I'm only sorry that it should have happened here. Fortunately Dr. Poffenberger was in the house, visiting Father, and he assures me there is nothing to worry about."

"Where am I?"

She laughed—a surprisingly girlish, carefree laugh. "That's supposed to be the first question, isn't it? You're in one of the guest bedrooms. Carl carried you upstairs."

I felt myself drifting off. "I'll go," I muttered. "I don't want to bother you. Your guests . . ."

"You are not a bother, and you mustn't think of going back to that wretched cottage. Just get some sleep; that's the best possible thing for you. One of the maids will sit with you tonight, in case you need anything. I must tell Paul you are better; he was so concerned. . . . Oh, here he is now."

I was almost gone, but I managed to croak, "Don't let him see me. I look . . . awful . . ."

The sound of her silvery laughter blended with the deeper tones of a man's voice—concerned, comforting, caring. I slid under the surface of sleep.

Morning sunlight roused me at last. Except for a

lingering dry taste in my mouth, I felt okay. I shifted position experimentally. Still okay . . .

A woman bent over me. I had hoped my attendant might be Maria, but this wasn't she; the face was older, a pleasant, smiling face with rounded cheeks and three chins.

"You are awake," she stated. "You are better."

"Yes, thank you. I'll get up right away."

"No, you stay. I will tell the lady."

She padded away. The door opened and closed.

I pulled myself to a sitting position and was relieved to find that the worst was over. Remembering how bad the worst had been, I grimaced in embarrassment. I certainly couldn't complain about the treatment I had received. This was the very quintessence of luxury.

Closed draperies glowed ruby red with sunlight, casting an eerie crimson light over heavy mahogany furniture and paneled walls. The bed was a four-poster, extravagantly carved. The sheets and pillowcases were trimmed with cobwebby lace. They weren't silk, but my nightgown was. I cleverly deduced it must belong to Mrs. Dunlap. The long sleeves and high neck, the demure Peter Pan collar and intricate smocking weren't my style, but the filmy fabric felt like heaven against my skin. I examined it anxiously but found no spots or stains. I don't know why that should have mattered, but it did.

I had no idea what time it was. There was no clock in the room. My watch was on the bedside table, but it had stopped. I saw no sign of my clothes.

A door on the far side of the room led, as I had hoped, to an ornately appointed bathroom. My clothes weren't there either. I was on my way back to bed when I heard someone at the door. I made a run for it and huddled under the blankets like a child almost caught disobeying orders.

The maid was accompanied, not by Mrs. Dunlap, but by another "lady," who introduced herself as Mrs. Adams, the housekeeper. She was much younger than I would have expected; and although she was wearing the conventional black dress, she didn't look at all like the housekeepers in horror movies. After feeling my forehead, she nodded approvingly and helped me sit up, propping the pillows behind me.

"Doctor Poffenberger said you would be fully recovered this morning, but you had better stay in bed until he comes, just to be sure. Are you hungry? He said you were to have anything you fancied."

"Hungry" wasn't the word. My stomach felt as empty as a limp rubber glove. Small wonder; I had emptied it thoroughly. I felt myself flushing at the memory, but she tactfully pretended not to notice. She beckoned to the maid, who placed a tray across my knees—a pretty white wickerwork tray like the ones I'd seen presented to the lady of the manor in nighttime soap operas. There was a vase with a rosebud in it, and a copy of the *Tribune* in a side pocket. I wondered, insanely, if the butler had pressed the newspaper.

I thanked them both and they withdrew. Then I fell on the food like a starving wolf. Fresh-squeezed orange juice nestled in a bowl of chipped ice, scrambled eggs with bits of chives and bacon, English muffins and tiny pots of marmalade and jam—I ate every bite and poured a second cup of coffee from the silver pot. This, I told myself, was living.

I had scarcely finished eating before the maid was back to remove the dishes, leaving me my cup and a fresh pot of coffee. This was living, all right. But it wasn't my style, and it never would be.

How had the maid been able to calculate precisely when to remove the tray before the dirty dishes could offend my delicate sensibilities but without hovering over me while I finished eating? Mrs. Dunlap would probably say that good servants developed a sixth sense about such matters. To which I would have replied, had courtesy not prevented me—bah, humbug. Perhaps people who took that kind of service for granted didn't mind paying the price—a sense of perpetual surveillance, of eyes watching to anticipate one's slightest want. But I would mind. I would hate it.

Yet if my theory proved to be correct, I might find myself offered the chance to live such a life. It was the first time I had really faced that possibility. How would Mr. Nazarian react if I claimed to be his granddaughter?

Now that I had met him, I knew what his reaction would be—cynical, suspicious, skeptical. He wouldn't believe I had no desire to become part of that indulged and oppressed household, that all I wanted was a sense of my own identity.

Reluctantly I conceded that he might have good reasons to be skeptical of such a claim. Stephen Nazarian had been on the run for several years before his violent, bloody death. Unquestionably there had been other women in his life. I had read enough about the radical groups of the sixties to know that a defiant sexual freedom was part of their credo. I might not be the only child—go on, use the word, the only bastard—he had fathered. There might well have been a long line of juvenile claimants, cuddled in the arms of hopeful mothers. Most women would jump at the chance to claim a relationship, any relationship, with a multi-millionaire.

Most women—but not Leah Emig Maloney. Not my mother. Surely not my mother . . .

The nasty taste in my mouth had nothing to do with physical sickness. I was relieved when a new invasion put an end to my train of thought.

This time it was the doctor. Mrs. Adams stood by while he examined me—blood pressure, pulse and heartbeat, temperature. He prodded my stomach and asked me a lot of personal questions before announcing that I was fully recovered. One of the questions was whether I was taking any medication which, combined with alcohol, might have brought on such a violent reaction. I was able to reply with perfect truth that I wasn't even taking aspirin and that I had never been allergic to anything.

It wasn't until after he had gone that I realized I hadn't been entirely truthful. I had almost forgotten the incident. It occurred while I was seeing Ann. We had hit a sticky spot in the analysis, I was having trouble sleeping, and Ann had prescribed a mild sedative. The first and only time I took it, I had been sick. Not as violently as this time, but sick enough to make Ann change the prescription.

When I asked for my clothes, the housekeeper informed me they had been sent out to be cleaned. If I would tell her what I wanted, she'd have one of the maids bring an outfit from the cottage. I refused with thanks, and with a vehemence that obviously surprised her, and after some argument she produced my raincoat. With Mrs. Dunlap's silken gown hitched up at the waist so it wouldn't drag, and my feet crammed stockingless into the pumps I had worn the night before, I sneaked out of the house and scuttled through the gardens to my cottage.

As soon as I opened the door I knew I had been right. This time the search had been done by a professional—at once more thorough and less apparent than the first casual inspection. I couldn't have pointed to a single smudge or misplaced object, but I knew that someone had been in the room.

After I had showered and changed, I folded Mrs. Dunlap's gown and left it lying on the bed for Maria. It was later than I had thought, and I knew I ought to make up for my performance by rushing to work, but I felt a shrinking reluctance to leave the false security of the four enclosing walls.

The fact that I had once had an allergic reaction to a particular brand of sleeping medication—I couldn't even remember the name of it—didn't prove that the same medication had been responsible for my illness the night before. But it would have been easy for someone to drop something in a drink. Almost everyone in the room had had an opportunity, including Margaret Maxwell; there had been moments when both of our glasses were side by side on the cocktail table. She had been drinking sherry, too.

Maxwell had had not only opportunity but a strong motive. Nothing would delight her more than seeing me humiliated in public—and what a public! My nominal bosses and my new patrons, plus some of Chicago's most distinguished citizens. I knew I had not imagined her gloating face or her insidious comments. If the doctor had not been at hand, or if my reaction had been a little less severe, my repulsive performance would have been written off as vulgar inebriation. I might well have lost my job as a result.

However, the second search of the cottage made simple malice only one of a number of possible motives. The end result of my collapse had been that the cottage had been left unoccupied all night. No one could have anticipated I'd have such a violent reaction, but any signs of illness or incapacity would have produced the same result; Mrs. Dunlap would have insisted I spend the night at the house. That's the kind of woman she was.

What in heaven's name was the unknown person looking for? The first cursory examination of my belongings had exposed the few personal papers I had brought with me; that's all there was, there wasn't any more. Apparently the searcher believed there was something more. I couldn't imagine what it might be. A marriage license—letters from Stephen to Mother, acknowledging paternity or betraying some dark family secret? I could have invented a dozen possibilities, but that's all they would be—inventions, products of a free-wheeling imagination. The most telling argument against any such theory was that there was no need for underhanded methods. If I were a blackmailer, the possessor of some unimaginable secret that threatened a member of the Nazarian family, I would have made my move by now; I had been on the premises for days. I couldn't imagine Mr. Nazarian being intimidated by me—or by anyone else, for that matter. He could kick me out or buy me off—or bump me off. . . .

I sat huddled in my chair, my brain buzzing with fantastic premises. I decided I was probably going crazy. I had not one scrap of objective evidence to prove the cottage had been searched or that I had been deliberately drugged. Even if I had solid evidence, what on earth could I do with it? Go to the police? To one of the people who were on my list of suspects?

A knock at the door penetrated the fog of confusion that engulfed me. I hadn't locked the door; before I could respond, Carl opened it. I knew what he was going to say. "How do you feel?"

I was getting awfully tired of that question, but I forced a smile. "Fine. Sorry I'm late. I was just—"

"Maybe you'd better not come to work."

"I want to." Grabbing my purse, I pushed him out the door. I didn't lock it. Why bother?

Carl trailed after me as I strode briskly down the walk. "Look, about last night—"

I didn't stop walking. "Let's not talk about it. I made a perfect exhibition of myself, which I bitterly regret."

"Nobody thinks that."

"I should thank you for carrying me to bed," I said, adding, "I hope I didn't throw up on you."

He caught my arm and swung me around to face him. "Cut it out, Haskell. We won't discuss it if you'd rather not, but I have to tell you you're not the one who should feel guilty. Paul is beating his breast, Dave has called twice already, and I . . . Maybe it was that last drink I brought you that did the job."

He looked sincere; even his muscles sagged. Mollified, I said more graciously, "I doubt it. What was that stuff, anyway?"

"That's the trouble, I don't know. I just grabbed a couple of glasses off the nearest tray. Dave will drink anything, and I didn't think you wanted—"

"Don't worry about it. I was never in any danger."

"Well—okay."

His concern seemed so genuine and his tentative smile was so friendly that I had to fight a sudden urge to confide in him. Carl couldn't be involved; he had no reason to wish me ill. Even if his friendliness was false and he wanted to see me fired from my job, he had other, more effective methods of undermining my position.

On the other hand, he was a subordinate, without power or influence. He doted on Mrs. Dunlap, he was dependent on Dave, and Victor Nazarian was paying his salary. He was also a terrible gossip. No; much as I yearned to tell all, it would have been the height of folly to pick Carl as my confidant.

The one person I trusted implicitly was the one person I didn't want to confide in. Whether Jon believed my story or whether he assumed I had succumbed to terminal paranoia, his reaction would be the same. He'd stop at nothing to get me away from Chicago.

That reminded me. "A friend of mine is supposed to pick me up this evening. Will they shoot on sight at the gate, or is it okay for him to come in?"

Carl accepted the change of subject without comment, but his eyes were as bright with curiosity as a squirrel's. "You'd better call the gatehouse and tell them when to expect him. You can use the phone in the office."

He showed me how to get the extension and pretended not to listen while I gave Jon's name to the guard. The man asked so many questions I became exasperated. "I don't know what kind of car he's driving—it's probably a rental. He's about six-two, dark-haired. . . . What? He's twenty-eight, why on earth . . . Oh. All right. Thank you."

I hung up the phone and turned, fuming, to Carl. "I'm

surprised he didn't demand a photograph and a birth certificate. Honestly!"

"Such are the penalties of your position," Carl said. As I settled myself at my desk, he added, "Another penalty is imminent. Paul wants to see you."

"Penalty?" I repeated uneasily. "What does he want me for?"

"I was just kidding. I don't know what he wants—he doesn't confide in me—but I'm sure it's nothing to worry about. Come on, I'll escort you."

We had to go outside and around to the main entrance. Carl explained, "You can get downstairs, to our offices, from the museum, but not the other way around, unless someone opens the door from the museum side. Security again. As is this . . ." He pressed a button and a buzzer sounded inside the building. It was answered, not by the guard I had expected, but by a woman. Though the doors were of glass, heavy grillework behind them obscured my view; I could see only her outline until she opened the doors.

Carl greeted her with a casual "Hi, Marge. Haskell, this is Marge Atwood, Paul's secretary. Marge, meet Haskell Maloney."

She looked like a TV version of an executive secretary— tall and model-slim, with shining blond hair shaped into an elaborate chignon. If I didn't miss my guess, her simple navy-blue suit was tailor-made; it fit as if it had been shaped on her body.

She gave me a cool smile and a cold hand and led the way across the lobby toward a door on the left. I didn't have time for more than a hasty over-all impression. The floor was marble, smooth and shiny as water; and the archway into the museum proper was flanked by a pair of red granite colossi. We entered her office; it was equipped with the latest thing in word processors. She crossed the room to another door, knocked, and opened it.

Paul's office matched his secretary—cool, expensive, handsome. Oriental rugs covered the floor, and his desk was a masterpiece of eighteenth-century craftsmanship. Its top was bare except for a telephone, a pair of "in" and "out" boxes, and, in the precise center of the gold-embossed leather insert, a single sheet of paper.

He rose from his chair and offered me his hand. Thank goodness he didn't ask me how I felt.

"Hello, Haskell. I understand you haven't yet seen the museum."

"Nobody told me I was supposed to show her around," Carl said quickly.

"That's perfectly all right, Carl. I'm glad you didn't, since it allows me the pleasure of doing so."

It was an experience I had long looked forward to and one that surpassed my expectations. There were six rooms in all, excluding the lobby; the last in line, counting from the entrance, was windowless and completely enclosed in steel and cement—a walk-in safe where the most valuable pieces of the collection were kept. Everything in the place was perfect: it had the latest in humidity and temperature controls, and every object was a masterpiece of its type.

The statues in the lobby were of Hatshepsut, the queen who had proclaimed herself king, and who had assumed the titles and image of a man. These showed her with a male body wearing the shendyet-kilt and nemes headdress; the royal uraeus crowned her brow.

"But they're perfect," I exclaimed. "Even the ones in the Met aren't this fine."

Carl moved slightly. "They have been restored," Paul said. "Rather extensively. Some people criticize me for over-restoration, but I see nothing wrong with wanting a work of art to look as it looked in its prime. Victor agrees with me."

As we passed through the other rooms, I realized that the same criticism or commendation could be extended to all the exhibits. There wasn't a scratch or a chip on the pieces of pottery; shawabtis and statuettes had had missing limbs and noses replaced. At least I assumed they had, since few of the smaller, more delicate pieces of sculpture have survived intact. Even a close examination failed to show what was original and what was not. Most museums do a certain amount of restoration of damaged objects, but modern practice is to use a material easily distinguished from that of the piece itself.

The solid foot-thick doors of the treasure room had been rolled back into recesses in the walls. I wondered whether they had been opened on my account or whether it was done daily for an audience that was seldom present. The museum was not open to the public. This entire building, with its complex lighting and ventilation and security systems, had been designed for the pleasure of one man.

I knew the vault must house the prize of Nazarian's collection, the most jealously guarded of all his treasures. It had never been published or properly studied. Only a few old black-and-white photographs existed. No one knew exactly where it had come from or how it had been acquired or even *when* it had been acquired. Rumors of scandal, of fraud, and of violence surrounded its scanty history.

The treasure consisted of Eighteenth Dynasty royal jewelry. In quantity and in quality it rivaled the collection of the Metropolitan, which is second only to that of the Cairo Museum. What made Nazarian's collection remarkable was that it had probably come from a single lost tomb, whose location had been known only to the illicit diggers who had stripped the princely mummies. Several other groups of royal jewelry had been found by archaeologists; hidden in secret caches, they had escaped the tomb robbers of ancient times. The Met's collection included several of these, purchased on the open market when such transactions were legal.

I moved slowly from case to case. Crowns and necklaces,

girdles, bracelets and rings mesmerized with the soft shimmer of gold and the symmetry of superb design. Even to an inexperienced eye like mine, it was obvious that the lovely things must have come from a single, multiple burial—perhaps from the workshop of a single master craftsman.

"It's incredible," I murmured. "Absolutely unbelievable. How something of this caliber could have been smuggled out . . . Is it true that no one knows how he obtained possession of it?"

The question might have been considered less than tactful, but Paul only smiled. "We haven't a clue. It was Anton Nazarian who acquired it, not Victor; by the time Victor began collecting in earnest, such a coup would have been impossible, even for a man as wealthy and—er—unscrupulous as he. Even Anton, who flourished during the bad old days of excavation, took some pains to hide his tracks. The entire collection was in a bank vault for decades; that's why we can't even be certain when he brought it into the country."

"That circlet"—I pointed—"is similar in design to the one in the Met. From the tomb of the three princesses Winlock found near Deir el Bahri."

"Except that this has a vulture's head instead of the head of a gazelle. That means that the original owner held the title of queen. Winlock's ladies were of a lower rank, minor wives or royal concubines." The light from the case cast a golden glow on his features as he brooded over the contents; his face was peaceful and calm, without the shadow of melancholy that usually marked it. Musingly, he went on, "It's a fantastic thought, isn't it—that somewhere in the cliffs, or under the sand, lies the violated tomb from which these beauties came. Perhaps no living man knows where it is. The thieves are long dead by now. And so is Anton Nazarian."

He glanced at his wrist watch and I said reluctantly, "I'm

sure I'm keeping you from an appointment. Thank you so much."

"The appointment is yours," Paul said, smiling. "Dave is joining us shortly to discuss future plans. Feel free to visit the museum anytime, Haskell. If I'm not here, Miss Atwood will let you in. I've placed your name on the list."

The list of the Sifted Few, I thought, as I accompanied him back through the quiet rooms. Carl followed, his hands in his pockets, his head bowed. He hadn't spoken a word.

Dave was late—"as usual," Paul said wryly. We sat down at a conference table and Miss Atwood served coffee. There were a number of eight-by-ten colored glossies arranged at one end of the table, and seeing me crane my neck to look at them, Paul gathered up a few and handed them to me. "These are for the catalogue. I've been working on it for—oh, an indecently long time! But I want it to be perfect—a model of what such a book can be, with unlimited time and care—"

"And funds," Carl said. His voice and his manner were perfectly respectful, but I had a sudden notion as to why he had been radiating silent criticism throughout the tour. The photos were fantastic—half a dozen views of each object, from every conceivable angle—even from underneath. The contrast between the museum in all its perfection and the dusty chaos belowstairs was striking.

I could understand Carl's feelings, but I wasn't sure I sympathized with his viewpoint. It was a basic and eternally unanswerable question: Does one spread the available resources of time, money, and skill to cover all the work that needs to be done, or does one concentrate on a single area?

If Paul was aware of the implicit criticism, he showed no signs of it. "And funds," he agreed readily. "I hope to include color photographs of every exhibit, plus, of course, detailed descriptions, measurements, chemical analyses when applicable . . ."

"It's a pity you can't be equally informative about the provenances," said Carl.

This time the criticism was more overt. Paul glanced at him, more in surprise than in annoyance, and I said quickly, "That's unknown in many cases, surely."

"Oh, right," Carl murmured.

"I wonder if there is anything about the jewelry in Anton Nazarian's journals?" I went on. "Sometimes he lets down his hair and chuckles over a slippery deal he managed to pull off. Wouldn't it be fantastic if I could find that?"

Paul collected the photographs and carefully restored them to their original places. "No more journals for you, Haskell. If I hadn't been so busy last week, I'd have found you something better to do. Not that it was a bad idea," he added graciously, nodding at Carl. "We'll want to transcribe the journals eventually—though I'm not sure how much Mrs. Dunlap will want to see published. At the present time, however—"

He was interrupted by voices in the outer office. To be entirely accurate, I heard only one voice; if Miss Atwood answered Dave's shout of greeting, her well-bred tones were too low to penetrate the closed door. Said door burst open, and Dave came in.

"I'm late," he announced in a surprised voice.

"Yes." Paul advanced on him with an ashtray but was an instant too late; the elongated ash on Dave's cigarette dropped to the rug. Dave ground it in with his foot. "Keeps the moths out," he explained.

"Sit down," Paul said resignedly. "You're barely housebroken, Dave; if it weren't for your winning personality, you wouldn't be welcome in any civilized house."

The discussion began. As behooved my inferior status, I kept quiet and listened. I couldn't have contributed anything even if my opinion had been asked, since I didn't know what they were talking about. It had to do with the legal arrangements for the trust and with certain administrative details. One thing was clear, however, even to me. Dying or on the verge of death, the old man still held the strings in his withered hands. His unwillingness or inability to reach decisions on specific matters was holding up the proceedings and would continue to do so until he was no longer around. I began to understand why everything I had seen and done thus far had such an air of indecisiveness about it. And above all, I wondered what the devil I was doing there, since I was the lowest person on the totem pole, and the least involved.

Dave wondered too. After a while he banged the table with his hand and declared, "The kids are wasting their time listening to this, Paul. They better get back to work. Come to think of it, I'm wasting my time, too. Let me know when the old devil makes up his mind."

"I'm sorry," Paul began.

Dave waved his hand, strewing ashes across the polished tabletop. "Not your fault. Talk to you later. Come on, you two."

He shooed us ahead of him. Instead of going out the main entrance, he crossed the lobby to a door opposite the one to Paul's office. It led to a landing and a flight of stairs. "You can't come up this way," he began.

"I told her," Carl said.

"Oh. Okay." His footsteps echoed eerily in the closed stairwell. A door at the foot of the stairs opened onto a narrow hallway, with several doors opening off it. There Dave stopped and proceeded to fall into a deep trance. He stared into space, lips parted and eyes vague. Carl, whose manner had relaxed considerably since we left the museum, grinned at me.

"He does this sometimes," he remarked. "He isn't dead, he's just thinking. It's a strain on him, so he—"

"Shut your face," Dave said equably. He shook himself. Ashes and dust rose in a fine cloud. "Let's stop screwing around," he said.

"Fine with me." Carl leaned against the wall, his arms folded. "What did you have in mind?"

"We need those files," Dave said. He glanced at me and explained, "The old museum files, from the period before Paul took over. He reorganized the museum and the records and had the outdated ones moved downstairs. Being Paul, he simply gave the order and the slaves carried it out. Now he says he has an idea where they are. Which is probably true. They may be as worthless as he claims, but they're better than nothing, and we need 'em. Let's go find 'em."

"What, now?" Carl exclaimed.

"Sure, why not?" Dave took off his coat, looked vaguely around for a hook to hang it on, and, finding nothing, dropped it onto the floor. He rolled up his sleeves.

"I can think of several reasons why not, starting with the fact that you told me I wasn't supposed to go prying around down there without a master plan and the approval of the trustees."

"I'm a trustee. Come on."

The next few hours were pure heaven. We rummaged and pried and shifted boxes and dived headfirst into packing cases. I couldn't believe Dave carried out an excavation the way he conducted that search; on a proper dig, every square foot of earth is supposed to be measured and photographed and staked out, and every square inch of soil is supposed to be sifted. There was a certain method in his madness, however; and Carl seemed to be familiar with his habits. Clipboard in hand, he followed his leader scribbling notes and writing down the disjointed sentences Dave shouted at him. By the time we stopped, Carl had a series of rough plans delineating the areas we had investigated and describing the general nature of the contents. But we hadn't located the files.

"Son of a bitch," Dave mused, wiping a hairy arm across his face and smearing perspiration and dust into a muddy mask. "Where do you suppose he put the damned things?"

"The most logical place would be in the basement of the museum," Carl said. He had used the tail of his shirt to wipe his face; it flapped loose, damp and brown.

"You could be right," Dave agreed.

"You know I'm right. You just wanted to indulge in a little treasure hunting."

Dave grinned. "It was fun, wasn't it?" he asked me.

"Wonderful," I agreed wholeheartedly.

We found the files, still in their original oak cabinets, at the back of one of the storage rooms in the museum basement. They were almost concealed behind piles of discarded office furniture, old typewriters, and moldering cardboard cartons. Perched percariously atop the pile, like the Nome King on his throne, Dave opened the topmost drawer and let out a whoop of triumph. "I knew it! Call a couple of the troglodytes, Carl, and tell them to get these cabinets upstairs."

"I'm going to call a pizza parlor and order some food," Carl said. "Do you realize it's after two o'clock?"

"It can't be," Dave said. "I have a committee meeting at two."

"Then you're late."

"Hmm. Looks that way."

Dave scrambled down, dislodging a carton, which burst apart, spilling moldy papers across the floor. Wading through them, he started rolling down his sleeves. "I guess I'd better get going."

"Like that?" Carl demanded. "At least wash your hands."

"And your face," I chimed in. "And your shirt, and—"

"Effete snobs," Dave said.

Carl got on the phone right away, and while we waited for George and another of the guards to carry up the cabinets, he called the kitchen to ask for sandwiches and coffee.

"I hate doing this, even though Mrs. Dunlap told me to," he said sheepishly. "Stupid attitude, isn't it?"

"No," I said.

By the time we finished eating, the file cabinets had been moved into the office, and we began sorting through them. I have seen messes in my time—the kitchen after Jessie had cooked a Christmas dinner for eight—dear, dizzy Dr. White's desk—or Dave's, come to that. But I have never seen anything to equal those files. I couldn't blame Paul for throwing up his hands and deciding to make a clean sweep of all his predecessor's works. According to Carl, the former curator had been an old crony of Nazarian's, who had been given the job as a reward for faithful service. He was an accountant—"Give you three guesses what kinds of services he performed"—with no training in archaeology or museum administration.

"What kind of services?" I repeated, puzzled. "An accountant keeps . . . Oh. Cooking the books?"

"Tax evasion is the least of the crimes the old man has been accused of," Carl said. "Ties with organized crime, illegal deals of all varieties—that Wall Street stuff is a mystery to an innocent like myself, so I can't give you the grisly details. Anyhow, nothing was ever proved, thanks in large part to good old Sam the accountant. Good old Sam was also an alcoholic. Victor didn't care; he wanted to run the place himself, and he was just as happy to have a drunken incompetent in the job instead of a man who would have tried to tell him what he was doing wrong. Since he had no experience either, and was too arrogant to take advice, he did a lot of things wrong."

"It's a good thing Paul took over when he did," I said.

"Yeah," Carl said unenthusiastically. "That was Mrs. Dunlap's influence. Nothing too good for her darling. . . . All right, all right, don't hit me; I'm sorry. Paul was an improvement, at any rate. And by that time, even Nazarian realized he was making a mess of things. He'd never admit it, so doing a favor for his dear daughter gave him a good excuse to bow out."

Though poorly organized, the material was voluminous—photographs, sketches, customs slips and receipts, you name it. We began sorting them, but we kept getting distracted. "What the hell do you suppose this is?" Carl would ask, showing me a picture of what looked like a Victorian chamber pot, photographed in a thick fog. I forgot about time; I forgot about Jon. But it was only a little after five when the buzzer at the back door sounded, and Carl, who had gone to see who it was, summoned me.

"Hey, Haskell. Someone to see you."

The odd note in his voice should have alerted me, but I was still chuckling over the receipt I had just found, for a case of Glenlivet Scotch. It was annotated, in a wavering masculine hand, "For professional entertainment."

The someone was Jon. He looked rather ruffled, though I don't suppose anyone who didn't know him as well as I did would have noticed. Towering over him, with the air of an incipient avalanche, was George.

"Is this the gennulman you said was coming, miss?" he demanded.

"Uh—yes. Yes, it is. Hello, Jon." George continued to hover, and I added, "It is all right, George. Thank you." My voice had the hopeful uncertainty of the owner of a very large, untrained dog suggesting, "Drop it."

Somewhat to my surprise, George did. He closed the door after him. Jon's free hand—he was carrying a briefcase in the other—moved to brush his sleeve. I didn't blame him; George and his brethren affected me the same way.

"You're early," I remarked.

"Am I?"

"I told you I'd meet you at the gate."

"You weren't at the gate," Jon said.

He transferred his gaze to Carl, who was staring at him with the rapt interest of a biologist examining a new species, and I introduced them. Names only; I assumed Jon was smart enough to figure out that Carl was a co-worker, and since I hoped their acquaintance wouldn't blossom into friendship, I saw no need to explain Jon to Carl. "Ex-fiancé" sounded so crude.

Jon transferred his briefcase to his left hand and extended his right. "How do you do. I'm Miss Maloney's former fiancé."

Carl blinked, examined his grimy palm, and grasped Jon's hand. "Hi. Lawyer?"

"How did you know?" Jon bared his teeth.

Carl bared his. "Intuition."

I suggested that Jon come with me to the cottage while I changed. Once we were out of earshot of Carl I muttered, "That was an unnecessary dig, Jon."

"I made the statement in the interests of accuracy. It was not a dig. The word 'friend' has too many—"

"Oh, never mind. But don't tell me you mistook the time; you've never done that in your life."

"I have some things for you. When I told Jessie I was driving, she asked if I would mind . . ." He came to a stop. "Damn. I forgot to bring them after all. Can you believe it?"

"It's hard to believe, all right."

"I have them," Jon insisted. "Two suitcases. The butler unloaded them along with my luggage, and I neglected to put them back in the car. I'm sorry, Haskell."

"Jon, what do the suitcases have to do with your being an hour early?"

I opened the gate; he stood back and insisted I precede him. "Not a great deal," he said in answer to my question. "The fact is I thought it might be advisable to suggest there were people in the great outside world who took an interest in your welfare. I had no idea it was as bad as this. Is old man Nazarian an ex-Mafioso or something?"

"I don't think so. Just an ordinary, common robber baron."

"That son of a gun searched me," Jon said indignantly.

"He's probably taking the car apart right now." I opened the door and waved him in. "I don't know how you ever got past the gate."

"I managed to convince the man on duty he was mistaken about the time. Thanks for notifying him I was expected; I'd probably have been shot on sight otherwise." He gave the room a searching survey. "So this is your new pad. Not exactly fancy, is it?"

"It's better than I had any right to expect. Sit down. Would you like a drink? All I can offer you is coffee or diet soda."

"Thanks, I'll take a rain check."

I took my clothes into the bathroom and dressed there after a much-needed shower. The quarters were cramped, and I bruised myself on the fixtures more than once; but I felt funny about parading around in front of my ex-fiancé half-dressed, though I have to admit it wouldn't have been the first time. When I came out, he had opened his briefcase and was perusing a sheaf of papers. Trust Jon not to waste a minute of his precious time.

"Researching a case?" I inquired politely.

Jon held up the papers, showing the bright cover of the latest issue of *Mad*. "The briefcase is camouflage; I figured it would add to my air of respectability. I'm on vacation at the moment."

He jumped up to help me on with my coat, and I said, "Oh. I wondered why you were in Chicago over the weekend."

"Morrie has been nagging me to visit him," Jon said. "Things are slow at the office right now, and he's house-sitting for his parents while they're in Europe, so this seemed like a good opportunity."

"The parental mansion—tennis courts, indoor pool, fully equipped gym?"

"All that and more."

I decided not to pursue the matter. "More" probably

meant little sister Miriam. Which was decidedly none of my business.

They had put the car back together. Jon headed for the Outer Drive, without asking for directions. He knew his way around Chicago, all right.

I was reluctant to introduce the topic that was uppermost on my mind, nor did he refer to it. Waiting for the proper moment, no doubt—when he had me in a public place, where I couldn't make loud noises. I asked him how Jessie was doing and he said fine, which ended the subject. Then he asked me whether I would prefer Greek food or Indian, or how about Vietnamese? I said I didn't care, and that ended that.

So we had Ethiopian.

The décor was delightful and the waiter greeted Jon by name. I knew he loved ethnic food of all varieties, and I knew he went often to Chicago, on business—as I had supposed—but it was a strange feeling to realize he had a life outside the one we had shared for almost a year.

The tables were low and the hassocks on which we sat were only a foot off the floor. Jon folded his long legs with perfect dignity. He could look dignified while being barbecued for a cannibal feast. He ordered for us, since I didn't know any of the dishes. The drinks, at least, were recognizable. He waited until I had had a sip of wine before telling me what I had wanted to know.

"I couldn't locate the official records on the case," he began. "Closed cases, old files—buried and forgotten. It was a stroke of luck that led me to the officer who had responded to the call. He remembered it because it was his first day on the job and his first . . . his first fatality.

"The car was totaled. It was impossible to determine whether any given part had been damaged before the smash. From the extent of the damage, the office concluded the vehicle was traveling at about sixty miles an hour. There were no tire marks on the pavement.

"His tentative conclusion, which eventually went into his official report, was that the steering had malfunctioned. It happened on a curve; even if she—even if the driver had hit the brakes, it wouldn't have stopped the car in time. Officer Kanofsky—who is now a lieutenant—believes she didn't have time, that her foot froze on the gas pedal. It was all over very quickly. Only a few seconds of actual time."

I stared at my glass. I wondered why I didn't feel anything. My hand was perfectly steady. After a moment, Jon added gently, "A routine search was made for broken bottles and beer cans, any evidence that alcohol was involved. Nothing of the sort was found. She had not been drinking."

"What about the autopsy?" My voice was perfectly steady too.

"There was no autopsy. The next of kin refused permission."

"My grandfather, I suppose. That fits; he wouldn't allow doctors to treat the living; why should he worry about the dead?"

"There was no need for an autopsy," Jon said. "No one else was injured; no other vehicle was involved. The car she was driving was ten years old—no question of a lawsuit against the manufacturer."

"So that's all."

"That's all. And," Jon added, with a touch of impatience, "it was a hell of a lot more than you had any reason to expect. Face it, Haskell. All the evidence points to the same conclusion. It was an accident, pure and simple. They happen every day—every minute of every day."

"Yes, they do."

"If you're not convinced—"

"I'd be very unreasonable, wouldn't I? I'm grateful, Jon; you went to a lot of trouble, and I appreciate it."

Jon said, "You're welcome."

• • •

I made him drop me at the gate. "There's no sense in going through that security routine again, Jon. This isn't Thornfield Hall, surrounded by miles of desolate moorland, with a maniac in the attic."

"Are you sure about that?"

The absurd, pseudo-medieval outlines of roof and towers bulked black against the night sky. A single lighted square of window, high up under the eaves, shone like a watchful eye.

"Cut it out," I said irritably. "The only nasty thing in the attics round here is old man Nazarian, and I really don't think he rises from his prolonged deathbed and prowls the grounds at night like a vampire."

"I wouldn't bank on that either."

"Damn it, Jon—"

"Okay, okay. Five minutes in this mausoleum would drive me bonkers, but if you insist . . . I'll drop those suitcases off tomorrow. No, wait a minute, I can't do it tomorrow."

"Yachting?" I inquired. "A little friendly match of polo?"

"Why the devil should you suppose I'm going to play polo? You know I can't even stay on a horse."

"I was only demonstrating that I am familiar with the casual amusements of the rich and famous."

"Oh," said Jon, in tones of mild surprise. "You were being sarcastic."

I was being nosy, but he didn't satisfy my curiosity. "I'll bring them Wednesday," he went on. "Can you get by that long without them?"

I had suspected his uncharacteristic lapse of memory was an excuse for a return visit, and I was determined he shouldn't get away with it. "I can get by without them, but I don't want you to go to so much trouble. I'll pick them up."

"Certainly not. It's a long drive to Winnetka."

"And from Winnetka."

The guard had emerged from the lodge and was staring suspiciously at the car. "You'd better get out before that character pulls out a submachine gun," Jon said. "I'll call you."

He leaned across me and opened the door. I said, "I'll call you."

"You have the number?"

"Yes." I got out and closed the door. The car shuddered as Jon slammed it vehemently into reverse.

The guard admitted me without comment, replying to my thanks with a slight nod. I couldn't remember having seen him before, and I wondered how many such men there were on Victor Nazarian's payroll. They were like robots, clones of a single, unpleasant type; and instead of making me feel secure, their presence had the opposite effect. I wished Jon hadn't started my imagination squirming with his dire hints. Madmen in the attics or living gunmen prowling the grounds, ready to shoot at anything that moved . . . My skin prickled as I hurried along the paths in the cool darkness.

I was getting ready for bed when the phone rang. It was Jessie, and Jessie was annoyed. "Where have you been? I called you three times."

"Didn't Jon tell you he was taking me to dinner? I thought he reported every move."

"Well, he doesn't. I wish someone would report something to me sometime, for God's sake. I've been worried sick about you. I can't sleep, I'm drinking too much, and I've gained five pounds."

A faint crackle on the line was almost certainly due to the usual mechanical difficulties, but it reminded me that every word we said might be overheard. "Stop drinking, stop eating, and stop worrying," I said lightly. "I am in perfect health and excellent spirits. I love the job and everyone is being very, very kind to me."

I had hoped the excessive enthusiasm would warn her to watch her words, but she didn't take the hint. "Did Jon tell you what he found out—in Indiana?"

"Yes. Jessie, I have to hang up. I'll call you—"

"I had no idea you felt that way, Haskell. It hurt like hell hearing it from Jon. Why didn't you tell me?"

"Jessie, please. We'll discuss it another time."

"She would never have done such a thing, Haskell. She loved you. And she wasn't the kind to run away from responsibility."

"I know. I feel better about it now, after Jon—"

"I'm glad *you* feel better. How do you think I feel? It was my car. I should have had it inspected before she left. One of the tires was a little worn; I meant to replace it, but she made up her mind in such a hurry. . . . It pulled to the right, you know. Not much, but . . ."

I forgot about possible listeners; I forgot everything except the dry controlled voice. I hadn't realized Mother had been driving Jessie's car. I had not realized, because it had never occurred to me to ask. I ought to have realized.

"The police said it must have been driver error, Jessie. She'd have known if there had been anything seriously wrong with the car; she wouldn't have risked driving it, she would have taken it to a garage—"

"Sure. I know. Don't pay any attention to me. I'm a little down tonight, and to top everything off, I got a call from your grandmother."

"I thought she didn't have a phone."

"She uses the neighbor's when she considers the situation an emergency. The last time was when your grandfather died. You didn't show up Sunday, and she was frantic."

"I told her I wasn't coming. I wrote her a note."

"Sometimes I wonder whether she can read," Jessie said morosely. "She wants you to come out there Wednesday and take her grocery shopping."

"For God's sake, Jessie! I have a job; I can't take an

afternoon off whenever it suits me. And it definitely doesn't suit me."

"She said it was important. She has something she wants to give you."

That put a slightly different cast on the matter, but the initial objection remained. "I'm on sufferance here as it is. I can't ask for a day off."

"I told her that, but I don't think I got through."

In other words, the ball was in my court. I hadn't the heart to go on grousing to Jessie, not after all the grief I had caused her. I promised I'd deal with the problem—somehow—and that I would call her soon. I told her I loved her. It didn't seem to make her feel better.

After I had hung up, I sat with my head in my hands wondering how and if I could ever make it up to Jessie. And wondering whether it was easier to believe your dearly beloved sister had committed suicide or died as a result of your negligence.

By contrast, the minor problem of Gran's grocery shopping amounted to comic relief. There was no way I could get in touch with her to tell her I wasn't coming, which left me with two choices—callously to ignore the two old ladies for (as they would believe) the second time, or to show up as expected on Wednesday.

A faint 40-watt bulb flickered in the general murk of my despondency. Jon had announced his intention of bringing my luggage on Wednesday. Perhaps the old ladies had given me a way out of that.

I reached for the telephone. By the standards of the merry youth of wealthy Winnetka, it was still early; Jon was probably whooping it up with Miriam and the gang. Sure enough, I heard the sounds of well-bred revelry in the background, and this time it was a servant who answered. I didn't give my name.

Jon recognized my voice, however. "What's wrong?" he demanded.

"Nothing is wrong. I just found out I have to go to Oak Park on Wednesday. So I thought, as long as I have to be out anyway, I could pop into Winnetka and save you a trip."

I might have known it wouldn't be that easy. "What do you mean, pop in? Winnetka is due north from you, and Oak Park is west."

"I don't care if it is straight up," I said, my patience fraying. "Tell me how to get there, and leave the suitcases with the butler or the third assistant footman. You don't have to hang around."

"You're going to visit your grandmother?"

"I have been bullied, blackmailed, and bamboozled into taking her grocery shopping."

"Suppose I meet you there."

"Suppose you don't."

"I'd like to meet the dear old soul."

"No, you wouldn't."

"What time?"

I knew the futility of arguing with Jon when he took that tone. Besides, a dose of Gran and Aunt Ella would serve him right. We settled the details, and that left me with only one little difficulty—explaining to my boss that I wanted a day off to take my grandmother to the grocery store.

8

Since I had a favor to ask, I made a point of being early to work next morning. I rang and banged on the door for some time without a response, so I concluded Carl had not yet arrived. I propped myself against the door and prepared to wait; when it swung open, I staggered in, straight into Carl's arms.

He had to catch me or leap aside and let me fall flat on my face. However, once he had caught me, he didn't have to kiss me.

It was the first time in over a year I had been kissed by anyone except Jon. The mustaches I had encountered in the days before Jon had been prickly or soggy or both. Carl's was a revelation—soft and silky as a kitten's tail and almost as active. It added a new dimension to a technique that had a great deal to recommend it even without the mustache.

I'd have kissed him back just because I wanted to, because I enjoyed it—for the fun of it. But there were other reasons for my instant, enthusiastic response. The hard warmth of his body was stability in a shifting world, comfort in the dark, something to cling to. The arms that held me were a shield against dangers I couldn't even define.

He didn't let me go; he pushed me away. I fell against the door in an ungraceful sprawl and saw Dave watching us. I don't know how long he had been standing there. He must have coughed or spoken. Carl couldn't have seen him; he was facing the other way.

Dave looked us over at his leisure. When he finally spoke, his words were even more devastating than his bland smile. "Please, children. Not on company time."

He then retreated, whistling, into the room from which he had come.

"Goddammit," Carl said. "I didn't know he was here."

He wasn't the blushing type. In fact, his tanned cheeks had paled, probably with consternation. I said rudely, "I assumed you didn't, or you wouldn't have done anything so rash."

"You're damned right I wouldn't," Carl agreed, with such sincerity that I was tempted to smack him with my purse. Belatedly he remembered his manners. "Sorry. It was a momentary aberration. It won't happen again."

As an apology it ranked with some of the insults I had heard. I knew I'd probably think of a devastating retort later, when it was too late, but at the time nothing occurred to me that wasn't vulgar. I brushed past him and went to my office. Carl didn't follow me.

I put my elbows on the desk and covered my face with my hands. I felt like a fool. Why did people do things to make me look silly? Jon hadn't helped, with that bland explanation of his presence—"former fiancé," indeed. The painstaking, humorless accuracy was typical of Jon, but another man might well have taken it as an invitation. "Go ahead, buddy, she's all yours."

I knew I was overreacting. It wasn't that single comment

or its aftermath that depressed me. I had had a bad night. It took me a long time to fall asleep, and when I did I was awakened by the same dismal dream—my mother walking slowly away from me along a dusty, endless road, never so much as turning her head in response to my cries.

I hated that dream. It could be interpreted in a number of different ways, but it had come to mean only one thing to me—failure. Whether it was her ghostly image or my own subconscious that reproached me was irrelevant.

Jon's discoveries in Indiana hadn't changed anything. I had never expected that they would, which was one reason why I hadn't bothered to follow that line of inquiry. There was no way of proving or disproving my darkest doubts. The fact that they had apparently never occurred to Jessie, or to Jon, only showed I must be loony to suspect any such thing. Poor Jessie, in particular, would have been desperate to grasp at any hope of shifting her burden of guilt onto someone else—someone like her father, whom she despised anyway.

But my grandfather wasn't the only person whose words or deeds might have had a fatal effect on a driver. Margaret Maxwell had hated Leah—the triumphant, happy young mother, proudly displaying her baby's pictures. And what of Stephen Nazarian? If he had been her lover and the father of her child, he had greater power than any other human being to hurt her. The line between life and death is so narrow; one false move, one instant of abstraction, and the line is crossed. The car goes out of control, the knife slips, the foot misses its step. If she had been a little more alert to the way the car was handling, could she have avoided the crash?

I would never know the answer. Jon had been right, as he always was. The only sane course was to forget my neurotic, unprovable fancies and do what he had suggested earlier: put my cards on the table, tell the truth, ask openly. What else could I do? I pictured myself searching through drawers and desks, looking for . . . what? What could I expect to find after twenty years? Love letters, faded mementos of romantic meetings, hotel or motel bills? . . . My lips curled in involuntary repugnance. No man would keep souvenirs like that; it was even less likely that his sister or his father would do so. Nor could I see myself playing burglar, sneaking and prying. I wouldn't even know where to look.

And now, after meeting these people face to face, I wasn't sure I wanted to know I was related to any of them. By going on as I had begun, I ran the risk of losing a great deal, including a job that was turning out to be far more rewarding than I had hoped. I enjoyed what I was doing, even the dull job of transcribing old Anton's journals. I had made friends, contacts who could be useful if I pursued the academic career I had always contemplated. Why risk a positive good for a dubious evil?

I was trying to nerve myself to return to work when Dave came charging into the office. I turned a startled face toward him; I suppose there were traces of the tears I had wiped away, because he put a hand on my shoulder and tried, not too successfully, to hide his smile.

"Come, come, time's a-wastin'. You aren't sulking, are you?"

"No. I just feel like a fool."

"Carl says it was his fault."

"How gallant of him." I felt better; Dave looked like a big rumpled brown bear, his arms folded and his cheeks creased into lines of laughter. "It wasn't anybody's fault."

"Who said it was? I don't know why you kids are so damned self-conscious about these things. Whatever happened to the sexual revolution? In my day . . ."

He broke off. "Tell me about it," I said.

"Damned if I will. I did read Carl a lecture, but I was kidding—well, half-kidding. I didn't think he'd take me seriously; he never pays any attention to my advice. I don't care what either of you does so long as it doesn't interfere with your work."

"It won't."

I started for the door. He held me back. "You're doing a good job, Haskell. I don't want you to blow it."

"I appreciate your interest, Dave, but I don't know why you're being so complimentary. All I've done so far is transcribe some old diaries."

Dave snorted. "You don't think I'd recommend you to Victor without checking up on you, do you? I called Alice White. She said some nice things about you. She also said you'd been planning to apply to graduate school here. Why'd you change your mind?"

"Didn't she tell you that?"

"She said you decided to get married."

"And I changed my mind about that, too. I don't sound very stable, do I?" I added, "History repeating itself, in fact."

"Oh—you mean Leah? There is a certain parallel. She wanted to come back, but . . ." He frowned. "You aren't getting morbid about this, I hope. The parallel isn't close. Unless—"

"If you mean am I pregnant, the answer is no. What do you mean, she wanted to come back?"

"That's why she was here that weekend." Dave sounded surprised. "I thought you knew that. She had decided to come back and finish her degree."

"No. I didn't know that."

"There was no problem about her being accepted," Dave said. "The problem was money. The fellowship had been awarded to someone else, of course, but she sounded pretty optimistic. She said something about . . . Hell, why am I rambling on like this? There's work to be done. Up and at 'em."

'No, Dave, wait—I want to ask you—"

Carl charged into the room. "He's coming. Paul just called. He wants us—"

"Wait a minute," Dave bellowed. "Who's coming? What's the idea of busting in like that?"

"Mr. Nazarian." Carl glanced vaguely at me, as if my face were familiar but he couldn't quite place it. "He's on his way. Paul wants us to come up and meet him."

"Bowing and scraping and tugging at our forelocks," Dave grunted. "Oh, hell, I suppose we'd better. Come on, Haskell."

I had to run to catch up with them. "Why is he coming here?" I panted. "I thought he was on his deathbed."

"He's been off and on it for ten years," Dave said. "He makes these little tours from time to time. The museum is his baby. Every time he shows up, he makes a speech about how it's his last visit and crap like that. One of these days, it will be his last. That's why I—"

The two of them were heading, not for the outer door, but for the one that opened onto the stairs leading directly to the museum. Obviously the routine was one they knew; the normally locked door was open, held by one of the museum guards. Dave went up the stairs two at a time.

Impeccably attired as always, Paul was waiting in the lobby. We joined him. Carl fidgeted, brushing at his tumbled hair, tucking his shirt in.

"Well, where is he?" Dave demanded. "Is he well enough for this?"

"Who knows?" Paul shrugged. "There's no stopping him once he decides to do something; and in a way . . ."

Dave smiled unpleasantly. "Yes, wouldn't it be touching if he had his final paroxysm here in the hallowed halls?"

Paul looked pointedly at Dave's bare arms and dangling tie. "I'm sorry I was unable to give you notice of his coming, Dave. You know how he is—"

"I know." Dave ignored the hint. "It's damned inconvenient, though. We found those files yesterday—"

"So I understand." That was all he said, but his tone of frigid disapproval indicated his opinion of Dave's proceedings. Dave was as unmoved by the disapproval as he had been by Paul's critical look at his clothes.

Paul stiffened. "Here he comes. Miss Atwood—"

Miss Atwood, cool as an ice cube, stepped forward to open the doors. The small procession approached. Jerry was pushing the wheelchair. The occupant, so bundled in shawls and blankets that his face was invisible, still looked like a mummy—one of the Peruvian variety that were swathed in cloth and buried sitting up. The nurse followed, looking bored, and Mrs. Dunlap trotted alongside the wheelchair. Her father's decision must have been a sudden one, for she lacked her usual elegance, her feet thrust into low-heeled slippers and her hair straggling.

I had noticed that there was a ramp in the center of the stairs but had thought nothing of it; most public buildings these days have accommodations for the handicapped. But this ramp had been designed for the convenience of one man. Like everything else in the museum.

Without giving a direct order, Paul had managed to nudge us into semimilitary order, he and Dave in the foreground, Carl and I a few paces to the rear. Carl stood stiff and straight, hands at his sides. As if feeling my eyes upon him, he turned his head and gave me a sickly, self-conscious smile. I moved a little closer.

"What's the matter with you?" I hissed.

"He scares the bejesus out of me," Carl muttered.

The wheelchair, a Cadillac of its kind, rolled smoothly up the ramp. Nazarian's head rose slowly out of the wrappings. The effect was absolutely grisly, like an old Boris Karloff movie. His wrinkled hands rested on a heavy silver-inlaid cane that lay across the arms of the chair. I was surprised to see it, because I would not have expected he was capable of standing even with its support. As I was soon to learn, it had another function. Once he was inside, he raised the cane and jabbed at Paul. Paul stood his ground, smiling stiffly. The old man croaked with laughter.

"All here, eh?" he said, skewering each of us in turn with a hard stare. "What are you doing here? Waste of time. Get back to work."

Carl jumped and turned on his heel. "Where are you going?" the old man barked.

"You said—" Carl began.

"Quiet." That took care of Carl, who froze in position. The beady black eyes moved on to me. "You here too? Heard you got stinking drunk the other night. Shameful."

"I wasn't drunk."

"That's what they all say." His mouth split in an evil smile. I smiled back at him.

"But most of them are lying."

"Father, please." Mrs. Dunlap tucked in a loose end of shawl. "You're tiring yourself. I do wish—"

"Quiet." He gazed around the room. His head was the only part of his body that moved, and one expected to hear gears grind and clash. "My last visit," he muttered. "My last look at my treasures."

Dave winked at me. It wasn't funny, though. It was both touching and macabre; the old man was putting on quite a performance, but he knew and we knew he might be speaking the literal truth. He looked worse than he had the first time I saw him. A bluish pallor lay like a plastic film on his wrinkled face.

He had heard about Dave's foray into the cellars, and he made a number of caustic comments, to which Dave responded by shrugging and looking bored. Then Nazarian demanded to see what we had found. This necessitated the use of the elevator—not the one I had seen, from the house to the tunnel, but another one in the museum itself, which had been intended to serve as a means of transporting objects from the basement to the exhibit rooms and vice versa. Like almost every other door in the house and museum, it was locked. With a look of great importance, Jerry produced a ring of keys and solemnly unlocked the doors.

Once down below, Nazarian went from room to room, commenting, adversely in most cases, on what had been done. The sight of the old files aroused an unexpected touch of sentiment about good old Sam, "the best friend I ever had."

Dave wasn't impressed. "Good old Sam made a god-awful mess of the place—not just the records, but the cellars. I wouldn't be surprised to find some vintage cognac among the antiquities."

The old man chuckled. "You won't find anything down there, Dave. It was me, not Sam, who decided what went on exhibit and what was stored. I knew what I was doing. No, don't argue with me; you've said it all before. I'm an old man. I haven't got time to listen to it again."

Dave, being Dave, argued anyway. Observing her father's cheeks darken and his voice rise, Mrs. Dunlap tried to intervene. A wild swipe of the cane missed her by a mile, but got the old man's point across. Turning to me, she said in an agitated voice, "This is so bad for him. He isn't supposed to exert himself."

I murmured sympathetically. "He must get awfully bored, Mrs. Dunlap. Maybe a lively argument will perk him up."

She had addressed me because I was the closest person to her; I don't think she was fully conscious of my identity until I spoke. She made an effort to regain her composure and her manners.

"I'm sorry, Haskell, I don't believe I even said good morning. How are you feeling? No aftereffects, I hope?"

"None. I never thanked you properly for your kindness—"

The wheelchair spun around. I suppose Nazarian had

some system of signals with Jerry, though I never saw him use one.

"What are you talking about?" he demanded. "Are you talking about me?"

"No, Father," Mrs. Dunlap said. "At least . . . Don't you think you've done enough for one day? Dr. Poffenberger said—"

"Stupid pill-pusher. What does he know? You're all alike, trying to deprive me of the few pleasures I have left."

Mrs. Dunlap's lips quivered. "All right, Katherine, all right," the old man mumbled. "I know you mean well. We'll go upstairs now. I want to see my treasures. That's why I'm here. Come along. No, not you!" The cane whipped out and caught Carl full in the stomach. "Get back to work. You, too, Dave. You don't appreciate art; stick to your dirty papers and pots."

"I have no intention of trailing after you," Dave said calmly. "Get the hell out of here so we can get some work done."

I assumed Nazarian meant me to remain as well, until a peremptory flourish of the cane indicated otherwise. Once we were upstairs, he dismissed the Dunlaps. Paul didn't trouble to hide his relief, but his wife looked hurt. Her tremulous lips and moist eyes softened the old man's response; he patted her hand, but he didn't revoke his order and he didn't explain why he had selected me to accompany him. He didn't have to explain to me. In the first place, I was a brand-new audience for the treasures he displayed to so few; it must have been a painful struggle between his wish to keep them all for himself and his need to revel in the admiration and envy of others. In the second place, I was a fresh victim, and one who had thus far remained impervious to his rudeness. He had tormented the others so often it wasn't fun anymore.

The exhibits were arranged chronologically, with the first room devoted to objects from the predynastic period and the early dynasties. I had noticed and admired several outstanding pieces on my first visit—a wooden stela carved in exquisite low relief, a pear-shaped votive macehead with scenes of pharaoh's triumphs in battle—but Nazarian whisked through without stopping, nor did he pause in the second room. The focus of the collection and of his own interests was the New Kingdom material. Some people considered the art of this period to be overly ornate, even decadent, especially in its later developments; but three of the six rooms of the museum were devoted to Eighteenth Dynasty objects, including the jewel room.

We went through the exhibits one by one and, for the most part, in silence. I was unable to repress a gasp of horror the first time Jerry opened a case and placed one of the exhibits—a translucent blue glass goblet with a white feather pattern on the shoulder—in the old man's feeble hands. Chuckling malevolently, he remarked, "It's mine, you know. My property. What's the use of owning things unless you can handle them—do what you want with them? If it breaks, who's going to complain?"

"If it breaks, one lovely thing is gone forever," I said. "There's no other exactly like it anywhere in the world."

"That's why it's here," Nazarian said complacently. "Everything here is unique. Here—take it."

"No." I put my hands behind my back. "If I broke it, you'd have me beheaded."

At his insistence, I touched some of the less fragile objects—a wooden box carved in the shape of a baby gazelle and a metal mirror whose handle was a graceful girl's body. It was an incredible experience, but I didn't breathe easily until each was back in its case.

Watching Nazarian, I had to revise my opinion of him; his passion for collecting wasn't pure acquisitiveness after all. Some of the objects brought an almost tender look to his face—a softening, as when he responded to his daughter. These he didn't remove from their cases or touch. He sat for a long time just looking at them. I was content to do the same. I asked only one question.

"Aren't the cases hooked up to an alarm system?"

"It's turned off whenever I'm in the museum." He gave me a sharp look. "So don't get any ideas, young woman. If you so much as breathed heavily on one of the cases at any other time, you'd rouse every security guard on the estate."

"If I were going to rob the place, I'd pick a time when you were here," I said, watching Jerry replace a small ivory carving of a bellowing hippopotamus.

Nazarian laughed till he wheezed. "And finish me off at the same time, eh? Good thinking. Why do you suppose I never announce these visits in advance?"

After we had made the rounds, we returned to the central exhibit hall, which had a pair of curved leather couches. Nazarian gestured at one of them, and I sat down.

"Well?" he said.

"It's fantastic. What did you expect me to say?"

He shook his head impatiently. "What's your favorite? If you were robbing the place, what would you snatch first?"

I hesitated, and he said impatiently, "The jewelry, I suppose. There's not a female alive who can resist gauds."

"No. There are several things I love, but that has to be my favorite."

It was in the central room—a carved alabaster head, slightly smaller than life-size. The translucent pallor of the stone glowed like the ivory skin of the young girl depicted. Once it had been painted, but most of the paint had worn off except for a blush of carmine on the full lips. The tinted glass inlays outlining the eyes and eyebrows were intact. The pupils were inlaid as well, giving a startling illusion of life. A few touches of black paint remained in the folds of the elaborate ringleted wig; on the forehead was the royal uraeus, a cobra raised to strike, formed of gold and precious stones.

"Nefertiti," the old man said.

"How do you know?"

"Who else could it be?"

"Any of the princesses; Smenkhkare or Tutankhamon; Akhenaton himself. They all look alike."

He had said practically the same thing himself, so he couldn't argue the point. He glowered at me, and I went on, "It's the lid of a canopic jar, isn't it? Obviously from the same period as the ones in Tomb 55 at Thebes."

"Think you're smart, don't you?" the old man grunted. "This one didn't come from Thebes. It came from Amarna."

"How do you know?" I repeated.

He grinned maliciously. "That would be telling. I acquired it in 1929; by that time it was illegal to take objects of that quality out of the country. Thanks to that damned fool Carter; I told him at the time he'd queer the game for all of us with his arrogance, but you could never tell Howard anything."

"You knew him?" I asked, impressed.

"Knew 'em all. Breasted, Petrie, Carnarvon. All gone now. All except me." For a moment I thought he had dozed off. His head drooped and the withered lids hid his eyes. Then he said, "I know where it came from. I bought it—never mind who from. What a scandal that would have caused. . . . Even worse than the one that blew up when I put it on display. They tried to get it back. Failed. My lawyers can handle any government, including this one. I won't let it go. You're right, girl, it's the pièce de résistance—the finest thing I own. And I found it. Everything I bought was the best. Not like my father; he couldn't tell a product of the Thutmose workshop from a modern fake. The stuff in the cellars is garbage; Dave's a fool if he expects to find anything down there. Modern fakes. Junk . . ."

Jerry had been standing at attention behind the wheelchair, proud as a general in his gold-braided uniform. He was no robot, though the old man treated him like one; more sensitive than I was to the weakening of his master, he cleared his throat in a bass rumble like distant thunder.

"Tired," he said. "Time to go."

"Not yet. Wait." Nazarian opened his eyes. "Well, girl? Are you going to thank me?"

"I do thank you. It was a wonderful experience."

I hadn't told him Paul had already shown me through the museum. It would have spoiled his fun and perhaps exposed Paul to his father-in-law's displeasure.

"You aren't afraid of me, are you?" he asked suddenly. "No."

"But you should be." The words came in a soft hiss; his eyes had narrowed to slits. "You should be kowtowing and genuflecting like the rest of them. My good will can mean a lot if you want to go into archaeology. That is what you want, isn't it?"

"Yes." I could have kicked myself. He looked fragile and half dead and he had moments of senile wandering, but the brain behind his mummy face was as keen as ever. His appraisal of people was completely cynical, and, in this case as in so many others, the cynical appraisal was the right one. Most people in my position would have crawled to gain his favor.

I added, with an attempt at lightness, "I'm trying a different approach. I figured you were tired of people jumping to attention whenever you cleared your throat."

"Hmph." He never blinked or wavered. "You're right about that. I wonder, though . . . There are other reasons for currying favor with me. Revenge, blackmail . . . Or were you thinking I'd take you to my bed like David with the Shunammite?"

My disgust showed clearly on my face. Nazarian laughed. "If you are up to any tricks, you'd better learn how to hide your feelings. They're as clear as print. But you wouldn't have been so finicky forty years ago—or even twenty. I could have had any woman I wanted. I did have most of them. . . . And it wasn't my money, either. No, by God, it wasn't. I had . . ."

Mrs. Dunlap hovered in the doorway. I wished she would interrupt; the sympathy I had felt for the old man had been buried under an avalanche of revulsion. It was Jerry who saved me. He didn't speak; he simply turned the wheelchair and pushed it toward the exit. Mrs. Dunlap swooped down. "Father, I told you—"

"Be quiet." He must have made one of his imperceptible signals; the wheelchair stopped, then turned. Nazarian croaked, "I'm not through with you, girl. Have to rest now. . . . Tired. But you come—come later. Hear me?" He was so short of breath, every word was punctuated by a whistling wheeze.

I said quickly, "Yes, sir. I'll come."

"Damn right you'll come. Five o'clock. They all come when I tell 'em."

The wheelchair and its horrible occupant glided away. Mrs. Dunlap came quickly toward me. I braced myself for recriminations, but instead she started to apologize.

"I hope he didn't offend you, Haskell. I couldn't help hearing him; he was speaking so loudly—and when he gets started on the women he's known, he can be quite—er—outspoken."

"No, that's all right. I suppose it's natural to boast when you feel your powers leaving you—including that one."

"Especially that one." She smiled ruefully and brushed back a lock of loose hair. "You do understand. I must run now; I want to make sure he's being properly looked after."

I walked with her toward the door. "He seems to have very devoted attendants."

"Oh, Jerry would die for him," Mrs. Dunlap said casually. "He does have a certain charisma, you know, when he chooses to exercise it."

She broke into a run as soon as she was out of the

museum. I stood at the door watching her and marveling at the wondrous diversity of human relationships. "Charisma" might not be the right word for what Nazarian had, but he certainly had something. I had felt it myself. And I prayed that the unwilling, occasional bond of empathy between us was based on our mutual love of beauty and not on something uglier.

The others were digging manfully through piles of rotting papers when I joined them, and Dave handed me a stack of my own. "Sort them by category—photos here, invoices here, letters, miscellany—and then by date," he ordered.

During one of his temporary absences from the room, Carl made his apologies like a gentleman. I waved them away. "It's no big deal, Carl."

"I was afraid you'd say that," Carl said mournfully.

Dave's return ended that exchange, and for the rest of the day we worked diligently. Dave was delighted to discover an envelope stuffed with sketches of pottery. Though brown and speckled with mold, they were marvelous examples of archaeological artwork. Accuracy is the most important consideration, but these had a delicacy and precision of line that made them a pleasure to look at.

"Damned if this doesn't look like Meg's work," he exclaimed. "I didn't realize she had ever done anything for the old man. I wonder where the hell—"

"Margaret Maxwell?" I asked.

"Yeah, she started as a draftsman. Too bad she didn't stick with it, she draws better than she thinks. What the devil do you suppose Paul did with this pottery? It's Naqada II—"

"You could ask him," Carl suggested.

"What's the use? He's not interested in anything but pretty pictures of pretty things."

It was grimy work, and at four o'clock I said hesitantly, "Can I go now? I should shower and change before I appear in public."

"Ah, another heavy date," Carl said. "You wouldn't believe this gal's social life, Dave."

I frowned at him. "This date is with Mr. Nazarian. He asked me to come see him. I don't know what he wants, or even whether he'll remember asking me, but I had better show up."

"He'll remember," Dave said briefly.

"And you damned well better show up," Carl added. "Dave, maybe you ought to go along as a chaperon. When I think of that poor, innocent girl walking alone and unprotected into the spider's web, the lion's den, the lair of the monster—"

"Shut up, Carl," Dave said.

Carl might be petrified of Victor Nazarian, but he wasn't a bit in awe of Dave. Something was bugging him; he couldn't seem to stop talking. Ducking Dave's halfhearted jab at his chin, he babbled on. "It wouldn't surprise me to learn that Victor's invalidism is a fraud. You know, like in those Gothic novels where the villain pretends to be paralyzed, but in the dead of night he prowls the darkened halls looking for victims—innocent housemaids, unsuspecting virgins. And that Neanderthal servant of his—"

This time he forgot to duck. The blow wasn't hard—it had not been intended to do more than sting—but it snapped Carl's head back and closed his mouth.

Dave didn't apologize.

"Jerry is an example of Victor's better nature," he said. "He's old Sam's grandson—"

"Sam the former curator?" I asked.

"Yes. As you may have guessed, he's an ex-fighter. A few fights too many left him in the state you see. His parents were dead and his siblings wanted nothing to do with him; if Victor hadn't taken him in and looked after him all these years, he'd be dead—or worse."

"I didn't know that," Carl said, absently rubbing his jaw.

"Yeah, well, there are a lot of things you don't know," Dave said sourly. "Smart-ass kid . . ."

But you were one yourself, I thought, as they smiled sheepishly at one another. The affection between them was plain to see; but how odd men were, expressing friendship with insults and blows.

"Get going, Haskell," Dave said. "Don't keep the old goat waiting."

As it had been intended to do, Dave's story made me feel more kindly toward Victor Nazarian and more sympathetic toward his forbidding attendant. It had also negated the uneasiness aroused by Carl's bizarre fantasies. Damn Carl, anyway; why had he tried to frighten me with nonsense like that? His cynicism had infected me, too. Much as I would have preferred to accept Dave's interpretation of Nazarian's motives, I couldn't help thinking that his careless kindness had been repaid a hundredfold by the devotion of a servant who was totally dependent on him.

Even after I had scrubbed them, my hands smelled faintly of mold. I changed into clean pants and an oversized tailored shirt that covered me like a tent. Nazarian's reminiscences and hints had been impersonal, nothing more than the pathetic boasting of any aged male chauvinist, but they had made me self-conscious. He probably hadn't exaggerated the extent of his conquests. With his millions, he could have been cross-eyed, bow-legged, and covered with long black hair and still attracted women. But not all women. Surely not all . . .

On my way out, I caught sight of the old photograph album, which was lying on the table. On a sudden impulse, I picked it up and tucked it under my arm. I can think of a number of reasons why I might have decided to show it to him; maybe I wanted to display the pictures of my young, radiant mother surrounded by young, attractive men to counter the old man's sexual innuendoes. But in the light of what happened afterward, a superstitious person might wonder. . . .

Assuming that the main entrance was reserved for formal social occasions, I went to the side door. I was expected; the guard passed me in and handed me over to his partner. As always, I was struck by the utter silence that prevailed. Already the house had the air of a museum; hushed, softly lighted, and almost empty of life. Even the servants remained invisible unless they were wanted.

As we reached the head of the great staircase and turned into the corridor that led to Nazarian's suite, I caught a glimpse of movement. Quick and oddly furtive, it was so out of keeping with the hushed atmosphere that it caught my attention; but when I stopped and turned my head, the person had darted out of sight. Probably one of the maids, I thought as I resumed walking; but the elongated form and awkward movements had reminded me of someone else.

Jerry was waiting outside Nazarian's room. I smiled at him and started to speak; he cut me off with a finger to his lips. "Sssh. We're sleeping."

"Oh. I'm sorry." He frowned and I lowered my voice to a whisper. "I'll come back another time."

The guard was already on his way to the stairs. I started to follow. Jerry's hand closed over my shoulder, bringing me to an abrupt halt and sending twinges of pain clear down my arm.

"No. You wait. Inside. Don't talk. Just wait till he wakes up."

I nodded dumbly—and then shook my head. That ought to cover all the contingencies; yes, I'll wait; no, I won't talk. Whatever Jerry wants, Jerry gets. I got the distinct impression that Jerry didn't like me. What did Dave have that I didn't have? Jerry had laughed at his corny badinage, but I didn't even rate a smile.

Holding me in a hard grip, he eased the door open. The nurse was waiting. She too put her finger to her lips.

"He dropped off a short time ago," she whispered. "But he will want to see you as soon as he wakes. Please sit there; it won't be long."

I took the chair she indicated, on the far side of the room and some distance from the bed. The curtains had been drawn around it, hiding the occupant from view; but I could hear him breathing in hoarse rattling gasps, and I marveled at the stubborn will that kept him alive when every physical function was dead or impaired.

Moving noiselessly on rubber-soled shoes, the nurse crossed the room and went through a door I hadn't noticed before. She left it open; I saw enough of the room beyond to realize it had been fitted out as a private surgery or small hospital. There was everything a patient might need except an operating table, and for all I knew, it might be there too, out of my range of vision. The spotless white enamel and tiled floor were an odd contrast to the luxuriousness of the bedroom. I had wondered why the old man had not been taken to a hospital. I ought to have known the answer; with his neurotic insistence on privacy and his boundless wealth, he had brought the hospital to him. The rows of bottles and jars on the shelves visible through the open door answered another question. There were probably enough drugs to make an addict happy for months. No problem finding sleeping pills in that house. . . .

The nurse came out, closing the door carefully behind her, and resumed her chair. Nazarian continued to snore. I turned my attention to my surroundings.

The chair in which I sat was a copy of one that had been found in an Egyptian tomb. (At least I assumed it was a copy; knowing Victor Nazarian's methods, I could only hope that the one in Cairo was the genuine article.) It was made out of highly polished cedar, with its arms and back heavily carved and covered with gold leaf. The tomb had belonged to Tutankhamon's grandparents, or maybe they were his great-grandparents, or maybe they weren't. It all depended on which scholarly theory you followed. Yuya, Master of the Horse to King Amenhotep III, had unquestionably been the parent of Amenhotep's chief queen; and her daughter, Princess Satamon, had presented the elaborate chair to Grandma and Grandpa.

It was surprisingly uncomfortable. I felt sure the princess had used cushions to protect her royal back and buttocks, but there were none on the copy, and the carvings dug into me when I relaxed. Bored and uncomfortable, I stood up, ignoring the nurse's frown, and looked around. The floors were bare or covered with light matting, but my sneakers made no sound.

Antiquities were everywhere—some under glass, some lying carelessly on tables and chests and windowsills, like ordinary ornaments. Mixed with them, in incongruous disarray, were more modern mementos, including a number of photographs. One was a studio portrait of Mrs. Dunlap. I had no difficulty in recognizing her sweet smile and wide eyes, though her hair was dark and the picture was obviously twenty years old. Another showed her and Paul in full wedding regalia; he looked gorgeous in tails, and the glow of happiness on her face made her almost beautiful. The dress was a knockout, even if it did overpower her with its billows of ivory satin and swaths of veiling. I smiled involuntarily at one enlarged snapshot, which showed a younger Nazarian with a very obese man whose rubicund face showed the signs of years of heavy drinking. Their arms were around one another's shoulders, and in their free hands they held glasses raised in a toast. Good old Sam, no doubt. Nazarian hadn't been bad-looking. There was a strong resemblance to his son, though his thinner, sharper features weren't nearly as attractive as Steve's.

An elderly couple attired in turn-of-the-century elegance had to be Nazarian's parents. The old man did look like a vulture; his wife's face was overshadowed by a huge hat piled high with ostrich feathers, bows, and puffs of veiling.

One photograph caught my attention because it was the only one of a child—dark-haired, approximately a year old, with the blank unfocused stare babies usually display to photographers.

There was no picture of Stephen Nazarian unless the child was he.

A change in the old man's breathing brought the nurse out of her chair and sent me back to mine. Jerry hastened to the bedside. Because of the bed curtains, I couldn't see what went on, and I was glad of it. The sounds I couldn't help hearing were both unpleasant and pathetic, and they reawakened the sympathy I sometimes felt for him. Why, I wondered, would anyone cling to life under such conditions?

Eventually the process ended. The old man had been free with breathless complaints and curses, and the nurse was visibly flushed when she came to the end of the bed and pulled the curtains back.

He'd wasted precious breath berating his attendants. Propped high against the pillows, he lay gasping, his eyes fixed on me. I knew better than to speak or move. Finally he raised a frail hand and beckoned.

Jerry moved another chair to a place near the bed, and I transferred myself to it. It was modern and overstuffed and much more comfortable, but I can't say I liked being so close to the old man. Despite the best efforts of his attendants, a faint unpleasant odor clung to the bed and its occupant.

Surprisingly light on his feet for such a big man, Jerry arranged more furniture—a table next to me, a silver tea set on the table, a lamp that shone directly on my face. I felt like a suspect about to be grilled.

"So," Nazarian said at last. "How long have you been here?"

"Only a few minutes."

"Then you heard. Nice, wasn't it? You see what you can look forward to."

"I may be lucky and die young," I said without thinking.

Jerry emitted a shocked, disapproving cough. The old man laughed. "Hear that, Jerry? Hear how she talks to me? Scandalous. The young have no respect these days."

He had revived amazingly; my half-joking disrespect did perk him up. The balance was delicate, though, and I regretted my thoughtless comment. "It was a stupid thing to say. What do I know? You seem to get some pleasure out of life, in spite of—I mean—"

"I know what you mean. Yes, I still enjoy life. Parts of it. Can't eat, can't drink, can't—" Another cough from Jerry stopped him, and he chuckled. "Can't even use vulgar language. It shocks Jerry. You wouldn't think, to look at him, that he was such a prissy old lady. Well, in a nutshell, I can't do much. Except . . ." The amusement faded from his face. He said with grim relish, "Power. That's the only thing that lasts, girl. Power over other people. I've still got that. I'll have it till I die. It's the only thing that makes life worth living in the long run."

"I don't believe that," I said.

"Didn't expect you would. What else is there? No, don't say it—I know what you're going to say. Love. Right?"

"Yes."

"Love," the old man repeated. The cynical contempt in his voice made it sound like an expletive. "Girl, that's the first thing that betrays you. Love is a trap. Love turns on you. . . ." He fell silent. I didn't argue. Even if I had seen any point in arguing, Jerry's inimical stare would have convinced me otherwise. Jerry definitely did not approve of me.

Finally the old man said, "What've you got there?"

I had forgotten the photo album. "Some pictures," I said. "I thought you might like to see them."

"Jerry, get the girl something to drink. Nothing alcoholic, mind. She's got a weakness, Jerry. Can't hold her liquor."

That kind of teasing didn't bother me. Smiling, I shook my head. "I've decided to go on the wagon. Could I have a cup of tea?"

The tea was steeping. Jerry poured and added hot water to the brew. His ham-sized hands and thick fingers moved delicately among the fragile procelain cups. I thanked him, but he only grunted in reply.

"You thought wrong about the pictures," Nazarian said. "I'm no sentimental old fool. I have no photographs of—of him."

"I noticed that."

"Burned 'em," Nazarian muttered. "Every single one. From the time he was a baby."

Then the baby picture wasn't of Stephen. Unless the old man was lying, to prove how tough he was. Oddly enough, I wasn't repelled by his statement. I could understand a frenzy of destruction caused by hurt and grief. But I had a feeling he might have regretted it afterward.

"Okay," I said. "I was wrong. You don't have to look at them."

"Damn right." After a moment he said grudgingly, "Might as well see them, since you brought them. Jerry."

Jerry adjusted the lamp, me, and his master. I ended up in a strained position, sitting sideways in the chair and looking at the pictures upside down.

I turned over the first few pages. "These are of people you don't know," I explained. "Before Mother entered the Institute. Here are the ones I was talking about."

His expression didn't alter, but when I would have turned the next page, his hand inched out to stop me. I'd have given a great deal to be able to read his mind. If he had been telling the truth, he had not seen so much as a snapshot of his son in almost twenty years. Without such reminders, one forgets. The most beloved features fade into a blur.

What an emotional experience it must be for him—and surely now, at the end of his life, the sight of that reckless young face must stir other emotions than anger. Regret for the senseless waste, possibly even a touch of remorse.

When he finally spoke it was not to me. "Get out, Jerry. You too, Miss What's-your-name."

After they had gone, Nazarian signaled me to turn the page. The shot of Dave playing satyr brought a sour half-smile to the withered lips and produced a muttered comment which I only half-heard. I didn't ask him to repeat it. His fingers crept, like a large brown spider, and touched one of the photos. It showed Mother with Steve Nazarian.

I really am a hopeless, sentimental idiot. Gently I suggested, "Would you like to have that one, and some of the others? I can get copies made—"

"Why the devil would I want copies?" Nazarian demanded. "To remind me of that crawling, treacherous little scum? You know what he did to me, don't you?"

"He died," I said with difficulty; my throat was tight with outrage.

"And left me without an heir. He didn't even have the decency to father a child before he blew himself to blazes over a cause as hopeless as it was moronic. The name ends with me, you know. The line ends with my daughter. That's the only immortality, the only real satisfaction I wanted—to hand on my wealth to a child with my blood in its veins. He deprived me of that. He did it deliberately, to hurt me, and I'll never—I'll never forgive—"

Alarm replaced my anger as his voice rose and his face writhed. "I'm sorry," I said. "I shouldn't have brought the pictures. Let me take—"

But his hand, abnormally strengthened by rage, held on to the book. "And Leah—your mother—she failed me, too. She could have saved him. He'd have given up his stupid cause if she had married him."

"You wanted them to marry?" I asked.

"Of course." The hot color in his cheeks faded. "Any girl would have done," he added callously. "Anyone young and healthy, who didn't have . . . But we didn't know about that then."

"What do you mean?"

He waved the question away. "I—liked—Leah." The word came with difficulty, like a sound foreign to his vocal cords. "She wasn't afraid of me either. Intelligent. Good genes."

"Maybe he didn't ask her to marry him."

"Oh, no, not the martyr. He didn't believe in marriage—in anything but the brotherhood of man. But she could have had him if she'd tried. Women know how."

"Come on," I said.

"Sure they do. That's how Katherine got that wimp she married. She chased him till she wore him out. I helped her; don't think much of him, but if that was what she wanted . . ."

I wasn't interested in his daughter. The enigmatic, unfinished statement had set my pulses racing. Didn't know what? About the dangers of Tay-Sachs—bad genes? Another statement had confirmed what I had suspected about Stephen Nazarian—that he wouldn't let a romantic attachment lure him from his chosen path.

Before I could frame my next question, Nazarian's hand slid from the page. His head fell back against the pillows.

"Shall I call Jerry?" I asked.

"No. No. Don't get much privacy around this place. Pour your own tea."

"I'm accustomed to waiting on myself," I said, stung. "That wasn't why I suggested calling him; I thought you were tired."

"No."

The remark about the tea hadn't been a polite invitation; it had been an order. Thinking he might want to compose himself without being observed, I got up from my chair and reached for the teapot. As I did so, I heard a whisper of paper as he turned the page. "That was the last of them," I said. "The rest are only—"

The sound went through me like a sword—a hideous, rattling croak. The teapot fell from my hand. It didn't break, but hot liquid spattered over the polished wood and stung the skin of my arm. I turned to the bed.

His mouth was wide open, a black square of emptiness. His face was purple, and the veins stood out like rope.

I screamed. Jerry came through the door like a charging bull. He pushed me aside; I would have fallen if I hadn't caught hold of the bedpost. The nurse was behind him. Their bodies hid the occupant of the bed as they bent over him.

I didn't have to be told to go. I ran—witless and panic-stricken as the murderer I felt myself to be.

I was sitting on the couch in my cottage with my head in my hands when someone knocked at the door. I didn't want to answer it. I was afraid of what the person on the other side of the door would tell me.

The knock came again, louder and more peremptory. Might as well know the worst, I thought drearily. I hadn't locked the door; the harbinger of evil tidings could, and probably would, walk right in if I didn't answer.

The sight of Paul Dunlap, looking even sadder than usual, confirmed my fears. He was holding the fatal photo album. Then he said, "My dear girl—" and the kindness in his voice did me in. I burst into a flood of tears.

We ended up sitting on the couch, with me bawling all over his beautiful gray suit and him patting me on the back. He kept repeating, "He's not dead, child; he may well recover from this stroke as he has from many others. It wasn't your fault. It could have happened anytime. . . ."

I went on crying. Partly because he was so kind, partly because I had so many stored-up tears to shed, over so many

different things. By the time I had rid myself of them, I was
a soggy, hiccuping mess; and after presenting me with a
hankie, Paul tactfully leafed through the books on the coffee
table while I put myself back together.

"This was your mother's, wasn't it?" he asked, opening
the worn copy of Gardiner's *Grammar*.

"Yes."

"There's a later edition, you know." As he must have
known, a safe, neutral subject distracted me and gave me a
chance to collect myself.

"I know. But this one was hers. It has all her notes and
comments—"

"She was a great note-taker," Paul said, smiling. "I
often teased her about it—she'd start writing the moment
she walked into the class and never stop till I quit talking."

"You were one of her teachers?"

"Oh, yes. They had me teaching history and beginning
Middle Egyptian back then. I was a very poor linguist," he
added, laughing a little. "It was all I could do to keep ahead
of some of my students, including Leah. Dave was the one
who really drove me up the wall. He was brilliant at
languages and would spend hours poring over Sethe and De
Buck so he could ask questions he knew I couldn't answer."

"You taught all of them, then. I guess I should have
known that."

"Yes, I did. Even your father." I started, but I don't think
he noticed, his eyes were fixed on the book. "He was only
in one of my classes, history of ancient Egypt. He wasn't
really interested in Egyptology; it was Leah who interested
him. They were all my students. You'll have to show me
those pictures sometime."

"Oh, damn," I said wretchedly. "Please, Mr. Dunlap—"
I thought of him as "Paul," but I had never addressed him
by his first name.

"Paul." He took my hand in his. "Stop berating
yourself, Haskell. I brought the album back because you

forgot it. No other reason. Jerry told me he was looking at it when he had the stroke, and I thought you might be blaming yourself."

"But I should have known! He said he had burned all the pictures of his son, that he wasn't interested in seeing snapshots of that—that crawling scum—"

Paul's handsome lips curled, but he only said, "He didn't mean it. I suspect it gave him genuine, if painful, pleasure to see them. Besides, it was his own choice. You didn't tie him to the bed and hold his eyelids open while you turned the pages."

"Well—no . . ."

"Case proved. Let's have no more self-dramatization." His smile removed any possible sting from the words. I smiled back at him. "You're very kind. And look what I've done to your nice suit."

The dark spots were conspicuous against the soft gray of his jacket. He said softly, "It will dry." He was still holding my hands.

He hadn't closed the door. We both heard the sound of footsteps, but Paul didn't let go of my hands. Carl came to a studden stop, staring. "Excuse me," he stuttered, and started to back away.

"Come in." Paul rose. "I must be getting back to the house. I hope you're feeling better, Haskell. Carl, I'll leave her with you; she's a little upset, so keep her company, will you?"

When he reached the door, Carl had to go in or out. He came in. I called, "Thank you so much, Paul," and Paul responded with a friendly wave.

"Maybe I should go too," Carl said.

"Please stay, if you've nothing better to do. You heard what happened?"

"Uh-huh. Word gets around fast when it concerns the emperor." Carl's hands had been behind his back throughout; now they came into view. He was holding two cans. "I thought maybe you'd like a beer."

I had to laugh. "Oh, Carl! As a matter of fact, there's nothing I'd like better. If you offered me a cup of tea, I'd probably break down and bawl."

"What have you got against tea?"

I explained. He had heard—from his little friend Maria?—about Nazarian's stroke and the fact that I had been with him when it happened; but he didn't know the details, and he was so intrigued by my story he forgot to drink his beer.

"You aren't blaming yourself, are you?"

The euphoria of Paul's comfort had worn off, and the beer had not replaced it. I said wretchedly, "I don't know, Carl. He was awfully angry. Not at me, at Stephen—and at Mother. But then he seemed to calm down—"

"It's a wonder his hate hasn't choked him long before this," Carl muttered. "Imagine harboring a grudge like that for twenty years—and the poor devil dust and ashes all that time. Why was he mad at your mother?"

"Oh, he wanted Steve to marry her and settle down. It wasn't too flattering to Mother, actually; he as much as said any healthy young female would have done. What he really wanted was a grandchild."

"Grand*son*," Carl corrected with a sneer. "So that the dynasty could continue."

"I couldn't help feeling sorry for him, though. That's not such an unreasonable thing to expect from life."

"I guess not." Carl smiled reluctantly. "My own mother has mentioned the subject from time to time. . . . Color me calloused, but I can't bleed for Nazarian. Even if it was his not-so-fond memories that choked him, you aren't to blame. The world is better off without him."

"That's terrible."

"I know. Oh, come on, Haskell, don't cry. He isn't worth

it. I know what you need—food and drink. Let's go out and grab a pizza. If you don't mind driving, that is."

"I don't mind. But I don't feel like going out. Why don't I whip up a little gourmet dinner?"

Carl's face brightened. "What've you got?"

"Well . . . Tuna fish and eggs are about it, I'm afraid. I make a pretty mean omelet."

"Got any tomatoes? Bacon? Cheese, onions?" I kept shaking my head. Carl clucked disapprovingly. "What good is an omelet without tomatoes, bacon, cheese, and onions? I happen to have all four. Suppose I get them and the rest of the six-pack, and you can cook."

He helped me chop the vegetables and grate the cheese, and then retired to the couch; there really wasn't room in the kitchen for two people. Like Paul, his attention was caught by the books.

"Hey, you know there's a newer edition of Gardiner?"

"Yes, I know!"

"Oh." Carl had found Mother's name on the flyleaf. "Good notes," he said after a while. "Yours?"

"No. Hers."

There were a number of papers tucked into the book, copies of hieroglyphic texts that had been assigned for translation. Some she had copied herself, leaving spaces under each line of text for the transliteration and the translation. Studying them, Carl produced another compliment. "She had a nice hieroglyphic hand."

"You don't have to pour on the flattery," I said.

"No, I mean it. This is a rather unusual reading of Spell 146."

"What?"

"Coffin texts."

I wandered into the room to see what he was talking about. "I wouldn't know. I never got that far."

"Hmph." Carl brooded over the paper. "She's noted a

couple of parallels. . . . I don't suppose you happen to have a copy of the *Wörterbuch* handy?"

I burst out laughing. "Sure, I always carry all five volumes around with me. In fact, I have several copies, at a mere thousand bucks a shot—"

My feeble attempt at wit passed unnoticed. Carl reached for a pen and notebook. "Mind if I copy these references?" I don't know why he asked; he was already doing it. "I can check 'em out tomorrow, if Paul will condescend to let me into the sanctum sanctorum."

"The what?"

"The library. I guess you didn't see it."

"There were a lot of books in his office."

"Just the tip of the iceberg. There is a separate library, and a damned good one. It adjoins Paul's office. We have access to it anytime; all we have to do is deposit a couple of quarts of blood and sign a document leaving our unborn children to the museum."

I snatched Gardiner out of his hands and laid the book aside. "The omelet should be ready. Maybe it will improve your disposition; I'm tired of sarcastic remarks about Paul Dunlap."

I stormed into the kitchen without waiting for his reply. As I slapped the omelet onto plates I heard him say, "I might have known you'd succumb to the famous charm. It gets 'em all."

"He's been very nice to me."

"I noticed that."

I advanced on him, balancing the plates. Carl cringed against the cushions, raising his hands defensively. "Don't. It would be a waste of a good omelet. I'm sorry, okay?"

"You have a filthy mouth and an even filthier mind. How anyone could possibly suppose—"

"Okay, okay, I said I was sorry." He got the plates away from me and onto the table without incident.

I sat down, glowering. "He came here to reassure me. It

was a kind, sensitive, caring gesture. And, believe me, I needed reassuring."

Carl's head was bent over his plate, and he was shoveling in food as if he were being paid by the mouthful. He glanced up at me over his glasses and under the lock of hair that had tumbled across his forehead. "I took your mind off it, though, didn't I?"

"I'd like to believe that was your sole reason for being bitchy." But my tone was milder; he looked rather sweet, squinting nearsightedly through the slit between his glasses and his hair.

"It was. It really was. I love Paul Dunlap like a brother. Or a son."

"You've got egg in your mustache," I said.

Carl's eyes narrowed. "That gives me a great idea—"

I couldn't help laughing, but I avoided his outstretched arm. "Some other time, perhaps. I'm not exactly in the mood."

"This has hit you hard, hasn't it?"

"For God's sake, Carl, I was right there when it happened. It was absolutely horrible, and I may have done something, said something . . ."

"That's foolish," Carl said gently.

"I know." I glanced at the telephone. "Someone would call, wouldn't they, if . . ."

"I don't know. Why don't you call?"

"I'm afraid to."

"Better to know, one way or the other, than sit here getting yourself in a frazzle." He reached for the phone.

I wasn't sure I agreed with his philosophy, but it cast an interesting light on his character. I listened, hands clenched, while he carried on a brief conversation Then he turned to me, smiling broadly.

"He's better."

"You're kidding."

"Honest Injun. Still on the critical list, but it looks as if the old bastard may beat the odds again."

"I'm so glad!"

"I'm glad you're glad," Carl said. "Otherwise, frankly, my dear, I don't give a damn." He got to his feet. "Since you refuse to kiss the egg off my mustache, I may as well go home. Why don't you take tomorrow off? You look beat."

"No, I'd rather . . . Oh, Lord. So much happened today, I forgot to ask you. I promised my grandmother I'd take her shopping tomorrow. I mean, I didn't exactly promise, she just assumed I would, and since she doesn't have a telephone—"

"You're babbling," Carl said with a grin. "Start again and take it slow."

I told him about Gran. I didn't mean to be funny, but Carl howled with laughter. He especially enjoyed Aunt Ella and her hidden bottle. "By all means go and do your duty," he said, chuckling. "I'm sure it will be okay with Dave."

"Thanks, Carl. I don't want to go, but I'm stuck."

"Yeah, I see that. The old lady has quite a technique. I'd like to meet her sometime."

"No, you wouldn't," I said.

After he left, I realized I had carried on the same dialogue with Jon. Quite a coincidence. Or maybe it wasn't. . . .

9

Despite my improved status, I had not been given keys to the museum. I had to ring for entrance; the following morning I rang three times before Carl finally appeared.

As soon as he opened the door, I heard voices raised in a heated argument. One was Dave's; that baritone bellow was unmistakable. Running through it like a duet was another voice, shrill with fury.

"What on earth—" I began.

Carl was grinning, but anxiety shadowed his eyes. Before he could reply, the argument ended in a piercing scream of rage, operatic in its intensity, and Margaret Maxwell darted out of Dave's office. She rushed down the hall like a steamroller; if Carl hadn't pulled me aside, I think she might have run right over us. She was not so blind with anger that she failed to notice me, though. She kept staring at me while she wrestled with the door and gave me a final, concentrated glare before she ran out.

Dave was the next to appear. Framed in the open office

doorway, he raised clenched fists and shook them at Carl. "What the hell is the idea of letting that demented female in here?"

"I didn't," Carl said. "I swear, Dave—"

Dave slammed his fist into the wall. "So help me God, one of these days . . ." He broke off, his eyes widening, and began wringing his bruised fingers. "Damn. That hurt."

"He's broken his hand twice since I've known him," Carl explained, relaxing. He knew the worst was over.

The furious crimson in Dave's cheeks faded, and he said plaintively, "If people didn't make me mad, I wouldn't hit things. I told you never to let that woman in my office."

"I don't know how she got in," Carl insisted. "It wasn't through the back door; I guess she must have come down from the museum. You know her, Dave, she's all over the place—scuttles from corner to corner like a rat and pops out of holes when you aren't looking."

"Uh." Dave sucked his knuckles. "Yeah, I know. She's got Katherine buffaloed. And Paul's too damned polite to kick her out. Shit."

He went back into his office. Carl grinned at me. "Nothing as touching as two old friends getting together."

"What's she mad about?" I asked, following him toward Dave's office.

"Everything," Dave shouted.

"Want some coffee?" Carl asked, pausing in the doorway.

"If you haven't got anything stronger."

"I'll get it," I offered.

Carl trailed after me, ready as always for a chat. While I started the coffee maker and looked for a cup, he explained. "Meg is furious because she wasn't named as one of the trustees. She hangs around flattering Paul and making helpful suggestions to Dave."

I watched the thin brown stream pour down into the pot. "Why should she have been made a trustee?"

"She shouldn't have been. I told you, she has an exaggerated opinion of her abilities. Besides, the old man can't stand her."

"But I thought . . . She implied that they had been on close terms for years."

Arms folded, Carl leaned against the wall and let the gossip flow. "They've known each other for years, but he doesn't think much of her. He doesn't approve of women in academic positions anyway, and Meg isn't his type."

"Where the hell is that coffee?" Dave roared from across the hall.

"Coming." I filled a cup, added milk and sugar. "She isn't Dave's type either?" I asked, lowering my voice.

"Meg isn't anybody's type."

Mutual antipathy, a basic conflict of personality? From what I had seen of Maxwell, she would rub a saint the wrong way. And Dave was no saint. But I wondered if there was another reason, a more specific reason, for her antagonism and his dislike.

Dave was in no mood to answer questions. Even Carl refrained from his usual jokes; neither of us mentioned Margaret Maxwell.

I asked about Mr. Nazarian and was told that he continued to improve. According to Dave, the old man was even then closeted with his lawyers, and although his speech was so distorted as to be almost unintelligible, none of us doubted that he was making his views known.

Hardly daring to believe it, I argued, "He must be in pretty bad shape if he's talking to a lawyer."

"That's a terrible thing to say about a worthy profession," said Carl with a meaningful look.

"Victor changes his will, or threatens to, about once a month," Dave said. "It's an empty threat; Katherine is his only heir, and he'd never cut her out, so the only people who stand to gain or lose are the members of various charitable organizations."

"It's Paul whose nerves he wants to frazzle," Carl said. "Face it, Dave, the only reason Paul is one of the trustees is because Nazarian insisted. If he withdrew his support, Paul would be out."

"Surely he wouldn't do that," I exclaimed.

"He might," Dave said thoughtfully. "He's not one of Paul's biggest fans. He's always blamed Paul for the fact that he doesn't have grandchildren."

"That's so unfair."

"Not as unfair as blaming the woman," Carl said.

"I'm ashamed of you two," Dave declared. "Gossiping like a pair of old ladies."

"Well, you were—" Carl began.

"Speaking of old ladies," I said.

Dave grumbled when I asked if I could take the afternoon off, but it was only one of his token grumbles. I was in fairly good spirits when I left. Nazarian was bound to die, sooner rather than later; but if he held on for a few more weeks, I could tell myself I wasn't responsible.

My cheerful mood evaporated when I pulled up in front of the house on Kenilworth Avenue and saw Jon's car already there. Few men would give up the charms of tennis courts, swimming pools, and hot and cold running servants, not to mention Miriam, for an afternoon with two old ladies, much less be early. But Jon had a soft spot for old ladies, also for little boys with freckles and missing front teeth, little girls with pigtails and dimples, fuzzy pussycats, and awkward puppies. He was too bloody sweet for words.

Gran's face was pink with excitement under the black bonnet when she opened the door. "Such a nice young man," she whispered. "Ella didn't want to let him in at first—you know what a scaredy-cat she is—but he looked so respectable, and he gave us a business card, and explained he was your young man—"

I doubted that Jon had used that expression. I also doubted that Ella had balked at admitting him. Not Ella, bored to her back teeth and as naïve as Gran about the wicked world. They locked the place up like a fortress and professed great fear of crime, but any smooth-talking stranger could probably get in.

Jon was sitting at the kitchen table, in his shirt sleeves, his coat hung over the back of the chair and a napkin tucked into his collar. He was eating cherry pie, and as I entered the room, he said to Aunt Ella, who sat across from him, "This is the best pie I've ever eaten, Mrs. Schafer. You certainly have a wonderful hand with pastry. If you ever decide to go into business, let me know; I'll draw up the papers for you, and invest in the firm."

Ella beamed. "Eat, eat," she urged. "There's plenty more."

"Hello, Aunt Ella," I said. "Hello, Jon. Doggoned if you aren't early."

"I felt sure I could talk these ladies into some food," Jon explained winsomely. "I've heard you brag about what wonderful cooks they are."

He hadn't heard me brag about what wonderful cooks they were. All I had done was complain about them. As penance, I ate a piece of pie too. Some penance.

Jon turned down a second piece. Patting his flat stomach, he declared he was stuffed. Aunt Ella said maybe he'd fancy some more when they got back or else she'd wrap up a slice for him to take home. I could see Jon sauntering into the fancy house in Winnetka carrying a paper plate covered with plastic wrap and oozing sticky juice. He was just the man to do it.

After a lot of fussing with pocketbooks and bonnets, the two ladies declared they were ready to go, and Jon declared he would drive. While Gran locked the house, Jon opened the trunk of his car and displayed two suitcases. "You thought I was kidding, didn't you?"

Ella had followed us, so I couldn't express myself candidly. "I do appreciate your bringing them," I said.

He transferred the suitcases to my trunk. Gran and Ella got into an argument as to who was going to sit where; Jon settled it with the same mixture of charm and logic he would have used with two quarreling children. "You sit up in front with me, Mrs. Emig, so you can give me directions. Mrs. Schafer can sit with me on the way back."

I didn't think we were ever going to reach the grocery store. Gran didn't know her left from her right and Aunt Ella kept contradicting her. We finally pulled into the parking lot, and then Gran announced she had forgotten her shopping list.

"I know I put it in my pocketbook," she muttered, rummaging in the black depths.

"I'll bet you left it on the kitchen table," piped Aunt Ella. "You always do that. I told you I should keep it, but no, you wouldn't listen—"

"You're the one that leaves it on the table all the time," said Gran, continuing to rummage.

I gently suggested that perhaps for once they could do without a shopping list. They both reacted as if I had proposed that they leave the house without their clothes. Jon said we'd drive back and get the shopping list.

"It's quite all right, Mrs. Emig. It isn't far, and I think I know the way now."

I knew perfectly well this was just another device of the old ladies to keep us longer. It would have been cute if it hadn't been so maddening. I would miss a whole afternoon of work, I wouldn't know how Mr. Nazarian was getting on, and I especially didn't want to spend hours watching Jon be saintly to two dotty old ladies. It had a demoralizing effect on me.

We stopped in front of the house. Jon got out and opened the door for Gran. "We'll wait in the car," said Aunt Ella, clutching me in case I had any inclinations toward escape.

I didn't. The fewer people inside, the less time the business would take. Jon took Gran's arm and matched his long stride to her mincing steps. They looked just adorable, the sweet little old lady and the tall, attentive young man.

Aunt Ella had been dying to get me alone. Her bonnet bobbed energetically as she turned to face me. "He's Jewish, isn't he?" she hissed.

"Yes," I said shortly.

"Well, I guess it doesn't matter," said Aunt Ella. "He's certainly charmed your grandma. It wouldn't of worked on your granddad, though."

"That," I said, "would have been too damned—darned—bad."

"He didn't approve of anybody," Aunt Ella mused. "Jewish, Catholics, Lutherans. There was a Methodist once, came courting your mama. Poor boy, how your granddad did rave at him."

"I can't imagine anyone having the nerve to court Mother—or Jessie," I said.

"Jessie wasn't popular with the boys. Your mama, now, she had them hanging around all the time, but none of the others had the nerve to come to the house. Your granddad had a husband in mind for her, a friend of his from downstate. . . ."

This was a new light on my mother's past, but I paid less attention than I might have because I was so exasperated with the tedious slowness of Gran's progress. I'd seen her bounce up and down those porch stairs several times, but with an attentive young man to lean on, she tottered and wobbled. Finally she got the door open and they vanished inside.

"He was a widower," Aunt Ella went on, "and twenty years older than Leah if he was a day, but he was a member of the church, and that's what counted with your grand-dad."

It was no wonder my mother had run away from home. I

was about to say so when Gran came flying out of the house as if she had been shot from a cannon. She rocked to a stop on the porch and stood there wringing her hands and emitting steady shrill shrieks like a mechanical alarm.

I flung off Aunt Ella's clutching hand and ran up the walk. I didn't stop to ask Gran what was wrong. The front door stood wide open; from inside the house I heard sounds of a struggle. It ended abruptly and ominously, with a thud and a crash of glassware.

Gran clutched at me as I tried to pass her. "Don't go in there, don't go in—help, help!"

Her grasp had the frenzied strength of panic. It took me several vital seconds to detach her fingers without hurting her, and all the while she kept shrieking for help. By the time I reached the kitchen, it was too late. Jon lay face down amid a ruination of broken dishes; the kitchen table had been overturned and the back door was standing open. As I dropped to my knees beside Jon, I heard a car up in the alley behind the house. The tires shrieked as it took off.

Kneeling had not been a conscious decision; my legs gave way and I didn't even feel the sharp edges of china cut into my skin. He stirred and groaned when I touched him, and the relief that washed over me was so all-pervasive it even affected my voice. "Don't move," I squawked in a shaky falsetto.

"It's all right." He rolled over and sat up. His face was bleeding in half a dozen places, but after a horrified gasp I realized the cuts were shallow, probably from the shards of pottery. His hand went wincingly to his jaw. "Damn," he muttered. "I suppose he got away."

"He's long gone." I put my arms around him. "And you aren't going anywhere, except to a doctor."

"I don't need a doctor." His head was heavy against my breast, but somehow or other his hands had moved, holding me, and I wasn't sure who was supporting whom.

"If you don't need a doctor, why don't you stand up?" I asked weakly.

"I like it here."

At that inauspicious moment the old ladies turned up in the doorway, screaming in unison like the chorus of an avant-garde modern opera. I think I would have maintained my cool had it not been for one small incident. Gran and Aunt Ella both disappeared for a few minutes; when they returned, each carried a bottle of wine. Gran's was Manischewitz Grape. The sight of their faces, openmouthed with mutual indignation, was too much for me. I broke into hysterical giggles and didn't stop until Jon, yielding to understandable exasperation, slapped me on the cheek.

After we had called the police we all had a glass of wine, except poor Jon, who needed it most. He said he was afraid to drink alcohol after a possible head injury, but I think it was the labels on the bottles that put him off. In fact, his injuries weren't severe. The cuts were shallow and the worst damage wouldn't be visible to the naked eye until later—bruises on his body, when he had grappled with the burglar, and a reddening spot on his jaw, from the blow that had laid him out. "A nice neat uppercut," according to Jon. Trust him to give credit where credit was due, even to a burglar.

On the whole, Gran and Aunt Ella rather enjoyed the excitement. Nothing had been taken, and except for a few broken dishes, there was no damage; the intruder hadn't been there long when we came back.

The police officer was severe with the old ladies. "People like you are perfect robbery victims, keeping to a strict schedule the way you do. Looks like everybody in the neighborhood knows you always go shopping on Wednesday afternoon. Hadn't been for you forgetting your shopping list and coming back early, he'd have finished his job and been out of here. And where was the dog while this fellow was breaking in the back door?"

"We always put him in the basement when we're gone," Aunt Ella explained.

The officer gave the beagle, panting and drooling in Ella's arms, a disparaging glance. "Wouldn't have been much use anyway. Well, ladies, I'll report this."

"You'll let us know when you catch him, won't you?" Gran asked innocently.

"Why, you bet, ma'am. But without any better description than this gentleman can give us—"

Jon grimaced. "All I can tell you is that he was big—taller and considerably heavier than I am. But even that may be colored by personal prejudice. I think his hair was dark, but I can't be sure; those handy stocking masks conceal features, hair, even ears."

The officer closed his notebook. Aunt Ella demanded, "Aren't you going to dust for prints?"

Obviously one old lady watched something other than evangelists on TV. The policeman grinned. "According to this gentleman, he was wearing gloves."

The ladies followed him to the door, twittering; he made the standard reassuring remarks about keeping the house under observation. I looked at Jon. "Are you sure you're all right? Maybe you shouldn't be driving. Why don't you let me—"

"I'm perfectly capable of driving," Jon said irritably. "Don't nag, Haskell. I hate it when people fuss at me."

I smiled at him. "So do I."

"Hmmm," said Jon.

The old ladies wanted to sit down and discuss the whole exciting adventure over cherry pie and milk, but I put an end to that idea; Jon seemed to be functioning properly, but he'd had a nasty experience and the sooner he was back in Winnetka, the better. Gran then pointed out that the grocery shopping was yet to be done. I squelched that subtle suggestion too, before Jon could nobly offer to try again.

Aunt Ella supported me. "We'll just call a taxicab, like we usually do. That poor boy ought to be home in his bed."

Jon left first; I was about to follow him when Gran came trotting down the walk, carrying a parcel. "You almost forgot this, Haskell."

It was the "important thing" she had promised—half a fried chicken, a loaf of homemade bread, an apple pie, and six pink pickled eggs.

The traffic was horrendous, and by the time I reached the gates, twilight was well advanced—but not in the garage area, which was lit up like a stage set under lights. There were several unfamiliar cars; I couldn't have pulled into the garage even if I hadn't known better than to try. When I went to open my trunk, the guard on duty joined me. His manner was casual, but his hand hovered near his belt.

"I'll take those suitcases for you, miss," he said.

One of the suitcases felt as if it were filled with bricks— probably the books I had requested. I took the shopping bag, with Gran's "important things." "I can handle this one."

The guard took it from me, politely but firmly. "No need for you to carry anything, miss."

He meant to search the bags, of course. I should have known; I guess I am a slow learner. "Don't take long," I said. "I want to unpack."

"It will be a few minutes, miss." He didn't blink. "I'll have to wait till someone relieves me. We're a little upset tonight."

The meaning of the strange cars and the unusual number of lights in the house suddenly dawned. "Is he—is Mr. Nazarian—"

"Taken a turn for the worse, they say."

"Oh, God. Is there anything I can do?"

"No, miss. I'll let Mrs. Dunlap know you're back. She

was asking for you—concerned about you being out after dark.''

His hard features weren't capable of displaying much emotion, but his voice softened when he spoke her name.

For what seemed like hours, I paced the floor waiting for the phone to ring. Surely someone would let me know. No one called and no one came. I told myself they had other things to think about, but my anxiety increased. I unpacked the suitcases, put the clothes away, stacked books on the table. I left Gran's "care package" on the kitchen counter, thinking I ought to eat something; but my stomach turned at the sight of the food. I kept trotting to the door and looking out. There were no lights or other signs of life at Carl's cottage. He must have gone out to supper. Once I ventured as far as the garage. One of the strange cars had gone; the other was still there. Doctor or lawyer?

When the news finally came it was from a completely unexpected source. I flew to answer the knock, expecting Paul or Carl. It was neither. It was Jerry. The look on his face told me all I needed to know. He was crying, as openly and unrestrainedly as a child. His cheeks glistened in the light. But there was another expression on his face besides grief—an expression that made me want to retreat and slam the door.

I said, "Is he . . ."

Jerry swabbed his wet face with his sleeve. "He said I should give you this. After he was . . . Here."

He thrust a small packet into my hands.

His unconcealed grief roused such pity I forgot to be afraid of him. There couldn't be many people, even in that house, who would mourn for the old man.

"Jerry, I'm so sorry—"

His lips drew back. "You aren't sorry. You didn't like him. You made him sick."

He loomed over me like a mountain. I stepped back. "No, Jerry, that isn't true. He was already sick."

The hands he had raised fell to his sides and the anger faded from his face, leaving it empty of everything except pain. "He said I should give it to you. After he . . ."

The long vowel trailed off into a desolate keening sound. I slammed the door; even through the closed panel I heard the sounds of his blundering retreat and his high, shrill crying.

My hands shook so that I could hardly turn the key in the lock. Not until after his wail of woe had faded into silence did I remember the package.

It was enclosed in a manila envelope folded over twice and tied with dirty string. The envelope itself was worn and tattered. There was no writing on it.

Inside were half a dozen brittle, faded snapshots. Pictures of an infant, dark-haired and toothless, like most babies. I knew them, though. They were pictures of me.

I had to look in the album to make sure, even though common sense told me these could not be the same photographs. They were copies of mine.

My brain had gone into slow motion. I looked from the pictures in the album to the pictures in my hand, not once but half a dozen times before the truth dawned. The second set of photos was the one my mother had taken with her to Chicago. She had shown them to her parents and to her friends at the Institute. They had ended up here. For twenty years they had been in Nazarian's possession. The implications were almost too much for me to absorb, but something stood out, bright as neon, loud as a shout. It must have been from this house that my mother had set out on her last journey.

Nazarian was dead, and one of his final acts had been to take the photos from their hiding place and give them to his trusted servant. It was like the old man to hedge his bets. He may have hoped for another of those miraculous recoveries, in which case he could have retrieved the photos. They were not to come to me until he was gone. Jerry was the one person he could trust to carry out instructions without questions or delay or equivocation.

I should have felt guilty. Maybe I had shed all my tears the night before. Maybe I had come to a more sensible and cynical appraisal of my role in Nazarian's death. There was no doubt in my mind about what had caused the fatal stroke. Not the angry memories of his son, revived by the snapshots, but my own baby pictures. Unquestionably of me, not only because they were in the same album but because Mother had labeled them.

Only one thing could explain the enormity of the shock he had received. He had not known the identity of the infant whose photos he had found among his son's possessions after Stephen was killed. They must have represented the ultimate frustration—evidence that perhaps after all Stephen had given him the grandchild he wanted. But the evidence wasn't conclusive and there was not the slightest clue as to the child's whereabouts or maternal parentage. Steve had known many women. Anonymous in unisex wrapper and diapers, the baby might have been male or female. Though I felt certain that it was Nazarian who had directed that my cottage be searched, the object of the search had probably been general rather than specific. Find out if this woman is who she claims to be; make sure she's not a reporter from some scandal sheet or a hired gun. . . . A ludicrous suspicion, but perfectly in keeping with Victor Nazarian's outlook on life. The photo album wouldn't have meant anything to the searcher, except in so far as it confirmed my claim to be Leah Maloney's daughter.

Carl turned up a little later, banging on the door and announcing himself in stentorian tones. I tucked the snapshots in a drawer before I went to the door.

He looked past me, to see if anyone else was there, before he came in. "You heard?" he asked.

"Yes."

"Paul?"

"No," I said. "Jerry."

"Jerry?" He looked a little surprised, but mercifully didn't pursue the matter. "Poor devil, he's probably hit harder than anyone. But he'll be all right; Mrs. Dunlap will look after him."

"Oh, sure. Dear Mrs. Dunlap."

"She's been very kind—"

"It's easy to be Lady Bountiful when all it takes is a smile and an order delegating the dirty work to servants," I began. "Oh, hell; that was a stinking thing to say. I take it back. I'm not myself."

"You seem very much yourself," said Carl with a trace of sarcasm. "I thought you'd be bathed in tears. You sure you wouldn't like to collapse into my arms and weep on my shoulder?"

"I'm sure."

"How about holding me in your arms while I weep on your shoulder?"

"What about?"

"Hunger," said Carl, wandering purposefully toward the kitchen. "My cupboard is bare."

"I thought you were out to supper."

"Ah, so my absence was noted. That's consoling. I was working late. What's this? Your supper? You ought to eat something."

"I'm not hungry."

Carl got out plates and began piling the food on them. "Looks like Grannie's contribution. Mind if I—"

"Help yourself."

I knew he was trying to distract me. Part of me wanted him to go away and leave me alone to absorb the startling revelations. But another part wanted companionship, easy talk, jokes. When he carried the food to the table and made coffee, I ate with him. He loved the pink eggs and devoured four of them.

Only when the inner man was replete did he turn his attention to the books and papers I had stacked on the table. "Aha," he said, pleased. "More of your mother's? I didn't see these last night."

"I only got them today. My aunt sent them."

"Hmph." Carl was absorbed in a copy of *Kingship and the Gods*. "I am sorry to observe," he observed, without looking up, "that your mom was one of those people who scribble in books. Talk about copious commentaries. . . ."

"Paul said he used to kid her about her compulsive notetaking."

"These aren't notes; they are critiques. Interesting . . ."

I didn't answer. I wished he would go away. My need for companionship was swamped in a sudden, overpowering fatigue. The implications of what I had discovered that evening had not fully sunk in. But the basic facts were clear; the answers I had sought for so long were now in my possession. Stephen Nazarian had been my father. My father . . . The words were just words; they didn't mean anything.

Carl tossed Frankfort et al. aside and picked up one of the thin notebooks encased in blue paper that were used for exams. He frowned.

"Would you like some dessert?" I asked politely.

"I already had some." Carl turned a page.

"More dessert?"

"No, thanks. Just coffee."

He spoke as he might have spoken to a waitress in a restaurant. Breathing silent curses, I heaved my weary body out of my chair and went to put the kettle on. When I returned with the coffee, Carl was still scowling; but now he was deep in a paper whose sheets were held together with a rusted paper clip.

"You're off duty," I said. "You don't have to grade the damned thing."

"Huh?" He looked up, blinking. "She was good, you know."

"I know. Here's your coffee."

"Thanks." Carl put the paper aside. "What was her field?"

I shrugged. "Egyptology."

"Her specialty. Archaeology, history, philology, art history . . ."

"I have no idea."

"She was working on her doctorate, wasn't she? What was her dissertation topic?"

I shrugged again. Carl looked disgusted. "Her master's thesis?"

I knew the answer to that one. I recited, "'The development of the queens' titulary and its significance with regard to inheritance.' I don't know why academic dissertations have to have such dull, pompous titles."

"What would you have called it? 'Sex and perversion among the pharaohs'?"

"Why not? I have a copy, if you're interested. Jessie didn't send it, but I can ask her for it."

"There's probably a copy on file at the Institute."

"Oh, yes." I yawned.

"Am I boring you?" Carl asked politely.

"I'm sorry, Carl. It isn't the company. I'm absolutely bushed."

"I guess it has been a hard day for you."

He didn't know the half of it. I nodded and yawned again, and Carl stood up. "Mind if I take a couple of these with me?" he asked, indicating the blue books.

Surprise almost shook me out of my lethargy—almost, but not quite. "Be my guest," I said. "I don't know why Jessie sent them, actually; I asked for Mother's class notes and I guess she wasn't sure what I meant."

Carl was also gracious enough to accept a slab of apple pie. "Physical as well as mental sustenance," he remarked poetically. "I am forever in your debt, madam. How about if I start paying you back right now?"

His lips were cool and firm and very skillful. When I pulled away from him I saw he was still balancing the blue books and the wrapped piece of pie. He'd done very well with only one arm. . . . Why hadn't I responded? The time and the place were inappropriate, but it was more than that. Not distaste or dislike; I liked him and I liked having him kiss me. Rather, it was something missing. Maybe it was me. Maybe all my normal instincts were frozen.

His reaction only increased my fondness for him. Instead of persisting, or looking hurt, he smiled. "Wrong time, wrong place?"

"I guess so."

"Okay. Sleep well, my dear, and dream of me."

I made myself take the dirty dishes to the kitchen, but I didn't have the strength to rinse them. I didn't brush my teeth or wash my face, I just got into my pajamas and into bed; and I fell asleep while sorting through terms for homicide. If killing your father is patricide, and killing your mother is matricide, what was the word for doing in your grandfather?

I dreamed, but not about Carl. It started out the same way—my mother walking slowly away from me, ignoring my calls. I knew she couldn't have heard me this time, my voice was as thin and frail as a bird's. Then it happened. The retreating figure stopped. Slowly it turned, and I saw the face. It wasn't the young girl's face I knew from the photographs. It was hers, unmistakably hers, but it was the face of a middle-aged woman, lined and grim, framed in graying hair.

I would like to think she was trying to warn me. But most likely it wasn't the shock of her altered face that woke me; it was the shouting and pounding from outside the cottage.

I came awake choking and coughing; I couldn't draw a deep breath. Even before I forced my heavy lids open, I could see light; it beat against my eyelids. The room was like my grandfather's notion of hell, bright red from the flames that had engulfed the entire kitchen area. The old dried wood of the framing and counters and floors burned like tinder, but there was plenty of smoke, enough to sting my eyes and fog my brain. Someone was banging at the door and yelling, but I was hardly aware of that; I only knew I had to get out.

All the warnings, like those jolly little cards in hotel rooms, tell you to keep low when there's a fire. The air is better close to the floor. I rolled off the bed and began to crawl. Halfway to the door I knew I wasn't going to make it. I went on crawling anyway. The key was in the lock. I could see it clearly, despite the smoke; the flames made the room bright as day, and I felt the heat on my back as I pulled myself up, palms pressing against the splintered wood of the door.

I turned the key. At least I thought I did—but the door wouldn't open. I was pretty groggy by that time. I don't remember what I did next. I ended up flat on the floor with my lips pressed to the narrow crack under the door. It was old and warped, enough fresh air came through to give me a deadly sort of second wind. I couldn't hear anything but the sound of burning. It is a strange sound, a mingled roar and crackle; it drowned out the crash of breaking glass. I didn't know he was there until he stepped on my hand.

He dragged me toward the fire, and I fought feebly to break free. The flames reached out like hungry red tongues. One of them licked my leg as I was lifted and pushed across a jagged surface. I fell, but I never hit the ground.

d

10

Hell is for all eternity, and that hellish interlude seemed to endure forever; but the whole thing couldn't have lasted more than a couple of minutes, from the moment of my awakening till I came back to consciousness and found myself outside. The ground on which I lay was as cold and clammy as a grave and someone's lips covered mine, pumping air into my straining lungs. His face was only a blur. I didn't recognize him until he rolled off me—and then only with shock and disbelief. One side of his face was black with smoke, as was his hair. Singed wisps stuck out forlornly, and half his beautiful mustache was gone. His feet were bare and so was his torso; the tattered remnants of his pants stank of burned cloth. His back against the wall, knees drawn up and arms hanging limp, he replied to my horrified stare with a feeble attempt at a smile.

I could see quite clearly. The cottage was engulfed in flames that cast a ghastly, vivid light. Silhouetted against the fire like demonic attendants were the dark forms of several men. One held a hose, which he was playing, not on the burning house but on the one next to it, wetting down the walls and extinguishing sparks. The others didn't seem to be doing much of anything. There wasn't much they could do, I suppose, but their negligent attitudes annoyed me, especially when I turned my attention back to my heroic rescuer and realized that the dark stains on his chest weren't smoke.

"My God," I croaked.

Carl coughed. "You mean I look worse than you do? I don't . . . believe it." He toppled over sideways and lay still.

His burns weren't as bad as they looked; he had passed out from shock and loss of blood. His bare arms and shoulders and the skin on the front of his body had been slashed in a dozen places when he crawled in through the broken window.

It took me a while to get that sorted out. Paul arrived on the scene while I was screaming at the rotten bastards who were watching the fire, trying to get them to help Carl. I must say Paul's comments were as vehement as mine.

Paul insisted on carrying me to the house. Two of the bastards followed, with poor Carl dangling between them like a sack of potatoes. The nurse didn't need my hysterical insistence to take care of him first. He was dripping blood all over the scenery when they carried him into the hospital room and dumped him on a gurney. She patched him up, but announced that though she didn't think he was in any danger, he should be taken to a hospital. I thought they would call for an ambulance. Stupid me. They had an ambulance—or at least a limo that could be converted into a reasonable facsimile thereof.

Paul sent one of the thugs to bring the car around and then laid firm but gentle hands on me. "Haskell, if you don't let Miss Brooks attend to you, I'll spank you. I'm not at all sure you shouldn't be going to the hospital, too."

I was hanging over Carl, who hadn't stirred or opened his eyes—wringing my hands and in general carrying on like a jerk.

"He pushed me through the window first," I said. "That's why he's burned and I'm not. He got the worst of the glass, too, when he came in. . . . Oh, Carl, why the hell don't you say something?"

His blistered lips parted. "I don't want to move anything. It hurts."

Miss Brooks bent over him. "I've given you an injection. You'll feel better in a little while."

"Hah," Carl said skeptically. "Haskell—are you—"

"Fine. Fine. Thanks to you." I took his hand. He let out a yelp and opened his eyes. "You don't look fine," he said, after a pained scrutiny.

"That's what I keep telling her," Paul snapped. "Miss Brooks, will you please—"

"Yes, of course, Mr. Dunlap." She twitched off the blanket she had wrapped around me, just as the door opened and the two thugs entered with a stretcher. They got Carl onto it, though they almost dropped him, they were so busy leering at me. There wasn't much left of my pajamas. Paul gallantly turned his back while Miss Brooks removed the shreds and went to work. I had a couple of deep cuts across my stomach—I had gone through the window headfirst and facedown, but poor Carl's hasty entrance had cleared away most of the shards.

I was still lying on the table stark-naked and shivering, when Mrs. Dunlap made her appearance. The sight of me struck her dumb.

I said idiotically, "Hello, Mrs. Dunlap."

Her eyes moved to her husband. "I heard voices—footsteps. What in heaven's name . . . ?"

Paul explained. "Fortunately no one was seriously hurt. I've sent Carl to the hospital; Miss Brooks says he'll be all right."

Mrs. Dunlap passed a shaking hand over her mouth. "Why didn't you call me?"

"I did look in your room, darling, but you weren't there."

"I was with Father," Mrs. Dunlap said quietly.

From the look on Paul's face, I knew he had forgotten about the old man's death. He moved to her side and put his arms around her. I felt a queer spasm of something that could not possibly have been jealousy. Rational annoyance, more likely; the dead were beyond any need for care, but I was still alive, and I was freezing. I said clearly, "Could I have a sheet or a blanket, or something?"

Immediately Mrs. Dunlap was her usual gracious self, concerned and apologetic. I ended up in the same guest room in another silk nightgown—pale blue and sleeveless, lavish with lace. As the soft fabric caressed my aching body, it struck me that I didn't have a stitch of clothing left, not even a pair of shoes. My mother's books and papers were gone, too, and so was the photo album. I had had so little of her, and now even that was reduced to blackened ashes.

A warm summer dawn was breaking before I fell asleep. I was rudely awakened by Dave only a few hours later. His voice was loud enough to have aroused any sleeper within a block. At least he wasn't yelling at me.

"Why the hell didn't you tell me? Why am I the last person to find out about these things?"

I heard a voice answer him. It sounded like Paul's, but I couldn't make out the words.

"Yes, I was," Dave shouted. "I worked late and fell asleep on the couch in the office. Slept through the whole damned thing. Went looking for Haskell this morning, thinking I'd talk her into cooking breakfast for me—Jesus Christ, I almost had a heart attack when I saw that pile of burned rubble."

I rolled over and sat up. Dave was backing into the room;

the farther he got from the person he was addressing—Paul, I assumed—the louder he yelled. I put my hands over my ears.

"Please," I croaked. "I have a headache."

Dave sat down on the side of the bed. "Is that all?"

Suddenly he reached out and took my face between his hands, staring as if he were trying to memorize every feature. It was like having my head squeezed in a vise. I thought the top of my skull would blow off.

After a moment he released me and sat back. "You don't look too bad. A little scorched around the edges."

I rubbed my aching cheeks. "You don't look so hot yourself." Hollow-eyed, unshaven, his eyes dark with fatigue and worry, he must have worked most of the night. But I had lied. He looked wonderful.

In the distance I heard a door slam, and deduced that Paul had gone back to bed. He was entitled.

Dave had to know exactly what had happened. Midway through the recital, the maid arrived with a breakfast tray. Dave ate most of it, which was all right with me. I wasn't hungry.

"Things have certainly livened up around here since you arrived," he remarked.

I winced. "You could say that."

"Fire started in the kitchen, did it?"

"I guess so. The fire marshal should be able to tell."

Dave snorted and started on the last piece of toast. "Don't kid yourself," he said thickly. "There won't be any fire marshal or any report. You think they'd let a bunch of outsiders in? They have their own fire-fighting equipment."

"I noticed that. But what if the museum—"

"They have enough sprinklers in that place to flood the grounds. Oh, sure, if the main house or the museum caught, they'd summon help, but for a run-down shack like the cottage . . . Did you get soused last night and forget to turn off the stove?"

"I had two beers. You can ask Carl. He saved my life, Dave. I have to call the hospital—"

"I already did. They wouldn't let me talk to him."

"I should think not, at this hour. Honestly, Dave, I'm sure I didn't leave anything on. It must have been defective wiring."

"Maybe." He was silent for a moment, his eyes narrowed. "I'm going to see Carl," he announced. "Want to come along?"

"Yes, please . . . Oh, dammit, I forgot. I don't have any clothes. What am I going to do?"

"Borrow something," said Dave, with the vast indifference of any man to such minor details as fit.

"I'll have to go shopping."

"In that?" He grinned, indicating the flimsy nightgown.

I pulled up one of the fallen straps. Mrs. Dunlap was a good deal larger in the bust than I. "Dammit," I repeated.

"What are you doing, sprawled all over the girl?" a voice demanded from the doorway.

Paul had not gone back to bed. He was freshly shaved and fully dressed, including vest, coat, and tie. He went on, "I suppose you've eaten her breakfast, too. I shouldn't have let you in the house; you're enough to send a convalescent back into shock."

He was smiling, but I detected an undercurrent of genuine anger under his light tone. "Oh, sorry," said Dave. He removed himself to a chair. "She hasn't got any clothes," he explained, gesturing.

"I am only too well aware of that," Paul said.

I tried to squirm farther down under the sheets. The tray tottered, and Paul picked it up. He watched approvingly as I pulled the coverings to a modest height. "How are you this morning, my dear?"

"Fine," I said, wondering how many more times I would have to repeat that word. "I'd like to get up, but . . . Do you suppose one of the maids could lend me a dress and some shoes?"

"Mrs. Dunlap anticipated your problem," Paul said. "I'm afraid we mere men don't think of such things. She has selected something she believes you can wear temporarily. Of course, you must let us replace your wardrobe. Would you rather have a selection of garments brought here, or does shopping give you a psychological boost?"

From his pocket, he took a wad of bills as thick as my thumb. I swallowed. "Oh, no, I couldn't possibly—"

"Why not?" Dave demanded. "He can afford it. Besides, it's his fault you were in that firetrap to begin with."

It wasn't Dave's rude comments that persuaded me; it was Paul's insistent kindness—that and the reminder that my cash and my checkbook had also gone up in the blaze. I'm sure it's the same with people who lose everything in a hurricane or other natural disaster; it isn't until they reach for some familiar object and find it gone that they fully comprehend the extent of their loss. Lipstick, pencil, driver's license . . .

Even if I had been willing to risk driving without a license, I was still a little shaky. Paul had anticipated that problem, too; he tried to put one of the cars and chauffeurs at my disposal, but Dave—not I—brushed the offer aside. "I'll drive her. She'll take all day if somebody doesn't hurry her along. Come on, Haskell, get moving."

There was no need to hurry; the stores didn't open until ten. Dave fussed about that, and made rude remarks about my appearance; Mrs. Dunlap's dress was too big for me in every dimension except length, and her shoes wouldn't go on my feet at all. I had to borrow a pair of sandals from the nurse. At least I didn't have to argue with Dave about where to shop. Paul would have assumed I was heading for Field's or one of the fancy stores on the North Side; without even asking, Dave drove me to a shopping mall not far from the university, where I found a couple of the moderately priced

clothing chains that crisscross the country. He was a pain in
the neck, pacing and staring at his watch and asking every
few minutes how much longer I was going to be. He'd have
blown his stack if I had done what Paul expected me to do—
spend all his money without regard for price or need.
Obviously I couldn't do that, since I intended to repay him,
so I confined myself to basic necessities, two sets of them,
and a cheap cardboard suitcase in which to put the extra set.
I was beginning to get rattled by then—not only because of
Dave's incessant nagging, but because I was anxious about
Carl—so I rushed through the drugstore, picking up combs
and brushes and toothpaste and a motley collection of
cosmetics, most of which weren't the brand I normally
used, but never mind.

"Is that everything?" Dave demanded, looking
martyred, as I stowed the suitcase in the car.

"No, not nearly everything. But it will have to do for
now. Remind me never to let you go shopping with me
again."

"With pleasure." Dave slammed the car into gear and we
darted into the traffic. "Time for lunch."

"Aren't we going to see Carl?"

"Later. You look a little green around the gills. Don't
want you passing out on me."

"I'm not going to pass out." I let my head fall back
against the headrest. "Do you mind if I cry a little?"

"What about? You're alive and you've still got a wad of
cash left."

The last crack made me so mad I forgot about crying. I
sat up and glared at him. "I'm going to pay him back.
Every penny. Why do you suppose I went to The Limited
instead of Saks or Neiman-Marcus? If you think I'd take
money from Paul after what I've done—"

"Aha, oho, and well, well, well," said Dave.

"Watch out," I shrieked. Dave glanced back at the road
and turned the wheel, narrowly avoiding a truck coming

straight at us. "What are you so nervous about?" he asked curiously. "Do go on with that most interesting confession."

"It was not a confession."

"It was heading in that direction. After what you've done . . . What precisely *have* you done?"

"I killed his father-in-law."

"No, you didn't, and if you had, he'd insist you keep the money as payment for services rendered."

"You ought to be ashamed of yourself."

"What for, telling the truth?"

I wasn't paying much attention to where he was going, and it was not until he stopped—in a No Parking zone—that I realized we were in front of the Oriental Institute. Dave opened his door. "I have to pick up some things in my office. Back in a minute. Keep an eye out for cops."

He bolted up the stairs, shirttail flapping. I slid down in my seat and stared moodily at the rearview mirror. I wasn't entirely clear as to what I was supposed to do if I did see a traffic policeman; he had taken his keys with him.

Absorbed in following orders, however senseless, and in my own meditations, I didn't see the face at the window until she rapped imperatively on the glass. It gave me a horrible start to see her; her nose was flattened and whitened as she pressed it to the window, greedy as a child at a candy store. Greedy, yes; but not childish, that scowling face.

She kept banging on the window until I rolled it down. I started out being polite. "Hello, Dr. Maxwell."

"What are you doing here?"

That finished my attempt at good manners. "Why shouldn't I be here?"

"I thought you were . . . They told me there was . . ."

"A fire? Yes, that's right. What do you know about it?"

Her lips drew back, baring crooked teeth. "Is that an accusation?"

Rudeness didn't intimidate her; it only fed her phobia. I said wearily, "No, of course not. The fire was an accident."

"You think so, do you?"

"Is that a threat?" I mimicked her voice.

"A warning." She thrust her face in the window. I recoiled; her skin was unhealthily flushed, as if with fever, and her breath felt hot. "Why don't you go back where you belong? You have no business here. It will be your own fault if something happens to you."

I had always considered her eccentric and annoying, but not dangerous; now I understood how she had earned her nickname. She *was* a little mad, not far from a breakdown of some kind. She didn't frighten me—not much—but when I saw the heavy door swing open and Dave's familiar figure appear, I let out a little sigh of relief.

She turned her head. Seeing him, she took off, almost running. Dave stopped and stared after her; then he went around the car and got in.

"Was that Meg?" he asked.

"Mad Meg," I said.

"What did she say?"

"Damned if I know." His sturdy, common-sense presence had reduced the woman to ordinary terms. "I think she wants me to leave town."

"Join the club," Dave said.

"What has she got against me? I can understand why she hates your guts—"

"Thanks."

"Oh, you know what I mean. You've challenged her professionally and . . ." I broke off, as a new idea struck me. Dave concentrated on driving, his face studiously blank, but there was something about the way he looked. . . . "Oh, no," I said. "Don't tell me she—and then of course you— No. I can't believe it."

"Of all the damned insults I have ever received, that is the worst," Dave said. "What is it you can't believe—that any female would be desperate enough to make a pass at me, or that I'd be fastidious enough to reject it?"

"Neither one," I said, surprised at his tone. "What are you so sensitive about? I'll bet all the female students in the department are lusting after you. In fact—"

"Never mind. As for why she detests you, that should be obvious to the dullest intelligence—even yours. She was insanely jealous of Leah, and now you're repeating the pattern. Charming every male in the vicinity."

"Me? Charming?"

"In your own peculiar way. Don't worry about Meg; she can't hurt you. All she ever does is talk and nobody pays any attention to her."

He swung into the curb so abruptly that the seat belt caught me across the middle and scored across my cuts. I doubled up to the extent the seat belt allowed, moaning. Dave opened his door. "Sorry about that. Got to grab a parking space when one appears. Here, let me help you out."

"Wait till I unfasten the seat belt," I said through clenched teeth.

The place he had selected was a pizza parlor, redolent with the odors of baking crust, pepperoni, and stale beer. Dave sniffed as if it were the finest perfume.

"Dave, I'm not sure I'm up to pizza," I began.

"Oh." He looked puzzled. "How about a hoagie?"

Once I started laughing I couldn't stop. The waiter who came to take our order grinned sympathetically; Dave leaned across the table and remarked, "Maybe I should slap you? Is it hysterics or honest mirth?"

"I think it's mirth. Damn, I forgot to buy tissues."

He plucked a paper napkin from the container and handed it to me. That almost set me off again, as I remembered the exquisite linen square the last comforting male had offered me, but I managed to control myself.

"It couldn't be that you are laughing at me, could it?"

Dave asked, with the air of a man who has just made an astonishing discovery.

"You're hamming it up on purpose," I said affectionately.

"Just my little way." He began crooning in a horrible off-key voice. "''Tis better to laugh than be sigh—ighing. . . .' I told you, there's nothing to cry about. Just because you lost all your clothes, your money, and your personal possessions—"

"I could cry over some of them. All Mother's things, Dave. Her books and papers—even the pictures."

"Maybe it's just as well."

"Oh, don't give me that crap about burying the past," I said crossly. "What's wrong with fond memories?"

"Nothing, if they're yours. You should be building up your own senile reminiscences. What do you want on your pizza?"

"Extra cheese, mushrooms, and sausage. But no beer, please."

When we arrived at the hospital, we found Carl's efforts to get out of bed being frustrated by a nurse about half his size and twice his age. His roommate, a timid little man whose foot was in an enormous cast, watched in alarm.

Carl greeted Dave with a cry of "Thank God! Have you got any money? They won't let me out till I pay."

"Ah," said the nurse menacingly. "Are you friends of his?"

"Sort of," Dave admitted.

"Yes," I said.

"He keeps getting up, and he isn't supposed to; the sedative hasn't worn off and he—" She broke off with a grunt as Carl made another abortive attempt to escape her grip. "He keeps falling down," she finished, yanking Carl back into bed.

"I wanna go home," Carl said.

"Can he?" Dave asked.

"You'll have to speak to Dr. Rama." The nurse straightened her cap. "He certainly can't be alone; he's still groggy."

"I'll take care of him." Dave sat down on Carl's legs. The nurse marched out. Carl subsided; the struggle had tired him. "I wanna go home," he repeated.

"Hospitals are no damn good when you're sick," Dave agreed. "I'll spring you, kid. You can come home with me. What do you need?"

"Now wait a minute," I began.

"My wallet, my money, my insurance card—"

"And some pants."

"And some pants."

"Okay. If you promise to be a good boy and quit annoying the nurses, I'll go get your stuff. Say hello to Haskell. She doesn't have any clothes either."

' Hi, Haskell."

"Hi, Carl."

They had trimmed the burned hair. He looked lopsided—half a mustache, waving locks on one side of his head, and a Marine cut on the other; right cheek red and blistered, the other only a little singed. The hospital gown was one of the tasteful garments that are open all the way down the back. It hid the bandages, if there were any; from what I had seen the night before, I surmised that there were. Carl's struggles had hiked the thing up to a level even more revealing than usual. My interested stare brought this to his attention, and he tried to pull his skirts down. If he blushed, I couldn't tell; his face was already crimson.

"You look terrible," I said.

"Thanks."

"Only your face. Not those gorgeous legs, or—"

"Thanks. Dave, are you going to get me out of here or not?"

I began, "I don't think—"

"Sure." Dave stood up. Carl grabbed for the sheet and pulled it over him. "Stay put," Dave said. "I'll be back. Coming, Haskell?"

"In a minute."

"Tactful as always, I will leave you alone," Dave announced.

He went out. I stood staring dumbly at Carl; I couldn't think what to say. "Thank you" seemed inadequate.

Carl smoothed the blanket over his lap. "You don't look bad for a girl who almost got barbecued last night."

"Thanks to you, I wasn't."

"Yeah? Was I a hero?"

"Don't you remember?"

"Things are a little fuzzy. They've got me doped up."

Dave poked his head in the door. "Hurry up and kiss him. I haven't got all day."

"I'm not going to kiss you," I said to Carl. "Not with those blisters. I couldn't do myself justice."

"Anyhow, I refuse to kiss women when I'm wearing a skirt."

"Rain check."

"Right. Uh—right, please."

It was the first time I had seen the interior of Carl's cottage. The furnishings were like my own, a mixture of discarded antiques and modern make-do. I assumed Maria must clean the place from time to time—probably more often and more diligently than she cleaned mine—but she had not been there that day, and there was debris strewn over every flat surface, including the floor. The clothes he had worn the previous day lay crumpled by the bed. I picked up a sock. It had a gaping hole in the toe. I threw it in the wastebasket.

Dave had gone to the kitchen. "What are you doing?" I asked.

"Nothing useful. Forget it." He picked up Carl's wallet

and put it in his pocket. Then he opened a dresser drawer and began rummaging.

"Don't forget shoes," I reminded him.

"Yeah, right."

I knew what he had been doing in the kitchen—looking for signs of defective wiring. As he had said, it was a useless inquiry; only an expert could have found a problem.

Among the miscellaneous papers on the desk were two blue books. I had forgotten Carl had borrowed them; I exclaimed in delight as I picked them up.

Dave glanced at me. "That's a funny way of demonstrating your devotion to your wounded lover—caressing his exam books."

"He's not my lover and these aren't his. They belonged to Mother. At least I have something of hers left."

Dave shoved the clothes into a shabby backpack and took the booklets from me. "Egyptian history. Hmmm. Pretty good. A-plus."

"Haven't you seen them before?"

"We didn't sit around reading one another's exams," Dave said caustically. "Come on, Haskell, move it. I have a hell of a lot to do."

Once outside, Dave's need for haste seemed to desert him. His steps slowed.

"Where are you going to sleep tonight?"

"I don't have much choice. Hotels aren't keen on guests who don't have luggage or credit cards."

"I have a day bed."

"You already offered it to Carl, remember? And don't make any lewd suggestions; they would be inappropriate as well as vulgar."

"You could sleep on the floor."

"Why should I, when I can sleep on silk sheets and have breakfast in bed?"

Dave took my arm in that bruising grip of his and towed

me toward a bench overshadowed by trailing roses. He sat down.

"I'm not so crazy about that idea," he said.

"Why on earth not?"

Dave scratched his bristly chin. "If I could tell you why not, I wouldn't be so uneasy."

"Are you going hysterical on me?" I tried to speak lightly, but his words had aroused an answering vibration of discomfort in me. "Ask the tarot cards. If you have them. You were kidding about that, weren't you?"

"No." He glanced up and said irritably, "Sit down; you make me nervous, looming over me."

"I make *you* nervous?" But I did as he asked. A flowery branch curled over my shoulder; the strong, sweet scent of the old-fashioned flowers almost overcame the stench of burned wood. "What's the matter with you, Dave? You act like a mother hen with two chickens."

"And the chicks are running in opposite directions," Dave mumbled. "I was planning to work late tonight, but I suppose I ought to stick with Carl, make sure he's all right. . . ."

Over the walls and trees and shrubbery, brilliant in fresh green, I could see the battlemented towers of the house against a sky blue as summer. To many people it might have looked charming and gallant in its defiance of the humdrum city that had tried to overwhelm it. To me it had a different aspect. I didn't want to stay there any more than Dave wanted me to.

"There's Carl's cottage," I suggested. "He won't be using it tonight."

"And neither will you, kid. A fine restful night's sleep you'd have, after what happened."

He was right about that. I needed sleep, too; my eyelids were scratchy with the lack of it. I thought of a quiet anonymous hotel room, of falling onto the bed and sleeping for twelve hours. Of having peace and quiet and time to deal with the dozens of small tasks that needed to be done. I couldn't avoid or postpone telling Jessie about the fire. I needed more clothes, a new driver's license, checks—there was hardly anything I didn't need; and unless I accepted Paul Dunlap's money, which I had no intention of doing, there was no sense in replacing clothes that were in my room in Philadelphia. I was going to need all the money I had left for school next fall—if I could make up my mind where I intended to go and what I intended to do with the rest of my life. The only certain fact was that I could not stay in Chicago.

Dave looked as if he had settled down for the rest of the afternoon. He had shoved the pack behind him like a cushion; the clothes were getting thoroughly mashed, but I didn't suppose it would bother him, or Carl either.

"Dave," I said.

"Uh?" said Dave.

"Talk to me. Don't sit there looking gloomy and enigmatic like Mr. Rochester. What's bothering you?"

He swiveled a quarter-turn and faced me. "What's bothering *you?*"

It might have been physical exhaustion, it might have been the kindness in his dark, deep-set eyes. All of a sudden my tongue had to move; it wasn't me talking, it was someone else.

"Stephen Nazarian was my father."

Dave was silent for a moment; it wasn't the silence of surprise, but of thought. I had never fully appreciated the astonishing quickness of his mind; he put the pieces together with the speed of a computer. Instead of asking the questions a less intelligent man might have asked, he went straight to the point.

"Does anyone else know this?"

"No. But I think—I'm sure—Mr. Nazarian had figured it out. That was what brought on his final stroke."

"What are you going to do about it?"

"Nothing. What would be the point? I don't want anything from them, even if I had a legal claim, which I don't."

"I should have known," Dave muttered. "I knew you were up to something."

"You *did* know. You weren't surprised. Why didn't you tell me?"

"Oh, come off it, Haskell," Dave said impatiently. "What the hell was I supposed to say? 'How do you do, Miss Maloney; it is my pleasure to inform you that you are not your father's child'? I suspected the truth, but my reasons were completely unscientific."

"You must have known Stephen was her lover."

Dave shrugged. "I knew she was in love with someone. The glow is unmistakable. But it could have been any one of several guys."

"Damn it, Dave—are you saying she was—"

"She was young and attractive and loving—that's what I'm saying. What kind of pious prig are you, Haskell? Too stupid to admit your mother was a normal, healthy female? How the hell do you think you got here?"

Jon had said much the same thing, only he had said it more politely. My eyes fell.

"Sometimes I hate you, Dave. You know what you are? The re-embodied voice of the conscience I tried to smother."

"Why did you try to smother it?"

"Because it was always telling me the truth."

Dave laughed. "I know what you mean. But it's no good, Haskell; I've tried to kill mine a dozen times. It has more lives than a cat."

"I'm not being priggish," I insisted. "At least I'm trying not to. It's a little difficult to think of your own mother as a normal human being, especially when you've known her only as a distant, idealized image. I see her much more clearly now. I only wish she had chosen someone who could have made her happy. Loving Steve Nazarian brought her nothing but pain in the end."

"Maybe it wasn't Steve. She never discussed her love life with me. It might have been one of the others."

"Or you?"

He hesitated, his eyes abstracted, as if he were listening to a voice only he could hear. Then he laughed harshly. "When I told you I wasn't in love with Leah I was somewhat less than truthful. Keep in mind that I was barely sixteen—the infant prodigy as well as the enfant terrible of the department. She treated me like a kid brother. Oh, I can see now that it was nothing more than a bad case of puppy love, but it hurt like hell at the time. I grew that stupid beard because I thought it would make me look older, and I acted like a horse's behind because . . . well, you can guess why."

The clown, the comedian—a form of protection, a wall defending against hurt. "If I'm already laughing, you can't laugh at me. You can only laugh with me."

"I understand," I said softly.

"Then you can also understand why I was the last person in the world with whom Leah would have discussed her love affair. The only thing I can be certain of is that I was never her lover."

I began impulsively, "I wish—" and broke off with a gasp.

Dave eyed me curiously. "What's the matter?"

"I . . . Nothing. My stomach hurts."

It did, too. The revelation had hit as hard as a physical blow.

"You shouldn't have had that sausage on your pizza," Dave said absently. "What about the other men in the group? Vlad, and Phil Cartwright?"

"I meant to check them out. But I got distracted . . . and Steve seemed so much more likely. . . ."

"And a radical rich boy is so much more romantic than an electrician or an insurance salesman," Dave said. "Are you by any chance a snob, kid?"

"Don't call me kid! And don't—don't keep exposing me for the fool I am . . . was. . . ." I put my head in my hands. "I'd be happy to settle for a nice honest electrician."

"I doubt Vlad would share your enthusiasm. He has eight kids and a very suspicious wife."

"You keep in touch?"

"Yeah, we get together now and then for a few beers and some senile reminiscences." He turned away and slapped at a trailing branch. "Damned roses. Covered with thorns. I'd better go, Carl will be having twenty fits."

I went with him. My suitcase was in the car; I had to retrieve it. It occurred to me that I did have luggage, of a sort, and plenty of cash. I could go to a hotel if I wanted to. Did I want to?

I asked Dave. His shrug had an uncharacteristic element of helplessness. "I don't know, Haskell. This news of yours has thrown me off-base; I guess I've been behaving like a fidgety old woman. Suppose you sleep on it, and we'll discuss the situation tomorrow."

The door of the guardroom stood open. No one came out, but I heard voices and an occasional burst of laughter within. The careless mirth jarred on me. Dave didn't like it either. Handing me my suitcase, he said, "Don't stay at Carl's tonight. The king is dead and I don't trust those characters. Not that I think they'd do anything, but if they have a few drinks . . ."

"Right. Thanks, Dave."

"What for? I haven't come up with any useful ideas." He got in the car and started the engine. Then he put his head out the window. "I'll call you later. If you decide to go to a hotel, let me know."

"All right."

"Here's my number." He tore a page out of his notebook, scribbled on it, and handed it to me. "Don't lose it. Memorize it—tattoo it on your arm. . . ."

"Okay."

I wondered why he had been so insistent about the telephone number. Even if he wasn't in the book (those pesky female students?) surely someone at the house would know how to reach him. Perhaps he didn't know, any more than I did, what he was doing or why; but the gesture, the willingness to make himself available for my needs, gave me a warm feeling.

Another burst of laughter from the guardroom made me beat a hasty retreat. Even without Dave's warning I would have avoided those men; they had always made me nervous.

The suitcase felt as if it weighed fifty pounds. I was so tired, every step dragged; but instead of going to the house, I wandered aimlessly through the grounds until I found myself once again in the enclosure of the cottages.

The dead square of burned rubble was an ugly reminder of what might have happened to me. I picked up a fallen bough and poked idly through the debris. A twisted scrap of metal sent up a flash of reflected sunlight. I couldn't tell what it might have been.

Had the fire been an accident? Seeming accidents loomed rather large in my life lately. Once—even a few days ago—I would have laughed at the idea that anyone hated me enough to kill me. Several candidates had emerged since then; and though their motives seemed completely inadequate for something as drastic as murder, a killer's motives usually seem inadequate to everyone except the killer.

I don't know how long I stood there. I must have fallen into a semi-doze, leaning against the wall. When I came to my senses I was aware of the sun sinking below the treetops and evening approaching. It was no wonder I couldn't think clearly; I was drunk with exhaustion, and the sight of that unholy square of burning didn't cheer me. But for the grace of God and Carl Townsend, my blackened bones might have been smoldering there.

Carl might have died in that fire, too. I wasn't in love with Carl. But I liked him. I liked working with him. He wasn't my ideal man, but I even liked his human imperfections. I had had enough of perfect men.

I could call Jon. I *should* call Jon. But then I thought, why should I? He'd only fuss and carry on and feel duty-bound to rush to the rescue. He might even suggest I come to Winnetka. What fun that would be, with dear Miriam playing the polite hostess, taking me in like a stray cat and asking tactful questions that would emphasize what a mess I had made of my life.

I would have to spend one more night at the house. I figured I had just about enough strength left to get there: I certainly didn't have enough to get any farther. That wouldn't inconvenience the family; if I kept out of sight, they might not even know I was there. I would leave in the morning—in daylight—after a good night's sleep and, hopefully, the restoration of my ability to think sensibly (about a lot of things). I'd leave a courteous note for Mrs. Dunlap, expressing my condolences and thanking her—and Paul. It gave me a queer, empty feeling to think I probably would never see Paul again. He had been so kind.

The butler answered my ring. His long face, set in the lugubrious expression that befitted a house of mourning, took on a trace of animation when he saw me.

"Mrs. Dunlap has been asking for you, miss. She is in her boudoir; I'll show you the way."

I didn't want to see Mrs. Dunlap. What I wanted to see was a bed, any bed, in any room—but I could hardly say so. I indicated my suitcase; the butler took it from me. "This way, Miss Maloney."

The house stank of flowers—the overpowering, sickening, sweet smell of death. They were everywhere—huge baskets and ornate wreaths, elaborate, expensive bouquets. They had come, and would be coming, from all over the world. From financiers and heads of state, from politicians and corporation leaders, and probably from a few gangsters. As I stumbled after the butler's stately form, I noticed one particular floral tribute worthy of Al Capone himself—an enormous horseshoe of purple orchids and white roses, crossed by a lavender ribbon with gold lettering that read, "Safe in the Arms of Jesus." Well, I certainly hoped so, but I had my doubts.

After climbing the stairs, we turned left instead of right. I had not been in this part of the house before; the old man's suite and the guest room I had used were in the other wing. So it had been Margaret Maxwell, calling on her dear friend Katherine, whom I had seen scuttling across that corridor. I hoped she wasn't with Katherine now, patting her hand and emitting sympathy. Maxwell was high on the list of people I particularly didn't want to encounter.

I have no clear recollection of the room, only an impression of pale pink flounces and antique lace, of crushed velvet chairs and tiny inlaid tables. Think boudoir, think money, and you've got it. Swathed in black from throat to ankles, Mrs. Dunlap sat at a mother-of-pearl inlaid desk, writing. The desk was piled with letters and telegrams and cards.

When she saw me, her ravaged face lit up, and she rose. "My dear girl! I've been so worried about you—where have you been?"

Her maternal concern would have been touching if it had not been so ironic. I wondered what she would do if I flung my arms around her and addressed her as "Aunt Katherine." Imagination reeled—so did I. Seeing me sway, she took my hands and led me to a couch. It was soft and pink; it enveloped me like a sunset cloud.

I made some noncommittal answer and then forced myself to coherence. "I've never said, Mrs. Dunlap, how sorry I am about your father. He was . . . I was . . . Knowing him, even briefly, was an experience I'll never forget."

"Thank you." Mercifully she hadn't noticed the ambiguity of my tribute; I had not been able to bring myself to voice the traditional platitudes. She touched a dainty handkerchief to her eyes. "You must think I'm foolish to be so upset. He was an old man who had had a wonderful, full life, and his helplessness in recent years was a terrible burden for him. But one never adjusts to losing a parent, does one?"

"I guess not." And who should know better than I, still weighted down by the burdens of a twenty-year-old loss?

Mrs. Dunlap continued to dab at her eyes, and I tried to think of a graceful way to escape. There were a good many things that needed to be said, but this seemed hardly the time to explain that I meant to repay the money her husband had lent me or to offer my resignation. It did seem appropriate, however, to offer to leave at once. Jessie would have said that was plain, basic good manners. I wasn't as resigned to staying as I had thought. Perhaps it was the memory of Mad Meg, lurking and spying, that had aroused resurgent fears.

"I'm glad I had a chance to say good-bye," I said.

The handkerchief dropped to her lap. Her eyes widened. "Good-bye? You aren't leaving?"

"Oh, I hope to see you again before I . . . That is, later. But I certainly won't intrude at such a time."

"My dear girl—you can't go." Her hands reached for mine. They were small white hands, but they clung with an urgency more effective than physical strength. "You mustn't go. Where will you go?"

If I said I was going to a hotel, she would feel obliged to protest. A new idea occurred to me; I wondered why I hadn't thought of it before.

"To my grandmother's. She and Aunt Ella live in Oak Park."

"Is she expecting you?"

"She always expects me." Mrs. Dunlap looked blank, and I elaborated. "She's rather—well—old-fashioned. They don't have a telephone, so it's impossible for me to let them know in advance. I just show up on the doorstep, and they take me in. They think I ought to be there anyway. . . . Sorry, I'm not making much sense."

"No. You look absolutely exhausted."

"I am a little tired." I was thinking about what I had said—straight from the subconscious and definitely incoherent, but oddly comforting. "I show up and they take me in." That's the definition of home, isn't it? "The place where, when you go there, they have to take you in."

"You can't possibly drive all the way to Oak Park this evening," Mrs. Dunlap said. "You're in no state to drive. I'd never forgive myself if you had an accident. You can make whatever plans you like tomorrow, but I insist on your staying here tonight. Besides, I thought you might like to see Father before they take him away."

"You mean the—he—he is still here—in the house?" I had assumed the old man's body was at a funeral home, promptly tidied away, as is the custom in our antiseptic society. Another reason for getting the hell out of there as soon as I decently could. Dead or alive, his presence cast a pall.

"It was his wish. The people from the mortuary will come late tonight, in secret. We have to take precautions, even now; he had enemies, and some of them might try . . ."

Her voice trailed off, but I knew what she meant; the tremor that shook her body ran through her hands into mine and aroused an answering frisson of horror.

"We'll go now," Mrs. Dunlap said. She rose to her feet, drawing me with her.

I hung back. Good manners be damned; my reluctance was total and instinctive. "Please—I'd rather not."

"I won't insist," Mrs. Dunlap said. "But I think Father would have wanted you to see him. And it would comfort me."

I didn't ask her why. I was caught; there was no way out of it.

Her soft white fingers twisted around mine; we went hand in hand along the hall like sisters—or aunt and niece. She stopped before the door I knew so well and opened it.

A dark form slipped out as we entered—one of the servants properly attired in funeral black. They kept to the old customs here; the dead must not be left unattended. Mrs. Dunlap closed the door.

There were candles all around the bed, burning clear and pure. That was the only illumination, and the resemblance to an ancient tomb was now complete. The movement of the door as we entered set the flames flickering; shadows crawled across the painted walls and the gold-inlaid furniture, as ornate as any buried pharaoh might have owned. The rigid body on the bed wore a long purple robe. His hands were not folded in prayer; they had been arranged in the hieratic pose of ancient Egypt—crossed on his breast, hands closed as if holding the scepter and the flail. Death had not softened the features highlighted by the candle flames. The lines of power and pride that had marked his living face were intensified and preserved for all eternity.

She didn't have to tell me that this was how he had wanted it to be. He had probably put it in his will. Fantastic images swam in my brain—visions, not of sober modern undertakers but of white-robed priests busy about their gruesome tasks. The heart, which was the seat of the intelligence, was always left in place, but the brain was removed with long hooks, inserted . . .

It was then that the only truly inexplicable, uncanny moment of the whole affair occurred. I didn't hear her thoughts or read her mind. Rather, our linked hands formed a passage through which understanding flowed in a silent current.

"You know, don't you," I said quietly.

And in a voice as quiet, as removed from emotion, she answered, "I've always known."

11

When Mrs. Dunlap spoke again, her voice was cool and politely curious; we might have been discussing the high price of groceries. "How did you find out? Did she tell you—that woman—her sister?"

"Aunt Jessie? No. She didn't know—she still doesn't know. I didn't know myself until after I came here."

"Really? How curious."

"I found out that Kevin Maloney couldn't have been my father. I carry a certain gene, or allele, or whatever it's called—Tay-Sachs. So I came here looking for him—my real father. It wasn't until a few days ago—last night, really—that I discovered it was your brother."

"Stephen." After a moment she repeated musingly. "Poor Stephen . . ."

"You needn't worry, Mrs. Dunlap. I have no intention of presuming on the relationship. In any way."

She didn't seem to hear me. "Did you tell Father?"

"Not exactly."

"He must have known. He knew everything. . . ."

I didn't answer. She had released my hand; my fingers were tingling. Surreptitiously I flexed them. "I'm going away," I said. "Away from Chicago. I didn't mean to cause so much trouble."

"You'll have to stay until after the funeral," Mrs. Dunlap said. "And the reading of the will."

"What?" My voice was too loud; it shattered the silence. I lowered it. "No. There's no reason—"

"There are a number of excellent reasons." Mrs. Dunlap's manner had undergone a startling change. Except for the flowing black draperies, all signs of grief were gone; her voice was quick and urgent, and the candle flames reflected in her pupils made them dance. "I never gave the matter a second thought because Father was always calling for his lawyers. But if he believed you were Stephen's child . . . You must know what that would have meant to him, how desperately he wanted an heir of his own blood. No, wait, don't interrupt me. I'm still trying to think this through; it's much more complex than I realized."

She didn't know the half of it. But I was in no condition to cope with anything more complex than a bed and a pillow—no, never mind the pillow, I'd have settled for a flat surface and eight hours of oblivion—especially not in that eerie cavern of a room, with my dead grandfather's marble-white features quivering as the candlelight flowed across them and shadows stirring in the corners. . . .

I started. Mrs. Dunlap's fingers tightened on my arm. "You're half asleep already. You need rest."

"It isn't that. It's this room. I'm sorry. . . . I thought for a minute someone was there, behind the bed. Jerry."

"He's not here," Mrs. Dunlap said abstractedly.

"No, it was just my imagination. I expected he would be here. I know I'm silly, but I've always been a little afraid of Jerry."

"Jerry? Why?"

"He hasn't been very friendly. I think he blames me for Mr. Nazarian's illness—that last stroke. I was here when it happened, and I . . . Mrs. Dunlap, I can't stay here any longer. I have to get away, I really do. I'll go to a hotel—"

"No. Wait." She was silent for a moment, frowning. The shifting light didn't flatter her; it sketched lines in her face I hadn't observed before. "What was that you said about Jerry? That he—blamed you—for Father's death?"

"He never actually said that." My head was spinning. "I don't remember what he said, but he frightened me. Please, I don't want to stay here."

"You don't understand. I'm just beginning to realize . . . Jerry disappeared last night, after Father died. He's done it before when something upset him—gone into hiding, like a sulky child. He kept talking about you—about fire, and the wicked burning in hell. . . . We had trouble with him some years ago, when he went through a period of setting fires—he liked watching the flames dancing. You don't suppose . . ."

"He . . . Are you implying he set fire to the cottage?"

"I had everything checked before you moved in—wiring, appliances, plumbing. Oh, Haskell!" Her nails bit into my skin. "If he is capable of doing something like that . . ."

"I have to get out of here," I muttered. "Right now."

"No, it's too late. I don't know where he is. He could be anywhere—out there in the dark. He could have done something to your car. He might have a weapon. There are guns in the house, Father insisted we have them. . . ." She pressed her hand to her forehead. "This is absurd. I'm getting myself worked up about nothing, and I've frightened you to death, poor child. What I'd really like to do is hide you away in a secret place, like Father's treasures."

I couldn't have agreed more. She was right; we were both over-reacting. Stress and grief and fatigue had left neither of us capable of sensible thought. All the same . . .

"It will be all right," she said, as if trying to reassure

herself. "You can lock the door of your room, and I'll ask Mrs. Adams to stay with you."

A fine lot of help Mrs. Adams would be if a berserk ex-boxer decided to break the door down and strangle me. I didn't doubt Jerry could do it. There was no way anyone could stop him if he wanted to do it; the house was a maze of rooms and corridors, and he must know every foot of them.

Her comment stuck in my mind. *Father's treasures . . .* "The museum," I said. "Why can't I spend the night there?"

"What?"

"In the office, the basement. There's a couch there; Dave spends the night sometimes. The whole building is wired with alarms that would go off if a squirrel approached."

I could see the idea appealed to her, too. "But you'll be uncomfortable."

"I have everything I'll need already packed in my suitcase. There's a coffee maker there, food, a bathroom. All I really need is a couch; I'm so tired I could sleep on the bare floor."

"Well . . . Do you really think . . . ?"

"I can't think of any place where I'd feel safer."

"I think you're right." Her face relaxed. "I'll take you there myself and lock you in."

She didn't so much as glance at her father's body when she left the room. I did. The still, remote profile ignored me, indifferent to my safety. Before I could summon up any emotions, sentimental or sardonic, Mrs. Dunlap caught my wrist and pulled me away.

We retrieved my suitcase from the butler, and Mrs. Dunlap sent him off on an errand. "I'd rather no one knew where you were," she explained, leading me along the corridor to the elevator.

"What about Paul—Mr. Dunlap?"

"I'll tell him, of course. He's out just now—making

arrangements. But don't open the door, not to anyone. And perhaps you had better not use the telephone."

She had fetched a set of keys from her room before we went downstairs. They were needed; doors that had been unlocked during the working day were now secure, even that of the elevator. I noted this with approval. Then I remembered. "Dave. He said he'd call later."

"I'll have all incoming telephone calls switched to my room." She used another key to open the door from the lower corridor into the museum basement, and turned on the light. Without pausing, she walked purposefully to the end of the corridor and began unlocking doors, glancing quickly into each room before she relocked it. She was making certain that no one could have concealed himself, and when she had finished the job I said admiringly, "You think of everything."

"It's amazing how clever one can be when circumstances demand it," Mrs. Dunlap said with a wry smile. She placed her hands on my shoulders. "Now. Have you everything you need?"

"I'll do without if I haven't. It's only for one night. I can't thank you enough."

"Don't thank me." Her hands tightened. For a moment I thought she was going to embrace me, but apparently our new relationship was as awkward for her as it was for me. Her hands fell, and she turned away. "Good night, Haskell. Sleep soundly."

"Good night."

The lights in the hallway burned bright, as did those of the rooms she had left open—Dave's office, the bathroom, and the office Carl and I shared. The utilitarian starkness of the hallway couldn't have contrasted more strongly with the dimly lit house—and they couldn't have appealed to me more. No one could hide here; there were no shadowy corners.

I wandered into Dave's office. Dust lay thick on the

artifacts crowding the bookshelves, and ashtrays overflowing with cigarette butts had spread a film of ashes over the clutter of books and papers.

The couch resembled a hummocky plain. It was probably just as hard, but I didn't care; a blanket thrown across it and a pillow, thin as a soda cracker, provided me with all I would need. I put my suitcase down by the couch and crossed the hall to the other office. I had intended to make coffee, but on second thought, I decided I didn't want any. My stomach felt slightly queasy. I knew I ought to eat something, though. The small refrigerator held cans of soda and a chunk of cheese; there were crackers and cookies on the shelf beside it. I made a frugal but adequate meal and returned to Dave's office.

After opening my suitcase, I realized I had neglected to buy pajamas or a nightgown. No matter. I brushed my teeth and washed my face, using paper towels to dry it. I kicked off my shoes and lay down on the couch. I pulled the blanket over me. I adjusted the pillow under my head. I closed my eyes.

A few minutes later I opened them again. I had left the overhead light on, but light should not have kept me awake. The couch was as hard as I had expected, but that should not have kept me from sleeping. My body yearned, ached, pleaded for sleep, but my mind wouldn't let go. Like a tape run over and over, like an endless series of instant replays, it reviewed the revelations of the preceding hour. There were so many questions I would have asked if I had had time—if I hadn't been tired and frightened and running for cover like a hunted animal. She had said, "I've always known." How? Had her brother confided in her, shown her the pictures? I felt an urgent need to know the answer, though in my confusion I couldn't have explained why it was so important.

Something else she had said, about the old man's will, nagged at me. She seemed to take it for granted that I would be mentioned in the will. The idea made my skin crawl. I wanted nothing to do with the Nazarian family—no acknowledgment, no status, and especially no inheritance. Surely he wouldn't have done such a thing. Wills were legal documents, and legal documents aren't based on supposition—on baby pictures. I was certain I was Stephen Nazarian's daughter, but there was no way of proving it. Thank God, there was no way of proving it. I had come looking for a father and had found only a posturing shadow, without warmth or substance.

The pillow smelled of cigarettes. I buried my face in it; it reminded me of Dave. Dave . . . He was the real reason I had thought of the museum office as sanctuary. It was permeated with his presence, with the feeling of safety and comfort he gave me.

I rather wished, though, that I hadn't let Mrs. Dunlap hustle me into my self-elected prison so hastily. I ought to have called Jessie. I ought to have called Jon, if only to make sure he had recovered from his adventure. That seeming coincidence might not be so coincidental after all. Victor Nazarian, who knew everything, undoubtedly knew about Gran; the burglar might have been one of his hirelings. Not Jerry, Jerry hadn't the intelligence to carry out such a search, but there were plenty of others—hard, tough men who would perform any task for money. Why hadn't I had the decency to telephone Jon? Miriam be damned, she was nothing to me; what did I care what she thought?

I threw the blanket back and sat up. I was so on edge that every inch of skin itched, like a case of poison ivy. Mrs. Dunlap had suggested it would be wiser not to use the telephone, but surely one call couldn't do any harm. I wanted to talk to Dave. If I could talk to him, hear his voice—find out that Carl was all right—then I could sleep. Outgoing calls didn't go through the switchboard, at least I didn't think so; all I had to do was dial a number to get an outside line.

He answered on the first ring. "Haskell! Where the hell are you? I've been trying to reach you."

"I'm in the museum. In your office."

His response was blasphemous and unprintable. Summarized, and with the obscenities deleted, it amounted to, "Why there?"

"It's too complicated to explain," I said. "A lot has happened since I saw you. Is Carl with you? How is he?"

"Fine. Babbling of green fields and the like. He's doped up to the eyebrows. Never mind Carl. What's been going on? You sound . . . peculiar."

"I feel peculiar." My attempt at a laugh wasn't very successful. "But I'm all right. Really I am. I just wanted to let you know I'm set for the night, and ask how Carl is doing, and . . ."

"Haskell." Dave's voice cut through me like a knife. "How did you get into the museum basement? You don't have a key."

"Mrs. Dunlap. It was her idea. No, it was my idea, actually, but she—"

"Now you're babbling," Dave said. "Just answer my questions. What made you two loony ladies decide that the lumpy couch in the office was a suitable substitute for a bed?"

"Jerry."

"Jerry?"

"I said it was too complicated to explain. . . . Oh, damn it, Dave, I should have known better than to call you. Jerry is missing, he ran off last night, and he's gone out of his mind, he blames me for Mr. Nazarian's death, and Mrs. Dunlap was afraid—"

"Oh, Christ," Dave shouted. "Of all the lunatic theories . . ." He broke off, breathing hard; in the background I heard a voice exclaiming, "What? What?"

like a bad imitation of a stage Englishman. "Shut up, Carl," Dave said. "Listen to me, Haskell. Stay put. I'm coming to get you."

"No, you're not. There's no need. As you said, it's probably a lunatic theory. I'm so tired, Dave. I just need to sleep."

There was a long silence. I heard Carl's voice, sharp with curiosity, but I couldn't make out what he was saying. Finally Dave said, "Haskell."

"What?"

"Something I forgot to ask you this afternoon. You said you learned . . . you know what I mean. How did you find out? Was it Jessie who told you?"

"What do you want to know that for?"

"Your grammar is as befuddled as your reasoning," Dave said cuttingly. "Just answer the question."

"Tay-Sachs," I said.

After a very brief pause, he said, "You're a carrier?"

"Yes."

"I see. Hmmm. I have to think about this."

"You don't have to, but you're free to speculate if you like. I'm going to bed. Next installment in the morning."

"Huh? Oh, yeah. Sure."

"Good night, Dave. Give Carl my love."

"Yeah, sure," Dave said.

I started to hang up. A mumble from the telephone brought it back to my ear. "What?"

"I said, lock yourself in."

"I am locked in. You know what this place is like."

Dave said, "Uh."

I could see him staring blankly at the telephone, his jaw bristling and his forehead corrugated. It was a beautiful picture, and it stayed with me, displacing uglier thoughts as I curled up under the blanket and let myself drift off. Going, going . . .

It seemed to me that I hovered in the half-world between

sleep and waking for a long time, but I must have fallen
asleep because the sound woke me, suddenly and shocking-
ly, and brought me bolt upright, shaking in every limb.
Such an innocent sound, under other circumstances—that of
a door opening.

Footsteps sounded along the corridor. He made no
attempt to creep up on me. I was huddled against the wall,
the blanket drawn to my chin, when he appeared in the
doorway.

"I'm sorry," he said. "Were you asleep?"

He wore one of his elegant, expensive suits—dark
charcoal gray this time, with a black tie discreetly figured in
gray. Mourning. Mourning for his father-in-law, now lying
in state with candles at his head and feet. He had every right
to be there. He was the only person aside from his wife who
had a right to be there, who knew of my presence, whom I
might have expected to see. There was no reason why I
should have been frozen with terror. I felt my teeth
chattering.

Paul pulled up a chair and sat down.

"I was in my office, upstairs," he explained. "I won't
have many more such opportunities. They'll read the will
day after tomorrow."

He seemed to think I understood this mystifying statement; he went on, without pausing. "I heard my telephone
give an odd little buzz. There's something wrong with the
connection; it does that whenever another instrument in the
building is used. I had no idea anyone was here; naturally I
picked it up."

I had to moisten my lips before I spoke. "You heard."

He nodded gravely. "Yes. So I thought I had better face
you with the facts before Dave does so. It won't take him
long to figure it out; he's extremely intelligent. And, you
see, he knows about the child."

"The—the child?"

"Ours. Katherine's and mine. Victor Nazarian the Second.'' My bemused expression exasperated him; he frowned slightly. ''You saw the photograph in Victor's room. He kept it there, prominently displayed. To remind us of our pain and our failure.''

The dark-haired child with the strange look . . . I had observed the incongruity without understanding it. A child of a year or more should have lost the unfocused stare of infancy.

Paul crossed his legs—even then he didn't neglect to adjust his trousers so the crease wouldn't be spoiled. ''Can you believe,'' he went on conversationally, ''that he wanted us to 'try again,' as he put it? He kept insisting that mathematically the odds were in our favor. Of course that was true. One chance out of four that another child wouldn't carry the gene, two chances out of four that it would be a carrier but not affected. But mathematical odds are meaningless against a possibility that we might have to endure that agony a second time. This was before amniocentesis. I saw what she suffered during that final year of little Victor's ghastly life. I would have killed myself, or her, before I'd let her go through that again.''

''But you—I never would have suspected—you aren't—''

''I never suspected it either. At that time the research on Tay-Sachs had barely begun. I know now, as you should, that other groups carry the allele. I was born in Canada—''

''Nova Scotia.'' A forgotten, meaningless sentence from the books I had read came back to me.

''My mother was Nova Scotian.'' He glanced casually at his watch, one of those thin gold masterpieces that exemplified the life style he had chosen. ''It was the snapshots that gave me away, I suppose? Your baby pictures.''

My head was spinning. Gave him away? Certainly not to me. He took my stupefied silence for agreement.

''Leah left them with me—at my request.'' His melancholy face softened in a ghost of a smile. "You were a pretty baby, Haskell. Victor was a year old then; he had been born shortly after your mother discovered she was pregnant. When she came back to Chicago, the doctors had diagnosed his illness. He had at best—or at worst—two years of life. Blind, paralyzed, retarded, in pain. Can you wonder that I risked keeping your pictures? I knew you were the only child I would ever have."

And that was the answer to the question I had never really considered: Why hadn't my mother married the father of her child? The simplest, most obvious answer: Because he was already married, to a woman desperately in love with him and about to bear his legitimate child. When she returned, after Kevin's death, it was to learn that the child was doomed and dying. Only a monster would have demanded that Katherine's husband desert her then. Afterward . . . But there had been no afterward for my mother.

"Victor found the pictures," Paul said. "I was careless about hiding them, and when he was ambulatory he snooped everywhere; nothing escaped him, the old swine. He never said a word to me, but I knew he must have taken them; no one else could have done so. He meant to hold them over my head and keep me in suspense, never knowing when the ax would fall—but for once his filthy schemes backfired. He underestimated her, you see. She . . . Now, even in the grave, he'll have his revenge. I'm not mentioned in his will. He told me that, years ago. Once his support is withdrawn, the other trustees will find a way to get rid of me. You've provided them with the weapon they need, and Dave won't hesitate to use it. He's always despised me. I don't know why. I'm certain Leah never told him. She swore to me that she hadn't, and I'm sure she was telling the truth. I should never have published that article. But I needed something to prove to Victor that I deserved academic respect. I hoped Leah wouldn't see it. But she did. That's why she came back."

He stopped, looking at me as if he expected a reply. "Article," I repeated. "What article?"

It was the right response, though I had no idea why. Paul smiled. "She didn't betray me then. It must have been something else that gave me away. I doubt you could prove anything. I had most of her papers, and the few you had were burned, but the mere suspicion will be enough to destroy me. That's what it will amount to—my destruction. I'll spend the rest of my life in the lap of luxury, my wife's kept man; but the work that gave my life meaning will have been taken from me."

He rose to his feet, shrugging to settle his coat across his shoulders. "There is only one thing left, and I'll do anything I must to preserve it. That's why you have to go, Haskell. Now. Tonight. I won't see the effort of twenty-odd years go down the drain, even for you."

He started toward me.

I hadn't understood half of what he said. The last part of it was irrelevant and immaterial; my entire consciousness had focused on a single overriding fact and the conclusions that followed it as inevitably as fate.

His hand had almost touched me when I moved, flinging the blanket over his arm and rolling ways, off the couch onto the floor and up again in a single motion. My wild throw served me better than I had hoped; the hanging folds of cloth must have wrapped around his feet. I was out the door before he untangled himself and came after me.

I didn't have to waste time deciding which way to run. The back door leading to the stairs and the out-of-doors could only be opened with a key, which I didn't have. The other rooms in the basement were locked or unlockable; I had no keys to the offices either. The elevator was no use to me. Even if Mrs. Dunlap hadn't secured its door, it would take too long for it to return from the upper floor where she had presumably left it. My only chance was the door that opened onto the stairs to the museum itself—if he had left it open.

I didn't dare look back; a stumble would have been fatal. The door was open. As I reached it, I heard a voice. "Haskell! Come back, don't run away!" The enclosing walls gathered his voice and hurled it at me like a missile; he might have been only a step away.

I pulled the door shut behind me and heard his breathless exclamation; it must have just missed his outstretched hand. A locked door wouldn't delay him long. He had the key. I was only halfway up the stairs when it opened. He called. "Haskell. Child . . ."

That treacherous word gave wings to my feet. Followed by my father, my murderer, I plunged through the door into the lobby of the museum.

Soft lights burned in the niches behind the giant statues. Hatshepsut, divine monarch, gazed serenely down at the panting, gasping human insect at her feet. It was animal instinct, not human reason, that directed my next move. I ran to the right, into the first exhibit hall.

The normal bright fluorescents had been replaced by dimmer night lights. They weren't dim enough to hide me in darkness. There was no place to hide, only rows of glass display cases raised above the floor.

He followed, still calling my name. The next room, like the first, offered no concealment. The line of rooms ended in the metal-enclosed vault that held the jewels. Perhaps that was where he wanted me to go. Once I was inside, he had only to close the doors. No one would think of looking for me there. It might be days before I was found. He had the power to ensure that it would be a long time, long enough to finish me. I would be written off as a cheap little thief, caught in the trap of my own greed.

The third room was not much larger than the others, but it gave an illusion of greater space because there was only a single line of exhibit cases on either side, against the walls.

The central space was occupied by the low couches and by the case containing the old man's pride—the head of the Amarna princess. She was so beautiful. The inlaid eyes seemed to follow me with a look of compassionate interest, but she couldn't help me, she could only warn, "Don't go any farther. It's a dead end. There's no way out. Stop here, catch your breath, try to think."

I pressed myself into an alcove between two of the wall cases. There was only one possibility of escape, so slim it was hardly worth considering—but any hope is better than none. I couldn't get out of the building. The walls and locks designed to bar intruders served equally well to prevent escape. The windows were covered with wrought-iron grilles, delicate as lace and hard as steel. The alarm system must have been turned off, as it always was when someone was in the museum. No one would come to my rescue. Mrs. Dunlap thought I was safely locked in for the night. In my infinite cleverness, I had refused Dave's offer to come for me.

Where were my gallant heroes when I needed them? I knew where they were. One was recuperating from the damages he had already incurred in trying to rescue me, and the other was miles away soothing his damaged ego in the smiles of another woman. A heroine as inept and reckless as I needed a dozen heroes, not just two.

My best and only hope was Mrs. Dunlap, if I could reach her. That moment of communication between us had been illusory after all; not until I mentioned her brother's name did she realize I was on the wrong track. I couldn't blame her for failing to enlighten me. She had done her best to keep me safe without betraying the husband she loved in spite of his failings. Little failings like murder . . . Perhaps she couldn't admit even to herself that I might be in danger from her husband, my father. But it was Paul from whom she had concealed me—not Jerry. She had not told him where I was. His own words had made that plain.

I heard him coming, his footsteps slow and firm against the marble of the floor. He knew I was trapped, that there was no need to hurry.

He stopped in the open archway. He wasn't even breathing hard. His eyes searched the room.

"Haskell, this is ridiculous. You can't get out of here unless I let you out. That's what I meant to do, you foolish child. I'm trying to help you."

The way you helped my mother when she came to you twenty years ago. She could have exposed you—not only your infidelity but your betrayal of scholarly integrity. The articles you published, the ones that made your reputation— they were hers.

"You killed her." I spoke aloud. He had seen me; his eyes were fixed on the alcove where I cowered.

"Is that what you think?" The hollows at the corners of his mouth deepened. "No, Haskell. Even if I were capable of such a thing, I had no reason to harm her. She didn't come here to blackmail me. You wrong your mother by such a suspicion. She wanted my help in order to return to school and regain her fellowship. That was all. I was more than willing to do that. I would have done much more."

"But you didn't have to do anything. It was awfully convenient for you, wasn't it—that so-called accident?"

The contempt in my voice brought him forward in a furious rush. I slipped past him, but just barely; by the time I reached the couch, he had recovered himself and was on the other side of it, barring my way out. He was too quick. He was in superb physical condition for a man of his age; probably he worked out every day in the city's most exclusive clubs.

All I needed was a brief span of uninterrupted time—time to reach a telephone and place one call. But in order to ensure that he wouldn't stop me, I had to have a weapon. I knew where to find one. It was in a case in the first room, devoted to predynastic and early dynastic objects. The stone macehead which, thanks to Paul's belief in complete restoration, had been remounted on a stout modern wooden handle. I even knew how to open the case; I'd watched Jerry do it.

I darted to one side and back again, leading him. He moved with me, back and forth, unable to reach me across the width of the couch. My bare feet gripped the cold stone. Faster and faster, side to side—and finally the thing I had prayed for happened. His polished soles slipped. He fell forward across the couch, reaching for me as he fell; I circled the end of the couch and ran.

Through the archway between the lobby and the first exhibit room I saw twin fans of light spilling out across the floor from open doors—one to his office, the other, opposite, to the basement stairs. So seductive was the lure of the light that it was all I could do to make myself swerve aside and stop moving. There were telephones downstairs and in his office—but no hiding place and no way of securing the doors. I shrank from carrying out my desperate plan, even though it offered a chance of survival. Unless he had a gun . . . I doubted that he did. He didn't need one. He had his hands and his hard, fit body.

He stood in the entrance to the next room, watching me. The glass of the exhibit case offered no concealment. He had his temper under control again; his voice was smooth and persuasive. "Haskell, this has to stop. What can I do to convince you I mean you no harm?"

I couldn't think of anything. "Shoot yourself?" I suggested. My hands moved over the smooth surface of the glass, seeking the hidden bolt. When the alarm system was activated, moving the bolt would set off the alarm. My fingers found it and tugged it back. No sound. I hadn't expected there would be. Once unlocked, the case tipped back on its hinges.

Paul answered my suggestion with a humorless bark of laughter. "So help me, I would if I could. I don't have a gun; do you think I . . . Wait a minute. There is a gun in the bottom drawer of my desk. I've never used it; I only kept it there because Victor insisted. Go on, into my office. The doors are open. Get the gun. You can cover me with it while we talk.''

The idea would have appealed to me if I had known how to use a handgun and if I had believed him. My palms were so wet with perspiration they slipped on the glass. I wiped them on my jeans and tried again.

Paul went on talking. What an actor the man was! The very sound of his voice, deep and sincere and mellow, would have convinced most listeners. ''The last thing in the world I want is to see you hurt. . . .''

''I've been hurt.'' The words weren't planned; they just came out. My hands tightened on the glass.

''I know. Dear child, I know. It's my fault, all of it; I'll do anything I can to make it up to you. I just don't want my wife to find out—''

''She knows. How do you think I got into the museum? She brought me here.''

''What?''

It might have been a woman's voice that emitted the high, shrill syllable.

''She brought me here and locked me in. She was afraid you'd try something like this. If anything happens to me, she'll know you did it.''

The sound that came from him wasn't a word but a low, agonized groan. He moved toward me.

The case fell back, shuddering. I snatched the mace and raised it. His advance had brought him within a few feet of me, but as I swung the heavy stone, the enormity of what I was about to do made me back away.

''I don't want to hit you,'' I gasped. ''But I will if you . . . Don't make me do it. Please.''

My retreat changed our relative positions. Now his back was to the lobby while I faced it. He was making a frantic attempt to remain calm, but his breathing was ragged and perspiration streaked his face, glistening like trails of tears.

"What do you want me to do, Haskell?"

Turn around and stand still while I brought the mace down on his head? I knew I couldn't. No matter what he had done, no matter what he had planned to do, I could not strike the blow in cold blood. I swallowed. "Walk away from me. Toward the jewel room. Keep walking; don't turn around."

He considered the suggestion. "And what will you do?"

"Never mind."

"The telephone," he said, as if to himself. "You'll call, won't you? That's the only thing you can do. Not Dave, or young Carl, they're too far away. You'll call the house. And whoever answers, she'll be notified. That's what you're planning, isn't it? To ask my wife for help."

I couldn't answer. I had always thought that the expression "heart in your throat" was only a figure of speech, but something blocked my vocal cords and my breathing—a thick pulsing lump of suspense. He couldn't have heard her; she moved like a cat, her tiny feet velvet-shod. He couldn't see her. She had come up the stairs from the basement and through the open door. She was dressed in black—practical, utilitarian slacks and turtleneck, the kind of clothing I had never seen her wear—and her hair was hidden by a dark scarf pulled low over her forehead. But I recognized her. I knew her by her walk, and by the fact that it could have been no one else.

"I can't let you do that," Paul said. The sound of his voice made me jump. I had to speak, do something to keep his attention fixed on me, so that she could . . . What did she mean to do? Surely her presence was enough to restrain him. But as I hesitated, she put her finger to her lips. It was her left hand that moved; the right was behind her.

"Why not?" I forced the words past the lump in my throat.

"Oh, God," Paul muttered. He raised his hand to his face. "I'd tell you—I'd even do that—if I thought you'd believe me. She—my wife—"

I don't know what warned him. I didn't hear a sound, she moved so quickly on those dainty little feet. But he was closer, perhaps there was a rustle of cloth or a catch of breath. Or perhaps my eyes shifted, betraying her presence. He whirled around. The shock of seeing her jolted his entire body, like an electric current. He didn't even raise an arm to defend himself from the blow. It struck the side of his head, and as he collapsed, she threw her arms around him, holding him and sinking down with him, breaking his fall. My body sagged in sympathy, and my numbed fingers lost their hold on the mace handle.

"Thank God," I whispered. "Thank you—thank you. He isn't . . ."

"No." She straightened. "Only stunned. You don't think I would hurt him, do you? I love him."

"I'm so sorry. . . ."

"Why? Because I love him? Don't be sorry. I'm not. He's the only thing that made my life worth living. I don't intend to lose it now."

The words struck a faint sense of familiarity. Someone else had said that earlier. . . . She was still holding the gun by the barrel. Seeing my eyes focus on it, she smiled and said in a conversational tone, "Father insisted I learn how to use a gun. People said he was paranoid, but he was right—he always was. Except about Paul. He never appreciated Paul." She glanced down at her husband's sprawled body, and a look of infinite tenderness transformed her face.

"My poor darling. It wasn't his fault that women loved him. Men are different from women. They have a stronger sexual urge. When some trollop tempts them, they can't resist. But it would have distressed him to learn that I was aware of his little lapses, so of course I never said a word."

I'm not sure exactly when my feeling of gratitude and relief was replaced by a spreading coldness. Maybe it was the word "trollop" that did it. I took an involuntary step back and caught myself with a stumble and a cry as pain shot up my leg from my left foot. The mace must have struck it when it fell. I hadn't even noticed at the time.

Mrs. Dunlap nodded approvingly. "That's right. Go back, farther into the museum. I want to finish this before Paul wakes up."

She moved toward me and I retreated, one agonized step at a time.

"Where are they?" Mrs. Dunlap asked. "What did you do with them?"

"I don't know what you're talking about. I don't have anything you . . ." A rush of anger made me forget pain and fear. "You were the one who searched the cottage! Well, whatever the hell you wanted is gone now. Reduced to ashes, along with everything else I owned. That was you too, wasn't it—the fire? Not Jerry. Poor Jerry, he'd never do such a thing. Dave was right. . . ."

She heard only what she wanted to hear. She looked pleased. "Gone. That's good. That's a relief. There won't be any loose ends this time. I should have taken care of them years ago; but who could have anticipated you would choose the same career? Only an Egyptologist would see the similarities between her work and Paul's."

Mother's papers and notes. Evidence of deliberate plagiarism, the most serious charge that could be leveled against a scholar—particularly one as vulnerable as Paul Dunlap. Some of his statements came back to me now, with new and poignant meaning. The co-regency article, the romantic, "almost feminine" love poetry. Every solid piece of work he had ever produced had been stolen from her. The first searches of the cottage hadn't found her notes because they had not been there. I had not received them from Jon until Wednesday afternoon. And that meant it must have been

Mrs. Dunlap who had slipped the drug into my drink at the party.

"Sleeping pills," I said. "That's how you killed her."

"I was so happy when it worked," Mrs. Dunlap said brightly. "It might not have, you know. But I thought, why not give it a try? I knew Paul and she had had an affair. Father told me. He knew everything. But I didn't care. I was his wife. That was the important thing.

"I knew she was in Chicago that week, even before she came here. Margaret was the one who told me that. Dear Margaret—poor Margaret—she wanted a man so badly, any man. She hated Leah as much as I did. I knew the bitch would come to Paul and I was waiting for her. I heard every word they said to one another. I hadn't been aware of the other thing—the article he published, that she claimed was hers. When I heard that, I knew I had to get rid of her. Father was only too ready to believe the worst of Paul. She would be around Paul's neck for the rest of his life like an albatross, threatening his career and his reputation. Worst of all—she wanted to come back to Chicago—to the Oriental Institute. On my very doorstep, where I'd have to see her—and you—where she could see Paul whenever she chose. I couldn't allow that. I intercepted her after she left Paul's office and offered her a cup of tea. She couldn't refuse. I was very pressing. And she felt sorry for me."

The smooth façade of her face cracked into tight wrinkles, drawing her lips back in a snarl. "Sorry for me. She with her healthy, living child and her healthy body and her clever cruel mind . . ."

She strolled casually, following my limping retreat. She didn't seem to notice that we were moving in a wide circle, back toward the exit, where Paul Dunlap's body lay like a dark stain on the marble. No wonder he had tried to prevent me from calling his wife. He knew I was in no danger from anyone else; that if she had hidden me away in a place only a few could enter, it was for purposes of her own. He had been weak and corrupt but he had tried to save me—without betraying her. I could pity him now; his dilemma had been a horrible one. His sense of guilt must be overpowering. Everything she had done had been for his sake.

"What was I talking about?" Mrs. Dunlap asked. "Oh, yes. I was telling you how pleased I was that the sleeping pills worked. I'd have tried something else if that scheme had failed, of course. With Father's business connections, it wouldn't have been difficult to find someone to deal with the matter. Fortunately that wasn't necessary. I've never liked that part of his life. It's so—so crude."

I cleared my throat. "No one could ever prove you did it. You're safe. But if you—if you do something to me—"

"I'll still be safe," Mrs. Dunlap said confidently. I had never noticed the resemblance to her father, but it was there—the same arrogant I-am-above-the-law smile. "There will be another unfortunate accident. I have it all worked out."

"Paul won't believe it."

"He'll believe it because he will want to believe it, and because it will be a fait accompli. He's never been really sure about Leah. He thinks of me as gentle and submissive." She whipped the scarf off her hair; silvery curls shone in the light, framing her smiling face, flushed a pretty pink with excitement. "Who would believe such a dear little old lady could commit murder?"

I had a hard time believing it myself. This was one woman who probably could get away with murder; she could fill me full of holes and be found standing over my body with the smoking gun in her hand, and still get away with it. Good lawyers and enough money to buy a few juries wouldn't hurt, either.

Her smooth forehead wrinkled and her voice turned petulant. "Now will you please stop backing away? I'd rather not shoot you; that would spoil my plan."

Why not? I thought fatalistically. I couldn't run; my foot

was broken or badly bruised. She wouldn't hesitate to shoot if she had to. Unlike Paul, I was warned and ready for her. She was an old woman, surely I could hold her off and wrestle the gun away.

She was confident, but not careless. She edged toward me, her arm raised. As I faced what might be the last few seconds of life, a name formed in my mind. I must have called out because I heard the sound go echoing through the quiet halls. It was not a plea for help so much as an invocation, and it surprised me as much as it surprised Mrs. Dunlap.

Her pause gave me time to duck in under her arm and grab her by the wrist. Such a fragile, brittle wrist—but her muscles had the strength of hate and suppressed rage. She broke my hold with contemptuous ease and brought the gun down in a sweeping arc. It skimmed my cheek and struck my shoulder, numbing my left arm. I staggered back. My weight fell full on my bad foot, and it gave under me. I landed on my backside with a force that jarred me clear up to the top of my skull.

My back hurt, my leg hurt, my arm hurt. I thought for a second I was going to pass out; but the darkish fog clouding my vision gradually passed, and then I saw him walking slowly toward her. His hand was out, palm up, open and beseeching.

"Give me the gun, Katherine."

"No, I won't." She shook her head. Silvery curls fluttered.

It was her turn to back away. Her plump little hands clasped the butt of the gun; her soft mouth was set in a petulant scowl. Paul followed her. "Give it to me, Katherine. Please."

Perhaps if I hadn't moved, he might have persuaded her. But I had to move; it was humanly impossible to sit spread-legged and helpless and wait to see what would happen— not when my life depended on the outcome. The muzzle of the gun wavered from Paul to me and then back to Paul. I maneuvered myself onto my hands and knees.

The bullet hit the floor and sent marble chips flying. One stung my face. I forgot my bad foot and my aching body; I bounced up like a jack-in-the-box. They were locked in a lovers' grip. Even then, I think, he was trying not to hurt her. She was far beyond such considerations. A stream of hoarse obscenities poured from her lips; she kicked and squirmed and clawed at his eyes.

It was over before I could intervene. Their bodies muffled the sound of the shot. In the last few seconds, he managed to turn his head and look at me. His lips shaped a word. It wasn't my name. It might have been my mother's. It might have been almost any word. "Run," perhaps. Or, "Sorry . . ."

Then the pain gripped him. His lips writhed, his eyes widened until the whites showed around the dilated pupils. The last I saw of him, before they went down together in a tangle of limbs, were those glazed, fixed eyes. When she freed herself to crouch over him, keening and weeping, the gun was still in her hand.

I waited for it to turn on me. I was petrified, incapable of feeling. I didn't hear them coming, though the pounding of feet on the stairs must have echoed like thunder. One voice rising over the rest, yelling my name, finally reached me. She heard it, too. Rising with the agility of a woman half her age, she pointed the gun.

His arms encircled me with the bruising force of an applied Heimlich maneuver, lifting me off my feet and swinging me around. The bullet whined past overhead. It must have touched him; an explosive four-letter expletive, more expressive of outrage than pain, blistered my ear. Somebody giggled and then said idiotically, "One hero left . . ." Fortunately the person who held her dangling like a rag doll tightened his grip and cut off her wind.

Otherwise I don't know what stupid thing she might have done next.

I slept for almost twelve hours. It was past noon, on a good old typical gray Chicago day, when I opened my eyes and saw his face hovering over me like a gargoyle on a cathedral roof. A feeble sound escaped my lips, and the gargoyle scowled.

"You are developing a disgusting habit of giggling," he remarked severely. "And at singularly inappropriate times. What's so damned funny?"

"I was thinking of Sleeping Beauty," I explained.

"Hmmm," said Dave. "I get it. A prince I ain't."

"Oh, yes, you are," I said fervently. A tear leaked out of the corner of my eye and slid down my cheek.

Dave said, "Hmmm," again. "Want some soup?"

"Yes, please."

"Stay put. I'll get it."

He disappeared. I lay still, savoring the beautiful gray light and the exquisite aroma of cigarette smoke that permeated the sheets. So Dave smoked in bed. I'd have something to say about that; it was a very dangerous habit.

From the outer room I heard the murmur of voices. Faint as they were, I knew them. They brought back incoherent, disconnected memories of the night before.

Carl and Jon. Talk about odd couples. I still didn't know how they had happened to be there; in fact, I didn't know why Dave had arrived in the conventional nick of time. I didn't know anything except that I was alive, against all odds. I closed my eyes and tried to remember.

I remembered the blood trickling down Dave's face when he finally lowered me to the floor and turned me in his hands, like the puppet I resembled. I remembered seeing Carl bending over the motionless body of Paul Dunlap while Jon soothed the distraught widow and murderess. Nobody could do that sort of thing better than Jon. He had his arm around her and she was looking up into his face with a vague smile. I remember wondering what the hell he was doing there. . . .

Then there was a long blank space—mercifully blank. My next memory was of an emergency room in a hospital and Dave cursing imaginatively as a nurse slapped a bandage over the shaved spot on his head where a bullet had creased his scalp. I was lying on a table—a gurney—and I floated there, in placid detachment until the nurse turned to me. The sight of the needle in her hand brought me back to life. I asked her what it was; when she said, "Something to make you sleep," I started screaming and fighting.

Another longish gap in memory: vague impressions of a ride through darkened streets with lights flashing by; someone carrying me, voices, a soft flat surface, hands . . . I sat up with a start. I was wearing pajamas—not mine; I didn't own any. These were about six sizes too big; the sleeves flapped loosely over my hands. They were a sedate dark blue in color and they also smelled of tobacco. So I hadn't imagined those busy hands. I wondered uninterestedly whose they had been.

I pulled myself to a sitting position, though not without a few hearty groans. I ached all over. Further exploration turned up a bruise on my shoulder and another one on my derriere. My foot was swollen and green and purple and red all over. My toes hurt when I wriggled them, but at least I could wriggle them. The damage—to my body—could have been worse.

Even a brain duller than mine could have identified the owner of the bedroom. It was a ghastly mess. In addition to the standard bachelor clutter of dirty socks and stained cups and all-over confusion, the most outstanding litter consisted of books. Books on the dresser, the foot of the bed, the chairs and the floor. Old books, new books, skinny books, and thick books; books closed and books open. They weren't all scholarly books. I shifted sideways so I could read the titles of the ones heaped on the bedside table. Somehow I wasn't surprised to find an eclectic mixture— Eiseley, an early Heinlein, Steinbeck, a volume on the Shakespeare ciphers, a biography of Mozart.

The door opened and Dave came in. He was carrying a tray, which he deposited on my lap. The soup was a tinned variety. It was lukewarm and half of it had sloshed onto the tray. I ate it.

Dave stood watching, fists on his hips, forehead corrugated. "How is it?" he asked.

"Fine. Thanks."

"Want some more?"

I tried to be polite, but it was impossible to lie to Dave— not any longer. "No, it's awful. How about sending out for some pizza?"

"Would you settle for a pastrami sandwich? Carl's gone to the deli; he'll be back in a minute."

"Sounds great. Is—is Jon here, too?"

"Uh-huh."

"Oh."

Dave sat down on the edge of the bed. The tray tilted, spilling chicken noodle soup on the blanket. "You have to talk to him sooner or later. You'll have to think about it— sooner or later."

I started to say "later," but it was the other word that came out. Dave nodded. "That's my girl." He stood up. The tray slid sideways, spilling the remainder of the soup.

Dave said, "Oh, hell." He picked up the tray and looked helplessly around the room. Finding no surface unencumbered, he put it on the floor.

"Carry me?" I suggested. "My foot hurts."

He put his hands behind him. "It's not broken. Do you good to exercise it."

"I don't think I can do it, Dave."

He knew I wasn't talking about my foot. "The longer you put it off, the harder it will be."

I had to ask, even though I knew the answer. "He's dead, isn't he?"

Dave nodded. "If it's any help—we know most of what happened; you won't have to go over it again. You talked—God, how you talked!"

"Oh. Okay. I'll try."

"I wish you would. Your lawyer friend has expressed his intention of sticking around until you make an appearance, and I'm sick of the sight of him."

I pushed the covers back and stood up. The pajama pants slithered down my legs. Since the jacket reached to my knees, nothing showed; but a vivid blush spread from Dave's chin to his forehead.

I stepped out of the pants and left them lying on the floor. There didn't seem to be much point in picking them up. "Were you the one who undressed me?" I asked curiously.

The blush deepened. "No, it was your boyfriend."

"Which one?"

"The original boyfriend. I figured he probably . . ." Dave stopped. "Damn it, Haskell!"

"All right. I'm going."

The foot didn't hurt as much as I had expected. I made the most of my limp, but it had no effect on Dave; he didn't even offer me an arm to lean on.

Jon rose to his feet and put down the book he had been reading. I said, "Hello, Jon," and sat down, smoothing the skirts of the pajama top primly across my knees.

Dave followed, carrying a blanket. He tossed it across my lap. "I'll—uh—make some coffee," he announced, and went into the kitchen. A tactful banging of pots and pans followed his departure.

Jon took the blanket, arranged it, and tucked it in. Then he sat down. "How do you feel?" he asked.

"If you are referring to my physical condition, not bad. If you are referring to my mental state—forget it."

"Okay." The silence that followed gave me time to regret

my rudeness. Poor Jon, why did he always bring out the worst in me?

"I called Jessie," he said.

"What did you tell her?"

"Nothing about . . . this." His expressive gesture incorporated the whole messy situation. "I was afraid she'd read about Mr. Nazarian's death—it was in all the papers—and try to telephone you. That might have led to complications."

Such as learning that I had narrowly escaped being burned to death. I said meekly, "Oh. Thanks, Jon. That was nice of you."

"Nice," Jon said, without inflection. "Thank *you*, Haskell."

I couldn't seem to say anything right, so I stopped trying. "How did you happen to be Johnny-on-the-spot last night?"

"Oh, you noticed I was there?" I stared at him. He went on, in the same smooth voice. "I got in touch with Dave yesterday evening, after I learned of Mr. Nazarian's death. I knew you'd get yourself into some kind of trouble; you're so damned naïve you never see the possible dangers, and so damned stubborn you don't know when to admit you're in over your head. But it wasn't until after the break-in at your grandmother's that I really got worried. That's not a high-crime area. It was a little too much of a coincidence that the first such attempt should occur shortly after you became involved with the Nazarian family. Your telephone calls could easily have been monitored, and if someone knew you had agreed to take the old ladies shopping that afternoon . . ."

"Gran said she had something for me," I admitted. "Something important."

"I didn't know that," Jon said. "I didn't know about your possessions being searched. I didn't even know about the fire until Dave told me."

"I'm sorry," I murmured.

"It's a bit late for apologies. The more I thought about the burglary, the less I liked it, so I decided to do a little detective work of my own. You had settled on Stephen Nazarian as Leah's lover, but it seemed to me that Dave was a more likely prospect—"

A clatter of crockery from the kitchen made speech impossible for a moment. When it subsided, I said, "It was something Mr. Nazarian said that confirmed my hunch, Jon. He talked about wanting a healthy wife for Stephen, and then said, 'But we didn't know about that, then. . . .' I assumed he was talking about Tay-Sachs—"

"Another little piece of information I lacked," Jon said in his lawyer's voice. "Had I but known . . . Dave didn't see fit to confide in me either, the first time I talked to him."

A voice from the kitchen bellowed, "So why didn't you mention the Tay-Sachs factor? You didn't confide in me either, shyster. Just asked a lot of damned impertinent questions."

"Touché," Jon said, smiling. "None of us talked freely, and each had bits of the puzzle the others lacked. If we had—"

He was interrupted by a pounding at the door. Dave went through the room without looking at Jon or me and opened it. Carl edged in, balancing paper bags.

"Hi, Haskell, feeling better? Listen, I'm really sorry about—" He broke off with a grunt as Dave kicked him in the shin. "Come help me with the coffee," he said, winking.

"Damned if I will. I got the sandwiches, didn't I?" Carl sat down and began unloading the paper bags. "Pastrami, ham and cheese, liverwurst . . . Pickles. What have you been talking about while I was gone? You've been talking about me, haven't you?"

"Such conceit," I said. Carl was about as tactful as a tornado, but in my present mood I found that restful. He beamed back at me. He had trimmed his mustache. I looked from his scorched cheek to Jon's bruised jaw to Dave, whose hair stood up in tufts on either side of his shaved and bandaged scalp, and I let out a long sigh. "All right," I said. "I owe you—all of you. Let's get it over with. Jon was telling me how he happened to be with you last night."

"I hadn't finished," Jon said coldly. "It was Dave who telephoned me last night, after he had spoken with you. He suggested we put our cards on the table. He had arrived at part of the truth—"

"What do you mean, part?" Dave demanded. "I had it all. All I wanted from you was confirmation."

"Wait a minute," Carl exclaimed. "I was the one who figured out that Paul had plagiarized Leah's work. Some of her notes reminded me of Paul's articles, especially her theory about the co-regency. The love poetry was hers, too. I found a translation of one of the Chester Beatty songs in her copy of Gardiner—in her handwriting—practically word for word with the version Paul published."

"I suspected that a long time ago," Dave grunted.

"Oh, yeah? Then why didn't you say so?" Carl asked.

"What would have been the use? Leah was dead. I couldn't prove anything, and Paul had Victor Nazarian's influence behind him."

"But that didn't mean anything until I told you the other things I knew," Carl said triumphantly. "About the cottage being searched and the fire. The door was jammed. That made it a deliberate attempt at murder."

"What?" I exclaimed. "You never said—"

"I wasn't sure at first," Carl admitted, "I assumed you had locked the door; you always did. That's why I broke the window. But when I tried to unlock the door from the inside, it still wouldn't open. Why do you suppose I had to push you across that broken glass? I was in something of a hurry at the time, and for the next twenty-four hours I was so doped up I couldn't think straight. Dave kept me till I remembered that I had stubbed my toe against something on the doorstep, and that I really had turned the key—not once but a couple of times."

"That was when I called him," Dave said, with a jerk of his head in Jon's direction. "I told him about the fire and he told me about the burglary. The picture was beginning to look pretty ugly, and when I added the fact that you were in hiding from someone in the house, my hackles began to rise. I couldn't believe Jerry would hurt anyone. He might strike out in anger if he or his patron was threatened, but a deliberate, cold-blooded stalking of a victim—especially a woman—no. Carl and I were discussing it when Jon arrived."

"He must have driven like a bat out of hell," Carl said with a certain grudging admiration. "Took him less than forty-five minutes from Winnetka."

"Forty-three," Jon said.

"By the time he got here, Dave and I had already figured out three or four murder motives," Carl explained. "Assuming that Paul had stolen Leah's work, which we considered probable, he might go to some lengths to keep that fact a secret. Then there was the old man's will. If Victor thought you were Stephen's child, he might have cut you in for a tidy sum. Money is always a good motive for murder. Dave didn't believe Jerry would harm you, but I wasn't so sure."

"We weren't sure about anything," Jon said. "It wasn't until Dave mentioned the Dunlap child that it hit me. He knew about the child, and he knew its symptoms resembled those of Tay-Sachs, but he wasn't aware of the fact that the disease can be carried by others besides Ashkenazi Jews."

"I did know it," Dave said, scowling. "Logically—"

"You hadn't read the same books I had," Jon said. "Since Tay-Sachs is a recessive allele, both parents must carry it if the child actually comes down with the disease. That meant that Paul Dunlap must have been a carrier. Dave looked him up in the *Dictionary of American Scholars* and found that he had been born in Canada. I remembered the group mentioned in one book—the group in Nova Scotia. Actually we didn't need that to prove Dunlap carried Tay-Sachs; the fact that his child died of it made that a certainty. If Dunlap was your father, Haskell, he had a double motive to silence you. I didn't know about his wife's fanatical devotion; I thought disclosure of his identity might move her to seek a divorce."

Carl finished one sandwich and reached for another. He pushed the plate toward me, but I shook my head. I wasn't hungry any longer.

"That's about it," Dave said, after a long silence. "I called the house and had them ring the basement office. No answer. When I asked for Katherine, her maid said she had gone out. Paul, too. So we mounted our trusty steeds and rode off to the rescue. The only piece of luck in the whole business was that she had left the door at the top of the stairs open. I couldn't have opened that one; I didn't have the key for it."

"You didn't suspect her?" I asked.

Dave started to answer. Carl scowled at him and cut him off. "Dave is going to claim he did; he always does that after the fact. I sure as hell didn't. I couldn't believe it even when I saw her pointing the gun at you. I stopped in my tracks. If Dave hadn't rushed in like a bull into a china shop—"

"Thanks," I said. "Thanks to all of you."

"No problem," Carl said grandly.

Dave slapped his hand away from the plate of sandwiches. "Okay, hero, that's enough. Can't you see the girl is about to fall apart? Be tactful for once."

"Quite right," Jon agreed. He rose to his feet. "I take it you wouldn't mind staying here a little longer, Haskell?"

"I don't mind," I said.

"I hope it's all right with you, Dave?"

"It's all right with me," Dave said.

"That's probably best, then," Jon said. "I'll bring you some clothes, Haskell. I know your sizes—"

"My suitcase is in the museum office."

"Oh. Well, never mind, I'll take care of it." He stared pointedly at Carl until the latter stood up, brushing crumbs off his pants.

"I'll be back," he said.

"So will I," Jon said.

Nobody moved until Dave growled, "You can't come back until you've left."

They tried to go out the door at the same time and got stuck. Dave shoved them out and slammed the door.

"You can cry if you want to," he said. "Or get drunk. Or both."

"Neither, thanks. I don't feel anything. I don't know what's wrong with me. What's going to happen now?"

"To her?" Dave considered the question. "An expensive sanatorium. To the estate? That depends on the will and the lawyers. It will probably take years to straighten out. Do you care?"

"No."

"What's going to happen to you?" Dave asked.

"I don't know."

"Plenty of time to decide. But you'd better not delay too long; not even I can get you into the O.I. at the last damned minute."

I pushed the blanket aside and stood up. The sleeves of the pajamas slid down over my hands; I pawed at them, trying to roll them up, but my fingers were clumsy and unsteady so I gave up. Dave watched me pace. His face was completely expressionless.

"Don't try to play daddy, Dave. The role doesn't suit you."

He turned away from me, pushing his hands into his pockets as if imprisoning them. "I thought that was what you wanted, Haskell."

"Two fathers are enough, don't you think? One man gave me his name. It was good enough for my mother, so it should be good enough for me. The other . . . He wasn't all bad. He got himself caught in a trap he couldn't escape without hurting someone. Who am I to blame him for the choice he made? In the end, for whatever reason, he chose me. I can stand alone now. I don't need anything from the past."

Not even her. If she visited me again in dreams, I could watch her walk quietly down the long road into memory without trying to call her back.

"Standing alone isn't so great," Dave muttered. "You don't have to. Apparently your long-suffering admirers are willing to forgive your stupidity and give you a second chance. Which is more than you deserve."

"That's true, but it isn't very nice of you to say so."

"Nice is your shyster friend," Dave said. "Nice isn't me. So which of them is it going to be?"

"I don't know." I stopped pacing; tucking my hands in my sleeves, Japanese fashion, I glanced at him from under my lashes. "Which do you advise?"

"Don't practice your cute, coy glances on me," Dave growled. "You wouldn't take my advice anyway."

I wasn't trying to be cute; I was trying to hide my trembling hands. Clasping them around my wrists to steady them, I felt the pulse beating furiously under my fingers.

"How do you know I won't?"

"You never have yet. Well—in the words of the immortal Charlotte, 'Choose him who loves you best.'"

He dropped down onto the couch and reached for a cigarette. "Why, Mr. Rochester," I murmured, "'I will at least choose—him I love best.'"

The unlit cigarette broke between his fingers, but he didn't give me any help at all, not even when I stood right in front of him doing my best to look seductive.

"Don't get carried away, kid," he growled.

"That isn't in the book."

"It's a stupid book. What girl in her right mind would fall for a supercilious, ugly old bastard twenty years her senior?"

"Not me. You aren't that much older." I sat down on his lap. He was as rigid as a stone statue. It took all the courage I possessed to brush his lips with mine, but the moment they touched I knew that for once my instincts had been right. "Why didn't you undress me, Dave? That's a daddy's proper job, isn't it? Were you afraid to?"

His mouth was hard and unresponsive. I kissed the bunched muscles at one corner, then at the other. "Why wouldn't you carry the poor invalid with the bad ankle when she asked you to?"

"Don't do that!"

"But you have such beautiful ears, Dave; I can't resist them. I noticed them the first time I met you. What did you notice about me? Was it love at first sight?"

"Yes. No. Damn it—"

"All right, not your ear. How about this? Mmmm. That's nice."

He turned his head. "Stop it," he said hoarsely. "You don't know what you're doing. You're in an abnormal emotional state—"

"I know exactly what I'm doing. I could do it very well if you'd cooperate. You're reacting, Dave, don't tell me you aren't."

"Of course I'm reacting, I'm not dead yet. But I won't take advantage of a girl who—"

"Not a girl. A woman. The past is past, Dave. I'm not my mother and you aren't the boy who suffered from an adolescent crush. I didn't fall in love with you at first sight. I *liked* you. And the more I knew you, the more I liked you. Isn't that how it ought to be? Feeling comfortable with someone, laughing and arguing and being honest? It wasn't until yesterday afternoon that I realized my feelings had changed—no, not changed—grown and developed—into something more than friendship—but not less.''

He wouldn't even look at me. He was too honest to lie outright, but he wouldn't help. I said desperately, ''I think you've forgotten how. Look—one arm goes like this. . . .'' I reached back, took his hand, and drew his arm around me. ''And the other goes—''

He hadn't forgotten. As his arms tightened I braced myself, remembering how bruising Dave's casual, friendly grip could be. I needn't have worried. His hands were so gentle and his lips so surprisingly soft—at least until the very end, when he forgot himself and added a few more bruises to the ones I already had. I didn't feel them.

I curled up against him with my head on his shoulder. ''Why don't you give up and grow a beard?'' I asked, rubbing my scraped cheek against his shirt.

''Why bother? This can't last. You're crazy. You'll get over it.''

''So what if I do? We could at least give it a try.''

Dave surged to his feet, lifting me in his arms. ''You'd better get some rest. Things will be better in the morning—''

''For God's sake, Dave, it's two o'clock in the afternoon. I just woke up.''

''Oh, yeah.'' He stopped. ''That's right.''

''But don't let me stop you. You were heading in the right direction.''

''Haskell—''

''Try 'darling.' ''

''Darling . . . Oh, shit,'' Dave said.

''How romantic.''

''You don't know romantic yet, kid. If I weren't a man of iron control . . . Stop doing that.''

''No. I want—''

''I know what you want.''

"You want it, too. Why fight it?" I took his face between my hands. "I love you. I've loved you for a long time—"

"Five whole days."

"Ten at least. I was just a little mixed up about *how* I loved you."

"You're still mixed up."

"No. I'm not. I'll prove it to you, if you give me a chance. What kind of scholar are you if you refuse to test a reasonable hypothesis?"

"Well," Dave said. "Since you put it that way . . ."

BARBARA MICHAELS is the author of *Ammie, Come Home* and, most recently, *Shattered Silk*. She was born and brought up in Illinois and received her Ph.D. in Egyptology from the University of Chicago. In 1986, Ms. Michaels was named Grandmaster in the first annual Anthony awards given at Bouchercon. She lives in Frederick, Maryland.